Camp Supernatural: Eyes of Vermilion

Jonathan Solis

1st Edition

Esperanza Publishing
Edinburg, TX

Edited by: Naidelyn Ramos
Megan Johnson

ISBN: 979-8-9928647-0-0

Dedication

To my family, to my friends, to everyone who has believed in me and supported me through this incredible writing and life journey. Thank you to everyone who supported me through the madness of my creativity. Please enjoy this second chapter in the Camp Supernatural series.

Table of Contents

Camp Cabins

Atlas's Agony .... (Weight of the World)
Blunt Bear .... (Honest but Fearless)
Cathedral Cove .... (Come and See)
Daredevil Delinquents .... (Want to Bet?)
Elegant Eagle .... (Eager to Impress)
Forsaken Fox .... (Far Too Sharp)
Gloomy Gnomes .... (Gum up the Works)
Hollow Hill .... (Hauntingly High)
The Imaginarium Illusion .... (Mind Over Matter)
The Jaded Jester .... (Jokes on You)
The Kruel Kingdom .... (Would You Kindly?)
The Lost Lord .... (Last Seen Nowhere)
The Majestic Meadow .... (New Horizons)
The Ninth Night .... (Not Too Late)
Obnoxious Offspring .... (Original Pranksters)
Pyro Prison .... (Light the Fire)
The Qualified Queen .... (Quite Acceptable)
Rasping Raven .... (Raging Messengers)
Swan Song .... (Final Curtains)
The Tears of Titan .... (Heavy Rain)
The Underrated Unicorn .... (United Especially
The Violet Virtue .... (Viscerally Potent)
The Weeping Willow .... (Weather or Not)
Xiomara's Axe .... (Excellent Warriors)
Young and Yearning .... (Eager to Serve)
Ziggy Zion .... (Ground Control)

Prologue: Shelly Fargo

Shelly waited impatiently for the taxicab as she skimmed through the contents of the camp letter. Unlike her brother, she had not been formally invited to Camp Supernatural and it wasn't until a few days ago when she had received a letter of her own. She looked it over, reading the words on it her brother had claimed were on his.

I remember the one Lucas showed me had nothing on it. This one has everything including my name. Why did it take so long for me to get one?

She checked her phone repeatedly and saw the many texts and voice audios she sent her brother; all were left on **undelivered**. After putting her phone away, it began to rain and it wasn't long before she was drenched from head to toe.

Shelly looked almost unrecognizable, as if she were a few years older. She hadn't slept for days and it showed with her eyes weighing heavy below her brows. Her feet dragged with each step she took and every breath came off as a long-winded sigh.

It had been almost three months since her brother, Lucas Fargo, left for Camp Supernatural, and she wanted more than anything to find him. A terrible truth awaited him and Shelly had to be the one to tell him.

I hope he doesn't already know. Either way, I have to be strong for both of us.

She tried to call Lucas multiple times, but she always got his voicemail. When she sent too many, Shelly began to send text messages, with each becoming longer and more distressful than the last.

'How's everything going, Luke?' 'Why aren't you answering me?' 'Lucas, please answer me!' 'You need to call me right away!' 'Something happened to mom and dad.' 'Lucas!'

No sooner did the elusive taxi arrive when Shelly stuffed the envelope inside her backpack and took her place on the backseat.

Once she was inside, the door slammed shut, with the taxi immediately speeding forward. Shelly stayed silent as the taxi drove through the rain like a ship in a storm. Despite the speed of the vehicle, she showed neither queasiness nor discomfort. She didn't even act surprised when the cab driver revealed himself to be a talking skeleton named Francis.

"Hi there," said Francis, "Have you ever seen a talking skeleton before? It sure looks like you have since you're calmer than a clam."

Francis was perplexed by Shelly's unresponsive attitude towards him, but seemed to sense her uneasiness either way. Unbeknownst to the skeletal cab driver, something deep was troubling his passenger, and she made no effort to volunteer the information.

If only I knew how he was doing. I hope he was able to make friends.

Shelly's mind was on her brother, thinking how he had gone through a whole summer without any sort of contact with her. She feared the possibility that he may no longer be in camp, since summer was nearly over.

What if he left already? What if he returned home and I wasn't there? Or worse… she diverted her mind elsewhere to avoid the unsettling thoughts.

Francis was maneuvering past the rainfall as he began talking up a storm of his own.

"In case you didn't hear me before, my name is Francis and as you can see I am a real-life talking skeleton," Francis repeated as Shelly ignored him.

After about five minutes of silence, Francis tried another approach.

"That alone usually scares most people," he noted, awkwardly. "I'm not sure if you know, but camp only lasts till August and today is the last day of summer. Still, Henry is usually good about sending those letters ahead of time. Not sure why you're barely coming now. Tell the truth, I was surprised when my cab took me to you first instead of directly to the camp itself."

After another five minutes went by in silence, Francis finally had it.

"Say, young lady, can you at least tell me your name? You haven't said a word since you got here and, pardon me, but this seems irregular."

"Really, I hadn't noticed, sorry," Shelly said in a brusque tone.

Francis did not seem to notice the undertone.

"You seem familiar. Have we ever met before?" Francis asked, curiously.

"I doubt it."

Francis shook his bony head and clanked his jaw together.

"Look, I don't have eyeballs. Heck, I don't even have a tongue, but I can tell things about a person by their aura. Yours is vaguely familiar. Like an old song that you can't quite remember the name of."

Shelly wasn't paying attention. Her mind continued to be on her brother's wellbeing.

The sooner I get to Lucas the better.

"Are we close to the camp yet?" she asked, impatiently.

Francis nodded, as his bony jaw clanked against his exposed teeth.

"Why are you in such a hurry to arrive anyways? You got someone you want to see there?"

Shelly shook her head and stared out the window.

"I just want to get away from home. It's what I need right now," Shelly confessed vaguely.

Until I know more about this talking anatomy class and my brother's situation, I shouldn't say so much.

Francis did not understand her predicament, but tried to lighten up the mood.

"Hey, I understand. Most kids going to this camp feel the same. As a matter of fact, I knew this one boy who was terrified of me like he was ready to vomit when he first saw me talking," Francis remarked as he attempted to remember the kid's name. "You actually remind me a lot of him. Does the name Lucas ring any bells?"

Shelly's eyes widened at the sound of his name.

"Yes, he's my little brother," Shelly blurted out without thinking twice about it.

Francis suddenly let out a small chuckle.

"I knew there was something familiar about you, but there's also something different about you. I can't really put my bony finger on it."

Before Shelly could ask, the taxi finally came to a halt.

"Here we are. Maybe I'll see you again once we begin our rotations back. I'll save a spot in my taxi for you and your brother."

Shelly nodded as Francis added, "You should wait for the Camp Guardian. He'll make sure you find Lucas. It was nice meeting you, Lucas' sister. You can tell me your name next time we see each other."

Shelly let herself out of the taxi, slinging her soggy backpack across her shoulder.

The rain finally dissipated, with a fog that was very thick replacing it. Before she could ask Francis what the Camp Guardian looks like, the taxi sped away, leaving behind Shelly in the humid landscape.

How will I know what he looks like? Maybe he's got to have a nametag or something distinguishable about him.

She walked forward, hoping to find someone to help her reach Camp Supernatural.

Why couldn't he just take me all the way?

It took almost ten minutes of nonstop walking and thinking, but finally Shelly saw something.

She spotted a sign that read, 'Welcome to Camp Supernatural.'

That must be the camp's entrance, Shelly thought as she walked towards it.

However, before she could enter, Shelly noticed a giant figure standing near the entrance. It spotted her near the same instant she saw it. She approached with caution as the figure seemed to take form. It was huge, so towering and muscular that she swore it was inhuman. She noticed how its skin was a translucent yellow and that its face showed no form of emotion or warmness towards her. The monster also wore a purple shirt that was promoting the camp, though the fabric appeared to be tearing on the shoulders.

Is that the Camp Guardian? He looks like Frankenstein's Monster come to life.

Despite the monster's grotesque face, she forced herself to hide her fear and stared him in the eyes.

Those are actually gentle eyes, Shelly realized in astonishment.

"Who goes there?" the Camp Guardian demanded with a raspy voice.

"Are you the Camp Guardian? I need to speak to someone in the camp, please. Can you help me?" Shelly begged as her eyes began to feel heavy again.

Please Lucas. Please be here.

The monster gave her a suspicious look.

"I am the Camp Guardian of Camp Supernatural. Who are you looking for and where did you come from?"

The Camp Guardian's eyes watched her move forward and his immense size became more palpable as she got closer. Shelly didn't feel any bad vibes from the monster, but seeing him watch her like a spotlight made her feel vulnerable.

"I'm looking for a boy named Lucas Fargo. Do you know him? Is he still here? Please tell me he's still here."

The monster looked at her dubiously.

"How do you know Lucas?"

"Is he here? I have to tell him something, please," Shelly pleaded.

"Who are you to him?"

"I'm his sister Shelly. Please take me to him. I swear, it's important."

The Camp Guardian's closely lidded eyes went up as high as they could go. His opened eyes were bloodshot around yellow pupils.

"His sister…Yes, he's spoken of you! Very well, I will take you to him. Stay close to me until we find him," the creature instructed Shelly with both warmth and slight hesitation.

That was too easy.

The foggy atmosphere shifted to that of a sunny day with a group of campers huddled by the entrance with backpacks and suitcases. Some were in lines, others in rows, all preparing to leave camp at any moment.

They are already leaving, Shelly realized.

The campers who saw Shelly stared at her suspiciously, and some murmured out loud to each other. She turned to glance in their direction, but did not see her brother among them.

Where are you Lucas?

By now, Shelly was drenched in mud and rainwater, which she thought is why everyone was staring at her with uncertainty. She felt a sharp sensation on the left side of her head like someone drilling a hole there. It took what felt like a few minutes to regain her bearings, but judging by her surroundings, it was likely only a few seconds. The Camp Guardian noticed this and offered her his arm to rest on. Shelly reluctantly took it.

As they neared the cabins, a girl came over to the monster and Shelly. She had long black hair, olive skin, and wore a green camp shirt. She looked to be about Lucas' age, leading Shelly to believe she may know where her brother is.

"Hello, Camp Guardian. Who is this?" the girl asked the monster curiously.

Her eyes were concentrated on Shelly, with a look of friendliness and curiosity.

"She's looking for Lucas. Do you know where he is, Vanessa?"

The girl named Vanessa looked at Shelly, then turned her attention back to the Camp Guardian.

"I saw him about an hour ago. He was going to tell my brother about us," Vanessa responded as she began to blush slightly.

The Camp Guardian seemed to notice what she meant.

"You and Lucas?" the monster asked with a thin smile.

His teeth were crooked, which made his already grotesque face even more repulsive. Vanessa nodded in response and smiled happily.

Where's Lucas? I need to see him, is what Shelly wanted to shout out badly.

Impatiently, she asked the Camp Guardian, "Can you please take me to see Lucas right now?"

Vanessa turned her full attention back towards Shelly and this time her face shifted into a scowl.

"I haven't seen you around camp. Who is she? Who are you?" Vanessa demanded, seemingly to both the Camp Guardian and Shelly.

Before things could escalate, the Camp Guardian got in between both of them and introduced Shelly.

"She claims to be Lucas' sister Shelly. I don't know how she got here, but there's only one way she could have entered."

Vanessa took this information in like a cogwheel spinning.

"You're Lucas' sister, and if you're here, that means you're like us," Vanessa exclaimed. "It's really nice to meet you. But wait, how did you just get here?"

Shelly felt a lump form in her throat as she tried to swallow.

"Lucas has spoken very fondly of you since his time here," the Camp Guardian admitted in a soft voice. "He is eager to return home and with you here, his joy will be reinforced. How are your parents?"

Shelly's expression suddenly shifted and the sunny sky became engulfed by grey foreign clouds. Her eyes prepared themselves for the rain to follow and she withheld the rest of what she felt. Only two words managed to escape and find an audience as the rest of her feelings remained closed off for her brother's arrival:

"They're…dead…"

Chapter 1: What's Done is Done

Lucas was in his cabin, the Imaginarium Illusion, holding the beads that he earned last summer during his first year in Camp Supernatural. He had fashioned them on his wrist the way campers had theirs, and paid special attention to the one Henry gave him personally. The bead was the only one of its kind because it had his initials carved into it in the middle: *L.S.* All the other beads given to the other campers had a specific color scheme to them. His bead was olive-colored and the one next to it was a dark blue with what looked like bits of red scattered around, like tiny fireflies. The other two beads he had were yellow mixed in orange, and violet with a dash of red.

Bill told me last year what each bead colors mean, he reminisced. *Blue means stability, red luck, orange enthusiasm, yellow optimism, green hope, pink delicate, purple spiritual, black mystery, white pure, and grey neutral. But I have combinations, so what do those mean?*

It had been nearly a year since Lucas came to Camp Supernatural and learned that he is an Alter Child. Part of a group of kids whose abilities are related to their disabilities. At the end of last summer, his older sister Shelly arrived in Camp Supernatural unexpectedly and delivered the worst news of his life.

I never got to say goodbye...

He was now fourteen years old and life seemed to become a lot more complicated. Lucas found himself thinking about the last time he saw his parents alive.

'Leave now, you're a disappointment to us'...

The memory replayed itself in his mind like an old movie and he wished with all his heart that he could go back and change things somehow.

When they returned home, Shelly and Lucas were greeted by a caseworker named Darla, who was in charge of ensuring Lucas' well-being until he turned eighteen. His mental health history was taken into account as well and Shelly was forced to prove she could take care of not only herself but her brother as well.

Darla began making regular visits, coming at least once a week, and making sure that Lucas was keeping up with his medication. Shelly did her best to make time between her schoolwork and meeting the needs Darla put on both of them. However, Lucas began to miss out on scheduled appointments and forgot to take his medication regularly.

I didn't forget, I just didn't want to. That stuff makes me want to sleep all day and my powers don't work when I use them.

Settling out the will, Shelly's name was the only one listed as the sole beneficiary. Her little brother found himself surprised that he was excluded from the will.

I should be upset by that, but I'm not. I feel like I deserve it for being a lousy son. They probably changed it after what happened last year or maybe it was always like that.

They held a small memorial with the few acquaintances his parents had, while the funeral itself was just as desolate. The two siblings didn't have enough money for an open casket or proper funeral, so they had to settle for a closed casket and evening viewing. There was also a book for attendees to sign-in and when Lucas looked inside, there were no signatures.

Not even a 'sorry for your loss, here's a five dollar coupon to Denny's.'

Lucas tried to invite some of his friends from camp to attend, but no one was able to show up. To make matters worse for him, Shelly insisted that he return to school so he could have a future beyond camp.

My excuse had been that Principal Lowe would never let me back into his school after how I left things.

To both siblings' astonishment, Principal Lowe allowed him to return, but never once met in person with either of them. When Lucas asked his sister about it, Shelly denied any involvement in the principal's unusual change of heart.

If I had to guess: I'd say he was replaced with another copy of himself, a nicer version, though that's not likely. I just have to put up with him for one more year...

Despite his reservations Lucas agreed to finish middle school and the two resumed their education that fall.

Besides Darla the case worker, Lucas also had to deal with regaining his original physique and resuming his appointments with Dr. Hoffman. It was during this time when he also underwent behavioral therapy and was diagnosed as being on the autistic spectrum. Correspondingly, it was around this time when Shelly started to monitor her brother's medical intake frequently, while also beginning to take college level classes.

Being autistic would explain my fixation on things and trouble with social cues. When I asked if I was still bi-polar, they didn't say yes or no...

As the months went by, Lucas saw his progress and not only had he regained his original physique; he even gained muscle in his arms and legs when before they were dormant.

I'm also a few inches taller, he observed after a measurement.

Despite his healing, Lucas still struggled with occasional limps, body cramps, and aches by the time the holidays came around.

Everything still hurts. I hope it isn't a permanent side effect.

Lucas studied for his classes when he wasn't in physical therapy, which would prove to be a challenge. After he successfully completed taking the remaining hours he needed to advance to the next grade, Lucas began taking eighth grade classes by December.

In his free time, Lucas tried to keep in contact with his friends from camp such as Ashley, Hailey, Bill, Mike, Josh, Gary, and most notably his girlfriend Vanessa. They would use Facetime or talk and text for hours on the phone, but seeing his girlfriend in person wasn't always easy. Vanessa lived in New Mexico, while Lucas and Shelly were in Austin, Texas. On some occasions, Vanessa managed to come and visit, even staying for a few days. Unfortunately, Shelly worried that this would interfere with Lucas's studies. Because of this she would discourage them from spending too much time together and once described Vanessa as his 'summer fling.'

I wish Shell wouldn't call Vanessa that, Lucas thought in embarrassment.

As for some of his other friends, Lucas heard back from Bill a few times but it was mostly through Vanessa. He didn't say much beyond prepping for Camp Counselor training during the winter break and that he was dating a girl named Shannon.

He's pretty excited about recruiting campers at the end of May, Lucas noted when he read Bill's most recent text message.

Lucas also thought about trying to message Ashley, but each time he tried texting her something held him back causing him to inadvertently avoid her. He mostly heard from his former cabin mates, Mike and Josh, with the latter telling him that if he didn't reply immediately it was because his home-school teachers were scolding him, lecturing him, or all of the above.

At least he texts me back a good amount, Lucas noted. He began reading to himself some of Mike and Josh's most recent texts: ***'Hi Luke, hope all is well. Looking forward to camp in a few days. See you then.' 'Hi Luke, Sapphire arrived in camp today and she's loving the cabins and outdoors. I can't wait for you to meet her.' 'Hey Luke, I found this app that teaches you how to sign language. Give it a look when you have the chance. I enjoy reading lips as much as the next deaf person, but after a while, it's about as fun as watching a fish talk. Peace.'***

Shelly had made Lucas promise not to use his powers to better himself in school. Although he tried to keep this promise, he ultimately did not. *And not for lack of trying.* Sometimes, he would anticipate the answers to questions the teachers did not have a chance to ask out loud. Other times, Lucas would use his powers to get at least a passing grade, while being careful not to get too many correct answers so as to avoid drawing unwanted attention from both his sister and peers. It was during this time when Lucas began to experience difficulties with his mind-reading abilities. He also had the occasional lapse of reading more than one mind at once, causing him to hear more personal thoughts than he would have liked. To counter this, Lucas tried to use the breathing exercises he learned from his physical therapy.

I remember my therapists from before would always suggest stuff like that, but I never took it seriously until now.

At one point during the school year, Lucas decided to wear his camp shirt since he had a few from his time in camp the previous year. He was shocked when the letters in the shirt weren't visible to anyone else. Only the color of his shirt was all anyone could see.

I remember running my fingers through my shirt and feeling the letters, but they weren't there. Like the name tag from when I first arrived in camp…

During the Christmas break, Boris arrived at Lucas and Shelly's home late one night to take them to camp for a week. He had arrived using a strange stone Lucas had never seen before. The stone seemingly teleported them from their home to Camp Supernatural. Upon arrival, Lucas hoped to see Henry, but was disappointed to see that the Camp Director was gone. When he asked the Camp Guardian about it, Boris yielded no answers.

I really wanted to spend time with Henry without having to worry about his son, Daniel, being around. Plus, he didn't get to meet Shelly last summer with everything that happened in the end.

The camp itself was beginning to go through some infrastructure workings, including the addition of new buildings. Lucas noticed one called The Grand Hall, which looked newly built but also old at the same time (Bill had explained the last time it was refurbished was before his time). Other structures included a nicer playground for the younger campers who didn't have to do the same training as teen campers, a small petting zoo with no animals in it yet, and the camp forge appeared to be open and ready for business. The forge included a few refurbishments of its own, with tools lining the walls like guitars in a guitar shop. Another building that was being added was similar in its structure to the Camp Director's home, but also looked to be about the same size as the tents the Camp Counselors occupied.

After a vote had taken place before the camp's closure last summer, Lucas was voted as the new Cabin Leader for the Imaginarium Illusion. His initial thrills for the ideas were dashed quickly when Bill warned him over the phone that the meetings were dreadfully boring. Most of the time, the council spent the meetings debating small insignificant things such as who gets to use the training field before someone else, and who gets to sit where in the cafeteria.

Another thing they argue about is who should wear what colored shirt for which cabin. Sounds exciting already. I thought the tables were already marked for everyone in the cafeteria, but maybe not for the Camp Counselors.

There were less than forty campers remaining, which included Mike, Lucas' cabin mate, and his little sister Sapphire. Last year, Lucas learned that she had been miraculously cured from her bedridden illness and was now living with Mike in Camp Supernatural. Her power manifested itself rather quickly when Lucas first met her. Her ability was to turn her body into a diamond-like form that made her body translucent. It also gave her fast agility and stamina for a short duration. The downside to the ability was that she got tired rather quickly and Mike attributed this to her size and age. Instead of having to worry about training, Mike revealed that Sapphire would be placed with kids her age and participate in activities with them.

I have to admit, her power is really cool. Makes me almost jealous. Emphasis on almost.

Shelly and Sapphire became close during that week they spent together in camp. This was mostly due to Shelly looking after Sapphire while Mike would go out on missions with the other camp counselors.

I wonder why Henry is letting him get that kind of training. Maybe it's because of how useful his ability is for missions in general? It also helps that he's living in camp now vs. me who has to go back into the real world like someone without abilities.

Lucas decided to ask Mike about why he was going on missions and his cabin mate assured him they were not part of the training portion of the camp.

"I still have to go through the training like everyone else. The only difference is once I finish, I'll go straight to Camp Counselor and not in-training like Bill is," Mike noted. "Henry lets a few Alter Children do this, notably the ones who don't have homes to go back to."

I didn't know that was possible. I wonder when that was mentioned. Maybe I can talk Shell into letting me stay here for at least a year once I finish middle school in May. If I can get all A's, without using my powers or without Shell knowing, then maybe there's a chance.

When Lucas asked about school, Mike explained that after Henry took him and Sapphire in, he legally adopted them, meaning their financial needs would be looked after by him. This also included the other Alter Children who remained in camp year round. Rather than having to worry about public schools, the two siblings would be receiving a formal education from Betty and Marcus. Both stayed in the camp as part-time teachers and were certified to teach in public schools. Betty was in charge of the younger campers while Marcus would help tutor the teen campers.

Lucky. I wish Henry could do that for me and Shelly. At least then we wouldn't have to worry about schools and mortgages.

When it was Christmas day, Shelly decided to surprise Sapphire with a special gift. The present was a DVD of the princess film, *Frozen.*

"It's really good," she told the little girl. "It has a lot of singing in it, a talking snowman, and a girl who can turn things into ice. She's kind of like you, but you're cooler because you can turn into diamonds."

Nice pun at the end, Lucas noticed, humorously. *Sapphire is the little sister Shelly always wanted me to be.*

Despite being ten years old, Sapphire did not physically look her age. She was unusually small, stood at about 3'8, and retained a very light squeaky voice. Her eyes were dark green with a bit of blue in them. She had an oval rounded face that made her look like an infant with long dark brown hair that Shelly took to tying in pigtails.

She looks more like a five or six year old.

Mike explained the reason for her youthful appearance was because she had been on medication for most of her life. Sapphire's physique was also halted by the effects of her illness. As a result, she had to receive regular hormonal shots to help with her growth, which her brother took responsibility for.

Another noticeable trait Lucas noticed about Sapphire was how hyperactive she often was. She had trouble sitting still for too long without pestering her brother or Shelly for attention.

When she received her Christmas present, Sapphire became especially excited and began to hop up and down like a bunny rabbit.

I know she doesn't mean to be that way, but she's very needy, Lucas thought, uncomfortably. *She also cries a lot when Mike leaves her alone for too long. She worries that he won't be back when that happens. Last time Shelly said she'd play with her in a minute, and when a minute passed, Sapphire started making a scene and calling Shelly a liar.*

Next, Lucas got Mike a video game that Mike already played and beat, but he still appreciated the gift. When it was his turn, Mike gave Lucas a scrapbook, which looked big enough to be mistaken for a textbook from school. Nonetheless, Lucas was grateful and promised to use it for the upcoming summer.

I don't even know what scrapbooks are for, he thought in embarrassment. *I think it's like a journal, but for guys, like how diaries are for girls.*

Sapphire made a sketch of herself, Mike, Shelly, and Lucas like a family portrait. When she finished drawing it, Shelly paid her five dollars to sign and purchase it.

Sapphire's looking at that five-dollar bill like it's a hundred, Lucas thought with a smile as the little girl held the money up like a trophy.

After this, Sapphire playfully told her brother, "You should marry Shelly so I can have a big sisto."

Mike flushed at the idea, but Shelly laughed it off, commenting on the age difference between the two. Mike was turning thirteen in January while Shelly was sixteen.

It's hard to believe he will be the age I was when my life changed, Lucas admitted, trying not to think too much about those intense feelings.

The final gift surprisingly came from someone unexpected; the Camp Director himself. There was a small cage in Lucas' cabin along with some bags of dog food. Inside the cage was a small dog that gave Lucas an eerie feeling of déjà vu.

That can't be… no way. I swear that's the same dog that Henry had last year when I was in the camp ward. He looks exactly like that dog.

The dog appeared to be a mixed breed between a Pomeranian and a Shih Tzu; a Shiranian. Its fur was light brown like bronze and its tongue waggled up and down in unison with its furry tail.

The gift was for Sapphire, and she decided to name her new dog Twinkle which Shelly thought was a cute but silly name.

Twinkle, like the song, Lucas heard Mike think.

I was thinking it's more because of the eyes. They twinkle like diamonds.

Mike received a vinyl record from *The Carpenters*, while Lucas got a book.

It's called 'Everything that Rises Must Converge' by Flannery O'Connor, Lucas thought in slight dissatisfaction. *I'm not really much into reading books as I am reading minds as it turns out.*

Shelly received a gift as well. It appeared Henry didn't know Lucas' sister very well since the present was a porcelain doll.

It looks like that doll from that one horror movie Shell said was lame because the doll barely came out in it despite being on the poster.

Shelly offered Sapphire the porcelain doll, which she took happily. At the bottom of the gift bag was a piece of paper, which made her face twist into a frown. When Lucas asked his sister about it, she dismissed it as being a note that welcomed her to camp.

"He just wrote, 'Thank you for accepting my invitation, and looking forward to a wonderful summer with you and your brother'."

That does not sound like anything Henry would say. But I'll take her word for it. I could always read her mind, but I want to trust whatever it is, if she felt it was important, she'd tell me.

After the holidays were over, Lucas and Shelly returned home. They talked about camp, what to expect, and the friends Lucas made while there.

From what I told Shelly: She should steer clear of Josh's flirtatious attempts. She'll be best friends with Ashley and Hailey easily. She doesn't hate Vanessa, but she doesn't like her very much either. Not 100% sure why. She might get along with Bill, although I don't know how much mingling he'll be able to do now since he's going to be a Camp Counselor. Gary should be cool with her, I hope. And lastly, I told her to avoid Alexia, even though we're supposed to be good after last year.

"As long as there's no ski-masked killer on the loose, camp sounds like it will be fun," Shelly said humorously. Lucas did not understand the reference and his sister shook her head in disappointment.

Lucas never told Shelly about the accident or about the two birds from the white room, but she did force him to tell her how he ended up in crutches. He told her the truth without saying the whole truth: That he fell from a cliff. Surprisingly, she found it harder to believe than he did.

On Valentine's Day, Lucas planned to take Vanessa out to a movie and dinner after. To his dismay, he soon learned that she had expensive tastes and expectations. She wanted the largest popcorn and largest soda, along with theater candy. For dinner, she expected a fancy restaurant as opposed to fast-food places. To top it off, they were not legally of age to drive so they had to be chauffeured around by Shelly, who stayed silent most of the time. She couldn't have gotten a word in even if she wanted when Vanessa began to bounce between topics of conversation like someone changing the radio station.

Shelly is trying to like Vanessa for me, but I can tell without reading her mind that she doesn't like her all that much. I've seen them talk a few times, mostly about girl stuff and even about Camp Supernatural, but Vanessa is definitely a conversation hogger. That's what Shelly thinks at least and as far as I want to know how she feels about it.

After they dropped Vanessa at the bus station, Shelly asked Lucas how much money he spent on their date. When he showed her the receipts, she was furious to learn that he had spent more than he was supposed to. While she tried not to show it, Lucas often heard her complaining in his mind. It was during these times when he felt the most pain in his head.

He lets that girlfriend of his spend money he doesn't have. He bought her popcorn, soda, candy, and she was still hungry for fancy restaurant food?! The worst part is she took the food to go, and all Lucas was man enough to ask for was the free breadsticks, he heard his sister think.

Lucas knew the stress was taking a toll on Shelly. Darla the caseworker was still checking in on the two siblings regularly, and she insisted that Lucas' sister take a part time job to cover necessities such as her brother's medical bills and home bills. Shelly found one at a local diner where her shifts were very late at night to accommodate her school schedule. She was miserable with the work demands and being constantly hit on by older men.

Despite the walls she put up, there were times when Shelly lowered them. One night, Lucas awoke to hear his sister sobbing in the other room and saw her clutching a family picture they had taken years ago. He wanted to comfort her but also knew that she needed to be alone to let out her feelings.

I've been crying a lot too… pretty often actually, Lucas admitted to himself as his throat began to tighten and he felt the urge to cry right then and there. *I can't though. I have to hold it in. We both need to be strong for each other…*

Similarly to Shelly's money problems, Lucas was fighting his own internal battle. He was unable to maintain control over his abilities without experiencing a sharp pain, even when trying to do something as natural as mind reading.

The pain is worse than when I couldn't read minds. It feels like something inside me is broken or wounded… and every time I use my powers it's like picking at the scab and not letting it heal on its own.

As spring break came to an end, Lucas finally decided to ask his sister about how their parents died. To his disappointment, Shelly would avoid the question and promise to tell him tomorrow. Then she promised to tell him next week.

Then next month.

Tomorrow.

Next week.

Next month.

All turned to never.

Many times, he was tempted to read her mind but knew that Shelly would hold it against him. Some days, when he woke up panting and sweating from a nightmare, his powers would shut down almost entirely. It was during this time that, no matter how hard he tried, he could not read minds. It got to a point where Lucas couldn't remember certain things and had trouble recalling where he lived once, but the confusion only lasted for a minute.

I knew having mind-based powers was going to be hard, but I didn't know it could also involve memory loss.

Finally, the end of May was near again, and Lucas was looking forward to the first day of a new summer in Camp Supernatural.

One of his New Year resolutions were to have a better year than last year, but Shelly reminded him that no one ever followed them through. When he tried to argue, she brought up the time when he was six and swore to forgo chocolate and caffeine, only to cave in a day later.

To be fair, it was her fault. She bought this huge can of chocolate pudding and just left it in the kitchen for anyone to get. Shell knew it was my favorite too, and it would have gone bad if it stayed there long. So, in a way, I did her a favor.

The day before they returned to camp, Shelly entered her junior year of high school and began applying for scholarships that were more than eager to accommodate her needs. She had her hair done the days before camp, straightening it, and cutting it a few inches shorter so it didn't curl. She also gave herself a bronde hairstyle to go against her natural dark brown hair. While Lucas was pleased with her joining him in camp that year, he began to think a troubling thought that settled in him like acid reflux.

It won't be long now before she starts applying to colleges. By next year she'll be a senior, and I'll still be in high school. Where does that leave me? Also, another pressing thought; she's like me, an Alter child, and she never received an invitation until late last year. What's that all about?

Shelly told Darla the caseworker that she and Lucas would be visiting relatives for the summer out of state and would be back by August. She promised to keep in touch regularly but hoped it wouldn't come to that.

Rather than the skeletal cab drivers, Betty showed up to Lucas and Shelly's address and brought them to camp. She had a similar stone to the one that Boris had used previously.

I was looking forward to seeing Francis and introducing him to Shelly, Lucas thought in slight disappointment.

Upon arriving at Camp Supernatural, Lucas was shocked that the other counselors were nowhere to be seen; even Mike was gone.

"Mikey left me here with Betty and with the rest of the counsal people," Sapphire told Lucas and Shelly when they found her in Mike's cabin. Her eyes were still rheumy from when she had been crying. Knowing Sapphire, the river her tears made could house many happy fishes.

Then, to Lucas' delight, Henry finally showed up in camp. He was quick to hide away in his house though and did not allow anyone to visit him. Even Lucas was denied entry. He tried at one point to enter, but Boris had to tell him that the Camp Director did not wish to be disturbed. Lucas felt more concerned than upset by this.

Why is he hiding in his office? Lucas wondered. *Does he know that I'm back? Does he care?*

Apparently, Henry decided not to summon the skeletal cab drivers this year. Instead, he sent the camp counselors to recruit the new campers when it was time for summer. Lucas was unaware of the reason for this, but suspected it had to do with why Mike left with them. Both Betty and Marcus were in charge of bringing back campers who had attended in previous years to expedite the process.

As Lucas was exiting his room, Shelly made her presence known inside the cabin.

"Hey, Lucas, Sapphire wanted to know if you're interested in seeing a movie with us?" Shelly asked him. "Please come see it with me. It's like the hundredth time she's seen that movie and I cannot stand that obnoxious song anymore. I can't let it go."

Shelly grimaced at the irony as Lucas shook his head.

"No thanks, but can we please talk, Shelly?"

His sister nodded and sat next to him on the couch.

"What's on your mind, Luke?"

Lucas had held off the questions about what happened to their parents, but he now wanted answers from Shelly.

"Shelly…what happened to mom and dad?"

Almost instantly, Shelly's skin went cold and she turned away from her little brother.

"Lucas… please don't make me talk about it," his sister pleaded as she took hold of his hand.

Brusquely, he withdrew his hand from her.

"I loved mom and dad too. I know I didn't always show it, but I loved them." Lucas insisted. "I didn't even… I didn't even get to say goodbye to them. At least you were there and got to be with them. So, tell me what happened. Please, Shell. I need to know."

After a few seconds, Shelly let loose in a way that made Lucas regret asking altogether.

"It was a brain aneurysm. They both died from aneurysms! Are you happy now?!" Shelly exclaimed angrily, as she began to sob.

Aneurysms? Brain aneurysms? But how, and why?

Feeling guilty, Lucas wrapped his arms around his sister in a warm embrace. At first Shelly wasn't receptive to it but relented after a few seconds.

"I'm sorry, Shell. I just needed to know, and I didn't want to read your mind to find out."

After hugging his sister, Lucas felt conflicted.

"I don't understand how they died. It shouldn't be possible for something like that to happen at the same time, right?"

Did punching my dad have something to do with it? The last time I saw him, he was hurt and my mom was afraid of me.

Lucas suddenly felt terrible for wanting to know the truth and hated himself for the last part he thought.

It makes no sense. Nothing about anything that has happened since last year makes any sense.

His sister shook her head and wiped her face clean.

"They loved you," Shelly confessed, sadly. "They loved you so much. I know they treated you harshly, more than me, but they weren't the same after you left. Mom and dad… they just slowly stopped. What happened to them… it didn't happen the way you think. They were fine for a little bit. It wasn't until July when… something happened… I can't remember it all… Anyways, you need to know the truth, Luke. You didn't hit dad. When I went downstairs to check on them, they were just… frozen."

Frozen, like when I used my power on Alexia.

"I tried to stop you from leaving, but you didn't hear me. So, I don't know what you think you saw, Lucas, but it wasn't what you thought. After whatever made them stop went away, they came to and thought you were still at home. It destroyed them to find out that you weren't there anymore. I'd never seen them behave that way, like they were in a trance, and something snapped them out of it."

But I remember it all. I swear what I saw was real. They stood still like statues? What the heck does that mean? Is it possible I imagined everything up until that point? None of it happened the way I remembered it… I don't know what to think anymore. If I had just gone back in when I heard my sister, and looked at my parents again, who knows, I probably never would have gone to camp to begin with. I never would have needed to.

That realization alone hurt him more than he could bear, but he felt a small semblance of peace now knowing the truth.

"I'm glad you were there for them, Shell," Lucas said through a pained smile. "I wish I could make things right, but it's time to try and move forward for both our sakes. We need each other, and I'll do everything I can so we can help each other. What's done is done."

After proclaiming this, Lucas hugged his sister again and pondered his own words.

Done, is what done…?

Chapter 2: A New Beginning

It was finally the first day of June. As the morning trumpet rang, Lucas felt his ears ringing like a telephone while his head flew from his pillow like a cannonball.

That's one way to start the summer off, he thought with a groan.

Once he finished rubbing his ears, Lucas decided to take a quick shower before heading off to the welcoming ceremony. He had to be careful with his nails as he scratched at his scalp.

I can't wait to see everyone again, Lucas thought excitedly. *The only person I've seen from last year was Vanessa but that's because she's, my girlfriend. I hope Ashley has been doing well.*

The Grand Hall had been completed and looked to be as splendid and enormous as Henry's house from an outside perspective. The roof looked like the top of fences, and the door leading into the hall was almost as tall as the Camp Guardian himself. If Lucas didn't know what the building represented, he would have thought it was a mini church.

In addition, one site had been built and another refurbished. The stable had small fences with grass barely growing, and a small litter of puppies that looked similar to Twinkle. Meanwhile, the blacksmith's forge had a small anvil that looked like it had seen the birth of many weapons. The weapons from before remained, but Lucas suspected that once camp went underway, someone was going to begin making more swords, shields, axes, and other medieval weapons he wasn't sure about.

I wonder who will use that forge. Maybe that guy from the camp gift shop and Alexia with her power goons.

Surprisingly, the camp shop was closed at the moment and looked to be going through some renovations similar to the blacksmith's forge.

Now where will we get shirts for everyone in camp to wear? Maybe it will be done by the end of the week. Also, why're there so many renovations this year? I was really hoping I could get a motivational mug that said, 'I read minds, but minds off limits.' I should coin that before someone else does.

When he turned a bit to the left of the camp shop, Lucas saw another building that reminded him of the Camp Director's home.

Even though this other house is new, it looks like it's had a bunch of owners, and whoever lived in it forgot to fix it up.

Its top and bottom were narrow and sharp, with edges that appeared as if they were drawn from the Victorian era. The windows were tilted and triangular, while the front door had a black doorknob and dark wood that seemed sunburned with small shades of brown scattered around. Lucas swore that a dark cloud hovered over the house like a flying saucer, but he attributed this to how strange the weather often was in Camp Supernatural.

Maybe that's why we have a forest nearby; because of how much it rains here.

Each cabin in the camp has a supernatural perk to it, with his cabin being able to create things out of the imagination from whoever was occupying it. Last year the occupants were Bill, who was now a Camp Counselor, Lucas himself, Mike, Josh, and Gary. With Bill's absence, and assuming the rest of the group returned, a new member would need to fill in the empty spot.

I don't like that idea. It's too much work to meet someone new and get them used to how things are in the cabin.

After Bill chose Lucas to replace him as Cabin Leader, he made him promise to keep the cabin in check and to make sure Josh didn't destroy it with his sonic waves.

The good news is if anything does happen to the cabin, at least I know who will get the blame.

Upon his return from recruiting other campers, Bill was going to have his very own tent along with the other Camp Counselors. He'd also take part in assisting with the training part of the camp next month.

I remember how excited he was about it last year. During the times we talked on the phone or through texting, Bill couldn't stop bragging about becoming a counselor.

When Lucas finished getting ready, he exited the cabin to join Shelly, Sapphire, and Twinkle, the dog wagging his tail excitedly at the sight of him. Sapphy was dressed in the smallest blue camp T-shirt Lucas ever saw with pigtails that Shelly had done for her. She was also holding the porcelain doll Shelly gave her for Christmas (which she named Barbara) in one arm and her free hand's thumb in her mouth.

The small girl had been crying because she had had a nightmare the previous night about a new movie Shelly saw with her.

"What's wrong, Sapphire?" Lucas asked with concern.

"The meanie man in the froggie movie got eaten by a big scary face," Sapphire said in-between sobs. She stopped sucking her thumb and began to impulsively pick her nose while making a squeaky sniff sound like a piglet.

I wanted to try and get Sapphire into another movie because I'm sick of that other one, Shelly thought in her mind, with Lucas suddenly feeling slightly annoyed. *She was fine at first, but then she started crying when that part happened. I just can't take that song anymore… Let it go, let it go…*

Lucas wanted to laugh at his sister's thoughts, but Shelly shot him a look that he was all too familiar with.

That's the look that says, 'Laugh and you'll choke on it.'

Mike was still away with the other counselors, so Sapphire needed someone to take care of her. Despite Shelly enjoying the little camper's company, there were days when Sapphire's needs were too demanding and excessive; this was one of those days. Shelly sighed in irritation as the little girl continued to weep waterfalls.

Maybe it was a good thing I never had a sister, because Sapphire is a lot sometimes, Lucas heard Shelly think. He felt uncomfortable with the thought. *Even when Lucas was a kid, he never got scared of the movies I liked, which were old horror movies. Sapphire is scared of even just the music by itself. If she can't handle voodoo dolls and dancing skeletons, she won't like anything else I can think of. Except for that talking snowman and that song…*

Lucas started to hear the song in his head and suddenly regretted his abilities.

Most people have the problem of hearing an uncomfortable song subconsciously. I am very *conscious when I hear them.*

In an instant, the sharp-stinging pain that Lucas had become acquainted with crept up as Shelly's voice continued to sound off in his head. He was grateful that it was mildly painful compared to the other times, when it hurt to read minds.

Twinkle began whimpering suddenly and huddled behind Sapphire's legs as Boris, the Camp Guardian, appeared before them. He was still the same as last summer, with his disfigured face and glossy mop of dark hair that fell to one side. The only difference was that he had nicer clothes from before and wore an orange camp shirt. It looked big enough to fit a gorilla in.

I don't see that shirt having a very long life with those tiny rips forming.

The outline of the monster's chest revealed a sunken stomach and rib cages that looked near visible past the orange from the shirt.

I hope Sapphire doesn't notice that, or we'll be expecting more showers, Lucas heard the thought enter his mind. He wasn't sure if it was from him or Shelly.

"It's great to see you again, Lucas, and you as well, Madam Shelly," Boris greeted them courteously with a crooked smile. "I am so pleased to see the both of you. The day is brighter now that you're here."

Lucas' eyebrow went up as his eyes glanced from Shelly to Boris.

I'm pretty sure he doesn't mean me in this instance, Lucas thought with a sigh.

"It's good to reacquaint myself with you as well, Sir Camp Guardian," Shelly said, trying to follow Boris's formal etiquette.

The monster laughed and shook his head. It was a sound Lucas was unfamiliar with laughter from the Camp Guardian. He found it oddly refreshing.

"Boris is just fine," the Camp Guardian said with a bashful grin.

Funny, it took me almost a whole month before I could call him that, Lucas thought with a hint of envy. *Plus, he likes Shelly already; it took me longer to win his trust. Not that anyone is keeping count.*

"I hope you haven't heard this before, but you remind me of Frankenstein's Monster," Shelly noted, to Lucas' embarrassment. The Camp Guardian chuckled and nodded. "I'm a big fan of classic horror movies so I had to mention it."

"Ironically, that film is where my namesake came from."

Shelly seemed confused by this, as did Lucas, until Boris explained.

"Boris Karloff is the actor who plays Frankenstein's Monster in the 1931 film."

Then it clicked with the two siblings as if both had been struck by lightning.

That actually makes a lot of sense. It's also kind of a cool reason.

"You know, now that I think of it," Boris continued as Lucas left his train of thought, "when you first came to the camp, Shelly, you walked in as if you belonged here all along. Only an Alter Child could enter the Camp as you did."

Shelly looked puzzled by this.

"Really? When were you going to mention this to me, Luke?" Shelly asked as she gave her brother a stern look.

Lucas shrugged helplessly.

"I forgot. We had a lot going on last year."

Shelly rolled her eyes and shook her head.

"Typical little brother."

I do one thing wrong and suddenly I'm 'typical little brother?' How typical of her to say.

"Are you aware of the ability you possess?" Boris asked Shelly.

Lucas' sister shook her head.

"I'm not sure. I don't have any physical or mental disabilities, unless you count blinking a lot. I used to do that as a kid, but not so much anymore."

Lucas thought about it and realized this was true.

She'd stand in front of the television screen and mimic whatever she saw while blinking her eyes like flashes from cameras. She was really good at pretending to be a dancer also, until she realized she had to wear a tutu to join ballet. I'm pretty sure that was the last time she danced.

Turning his attention to Sapphire, the Camp Guardian said in a baby tone, "Hello there, little one. It's so wonderful to meet you" He knelt down to level with her, while Twinkle began to softly whimper.

The small girl looked at Boris in bewilderment.

"Why do you talk like a baby?" she asked forwardly.

If I didn't know how nice of a guy Boris is, I would be terrified of his reaction to that.

Boris chuckled awkwardly and turned his attention to the puppy behind her.

"Who's this little fella?" Boris asked in a normal tone as Twinkle looked at him meekly.

"This is Twinkle. Say 'hi', Twinkle," the little girl instructed her dog.

The Camp Guardian stretched out his hand and the dog slowly crept up to him. Despite how grotesque his hand looked, with its moldy look and pieces of charred skin, Twinkle licked Boris's hand and barked happily. The little girl giggled at this and gave the monster a comfortable look.

"He likes you," Sapphire said with a small smile.

"I like him too," Boris said, blushing slightly.

Making his presence known, Camp Director Henry James appeared as if he had been there the whole time. Physically Henry still looked somewhat the same as last year, but his long grey hair appeared to be brittle, whiter, and his beard was longer now. He was also wearing a grey robe that had a hood stitched to it. The sleeves of his grey robe had lines of red and blue while the edges of the bottom were stitched with faded black.

That robe looks like he made it himself. I remember he likes to knit.

"Hello, Lucas, and welcome to Camp Supernatural, Shelly, and Sapphire," Henry greeted them with a warm smile.

Shelly nodded stiffly at him and gave him a puzzled look. Sapphire stared at Henry with a look of excitement and anticipation.

This is the guy Lucas couldn't stop talking about, he heard Shelly think. *There's something about him that seems off. Not sure what—*

After that, Lucas was not able to hear the rest of his sister's thoughts.

"Sapphire, I am assigning you to Underrated Unicorn. It's the cabin best suited for little girls, and your brother will only be a few cabins away should you need him," Henry assured the little girl, who nodded enthusiastically. "Shelly, after much consideration, I have decided that you would be best suited for the Weeping Willow cabin. If you would like to choose your own cabin though, you may. Cabins are ordinarily assigned to all campers, but I would like your stay here to be as amicable as possible."

Shelly nodded again as Henry handed her a list of cabins. She snatched it from him and glued her eyes to the page.

What's with Shell, Lucas thought, feeling uncomfortable. *She's acting like Henry did something to offend her.*

Sapphire recognized the Camp Director as the man who gave her Twinkle for Christmas and smiled meekly at him.

"Hello, Camp sir. Thank you for Twinkle. I love him so much."

Henry smiled at the little girl, knelt down, and patted her on the head gently.

"You are very welcome, my dear. I do hope you will take good care of him."

Sapphire scooped up Twinkle with both arms and kissed the puppy on the forehead.

"I will," Sapphire promised with a big smile on her face.

That's the happiest I've seen her since Mike left.

Henry also noticed the doll Sapphire was holding and asked where she got it from.

"Shelly gave it to me," the little girl admitted bluntly. Shelly looked slightly embarrassed by this, like she was being called out for stealing something as minor as a candy bar in a store. Nevertheless, Henry didn't seem to mind and instead laid a soft hand on Sapphire's small head.

"Take care of them both then."

Turning his attention to Lucas, Henry asked, "Lucas, would you kindly follow me?"

Finally, he wants to talk, Lucas thought enthusiastically.

As they were walking away, Lucas heard the uneasy thoughts Shelly had about the Camp Director.

I don't like this. That letter he gave me. I just want Lucas to— Shelly's voice became drowned out in static, and her brother was unable to hear the rest of her thoughts again.

He shook his head, feeling both uneasy about his sister's hesitation towards Henry, as well as his own inner turmoil.

Why is Shelly acting so weird towards Henry? He's shown me nothing but kindness since I came here last year. He's the reason I'm not in a hospital bed anymore… she doesn't know that though. Maybe she'd trust him more if she knew. Ugh, I wish this pain would stop already! It's not just my body; it's my mind that is hurting also.

Lucas saw Boris walk with Shelly and Sapphire towards the pavilion area where the platform was already being set up by Camp Counselors Betty and Marcus. When they spotted him, only Betty waved at Lucas. She appeared to be thinner than the year before and looked well off compared to Marcus, who looked like he hadn't slept in days. His eyes were sunken in, and stubbles decorated his cheeks like breadcrumbs.

He's thinking a lot about Naomi; where is she, how she is, what is she doing? Who is Naomi?

Lucas followed Henry to his office and upon entering noticed the re-decorations. Last year he saw dozens of books and records lying around, now he noticed they were all organized on a shelf for easier access. The record player still remained the same, playing another song from *The Carpenters*. Henry looked at it and smiled.

"*Yesterday Once More*, a classic amongst their discography," he commented proudly as the chorus in the song played.

I told myself I'd listen to the Carpenters more, but with everything that happened last year, I never got around to it.

Henry then beckoned for Lucas to sit. He did so eagerly.

"How was school this year?" the Camp Director asked as he adjusted his seat.

"Boring, nothing new," Lucas confessed casually. "I finished middle school but it's nothing special. I'm starting high school in the fall and Shelly is going to be a junior." After saying this, he realized how much time was beginning to pass.

Before coming to camp, I was halfway through middle school, and now I'm entering high school. My parents were also alive… no! Stop it! Not here.

Henry nodded and listened intently.

"That is good to hear, my son. Very well done. How has your sister adjusted to the events of last year?"

While Henry sounded caring, Lucas had trouble telling if he really felt that way. Oftentimes he seemed kind and compassionate, but other times the Camp Director appeared very disinterested, unemotional, and impassive. His long-lined face made him look like a melting wax figure.

He looks exhausted and older. I can't read his mind so I don't know what could be bothering him.

"Things… haven't been easy," Lucas began to explain. *I don't want to talk about it.* "But according to the will our parents left behind, there's enough money for Shell to start investing in college and to look after me." *Hogwash. Baloney.*

"Did they leave you money for college as well?"

Lucas nodded, gritting his teeth as if in pain.

No, they didn't, but Henry doesn't need to know that.

"It doesn't matter anyways. Maybe I don't need to go to college. I mean, I can literally read minds. I could go through high school and then just come back here and work as a counselor, right?"

Maybe not forever but at least until things get better.

Lucas gazed at the emotionless face of Henry as he waited for an answer.

If I wasn't sure before I am now; something is off. It's like he's trying to pay attention, but I can tell he's drifting off. He's behaving like someone who is half-awake and I know that feeling all too well.

As the song finished playing, Henry walked over to the record player and carefully removed the vinyl, putting it back into its sleeve.

After this, he walked to the shelves and placed it carefully in between some other musical records.

I wish I could read his mind. More than that, I wish he trusted me with what's on his mind.

Lucas was so deep in his own train of thought that he didn't realize the Camp Director was already seated across from him.

"How do you feel regarding the unfortunate passing of your parents?" Henry asked a bit more forwardly than Lucas would have been comfortable with.

Lucas suddenly felt his anxiety climbing the ladder of his mind rapidly and felt like retreating.

I don't want to talk about it. Not even with Henry.

"Sir, if it's all the same, I don't want to talk about it," Lucas heard himself say impulsively. He suddenly felt shameful, feeling like the Camp Director would take offense because of the way he said it. Instead, Henry simply nodded.

"I understand, my child. Forgive the inquiry. It has been a difficult year for you and your sister," Henry admitted. "But now is not the time to think about the past. It is time to enjoy yourself and to better control your abilities. I have faith in your capability to master your mind where others have failed," the Camp Director finished as he smiled benevolently at him.

Lucas could sense the wisdom in his words as well as the sincerity.

"This summer, you will also be able to take part in missions which will begin around next month."

"What are the missions like?" Lucas suddenly asked. He was disappointed when the Camp Director abruptly changed subjects.

At least that hasn't changed.

"Before we discuss anything further, do you know why I requested to speak with you at this moment?"

He shook his head as Henry continued.

"Something has come to my attention that needs addressing."

Lucas felt his hands begin to shake and his muscles tense as he feared what the Camp Director wanted to talk about. His eyes darted in every direction, avoiding direct eye contact.

Does this have to do with what happened last year? He felt the instinctive desire to pick at his skin but restrained himself to avoid calling Henry's attention to this new habit.

"As you are aware, today is the first day of summer camp. By now, we would have begun the welcoming ceremony and the induction of campers into their cabins. However, Daniel and the other counselors have not returned, and their absence is becoming a concern. Ordinarily we would have had the skeletal cab drivers picking up campers as with previous years, but this year that is not possible. Considering the number of known Alter Children has begun to dwindle in recent time, Daniel has proposed that we should first focus on bringing back those familiar with the camp before finding new children," Henry explained anxiously. Despite his tone, his face was too calm.

Only campers who are already familiar with the camp? Why them first? I get that new campers means new possibly good and bad abilities, but there's got to be a reason for that. Also, what happened to the skeletal cab drivers?

The Camp Director suddenly shifted moods with his face turning towards a brighter disposition.

"It's still early in the day. They may yet surprise us."

Lucas nodded, trying to feed off Henry's sudden optimism.

"Do you think Mike is okay? He's not a Camp Counselor, so why did he—"

Before Lucas could finish speaking, Boris burst through the door as if a bomb had just gone off.

"Camp Director James! We have a situation!" the Camp Guardian exclaimed urgently.

Henry quickly rose from his desk and showed strong facial concern.

"What is it, Boris? Have the counselors returned with the first wave of campers?"

Boris shook his head and swallowed uneasily before he replied.

"No, sir. They were attacked… and there is something else."

The monster took a moment to speak. His eyes hesitantly turned to Lucas.

"It's alright, Boris. Speak freely now."

The anxiety Lucas felt began to build up, as if his body had a mind of its own. He began to pick at his arm and was grateful that he was wearing a long sleeve. Lucas was grateful that Henry's attention was fixed on Boris and not him. No amount of anticipation could have prepared Lucas for the Camp Guardian's revelation.

"Counselor Zane was able to send out a message using the remains of his sanctuary stone. I'm compiling a list of casualties and wounded with Zane. Several campers were captured and… a counselor."

Chapter 3: Bloodshot

Mike followed the group ahead of him which consisted of Daniel in the lead, Jane, Alexander, Richardson, Bill, Shannon, and Connors, the last three being counselors-in-training. He was the only camper among them, and he knew why that was.

I can find most anything just by touching it, and the kids from camp always carry their beads from the previous years.

The other group of counselors that included Zane, Naomi, Margot, and Lucinda had split up to search for new campers to bring in before the start of summer camp. Daniel's group began a trek past the pre-summer wintery landscape with a group of campers they picked up in the north continent area.

I hope Sapphire is doing alright, Mike thought while he shivered underneath his various clothing. *She's too delicate like that power of hers.*

He was bundled up in two heavy-set jackets, jeans, and running sneakers. He hadn't cut his hair since March, so his bangs were nearly falling to his eyebrows even with a beanie on. Mike reached for the water in his pack, but hesitated, feeling how much was left in it.

Not as much as I'd like and there's no water foundations nearby. Mike threw back his head and let out a sigh. His breath painted a small cloud from his mouth like smoke. *Not that I'd actually drink from one of those disgusting filthy things.*

He was joined by Bill and Shannon. The two counselors in training were walking closely together with their bare hands clasping each other.

How they can do that without gloves is beyond me. In the cold they'll get splinters or they'll get sick from not washing their hands.

Part of Mike's training wasn't just to continue mastering his ability, but his OCD as well. He often felt compulsions such as needing to wear gloves, to avoid touching anything that seemed contaminated and fixated heavily on mental reviewing. The last time he felt this compulsion was in his cabin's room. He recalled tapping on the door repeatedly with his knuckles and pushing it with the back of his hand to make sure it opened and closed properly.

A door is a door when it wants to be adored.

Behind the group were about twenty children, each with varying abilities. Mike had found the majority of them by using the beads they had, while Daniel located five new campers with his glimpse ability. When Daniel tried to find more, his ability began to act up.

After this group, we should be heading back to camp soon, Mike thought happily. It warmed his heart to imagine seeing his friends again once the next group was brought in. He hadn't seen Josh or Gary among these kids but knew they wouldn't be far behind.

The blistering cold was getting to Mike, who was in charge of making sure the young campers following behind were doing alright. He instructed them to form straight lines and to hold each other together by the arms. Bill and Shannon were too busy talking with each other to notice how slow the young campers were progressing behind them. Connors helped Mike to rotate turns in keeping an eye on the children.

What if they get lost? What if one trips and brings down all the others? Why aren't Bill and Shannon doing anything but making googly eyes at each other!

To ignore the pain, he felt from the cold, and his intrusive thoughts, Mike began to think of poems that rhymed. He started with some of his favorites, which included *'The Tyger'* and *'Fire and Ice'*. His own words began to take form in his mind like a prophecy.

For what cannot be seen, will soon go green. When the blind walk alone, the deaf will be forlorn. Some enjoy the beauties of life, others struggle through strife. Compared to life above ground, both views remain sound.

This constant stream of rhymes helped to soothe Mike into a calmness he often found difficult when his symptoms for OCD worsened. Taking a break from watching over the young campers, Mike made his way towards the front where Jane was also heading in Daniel's direction.

Everyone was wearing heavy jackets and had their hoods up. To Mike, if he saw himself and the others from a distance, he would have thought they were nomads journeying to a faraway land.

If you can't make it to the top, you have to enjoy the goods before they drop. Get enough wood for a fire, so you can reach your heart's desire. Okay, that's enough rhymes. I'll try limericks next time. For real, I mean it!

The only two counselors who were not wearing a lot of clothing were Alexander and Richardson. Both sported matching green beanies, blue and red long sleeves with the camp's name on them, and heavy leathered boots. Alexander was rhythmically breathing as if he were preparing for a jog. Richardson's mouth was closed, his nostrils flared backwards, and his lips exhaled the breath that was taken in. Mike wasn't sure if it was the cold or the fact that his nerves were screaming, but he swore he saw small dancing sparks coming from Richardson's breath.

"How much further do we have to go, Daniel?" Jane asked him. Her newly dyed red chestnut hair was underneath her hood, and her eyes seemed to gleam in the reflection of Daniel's mismatched irises.

"We need to get out of this weather before using our sanctuary stones," Daniel assured. "There won't be enough charges to send everyone back at once. Some of us are going to need to stay behind until Zane's group comes to us."

Mike understood what Daniel meant. Sanctuary stones, though convenient, were not meant for large group traveling. Their charges required a few hours' rest before they could be used again and they could only transfer at most five people at a time back to camp. Even so, the safety number was three and the danger limit, five. Reckless overuse could render the stone inoperable.

There's eight counselors, and eight stones since Shannon, Bill, and Connor don't have one. We expected to find at most twenty or fifteen campers at a time. Daniel is pushing it by trying to find more campers than we can take back at the moment.

As Mike was trying to do the math in his head regarding who would possibly need to get left behind, Bill made his way towards him.

"Hey, Mike. How are you holding up in the cold?" Bill asked in a relaxed tone. "Are those gloves helping you at all? I can barely feel my fingers."

Bill had red goggles on to protect his eyes from the cold, a grey pullover hoodie, and carried a backpack filled with supplies for the counselors. Shannon and Connors both had similar packs with them.

Shannon made her presence known just as Bill had. She had a youthful face with medium length frizzy light brown hair that was buried underneath a blue beanie. Her lips were tight and forward, with a nose ring on her left nostril. She wore a red sweater with fur linings and fur boots. Underneath was a camp shirt with the words, 'Honest but Fearless'.

Mike nodded, touching his gloves to his face.

"They get the j-j-job done. With my new a-a-ability it doesn't do me good to be w-w-without them," Mike declared through chattering possessed teeth.

Camp is starting to sound nicer by the minute, and not just because my sister is there. Even if it is rainy and humid, I'll take that over the cold any day of the week.

Shannon giggled softly at Mike's comment and gestured to Bill for his attention.

"Those red goggles make you look like a robot," she noted playfully.

I've only known Shannon for a short time. Bill said they were friends before they started dating back in December. She seems nice, but a bit possessive of him.

Bill was pretending to be a robot when Connors joined the trio. He was a muscular boy with short cropped brown hair, a baggy jacket lined with fur, and cleats that made a crunching sound through the snow. Most of the people in the group wore boots, which struck Mike odd that someone packed shoes with spikes on them.

The only time I've ever heard of anyone having cleats is for soccer maybe, Mike thought in-between breaths.

"Some of the kids are complaining that they need to use the restroom out here," the muscular boy mentioned. Mike peered towards the group of children they had. Some had looks that ranged from annoyance to pain, and even anger.

"Well, it wouldn't be a good idea to pee out here, so they'll have to wait," Bill noted. His tone shifted from his usual easy-going attitude to one more professionally serious. "Last time I asked, Daniel told me we're near the rendezvous point where Zane and the others should be. In the meantime, just to try to keep the kids from getting lost or hurt in this weather."

Connors nodded but did not appear satisfied with this solution.

"I heard Zane's group also found twenty campers," Bill told Mike. Mike didn't hear Bill's comment, which caused his former cabin mate to repeat himself. "*I heard Zane's group also found twenty campers.*" Bill paused, hoping for a reaction, which he did receive, before continuing, "It's not like it's a competition, but with your new ability and Daniel's, we definitely have more of an advantage to find other campers before heading back. How exactly does it work again?"

Mike felt annoyed by the question until he realized Bill was trying to make conversation.

"Before I could find things by touching them, and now I can find people by either touching something they owned, like those beads from camp, or direct contact. But direct contact isn't preferable in my case." Mike examined his gloved hands.

Making contact with a person should be a last resort. Like if my life is in danger and I need some way of identifying a weakness in them.

Bill nodded approvingly, only to suddenly become skeptical.

"Sounds like a lot of work, but at least you know what you're doing. You know, I was against the idea of not using skeletal cab drivers until it was mentioned that we'd be going into the field. This is where the real action happens, Mike, and if you ever want to become a—"

Mike felt something inside him, a familiar sense that made his body vibrate and tremble like rippled water. He moved his hand as swiftly as the muscles in his arm allowed. Time slowed down, making Mike's vision appear as still as a picture.

When his gloved hand made contact with Bill, his eyes spotted an unidentified object shooting through the air with such speed that it was like a bullet. By the time he realized what it was, the object had impacted one of the children they were escorting to camp. The child fell backwards, screaming, and had a sharp gash appear on the top of his shoulder where the arrow narrowly missed puncturing him.

An arrow? Where did it come from? Up? Down? Left? Right? Side to side?

As Mike and Bill ran towards the boy, more arrows began to shoot out in their direction. Daniel and the other counselors were quick to react and began to shield the children with their abilities. Jane managed to pull the roots from the ground and used them like a giant wooden shield. With her arm becoming fused to this shield, she managed to catch the majority of the arrows. The few ones that got by flew past the campers and counselors.

While Bill tended to the injured boy's needs, Mike tried to keep the other children calm as they began to panic. Some of their abilities were beginning to show like soda cans ready to burst. One child had an ability that made him zip zap faster than Ashley, while another child bore beaver-like teeth that were beginning to burrow on the ground anxiously.

There were bits of snow fluttering around the air, like a mini-blizzard, and not the good kind you get at DQ.

"Everything will be alright." *This isn't good.* "Stay together, don't get separated in this weather." *I shouldn't be here.* "Keep close to a counselor. You five, with Richardson, you three with Alexander and the rest with me, Bill, Connors, and Shannon." *That's a lot of blood. I can't… high and low, steep and slope, do or don't, chocolate or vanilla.*

The children reacted fast, some did what they were told, while others scrambled around like headless chickens. The latter were the ones whose powers involuntarily were becoming activated.

During this time, Mike noticed Connors was no longer with the group. He looked around to see where the muscular counselor in training had gone but could not find him. Jane continued to hold off the remaining arrows, while Daniel tried to assist her by balancing her. In the ensuing chaos, Alexander and Richardson were trying to use their separate abilities to help as well.

Alexander breathed rhythmically, like the beating of drums, grabbed handfuls of snow, melted them, and refroze them into solid ice balls. Richardson inhaled a deep breath and exhaled to melt the ice in front of him. The ground beneath where they were huddled up began to reveal itself, which helped Jane with her ability to fortify the wooden shield.

Why is this happening? Who's attacking us? They'll overwhelm us soon! Make swarms of our skulls like worms.

Bill and Shannon were doing their best with the children who were hidden within the wooden shield but lost a couple of kids who were running in the opposite direction. Their powers were going haywire.

Shannon took it upon herself to try and retrieve as many of the kids as she could. She snarled at the threat around her before pulling her thumbs inwards and turning her hands into tightly clenched fists that put pressure on her thumbs and caused her body to morph into something resembling a humanoid wolf. Her teeth became sharp and her fingernails turned to claws protracting from the pressure of her squeeze on them. Dashing through the blistering wind, on all fours, she rushed at the kids who were farthest away and rallied them to her frantically.

Mike tried to look around, his vision was blurred by the cold wind. He concentrated on his new ability, called Peril Perception, to see if he could sense any nearby threats. His vision focused on a child who was lying on the ground, making what looked like a snow angel. Mike was about to call out to the child until he realized he didn't recognize him. He felt the trembling effect return to his body, telling him to be wary of this new child. Each time the boy's arms went up, the ice grew thicker, and each time his legs went down, the ice began to melt. His skin was unnaturally pale, and his eyes were pure white. Sharp pieces of ice began to rise from the ground where the rest of Daniel's group was. Richardson steadied his breath, until he emitted what looked like a low fire from his mouth, which gave him the look of a dragon.

He can breathe fire? I knew Richardson could make things very hot with his breath, but that's new.

Richardson's face turned red, his eyes watery, and the fire was fighting a battle to be released. While Richardson did his best to fan the flames from within, Alexander hurled solid snowballs at their attackers. Mike didn't know if it was because of the wind, but he could not hear any grunts from those who got hit by the solid snowballs. Jane's wooden shield began to weaken, as Daniel pulled a branch from it, and thrust it in front of Richardson's fiery breath. The wood caught fire and lit it like a torch.

"Now, Jane! Let it down!" Daniel instructed. She nodded and exhaustedly let the wooden shield down. Daniel momentarily waited for something before thrusting the fiery wood forward. The wind had suddenly changed directions, with the wind now fanning the flames even more so and caused their attackers to silently back off.

The brightness of the flames was so much that Mike was able to see their attackers. They were children, just like the ones the counselors were escorting to camp. But these ones looked more like goblins. They're skins were pasty, they all shook almost in synchrony, and had bags under their eyes. They looked neither fearful nor distressed over the flames; only momentarily taken aback. Jane was beginning to pull up her shield wall again when something unexpected happened.

The flames that at first held back the silent children began to subside, and, before anyone could react, a new fire engulfed Jane's newly formed wooden shield arm. She screeched in pain, and Mike could see that the flames had burnt her arms, shoulder, and part of her right cheek severely. Her screams were so loud that nobody heard or saw the person who teleported in front of them.

What? Who? How did he…? I didn't sense him at all.

Mike observed his unmoving body, which didn't react even when in the presence of the fiery man.

Even in the blistering weather, his appearance was undeniable. The fiery man's golden long hair flew in the wind with a mind of its own and his piercing smile showed someone who was about to have his definition of fun. He wore what looked like a velvet cloak with a long-stitched hood down. The golden-haired man moved so incredibly fast that it only took a second for Mike to realize he was near the cluster of children who were too frightened to use their abilities in self-defense.

"I'm taking some of these brats with me," he revealed. "If you value what remains of your limbs, I suggest you look the other way."

Daniel shook his head.

"Not a chance, you're not going to take any more of these kids over my dead body," Daniel declared, wielding his still burning wood like a blade.

The golden-haired man seemed to find this amusing.

"That's the plan actually. You're his kid right? Henry's wayward son?"

Daniel hesitated, looking at the golden-haired man as if he were contemplating what action to take before undertaking it. "I am. What of it?"

There was a shrill laughter that came from the golden-haired man, piercing, as he shot Daniel with triumphant eyes.

"I'd say this isn't personal, but it kind of is. Now play dead like a good dog."

Daniel prepared to charge towards the golden-haired man with his flaming wood. In an instant, Daniel was blindsided by another attacker who came between himself and his adversary. It was someone Mike had lost sight of until now.

Connors.

He looked like he was in a daze. His nose was bleeding and the veins in his temples were pulsating. The muscular counselor threw a wide punch in Daniel's direction, who dodged the attack carefully. Mike saw the Camp Counselor was using an ability he called Foresight, where Daniel could anticipate possible movements from others for a short time.

I saw him do it once during training, Mike reflected. *Lucas was still in a coma at the time, but Daniel could see movements, as he described them, like instant replay.*

Connors went in for another punch, nearly taking Daniel's head off when he miscalculated a step. Luckily, the deadly punch was blocked by Alexander's interference. He used his sheathed sword as a shield, and somehow this was enough to repeal Connors. This gave Daniel enough time to begin activating his sanctuary stone, against the advice of Richardson.

"We need to get to higher ground," Richardson advised, channeling his breathing so he could emit the flames necessary to melt the ground. "That won't work if we're too far apart from each other."

Despite her injury, Jane continued to hold the shield wall up. Whether it was by instinct or inability to subside, Mike couldn't tell.

Daniel activated his stone, a portal opening up that looked like a whirlpool in mid-air. Its winds began to suck in a few nearby campers, while Daniel made sure Jane was with them. It closed fast, as the stone in Daniel's hand emitted a low hum that subsided like a dead battery.

Richardson grunted, caught his breath, and proceeded to activate his stone as well. When the portal opened, he made sure several new campers were near it. They disappeared in a flash, and the portal was gone just as fast.

As this happened, Bill did his best to help several of the children who ran off, but the golden-haired man managed to ensnare a few in a ring of fire.

Who is this guy and how can he do that?!

The children trapped behind the fire could scarcely move and were in a panicked state when the golden-haired man sent Connors to them.

"I'll get the rest of those kids who are with Red Eyes over there," he gestured in Bill's direction. Giving a quick glance at Daniel, the golden-haired man muttered, "I'll be back for you after this."

Instantly, the golden-haired man was in front of Bill and the other children.

"Make this easier on yourself, boy," the golden-haired man told Bill. "Give me the rest of those brats and I'll let you all go scot free. You already have one injured counselor. Next time it won't just be burns."

Bill looked to Mike, who tried to figure out what he should do. Shannon was still too busy trying to round up as many campers as she could to notice the commotion that was happening. She fended off a couple of the silent children who tried to stop her, baring her canines at them and charging for them.

I don't know how her power works in the cold, but if she goes feral, we could have more than one problem.

"Like Daniel said, no way are you taking these kids. You'll have to kill me first."

The golden-haired man sighed and shook his head.

"So eager to die before your time are you?"

A pockmarked boy appeared from the winds themselves and moved in to attack Richardson with a weird, shaped knife. The knife's curve wasn't straight and resembled a hook that had been bent too much. Richardson turned his attention on the pockmarked boy, who didn't appear fearful of the flames.

"Took you long enough, Payne. Keep that one busy and try not to have too much fun."

This brief distraction gave Bill enough time to use his beams on the golden-haired man. They emitted themselves through his goggles with a steady, straight, piercing ferocity. But sadly, they weren't strong enough to repel against the flames that came out of the fiery man's hands.

While Bill managed to keep the flames from harming the other campers, some of the fire burnt his right shoulder and forearm. It didn't go past his heavily worn hoodie.

"That's a shame. I thought your beams would have been stronger than that by now," the golden-haired man mused to himself.

This is crazy… we're not trained for this… what's happening... I need to help…

Mike was about to rush in and help Bill when he felt a sharp pain in his leg. It was so fast and instant that his Peril Perception did not have a chance to activate. He found himself on the floor with an arrow that looked as big as an arm sticking out. He let out a loud scream and cradled his bleeding limb.

Ugh! Where did that come from…!

Mike's gloved hands remained on his leg, as he watched his companions being swarmed by the children who made no sounds. Mike saw Richardson, who had finally pushed back the pockmarked boy, attempt to help Bill. While Richardson was distracted, the golden-haired man teleported in front of him.

"Now this is interesting. I haven't seen one like you who can breathe fire. I can't even do that. Let's see which flames are stronger."

Richardson emitted his dragon flame on him, but the golden-haired man didn't flinch or attempt to move out of the way. When the flaming breath dissipated, the golden-haired man merely shrugged it off with a brush on his shoulder. Richardson's face was sunburnt red, and his breathing was very hoarse.

"How disappointing. My turn," the golden-haired man said through clenched teeth. He lifted a steady hand, and flames conjured themselves similarly to Richardson's, only with more ferocity. Richardson was still catching his breath and sweating profusely when he let out another breath of flames. His throat was becoming charred, and his mouth was looking unrecognizably burnt. The two flames were beating against each other viciously, until the fiery man's flames triumphed.

Richardson had only enough breath to let out a silent scream, which came off as a small sudden gasp, as the golden-haired man's flames engulfed him.

"Too bad he wasn't fireproof," the fiery man noted blankly.

When Alexander saw Richardson's lifeless charred body, he let out a loud scream. Alexander charged towards the golden-haired man, who saw him coming fast. After dodging his attack, the fiery man unsheathed a long boney blade that wriggled to life with a crunch and slashed Alexander's back with it. The cut was so deep it looked like Alexander's spine would pop out like a Jack in the box. The counselor fell to the ground motionless.

Daniel tried to fend off the silent children with another fiery branch as they encircled him and a few other frightened campers. The fiery man spotted him and returned to Daniel, twirling his boney sword and cutting the air around him. The silent children near Daniel subsided in the presence of their superior.

"See if you can foresee this," the golden-haired man beckoned with a sharp grin.

The fiery man brought his twisted blade forward swiftly and nearly decapitated Daniel. Daniel successfully dodged with little effort, until the golden-haired man did a blade switch. Daniel's foresight was not fast enough to dodge this one, as the blade made a steady sharp contact with his leg. He landed face first on the snow-covered ground and was out cold. While the wound wasn't deep Mike saw the gash that would become a long scar on Daniel's upper leg near his thigh.

Bill was still repelling other silent children when a pockmarked boy appeared in front of him. Like the flames, Bill's heat vision did not seem to bother him, and he advanced on him. Bill retreated and tried to keep his distance from the pockmarked boy and his silent companions.

In the meantime, Shannon continued to help the kids in her charge, but she was outnumbered by the silent children who were rounding them up. She turned to find her boyfriend and let out an agonized howl, preparing to charge in his direction.

This can't be how things end... please don't let it be how it all ends.

The golden-haired man was about to stab Daniel when Mike regained his senses long enough to see lightning from the sky.

A storm's coming? No. The sky's cloudy, but not enough to anticipate a sudden change in the weather. No, it has to be...

Mike's suspicions and hopes were both confirmed at once.

Zane's here. Thank the Gods, he thought, weakly.

He watched Zane rush in to assist a group of children, the few remaining, while the other counselors with him kept their group of children safely away. The girl he knew to be Naomi was grabbing bits of rocks and charging them up to be thrown at the silent children. The rocks appeared like burning coals until they made an impact and exploded.

"Well now, this is becoming mildly interesting. Looks like I'll have fun today after all," the fiery man screeched. He gave Daniel one last foreboding look. "I'll come back if you don't bleed out first."

Mike heard a defiant response from Zane but could not distinguish it from the ringing in his ears. All he saw was the flashing lightning the electrified counselor threw in the golden-haired man's direction. His flames and Zane's lightning conducted a sparkling orchestra.

While Zane fought against the golden-haired man, Mike's senses suddenly caught fire. Every part of his body went haywire like a faulty power outlet. He had a hard time differentiating between what his mind was thinking, his Peril Perception, and the newcomer a few feet from him. This person's features looked distorted by both the cold winds and the cloudy sky. The man's hair was long and silvery, falling over his face like a veil. His skin was pale, but what frightened Mike were the man's eyes.

Bloodshot eyes, with no hint of whiteness around golden irises.

The silver-haired man's nails were sharp, with several scars etched into his open palms. He wore a black long sleeve shirt with torn jeans and bare feet. Mike couldn't understand how the cold wasn't bothering the newcomer.

My mind's splitting… I…feel…unclean…so unclean…!

Mike started to viciously scrub himself with his gloved hands. He feared scratching at his skin and what would come out.

B…b…bugs…lots…lots…of… them…

Connors seemed to involuntarily react upon seeing the silver-haired man. He became his regular self but seemed to appear in a daze of sorts.

"What's happening?" he croaked, unable to say more beyond that. The newcomer ignored him and kept his attention on the children, particularly at Bill's group.

"We must have those," the silver-haired man muttered, pointing to the group Bill was protecting. "They will be silenced first. Keep the rest still."

The golden-haired man repealed Zane's incoming electric blast and stunned him with a fiery blast. Zane fell backwards, screaming, and Mike saw a burn etch itself onto his right shoulder.

The silver-haired man pointed towards Bill.

"Take that one. We will test his resolve."

The fiery man turned his attention to Bill, who was still fighting against the pockmarked child. Despite his beams having no effect on Payne, Bill managed to melt the ground below him, causing the boy to temporarily fall over himself. Just as it seemed he got the upper hand, the other silent children quickly surrounded Bill and removed the goggles from his eyes.

The pockmarked boy climbed out of the shivering pool of water, appearing unscathed, and knocked Bill out with a hard punch. While his wrists were being tied, Bill's eyes became engulfed by a damp heavy blindfold.

Shannon saw this and brushed aside the enemies violently. She made her way towards Bill, only to be stopped by Zane.

"Don't be stupid, girl!" Zane shouted. "We'll save him later, but for now we have to get out of here."

Shannon looked very feral by this point, appearing ready to bite Zane's head off. He snapped his fingers and touched her fur, sending a small volt of concentrated electricity through her body which immobilized her. Her sharp nails and canines subsided, and she appeared as herself again. Zane gave Mike and the rest of the group a quick glance and activated his sanctuary stone. He went through the portal himself and took the unconscious Shannon along with three more nearby campers.

Mike tried with great effort to rise up, but the pain from the arrow in his leg caused him to scream loudly and shiver uncontrollably. He still couldn't control his senses or ability, to the point where his struggles made his enemies remember his presence.

Door…floor…core…shore…languish…language…

"No use for damaged goods," the silver-haired man said, grimacing and rubbing at the sides of his temples with his knuckles. "Leave the soil where it was dumped. Tear out and bury the bones."

The golden-haired man nodded and gave Mike an unsympathetic look.

"In layman's terms, Jacob would have me do away with you," the fiery man revealed, "but I see your value more as a messenger."

I've heard that name before. Where have I heard that name before?

"You will deliver a message for me to your Camp Director and that little mind freak of his. Tell them if they wish to see that boy alive, along with the rest of the campers we're taking with us, Henry must surrender himself and Lucas Fargo to Alistair and Jacob. If he refuses, let him know that the camp will be taken one way or another. The hostages will be returned once the exchange is made. Got it, kid?"

Jacob seemed to disapprove of this idea, muttering incoherently to himself. Alistair gave him a reassuring look, as if the two were communicating silently.

I can't let him get away… I won't let him get away…

Mike grasped Jacob's ankle with his gloved left hand while his back was to him. His intention was to ensure the maniac would become distracted enough to lose his concentration, but what ensued was a series of images and flashes that caused Mike to feel like he was being electrocuted.

W.W.Wut…What…? I.I.Is hap..happy…happening to m.m. ME!

His head was filled with millions of voices, with words that were all jumbled and fast talking like news reporters. He tried to center his mind as he always did, listening to his Peril Perception, but felt something sharp and sudden overtake him. An even stronger force and feeling.

Mike screamed, his eyes opening to Alistair stomping his booted foot on the arm that held Jacob's ankle. There was a terrible crunch sound that was non-comparable to anything he had ever felt or heard before. Mike let out such a loud scream that made Jacob irritated. He began to scratch at his open palms and did not appear bothered by the blood that began to seep down into the snow.

"Cease this noise, unbearable, undeniable, unbroken," Jacob began to mutter and beat against his head like drums. "No noise, insufferably insolent. Be broken. Loose line!"

Jacob's rambling became a convenient distraction for Naomi to use her sanctuary stone. The portal pulled in Daniel, Alexander, and Mike towards her furiously.

"Zane's group is gone. The other counselors will try to save as many of the kids as possible, but we need to get out of here now!" Naomi shouted as she too was dragged into the portal.

The last thing Mike saw before disappearing into the stone's light was Bill being unconsciously dragged through the snow by a group of children who all wore the same empty expressions on their faces. Mike was shocked to see Connors with them, his eyes looking still and placid. While he was being engulfed by the portal, Mike's head began to throb, and he heard a voice that was not his own.

When next awakened, through eyes unseen will thoughts be heard. Looking through a murky lens, these words will appear: Cast… Below… Surface…Loom… Strewn…

Chapter 4: Aftermath

Lucas felt his world shake out of control at the news he heard. He impulsively replayed the words in his mind.

Alistair took Bill. He's the one I saw last year talking with Henry. Even though I don't know him, Alistair still makes me feel so scared and angry at the same time. His fists tensed up, as his nails began to dig into his palms. Lucas' uncut nails drew small trickles of blood.

After leaving Henry's home, Lucas walked towards the middle of the pavilion field as the wounded counselors made their way through the front entrance with the few campers they had with them.

Come on, Mike, where are you? Please be okay…

The wounded counselors were being helped through the entrance by Boris and hospital ward staff. The children who came through, none of which Lucas recognized, were being swarmed by nurses like paparazzi. One kid, who had an arrow on his shoulder, was being put on a stretcher and carried away to the ward.

That doesn't look good at all. I'm not a doctor but even I know that thing is going to hurt when it comes out.

Among the oncoming crowd of campers, counselors, and nurses, Lucas spotted Mike being carried by Daniel. He had a notable bruise above one of his eyes and was limping in pain. Counselor Jane was being carried by a group of new campers and looked like she was in the worst condition. She appeared to be severely burnt, with one of her arms looking both charred and still wooden. Nearly half her face was burnt, and one of her eyes looked like a cue ball because of the swelling.

Who did that to her? A fire-breathing dragon?

Lucas saw the other counselors, Margot and Lucinda, follow after Jane frantically.

A lone girl Lucas did not know was walking alone, with bruises and scratch marks on her cheeks. From the way she walked, she had a hunched posture with her head looking upwards as if to smell the air.

She looks like a stray dog, he thought as the girl glanced at him and continued limping away.

Lucas didn't recognize Alexander, who appeared severely injured and was strapped to a gurney. He was heavily bandaged across his chest and had an oxygen mask affixed to his face. The nurses attending to him looked like they were prepping for a worst-case scenario right from the get-go.

I don't see Richardson anywhere, Lucas noted as more Camp Counselors came into view.

He spotted the rest of the counselors, including two he didn't recognize from last year. No one looked like they had any serious injuries, but their eyes told the tale of an intense battle.

Not just their eyes, but their thoughts. Nobody is thinking clearly right now.

Mike sustained a broken arm that was hanging limply down, and his leg had a thick monstrous arrow sticking out of it. A piece of cloth was wrapped carefully around the entry wound. Mike's face was red and looked almost burnt underneath his beanie.

Please don't let Sapphire see him like this, Lucas thought.

Suddenly, his worst fear came true, as Mike's little sister spotted her brother in the crowd.

The little girl began to shake hysterically, breaking into tears as she ran towards her brother. Daniel handed Mike to the medical staff, who strapped him to a gurney and led him to the hospital while Sapphire walked closely behind them. Shelly saw what was happening and stopped the little girl before she could go further. Sapphire continued to whimper and cry out, causing her skin to reverberate from her natural skin tone to a diamond-like one.

I can feel what they both feel… and it hurts a lot. Mike is going through physical pain, but Sapphire's is emotional.

Before Sapphire could fully take on the diamond form, Shelly managed to calm her down and the little girl was reduced to sniffles.

Lucas noticed that Daniel's limping leg had a terrible gash on it, like a sword had slashed it and only scraped against the surface of his skin. Marcus came and hugged a female counselor who walked over to him.

That has to be Naomi. She's pretty for someone her age. How Marcus ended up with a girl like her is the same question I ask myself about Vanessa.

Another woman made her presence known and helped Daniel. Lucas noted that she looked pretty, prettier than Naomi.

She looks familiar somehow, but I'm not sure from where.

From the wounded, Lucas observed a Camp Counselor keeping to himself. While the distant counselor had fewer injuries than the others, he had minor burn marks on his arms leading down towards his hands, which were already wrapped in bandages. Lucas also noticed a scorch mark on the counselor's shoulder that didn't look serious.

No, it's his other left. That's right.

The mildly injured counselor walked over to Henry and curtly denied any further assistance from the nursing staff.

"Before you speak, let us find someplace away from open ears," Henry instructed the counselor, while giving Lucas a quick wary glance. The two walked off a short distance away, with the rest of the camp being too preoccupied by the injured campers and counselors to notice the Camp Director's absence.

Let me see if I can read his mind. Lucas' attention was on the enigmatic counselor, who looked about as interested in the moment as Henry on a good day.

The casualty's report is the following, the counselor thought rapidly. Lucas had to take a short pause before reading the rest when his head winced in pain.

He thinks the way Mike does, Lucas thought ruefully, noticing the rapid way the counselor thought. *I'll just pick up the main stuff.*

Counselor Bill has been captured by… Alistair… and his Silent Ones. Richardson is dead, unable to retrieve body. Alexander is in critical condition. Unlikely to survive past the day. Jane suffered severe burns. Counselor Connors lost to Jacob and Silent Ones. Mike was injured badly with a broken arm and wounded leg. Daniel suffered both minor and notable injuries. Overall, out of the forty kids found in total, only fifteen were brought back…

What's a Silent One?

Lucas remembered Richardson and Alexander from last year. They were best friends and known for being tough on the campers they trained.

Sure, yeah, they were tough, but they were also an important part of the camp. I remember when Richardson took part in helping arrange the cabins and participated in the activities. Those are going to be big shoes to fill.

Thinking this filled Lucas with a deep sadness. Between him and Alexander, everyone always preferred Richardson because he was more understanding and kinder to the younger children.

Maybe that's because he has a son of his own… oh damn.

The realization came as sudden as a splash of cold water.

His son, and the young lunch lady. When they find out that he's dead…

When the counselor had finished giving the Camp Director his report, Henry made an unceremonious exit. Lucas was so distracted with his thoughts that he didn't notice when the enigmatic counselor called out to him.

"Hey, kid, you lost?"

Lucas looked at him in confusion and tried to play obliviously.

"Me? You're talking to me right?" Lucas asked naively.

The rude counselor looked at the other campers who were being calmed by the hospital staff, then turned his attention back towards Lucas.

"You're the only kid I see standing around with no sense of direction. Did you get lost on your way to the little boy's room? It's that way." The rude counselor pointed towards where the facilities were.

Lucas shook his head defensively.

"I was just stretching my legs. It is a big camp you know," Lucas lied poorly.

The rude counselor did not look convinced. Before he could question Lucas further, a female Camp Counselor called out to him.

"Zane, get over here! One of the campers we brought back just fainted and isn't breathing."

"Get a move on, kid. Find something useful to do or get out of the way," Zane told Lucas and darted towards the unconscious camper.

Lucas saw the other campers who were nearby appearing frantic and panicked. One kid looked about ready to burst like a cherry bomb, but he began to calm when one of the nurses wrapped him in a soft embrace. Another child was being helped into a wheelchair which caused Lucas to experience a high degree of anxiety. All their distress and fear, mixed in with his own, made Lucas feel as if he were drowning with an invisible hand holding him down.

What the…? Agh, why is my head hurting so much now? I can't… hear… my…

Lucas' eyes began to flutter rapidly, and he fell to his knees. His fingernails began to impulsively pick at his right forearm, etching themselves across his skin as if they had a mind of their own. Even as he picked there was no pain. It was like his brain and body were on two different planes of existence.

He continued to scratch himself as Zane began to emit some form of electricity from his bandaged hands while rubbing them together carefully like defibrillators.

Zane beckoned for the others to stand back and shouted, "CLEAR!"

Zane pressed his hands hard on the unconscious camper's chest. The boy's body responded in a grunt upwards. When the boy did not respond, Zane did it again but was very careful not to fry the camper alive.

Whoa, his ability is to use electricity. That's shocking, Lucas thought as he regained enough of himself to stop picking at his skin. His newly awakened consciousness registered the pain a new cut added which would soon become a small scar along with the others he had.

Finally, after the third try, the boy camper awoke. Zane sighed in relief, waggled his hands, and turned to the female counselor who promptly thanked him.

"You're welcome, now get these campers to the ward. Make sure Mike is taken care of as well. That kid had no business being out there with the rest of us."

The female counselor nodded and directed the campers towards the ward.

Lucas suddenly remembered that Zane had been absent last summer, but he couldn't remember why. The two exchanged a brief look when Zane darted past Lucas. The way their eyes met gave Lucas a brief chill.

I want to say he reminds me of Daniel, but there's something different about him. It's like one enjoys conflict while the other makes it, Lucas pondered as he watched Zane walk off in a solitary way.

Lucas thought Zane looked to be as old as Daniel. His eyes were lighting yellow-green. His wavy dark brown hair appeared no longer than his ear lobes and parted ways on his forehead. He had a thin physique and wore a red long sleeve similar to Lucas.

He looks like a biker. Maybe that's what he does outside of camp.

The rest of Zane's thoughts were frantic and mixed with concern for the well-being of the wounded. Lucas picked up on all of it and began to feel the cuts on his arms and chest sizzle like cooked meat. Naomi had parted from Marcus and made her way to Zane. He shook his head to her and headed off towards another direction. Not wanting to be in the way, Lucas walked to where his sister was as she frantically held back an antsy Sapphire.

"What's going on, Lucas? What happened to the counselors?" Shelly asked as Sapphire tugged on her hands.

"Take me to Mickey, Shell," said the little girl, as she continued to try and pull away from Shelly's grip. Twinkle barked softly and was panting anxiously.

Lucas felt even more anxious around the little girl than he did around the other wounded campers and counselors.

Sapphire won't be able to keep Shelly's attention away for long. I should tell her enough so that she won't think to ask me anything for a while.

"Some guy named…Alistair… did all this. He took Bill, Vanessa's brother." Lucas struggled to say the man's name. He checked his sleeves to make sure they were covered and was relieved when they were. The sweat he felt made his arms itchy, but for that moment he ignored the feeling.

While he told her the truth Shelly looked like she was expecting more of an explanation.

That's about as much as I know at this point.

"Who is this guy Alistair? Why would he do this? I thought you said this camp would be safe," Shelly asked suspiciously. She noticed Lucas subtly winning when he heard that name. "And why are you making that sound when I say his name? Alistair?"

Lucas grimaced and nearly fainted when someone came to interrupt them.

Oh, thank the Gods.

To Lucas' shock, it was Zane. He gave Shelly a pointed look as if he meant for her to walk away without saying a word.

Like that's going to work.

It surprisingly did. As she left Shelly gave her brother a concerned frown.

"Just don't do anything stupid until I get back, alright?"

Lucas was about to nod until Zane seemingly answered for him.

"Don't worry, if he does anything stupid, I'll be sure to list you as his emergency contact," Zane said, with an ironic tone.

Shelly ignored him and walked away with Sapphire and Twinkle following very closely behind her.

"Now then, where did we leave off? Oh, that's right, you were looking at me and Henry talking. I know you can read minds, not lips, so tell me what you heard."

Lucas shrugged and tried to come up with an answer in his mind.

Who says I can read minds? Maybe you should mind your own business, Lucas might have said if he wanted to tell Zane off. *It turns out you were right; I heard what you were thinking about, but only part of it because my powers are not working for me.* That last thought sounded almost as ridiculous as the effort it took to conjure it up.

"I couldn't hear much because my powers are not working the way they did last year," Lucas heard himself say, while feeling strange at the admission whether it was intentional or not.

Zane nodded, confirming not only his suspicions but another working theory.

"I'm sure you heard enough though. Your Bill's best friend. Lucas Tango, right?" Zane asked to Lucas' annoyance.

"It's Lucas Fargo, not Tango."

"Right, that's right, Fargo, like that old movie," said Zane nonchalantly. "Henry's told me a bit about you but I'd like some more information straight from the source. Let's start with the range of your abilities and how far along you've gone in using them."

How far gone? Range of abilities? How range of abilities far along?

Shelly walked over to Henry's home and went to meet him as he requested in the note she found during Christmas.

I don't know why he wants to speak to me alone, but I don't like this. He has this way with him like he pretends to be nicer than he is. Doesn't matter. I should go along with it until I know what Henry's intentions are for my brother.

Shelly knocked on the Camp Director's door but didn't realize that the inside was just a straight-away towards the office itself. She hesitantly opened the door and was in awe by what her eyes beheld. When she entered, Shelly saw the amount of books and record vinyl that Henry owned.

He's either a hoarder, or he really gets around in the world. Records and books from bygone decades. I recognize so many of those movies and books. First editions also!

She was thinking this when Henry seemingly appeared from nowhere with an unmoving line of a mouth obscured underneath his grey beard.

"Hello, Shelly. Please have a seat."

Despite his welcoming appearance, Shelly felt something was off about the Camp Director. The doubtful feeling drove her to shake her head.

"Not to be rude, sir, but I think I'll stand. I don't expect this to be long."

Henry nodded and sat down himself.

"As you wish. I wanted to discuss our previous arrangement."

This confused Shelly.

"I'm sorry? What arrangement?"

"The arrangement that was in the note I left for you. In light of your parent's tragic passing, I wanted to make sure that you and your brother are well accommodated." Henry reached into his drawer and pulled out what looked like a check. When Shelly looked at it, she knew exactly what the numbers meant.

"This is enough money to attend any college you wish. Do not worry about expenses regarding a living arrangement. I will make sure that you are well established and that all your needs are met. The numbers on this check are more of a formality than what you will receive should you accept this offer. There is still time before you will need this, so consider it an advancement."

Shelly wanted to trust the Camp Director, but a part of her couldn't shake the previous bad feeling she felt from both entering his home and now from the note itself.

Something isn't right about this or should I say something feels too right about this.

"Thank you, Director James. But I don't accept charity, especially when I don't know what I've done to deserve it."

Henry nodded and understood.

"You are a bright young lady, as Lucas has so fondly told me on many occasions. I only wish for you to apply your set of skills in a more useful field. Since you are an Alter Child, albeit a latent one, you will receive training along with all the campers who come. However, I don't believe your future is here. Something I presume your parents would have felt similarly."

Don't you dare talk about them like you knew them, Shelly wanted to say, but instead she kept her composure.

"And what about Lucas? Where does he fit into this arrangement of yours?"

Henry's face changed now, as if what she asked had offended him.

"Lucas has a different path he must follow. This is ultimately where our arrangement becomes complicated."

Shelly did not like where this conversation was going.

"I know you love him dearly. You've spent the better part of your life protecting and keeping your brother from harm. For that I am very grateful. However, he cannot leave, not when he's come so far in his training and has the potential for more. Lucas has the capacity to become a powerful telepath with boundless potential. He has a good heart, a pure one that is willing to do the right thing at any cost. I have dedicated every moment since his arrival to making sure he meets that desired outcome. His powers are young and volatile, but in time I believe they can be harnessed for the greater good.

"At the end of the summer he must remain here to begin advanced training, and you must return to the world outside because your presence will cause a hindrance for him. I understand you are having difficulties with caring for Lucas after your parents passing. With the money I have provided, you will be able to take care of your needs, and I will take care of Lucas's needs." Shelly was beginning to seethe with anger.

I knew it… he wants me to abandon Lucas. That's what this is all about.

"You want me to leave him here with you?"

"Don't look at it that way, child. I only want what is best for Lucas, as I know you do as well. It is much to ask for, but if nothing else, I ask that you trust me. Think of this as a chance to do what you could never accomplish with your brother around. I think with everything that has happened you deserve a reprieve. Especially considering you have had to prove your competence as a proper caretaker for Lucas in the eyes of the law."

At this Shelly felt her body tense up and her eyes beginning to water with both shock and rage. Her and her brother's situation wasn't any of his business!

"Did you truly believe that the state would allow you to continue caring for Lucas on your own? The lady who oversees you both will not raise further alarms should you agree to my terms. I can give Lucas a home here where you may visit him while you are attending to your schoolwork."

Visit him? Like what? Like a prisoner in jail, except the bars are more luxury than confinement?

Shelly shook her head, tensing with anger. Her thoughts were suddenly louder now than the Camp Director's voice.

Why is he so quick to want me gone? To want Lucas to himself?

After pondering these thoughts, Shelly slammed the check on the Camp Director's desk.

"As long as I'm alive, where I go Lucas goes. I won't leave without him, and I most certainly won't leave him alone with you. I don't know what kind of games you're playing with him and everyone else here, but I'm not going to let him go through it alone. I already know he won't want to leave because of his friends here and because of you. You were all he talked about last year; how you helped him and were there for him. Believe me if I could have been here with him, I would have. Even if it meant… Just please, I am begging you,

Director James, don't hurt him. He's been through enough. We both have. I want to believe you're a good man so prove him right."

Shelly looked to be on the verge of tears but held them back as she turned towards the door. "Also, don't ever presume to know what our parents would have wanted. Just be the Camp Director who cares but doesn't overstep his bounds. I'm Lucas' family, not you."

Shelly was outside the house, feeling conflicted by what transpired, while Henry remained unfazed. He only reclined in his chair and sighed as he stared blankly at the check.

After a moment, the check's contents became blank, revealing a piece of writing paper.

"It appears the path has been set. Do you require further proof, or will this be enough for now?" Henry asked with exasperation.

A shadow took form to reveal a woman whose skin was translucent. Her hair was a deep unnatural shade of purple. She wore a gray robe with a hood over her head. When she removed her hood, the lines running down her cheeks from below her eyes looked notable. She softly bowed to the Camp Director.

"It is as you say," she confirmed, with a low tone. "Her purpose is here, for now. One cannot be without the other it seems. Now, would you like to know what I dreamt of the night before last?"

"If I must," said Henry as he pulled a small notebook from one of his drawers. He prepared to write as the pale woman spoke.

"I dreamt of a tree, large and lively. Its branches stretched outwards like veins. Roots so deep in the earth that water could not reach it even with the heaviest of rain. Its sap was black as the night sky. I saw an infant whose birth meant a great change awaited. Its life gave birth to death, as it was fed the black sap from the tree. The sap took root in the infant and became a new form. This form has many roots, but one source."

Henry pondered this for a moment and began scribbling everything the pale woman described and placed it back into his drawer when she finished.

"Thank you, Shanine. That will be all for tonight."

Shanine nodded and proceeded to walk away.

"Before I go, the prophecy has changed form once more: Two miracles, one's fate is sealed, while the other is yet to be revealed. One who supplants pretense, at the others expense. The one hears all, as the other one falls. The path ahead is shrouded in fear, but the object is clear. Balance is the key, to break the chains and be free."

She was about to exit the house when Henry called out.

"Be free from what? This prophecy changes every time you introduce it to me. By which hand am I led to believe in the path?"

Shanine smiled and nodded knowingly.

"As it was said the past time; choose your hand wisely, Henry. One hand is still soft and can be nurtured with care provided. The other hand is stiff and on the verge of undoing all you have prepared for with one careless stroke. You did well in preparing both for their roles, but now the path ahead bears no clear markers. You and those before you walked so they could run."

With that final premonition, Shanine retreated back into the shadows and was gone. Henry slumped into his chair with a heavy sigh and felt his hands begin to shake erratically.

It's too soon. Not yet. I'll know once the moment happens. That's when I'll know which path this is…

Chapter 5: Damaged Goods

After speaking with Zane, Lucas found himself wandering the camp aimlessly as if he were still waking up from a bad dream. His mind was a jungle of thoughts that kept running back and forth between what he knew, what he thought he knew, and what he tried to deny of the two. He did his best to ground himself and his thoughts, but his mind and body were at war with each other.

As much as I want to see my friends, I'm worried about how Vanessa will take the news about Bill, Lucas thought uncomfortably. During the last few hours of the first day, Lucas noticed he was being watched by the wolf-girl counselor. The way she prowled from a distance was like a predator eyeing its prey. Keeping this in mind, Lucas made sure not to be alone in the campgrounds and occupied his sister wherever she went. The wolf-girl counselor seemed to have abandoned her efforts after a while.

That night Lucas had a nightmare, one that had been recurring since his accident last year.

He was standing on the edge of a cliff, the rain pouring down on him ferociously. It was as if the skies themselves were weeping for him and the tragedy that was about to befall him. The Shadows made their presence known and the sounds they produced was akin to the mumblings a person makes when their lips are very slightly open. It was a sound that haunted Lucas.

Sssssssshhhhhhhhhhh. Sssssssssshhhhhhhh. Aaaaaaaaaahm. Aaaaaaaaaahm

Lucas blinked and silently fell into a never-ending abyss.

Standing above him was a man with golden hair and a sharp smile. His face was obscured by the shadows, but his piercing green eyes glistened through eerily, like the eyes of some ominous demon. He also had flames emitting from behind him that looked like a bonfire.

As he fell, Lucas muttered softly, while clutching his chest, *I don't want to die…I don't want to die…I don't want to die…*

Instantly the nightmare was over. The moonlight pierced through his window when Lucas awoke, covered in sweat, and felt his sharp nails digging deep into his chest where his heart nested. He removed his hand to see small crescent marks that his fingernails imprinted, already dripping with trickles of blood. When he searched for his camp shirt, the one he swore he had worn,

Lucas found it torn to shreds by the side of his bed. Bits of fabric decorated his bed and person like dandruff.

The remnants of his past trauma came in the form of the nightmares he continued to have of a man with golden hair who tries to kill him each night. Of shadows whose forms are shapeless, and whose sounds are trying to mimic a person. Of the talking birds who spelled misfortune and tragedy for his future. But why would a man he doesn't even know want to kill him?

Maybe I pissed him off and said the wrong thing. It wouldn't be the first time that happened, but it would be the first time someone tried to kill me for it.

Forgetting how sharp his nails had become, Lucas began to scratch at his bare forearms and opened a scab from a previous nightmare he had a few days ago. He barely noticed it and reflected that the cut on his chest from this past nightmare would form a broken lined circle where his heart nested.

It used to hurt. The first cut wasn't even deep enough to make a scar. It wasn't until the nightmares started happening more that the cuts became deeper and each began to hurt less and less. I wish I could feel something, anything but this… this lack of feeling.

It wasn't just feeling numb that bothered Lucas. He wondered why his body, despite the scars, wasn't healing properly. He didn't know if it was because of his accident last year, or the loss of his parents, or—.

That's enough. I don't want to think about it. What I'm doing helps me and isn't hurting anyone. Reading minds hasn't been working, and it hurts me. It's the only thing that hurts me now…

The thought began to fester in Lucas' mind, nagging at him, until he pushed them aside and forced himself to drift into the solace of sleep.

The next morning Henry had Zane, Naomi, and a few of the other counselors assist in bringing back the remaining campers. The objective was to strictly stick to returning campers rather than bringing in new ones. Cecilia and Darrell prepared the welcoming ceremony, while Boris was on patrol duty.

Lucas couldn't stop thinking about all the things that were happening at once even as he spent his free time with his sister and Sapphire. Each new fearful thought caused him to start scratching at his forearm, where his nails dug at his long-sleeved arm like a dog digging a hole.

If I was still on my meds, this wouldn't be affecting me as much as it is, he noted. Lucas found himself compulsively forgetting to take his medicine, even more so after last year. Shelly did not forget to pack his capsules and pills, which was something he only knew about because of reading her mind briefly.

Lucas thought about Mike and remembered seeing him being carted away, not knowing if he would live or die. The wound he suffered to his leg looked serious and it was very likely that he would suffer a lifetime injury.

I wish I knew what happened. Why would… That guy attack the counselors? It just doesn't make any sense to me.

Sapphire continued begging to see Mike, throwing a notable tantrum in one instance when her power very briefly activated. Shelly calmly assured the little girl that her brother was being well taken care of and that he needed to rest before she could see him. Even though this calmed her down, Lucas could see that his sister was running on fumes.

Shelly is doing her best, because I know I couldn't do what she does. I wouldn't have the patience for Sapphire's tantrums.

Lucas tried to go visit Daniel in the hopes of learning more about what happened. To his disappointment, he was absent from both his tent and the ward. When Lucas asked around, the best answer he received, from Zane, was that 'Daniel is taking some alone time to sulk'.

He blames himself for what happened. Lucas heard Zane think when he was leaving. *It was a bad idea, for sure, but no one could have known that it was going to turn out that way. I mean, Daniel can see into the future, but they're only possible glimpses, nothing concrete…*

Lucas groaned in pain and bit the side of his tongue by accident.

This really sucks right now.

The camp was put on immediate lockdown, meaning no one was allowed in or out except the counselors who were expected to arrive the next day with the remaining campers. A strict curfew would be enforced the following day as well that would require campers to return to their cabins by seven rather than ten at night.

It barely gets dark by seven, and full dark by close to eight. That's going to make campfire gatherings unlikely this summer.

That night Lucas feared the nightmares he had of the golden-haired man. When he finally did sleep, it wasn't the nightmare he dreamt of. He instead found himself in a different place, and in a different frame of mind…

Bill was hauled into a room that was dark and moldy. He registered the decayed smells which gave off a strong sewer stench. There was a tight cloth over his eyes and one that was fixed to his mouth. His wrists were tightly bound behind him with rope. Bill felt small against the strong hands that were on either side of him, moving him along with such strength that he could do nothing except struggle silently.

He found himself shortly thereafter attached to what felt like a gurney. His bound wrists were loosened and, before he could think to fight back, his feet and wrists were strapped together. Bill was wheeled down what sounded like a long-blackened hallway. He heard doors opening, closing, then he was inside a brightened room. With the cloth over his closed eyes the light made him see a wall of orange.

The doors opened again, closed, with fresh footsteps entering. Each foot made an echo that was almost in synchrony with Bill's heart.

What is this place? He thought. *Why can't I see?*

Bill felt another voice mixed in with his own but couldn't identify it.

He attempted to open his heavily bandaged eyes, but it was as thick as duct tape. The cloth on his mouth was loose though and could come off easily.

Before Bill could try, the one who entered the room announced their presence.

"Good evening, children," said the booming voice of a man Bill didn't know. He tried to wriggle free from his restraints, the straps on his wrists and feet as tight as the cloth on his eyes. "Today we have a very special guest. This young man is very lucky. You see, he'll be among the chosen from his group to receive the liquid which will determine his fate."

Fate? Liquid? What in the name of all that is sane is this?

Bill muffled protests while working his tongue and teeth with the cloth in his mouth. It came loose and settled on his bare neck like a handkerchief.

"What's going on here?" he cried out. "Why am I here? What are you going to do to me?"

The booming voice did not appreciate being interrupted from what could only be his grandeur moment. This was evident when he made a groaning sound and his footsteps approached the gurney Bill was strapped to.

"What's wrong with you? Didn't your parents teach you not to interrupt people when they are speaking? Such poor manners. Just remember; what's about to happen is the best-case scenario." The man whispered the last part. Bill felt something hairy touch his bare chest. It moved back and forth as if the man hovering above him was using a feather duster on him.

"Now where was I… Ah yes, of course. If we can forgo any further interruptions, this young man will know what it is like to experience true power."

Bill heard more footsteps enter the room. The feet sounded hurried and fearful. Something about them reminded him of how a mouse must feel when they see something bigger than it. The footsteps were gone just as fast as they had entered.

"I hold in my hand a special elixir of sorts," Bill's captor boasted with pride. "This is a rare honor indeed. It will go a lot easier if you don't fight it."

Bill began to panic, his dry mouth crying out for a drink, but not the one this man above him offered. He turned his head every which way, hoping to somehow loosen either his restraints or the cloth over his eyes. After what felt like a full minute, the man sighed and snapped his fingers.

"Gus, Bit, pinch his nose and hold his mouth open."

Footsteps approached Bill as his nose was pinched shut by one of the small boy's while the other boy's hands attempted to wrestle Bill's jaw open like a jar. He gritted his teeth, nearly biting his tongue. When the great puff came from his mouth Bill had only a second or two at most to enjoy the feeling before something gooey and slimy entered his mouth. His nose was still closed, but his mouth was wide open, welcoming the unknown substance that forced its entry down his windpipe.

Some of it spilled over his mouth and dripped across his cheeks and neck while caking the cloth that had rested inside his mouth just moments ago. Bill felt the putrid liquid slither into his throat like a snake. The liquid left track marks that were burns etching his insides.

When it was over, Bill took a long heavy sigh and attempted to cough out and regurgitate what he had been forced to drink. His mouth was dry, his lips beginning to crack, and his tongue felt swollen in his mouth. The two silent children walked away and disappeared.

"Wat's happenang to me?" Bill struggled to say. The tongue inside his mouth was threatening to obscure his airway. His heart began to make palpitations and sweat began to sprinkle his body like icicles. He felt himself convulsing; the strange liquid he drank having arrived at its destination. It bought the ticket, and Bill's life was the fare.

Even though he had lost consciousness, his mind was still awake. This allowed Lucas, his cabin mate of last year, to get a sneak peek at his horizons. Lucas too saw the orange wall that blocked Bill's vision, but he managed to stretch himself beyond it in order to observe his surroundings. He felt almost like a ghost, moving through his friend's subconscious and reading the room.

Lucas' eyes spotted a figure he feared, why he couldn't say. The man's golden hair was loose, and he was dressed in what looked like an expensive black suit. His face was angelic and his smile gave him a youthful appearance that also made him intimidating.

"Let's see if he lasts the night. While we wait, get the others ready," the man instructed. Lucas noted the audience in the room were children, many of which looked malnourished and sleep deprived. They moved like imps in a fairy tale and darted with speed outside the room that would only be surpassed by Ashley's ability.

Bill was coughing violently, the liquid commencing its work on him, as his eyes began to glow red beneath the tightly wrapped cloth…

Lucas awoke swiftly, his head flying from his pillow. His whole body was covered in sweat as if he had just emerged from the ocean.

What was that?!

His eyes were closed and when he tried to open them, Lucas feared what would happen.

My eyes! They're on fire! It's like they're melting in my sockets!

Lucas staggered towards the cabin's bathroom, filled the sink with cold water, and submerged his whole face into the small pool. He kept his eyes closed, feeling the water around his face enter his nostrils and begging entrance into his eyes.

I've never felt anything like this before in my life. This pain! It's not just what I feel; it's taking something away from me I can never get back. But it's not me; it's Bill.

When the pain finally calmed, Lucas pulled his soaking face out of the cold water. With great effort he opened his eyes and saw his normally dark green eyes appeared lighter this morning. There was even a little blue in his eyes that he had never noticed before until now. His eyes were also slightly bloodshot and the bags under his eyes gave him a black-eyed appearance.

Even when I sleep, I'm not sleeping, Lucas noted to himself.

What jolted Lucas back to himself was the bothersome trumpet ringing again, to signify the first *official* day.

It was the 'official day' the day before yesterday.

Lucas rubbed his ears so fiercely that his sharp nails were close to cutting his ear lobes.

How was I able to feel that? That went beyond reading minds; it was like experiencing whatever happened to Bill. Whatever that…guy… did to him.

Lucas thought maybe Henry would know something about it.

If I tell him about my eyes, then I'll have to mention the dream, and I really don't want to relive that experience again so soon.

When Lucas was done thinking, he got dressed and headed out. He was eager to greet his friends and girlfriend, despite wondering how the situation with Bill would be handled.

Henry has a plan. I know he does. He'll save Bill before I have to confront Vanessa about it… and before I have a chance to mention the dream.

Lucas' thoughts sounded more assured than he felt.

While I want to believe Henry's doing everything he can to help Bill, what if there's more to it than that? No, that's crazy talk. Bill's one of us and, more than that, he's a Camp Counselor now. So, he's important, definitely.

Lucas left his cabin and saw Zane and Naomi emerging from the entrance with the other campers, including, to his delight, his friends. He spotted them among the crowd of campers, many of which he knew only by faces but not by names. Lucas noticed Daniel approaching the campers with a cast on his broken leg and moving with the help of crutches. Close to Daniel was the girl Lucas had seen from earlier and had previously seen in a picture the Camp Director's son showed him last year. The girl helped Daniel walk and held his hand tenderly.

She's even more beautiful than in the picture, Lucas noted bashfully. Noticing her now, Keira had long brunette hair that was streaked yellow brown, with green eyes, and Lucas noticed her smile was similar to Ashley's.

She could be Ashley's sister for all I know. I've heard how siblings sometimes share the same smile. Shelly and I would beg to differ though.

Keira wore an orange shirt that read, 'Camp Supernatural, established in 1963', and a skirt with black leggings which made her look like a schoolgirl.

She looks younger than Daniel. He said they met while both were in high school, but she somehow looks like she's still there.

With his friends coming closer, Lucas noted Josh's clothing and appearance compared to the year before. He had grown a few inches taller, his bright auburn hair had grown longer as well. The wind's incoming breeze supported the waves in his hair, and he sported a light yellow short-sleeve hoodie over a black long sleeve shirt.

He looks like he's dressed for the winter instead of the summer heat. Still, I have to admit to myself, it suits him. Yellow might be his color.

Josh raised up his hand as if to slap Lucas when they neared each other. Both their hands found each other and pulled one another for a short embrace.

"Luke. Hey, man. How is life? Is it nice?" Josh's concentrated voice tone asked.

Lucas began to use sign language, something that surprised Josh.

A lot of it I got from his mind before my powers started acting up, and the rest I got from the internet.

Lucas tapped the back of his right hand with his opened left palm (Good). He then used his right palm to slide in the air to the side with his thumb up (Better). Josh looked at him both knowingly and also with a glint of humor in his eyes.

"Good. Better. You're good but can you be better?"

Lucas nodded, smiling for both him and Josh.

"Not bad," Josh signed appreciatively.

"Thank you. It's good to see you, Josh," Lucas remarked with signs amiably.

Josh had been one of the few friends he had kept in touch regularly with since camp ended a year ago. Despite the two friends coming into conflict the previous summer, their friendship endured and Lucas was happy for that.

I never thought after everything that happened last year I'd be so happy to see him again. Luckily he feels the same way.

Behind Josh came Hailey and Ashley. Hailey still towered over Lucas by a couple of inches but other than that she looked more or less unchanged. She wore her hair behind her in a bun that made her look almost masculine.

I'm sure if she lets her hair loose, she'll look more like herself, Lucas noted.

She smiled at Lucas and greeted him.

"Hey, Lucas. How have you been doing?"

"Good. Yeah, it's been good. Are you ready for the summer?" Lucas asked.

Hailey nodded.

Short but sweet. No wonder our texts never got beyond that point. Even when I asked her about Ashley, I never got past, 'She's doing alright' or 'She's doing fine.' I really really hate small talk.

There was an uncomfortable look that passed between Lucas and Ashley as if they were strangers now. Lucas was glad to see Ashley looked just as she did the year before. She sported a blue cap over her blonde hair with a red shirt underneath a green jacket. She wore a small bit of make-up on her eyes, but it was barely noticeable even with the morning sun's rays. Her freckles seemed almost to blend in with the sun like bits of sand on a beach.

Feeling bold, Lucas gestured for a hug to which Ashley complied softly.

They had been this way ever since the end of last summer. Ashley had asked Lucas to the Fourth of July dance, and although he agreed to go with her, he suffered a mysterious accident that left him in a coma for over a month. He had no recollection of the events leading up to the accident or the accident itself.

I only remember why I left; I felt so alone. There was so much going on. I just wanted to go home and be with Shelly. After what happened, I wish I...

While Ashley did not blame him for missing out on the dance, Lucas did choose Vanessa over her even after knowing that she was there for him at his lowest. He was about to say something when he heard her voice in his mind.

I hope he's doing okay. After what happened to his parents I can't imagine what he is going through. I wish I could have told him how sorry I was last year, but everything happened so fast that I didn't get the chance…

Lucas knew exactly what she was talking about and did not want to get into it. Just the very thought or inkling of it made him want to scratch at himself. He had to forcefully stop his hands, knowing there were others around him who would see.

Vanessa emerged from the crowd and towards Lucas. She wrapped her arms around his neck and planted a passionate kiss on his lips.

Why do I feel like that was more for Vanessa's image than for me? Also, why do I taste cherry?

"Hi, babe, I've missed you," Vanessa said happily after she stopped kissing him.

I wonder why he hasn't answered any of my calls or texts, Lucas heard his girlfriend think. This thought caused him a slight pain that went largely unnoticed.

Vanessa wore a pink blouse with her dark hair loose and falling on both sides of her shoulders. Since the last time Lucas saw his girlfriend, she had added an extra piercing to both her lobes (bringing the total now to four) and wore make up on her face including lip gloss and mascara. When Lucas touched his lips, he realized that was why he tasted the familiar taste of cherry.

While Lucas was happy to see his girlfriend, he was also very uneasy. She didn't know about Bill's disappearance, and he slowly began to realize he did not return her affection for him like before. A realization that first came to him after Valentine's Day, but Lucas decided not to do anything about it because he had no idea how to break up with a girl; especially when that girl still had feelings for him.

Shelly says it's not rocket science. Just to be straight-forward and truthful. Apparently texting or calling to break up isn't right, so I have to do it in person. What if she cries and makes a big thing out of it? I know we've been together since last year, but it feels much shorter than that. I mean, we only saw each other a few times outside of camp and now with Bill gone…

When he heard her thoughts in his head, he knew she was not ready for either truth.

This is going to be the best summer ever! I finally have a steady boyfriend, and my brother is going to be a counselor. I hope Shannon takes it easy on him. She can be more ba…rk…than bite, or the other way…bad…around…a…on…day…

Vanessa's last thoughts came up in Lucas' head, and he was unable to hear the rest of what she was thinking.

Lucas was so distracted by the broken thoughts that he didn't notice Shelly appearing beside her brother. Vanessa gave Shelly a friendly acknowledgement, which was exchanged for a similar yet empty gesture. The only one who seemed to be aware of this fact was Lucas.

I wish Vanessa and Shelly got along better. I know she doesn't like how bossy Vanessa can be, and the fact that she has expensive tastes. Shelly likes to remind me how we're not exactly swimming in the money our parents left behind.

Josh kissed Shelly's hand in a flirtatious manner as if she were royalty. She was flattered by it while Lucas rolled his eyes. Hailey thought it was a cute gesture but didn't realize that Josh was hitting on Shelly.

"You look like a magazine model come to life," Josh signed and said aloud with a wink towards Shelly's direction. She seemed less flattered by this comment, but she hid it well from all but her brother.

"Nice to finally meet you, Shelly," Ashley greeted her, amiably. "I'm sorry for last year. I wanted to give you both my condolences." While Lucas' sister was appreciative of this, Lucas was not. "You were all Lucas talked about last year and it's really nice to put a face to a name."

Shelly nodded bashfully at this.

"Do you know what your ability is?"

"I'm not sure yet," Shelly admitted. "I've been told I have one, but I haven't felt anything different since last year."

"No worries," Ashley said with a smile. "That's what this camp is for; to figure it out and how to use the ability, once discovered, properly. They'll be assigning cabins pretty soon. Are you familiar with how it works?"

Shelly shook her head.

"The Camp Director mentioned it, and he assigned me to the Weeping Willow. Is that a good one?"

Ashley smiled when she asked this, which made Lucas somewhat envious that she didn't smile for him.

"It's definitely a good cabin. That's where Hailey and I were last year. We're very happy to welcome you."

Hailey nodded in agreement. While Lucas felt uncomfortable about Shelly befriending the two girls, for the sake of his sister having more friends, he decided not to voice his discomfort or object.

I want to say it's fine, but I just don't like the idea of Ashley and Shelly talking about me behind my back. Ashley I trust to an extent but Shelly, she loves gossip as much as most middle-aged women love reality shows. Why did I just think that?

Ashley and Hailey led Shelly away, leaving Lucas with his girlfriend and Josh. Vanessa bit her lip, looked behind her boyfriend, and around him as if expecting someone to be there.

Where's my brother? Vanessa thought anxiously.

"Umm, Lucas, where is Bill? He should be here right?" Vanessa asked intuitively. "I've been trying to text and call him also, but his phone always goes straight to voicemail."

"Hey, Lucas, where is Bill? Shouldn't he be here?" Josh said steadily and signed furiously.

Josh did not understand that Vanessa had already asked Lucas that question.

I guess I better tell her what I know already.

As he was about to, Daniel came towards them with Keira by his side.

My luck's beginning to turn!

Keira smiled at them while Daniel looked at Lucas with a darkened expression.

"Mike is conscious and he wants to speak to you," Daniel said to Lucas stiffly.

When he noticed Vanessa and Josh around, he told Lucas in his mind, *it concerns Bill.*

Lucas suddenly felt tense at the thought of going to the hospital ward. He did his best to brush the memories of the previous year and his own fears aside as he followed Keira and Daniel to the ward.

Josh and Vanessa wanted to join them, but Daniel insisted that Mike wanted a private word with him.

I hope Mike is y…o…a…k, Vanessa thought with concern.

I wonder…who…Mike…happened…him…what…to…and…, Josh's thoughts trailed off as well, with Lucas feeling a sharp pain from both voices in his head.

What's going on with my powers? It's like I can still read minds, but after a while they start to become hard to understand beyond my own thoughts. I can't tell what is up or down when it comes to the flow or left and right when it comes to who's thinking what. Even my own thoughts sound like they are confused. It's been upended and downsized since the accident and I can't keep whatever is in my head from…

"…spilling out," Lucas muttered out loud. He was relieved that Daniel and Keira were too busy talking to each other to notice what he had said.

Keira and Daniel hadn't noticed Lucas' absence when he hung back. He looked up at the hospital and noted that, while it looked big enough to house a few dozen campers, it now appeared to be near full capacity. Lucas knew the ward was composed mostly of separate rooms for patients and little offices on the side for the staff members. With some of those offices being used to house the rest of the campers who were still recovering from their injuries. Lucas didn't want to go inside; he REALLY didn't want to go inside.

You have to, he told himself. *I mean I have to. For Mike. For answers. Who's though? Yours or mine?*

He shook his head compulsively and screamed. Lucas swore the whole world could hear him, but to his relief it was all in his head. When he looked around, no one was watching him. Keira and Daniel were still inside making their way to Mike's room.

Taking a deep breath, Lucas went inside of himself, compartmentalized, sighed, and entered.

Lucas spotted Melanie, the nurse from last year who had a crush on Josh, run past him. She didn't notice him and was tending to Alexander, who was still unconscious but somehow looked worse than when he was brought in.

Zane said he wasn't going to last long. It looks like he might be right.

Alexander was bedridden and appeared catatonic. His eyes were staring upwards while his mouth hung down like the end of a deflated balloon.

His thoughts are all over the place. He's thinking intensely about Richardson, and his last moments… Why Richardson… Why… That's not me.

Lucas found himself shaking again, his own thoughts at war with the ones surrounding him. Everyone's minds in the hospital were screaming and projecting onto Lucas like a conduit. It took all he had, gritting his teeth, scratching his clothed forearm, and blinking rapidly, to finally be composed enough to put one foot in front of the other in a solemn march.

When he reached the room Mike was in, Lucas nearly stopped himself from entering. He saw that Daniel and Keira were already there but couldn't bring himself to imagine a scenario where he would be able to be inside without having a full-on panic attack. Noticing how he continued to breathe rapidly, Lucas paused, steadied himself, then entered.

This is too much… too much.. is this… I can't… no… I can… this I can… I must…

Recalling his breathing exercises, controlling breathing, inhale, exhale, he entered the room.

Sapphire sat with Twinkle resting in her arms inside the room as she watched her brother with fresh tears trickling down her eyes. Her doll Barbara was sitting beside her like a silent companion offering emotional support.

That is so depressing, Lucas thought, as he began to feel what Sapphire was feeling. *If Mike doesn't get better…no… I can't think that way. He* will *get better for Sapphire. What if…no… I can't do that either. I promised Henry I wouldn't tell anyone about what he did for me.*

When he got closer, Lucas noticed how bad the damage was. Mike's face was covered with bandages, his broken arm was now in a cast, and his wounded leg was covered by a quilt. He looked like a half-finished mummy and was unconscious.

He also had restraints on his wrists and ankles, which perplexed Lucas.

It's like he was putting up a fight or something on the way inside.

Sensing their presence, particularly Daniels, Twinkle began to growl at him which made Sapphire shudder and come out of her daze.

"I'm sorry, mista Danny," said the small girl, meekly. "Twinkle, don't be mean. He's a good mista."

Daniel smiled warmly at her and limped towards her, while Twinkle bared his small teeth at him.

"Just Daniel or Danny is fine, Sapphire," Daniel said as he proceeded to pat Twinkle on the head. Instantly, the dog began to lick his hand.

He strangely seems enthusiastic all of a sudden. Twinkle took longer to be comfortable with me for some reason.

"Sapphire, this is my girlfriend Keira."

Daniel's girlfriend waved a friendly hand to both Sapphire and Twinkle. The little girl smiled brightly at the young woman.

"You look so pretty. Like a princess," said Sapphire. Keira blushed and nodded approvingly.

"Thank you, Sapphire. That is so sweet of you to say."

Daniel interrupted the two, putting himself in the middle as if to make his presence known.

"I thought Mike was awake. What happened to him?"

Sapphire shook her head and wiped a fresh tear from her eye.

"He was a wake a little bit a go," she replied hesitantly. "Doctor said stuff I don't know. Why is he like this? Who did this?"

Lucas sighed in disappointment. He shuddered and felt himself nearly stagger backwards when he spotted a bed pan near Mike.

Not that! No. I can't be here. Here I can't be.

Lucas gazed at Mike, sleeping soundly, and heard his friend's faint voice inside his head.

Mom…dad… where are you... don't leave us…. Mike mumbled in his thoughts incoherently.

Lucas winced in pain and he could not hear anything past the last word. He was momentarily grateful that Mike's words drowned out his anxious thoughts.

"Keira, why don't you take Sapphire outside for a quick bite? We'll be right here until you get back."

At first Sapphire hesitated on joining Keira until she promised to take her to where they had a new snack machine installed.

"Can I get a Honey Bun and Twinkie for Twinkle?" asked Sapphire excitedly.

Keira only chuckled as she led her and Twinkle out of the room.

"How many do you want?"

"A lot a lot. A bunch and a bunch."

When they were gone, Daniel turned his attention to Lucas.

"He suffered the worst out of us all," Daniel told him, miserably. "His arm's broken and what worries me more is his leg." He took a moment to speak further, thinking, then he continued. "The doctors are optimistic that he will be able to keep his leg, but he may have trouble walking on it for the rest of his life. When they brought him in, even though he was unconscious, he was fighting the nurses. It was like his body didn't want to be in here."

Lucas recalled noticing the restraints on Mike.

His thoughts are filled with fear right now…

"It's my fault he was out there. My father refused to use the skeletal cab drivers this year so we needed an alternative. Mike's ability allows him to track other campers from various places. He began to develop it last year during the time you were in a coma. He can only find people he's acquainted with based on personal items, but even then it isn't foolproof. I tried to overreach and the losses are the consequence for my actions.

"What I didn't see coming was Alistair and those kids he has with him. Even though all I can see are glimpses, I still didn't see them in any single one. Something felt off about this, even the idea of it was wrong somehow."

Lucas gulped, trying to think of a possible solution.

I know he's getting the best care possible, maybe he needs more than what even the doctors here can offer.

It took a moment for Daniel to notice Lucas' discomfort, which made him appear suddenly guilty.

"Oh, my Gods, Lucas, I just realized… I am so sorry. Are you doing alright? Being back here again after last year?"

Lucas shook his head, not wanting to open up about it to Daniel.

To anyone. I said I'd never talk about it and I won't.

"Do you think Mike should go to a hospital outside of camp? Maybe they can help him in ways that we can't," Lucas abruptly changed the subject.

Daniel noticed the evasion but did not press it or seem offended. He shook his head and sighed in resignation.

"The doctors here are not specialists or professionals. Most are like us and others are here out of the kindness of their hearts. Unless you know someone who can heal broken limbs and torn muscles, there isn't much medical expertise can do but save his leg altogether," Daniel admitted with a frown.

Lucas had the sudden urge to mention what Henry did for him, if only as a possible way to help Mike.

I know I would be breaking my promise, but shouldn't Daniel know what his father can do? I'm surprised he doesn't already.

"If you couldn't see it coming, then who could, am I right?" Lucas whispered to himself. To his horror, he realized what he said was supposed to be an inside thought and not something spoken for others to hear. Daniel heard every word, with his face becoming the way it had been the first time Lucas and him were alone together.

"What was that, Lucas? Are you making fun of me? Did something I say sound funny to you? Is that it?"

Daniel's tone matched the sudden burst of hostility he was suddenly displaying.

This kid is really starting to get on my nerves. I tried being patient with him last year, but now…wish…he…I…stayed…gone…would've…

"No, it's not like that," Lucas admitted defensively. "I was just thinking out loud about how that would be helpful, if you had seen the attack coming. But even with your abilities, maybe it was a fluke."

Keep quiet, Lucas heard himself think. *Shut up now. You moron!*

Daniel began to become increasingly annoyed. He gathered his composure long enough to avoid making a scene when Keira returned with Sapphire, who was holding a bag full of candy bars and Honey Buns. Twinkle also had a Twinkie still in its wrapper in-between his teeth.

"Look, Lukey, Ms. Keira bought me candy and Honeybuns. Mikey and I love these. I'll give him one when he a wakes up," said the little girl with a big smile on her face. The smile made her look younger than her age suggested.

Keira sensed the tension between Daniel and Lucas and inched towards her boyfriend. Her eyes were darting every which way as if to assess the situation calculatedly.

"Is everything alright, sweetie?" Keira asked Daniel with concern.

Daniel composed himself and nodded, looking like himself again.

"Yeah, hun, everything is fine. I was just about to go back to our tent. It's nearly time."

Keira nodded knowingly, as she put Daniel's arm around her and the two began to walk outside the room.

What's his problem? Daniel thought, as if he knew Lucas was listening to his thoughts. *I swear that if he makes a fool out of me… my…out…in…of…to…front…father…going…it…I'm…*

Lucas continued to groan in pain, while he tried his best to make out what Daniel was thinking.

Said too much, Lucas heard himself think fast. *Why did I say too much? Too much I say did I why?*

He didn't want to alarm the little girl, so Lucas went back inside himself again, bringing his thoughts with him, his fears, and, with his hands in his pockets, scratching the inside of his jeans. The sound irritated him, made him want to grit his teeth. It reminded him of the sound feet make when stepping on concrete.

Sapphire asked for the television to be put on and wanted to watch a show with talking dogs in it. After Lucas obliged her, he gave her a sly smile.

"Make sure to save some of that candy for Mike," Lucas teased, as Sapphire was already beginning to unwrap her third Honeybun. "Don't eat too many of those either. You'll get a tummy ache."

The little girl giggled enthusiastically.

"You sound like Shelly, Lukey. Okay, I won't eat a lot a lot. I promise."

Sapphire said this with all the innocence and youth she missed out in those years in the hospital. This thought made Lucas pity the future that lay ahead for Sapphire.

She's still too innocent to be with kids her age. Mike is the only person who can look after her properly. If he can't, even Shelly wouldn't be able to take care of both me and Sapphire… No, definitely not.

"What were you and mista Danny saying stuff on?" Sapphire asked Lucas.

"We were talking about how Mike looks like he's getting much better. He should be on his feet soon enough."

Lucas was lying to Sapphire just like how Shelly used to lie to him. One of her most notable lies was that their parents would go easy on him for whatever mistake he made.

'They will understand. They can only ground you.'

She always promised that the next day would be easier than the previous day.

It never once happened. Just like Mike will never be the same after this. I shouldn't have said 'on his feet.'

Sapphire had a troubled look that concerned Lucas.

"What's wrong, Sapphy?"

She shook her head and looked at him with her big hazel eyes.

"What will happen to Mikey's leg? I asked Ms. Keira and she said he's good. Then a mista Doctor said he might lose his leg. I don't want that for Mikey," Sapphire cried out, beginning to look like she was about to have a panic attack. She dropped the candy and Honeybuns she was holding and looked as if she were about to explode. Twinkle began to tremble and whine.

Her skin is becoming translucent like when she uses her power, Lucas noted in fear. *If I'm not careful with what I say next, she'll explode into a confetti of diamonds.*

Sapphire's eyes were beginning to well up with tears and she shivered as if she were cold. When Shelly entered the room, she saw Sapphire in a panicked state. She rushed towards her, wrapped her arms around the little girl and began to rock her back and forth.

"What's going on with her?" Lucas asked Shelly, who shot him a quick unreceptive look.

Just let this happen, Shelly thought for Lucas to hear. *Don't say anything.*

After a few seconds of this, Sapphire began to calm down, her skin returning to normal, but she continued to sob.

"Is Mikey going to be okay, Shelly?" Sapphire asked in-between sobs and sniffles.

"Of course, Little Sapphy. Who said otherwise?"

Twinkle began to bark with concern, which seemed to make Sapphire calm down.

"I'm okay, Twinkle," said Sapphire breathlessly. "Thank you, Shelly."

"What was that?" Lucas asked his sister.

"She just had a mild panic attack. Did you give her candy, Lucas?"

When Shelly noticed the candy, she became angry and gave her brother a disapproving look.

"What were you thinking?! She's scared enough about Mike and you give her something she shouldn't be eating!"

I didn't give her the candy. It was Keira.

Lucas was about to defend himself when Sapphire spoke up for him.

"It was me, Shelly. I wanted it for me and Mikey when he woke up. It's my fault."

Shelly's mood suddenly shifted and she went back to softly rocking the little girl.

Nice save, Lucas heard himself think. *Thanks for that, Sapphy.*

This was worse than last time, Lucas heard Shelly think. *It wasn't just the sugar intake; it was also…her…Mike…concern…for…*

"I'm sorry, Shell," Lucas said after Sapphire had calmed down enough for Shelly to stop rocking her. "Can we talk outside?"

Shelly nodded and seated Sapphire in the chair she was on.

"We'll be right outside okay, Sapphy? Just continue watching that show. It looks like a new episode," Shelly told the little girl. "I'll come join you in a bit."

Shelly took the remaining candies and honeybuns but promised to give them back to Sapphire when Mike woke up.

"I've got a bad feeling about something," Lucas noted, trying to make it so that he meant to say it out loud instead of thinking it. When they were outside the ward, he continued. "Mike is in worse shape than anyone wants to let on. Daniel told me so himself. But there might be a way to help him. I just can't say what it is…"

Shelly looked as if she was waiting for an explanation, but when Lucas didn't give her one fast enough, she said, "Since when can't you say anything to me?"

"Since this is something I made a promise about and it means a lot for me to keep it," Lucas said defensively, in a tone his sister wasn't familiar with.

"Then why even mention it at all?"

Lucas hesitated before continuing.

"I'm having problems with my powers," Lucas admitted to his sister. "When I read minds, they become jumbled up after a while. The words I mean. I get these headaches like someone poking the back of my neck with a sharp point. The worst thing that's starting to happen now is I'm saying inside thoughts out loud."

It's been happening for a while, but it's even more so now that Vanessa and my friends are back.

Lucas could tell that his sister didn't understand what he was saying fully. Regardless, she understood where he was coming from.

"I'm guessing you almost blabbed about that secret to Daniel, right? He looked like someone ran over his foot when I last saw him."

Lucas nodded shamefully.

"Luke, you know I'd do anything for you, and being here in this camp is more for you than for me. If you can't be honest with me, then please trust one of your friends with this. Don't deal with it alone when you don't have to."

He almost considered this, only to shake his head in response.

"I can't trust anyone with this. Not even you, Shell," Lucas heard himself admit.

Another inside thought.

"What is that supposed to mean? If you can't trust me or your friends with this, then who? Do you trust Henry with this secret?"

Lucas suddenly heard something in his sister's voice that he never thought he would hear.

She's suspicious. No, she's jealous.

I don't understand why he won't talk to me. I'm his sister and I love him. I can't stand the thought that Henry is using him. Lucas is too good...person...doesn't...deserve...a...of...

"It's not about Henry; not everything is about someone, Shell. Anyways, you just have to trust me on this."

"Oh, do I? Because ever since last year, I don't know what to think anymore. You come home after being away for three months, three long months, and you have these abilities that are somehow connected to your disabilities. You can read minds, you can control minds, and all of a sudden your powers aren't working anymore. I understand a lot of that has to do with losing our parents and I know it was very hard for you, but at least I was there for them. I tried to pick up the pieces after you left. I mean, that's all I've ever done when it comes to you. I pick up the mess you make, try to pretend it isn't there, but not this time. It's not fair for me, Luke.

"I love you with all my heart, but right now you're breaking it. You used to trust me with everything. You would tell me when things were bothering you and ask for help. To be honest, you don't need to read my mind to know this, I liked being there for you. It helped me deal with the worst days with mom and dad. While you were gone, I didn't have that anymore. I didn't have my little brother. How do you think that made me feel? I wish you knew, truly, because then maybe you'd think clearly before you say something so harsh to me. The one person in this world, Lucas, who will defend you against anyone and always support you."

Lucas was at a loss of words. He felt like anything he'd say would be the wrong answer and she'd bite his head off faster than he could finish his sentence.

I can't tell her. No matter how badly I want to. Henry would never trust me again. Besides, I owe him my life.

Ultimately, Lucas shook his head again.

"I'm sorry, Shell, but I can't," he declared.

Shelly sighed and shook her head in response.

"Okay, keep your secrets to yourself, Lucas. Just know this: Henry gave me a choice and I chose you. I will never regret that choice no matter what. I hope he can help you with your powers, because for the first time in my life, I don't know how to help you. All I can say is that I am here for you, and I am not leaving this place without you."

Before Lucas could say anything, Shelly turned around and reentered the hospital. He thought about going back inside the room if only to check on Mike, but knew his sister wouldn't appreciate it at the moment.

What did Shell mean by she chose me? What choice did Henry give her? She has no right to think so badly of him. Shelly doesn't know Henry the way I do. Maybe if she knew what he did for me, it would change how she feels about him.

"I promised Henry I wouldn't tell anyone; not even my own sister," Lucas said to himself. He shook his head, wincing in pain, and began to rub his eyes compulsively. When that didn't calm him, he began to scratch at his clothed arms and felt a small rip in the fabric from his nails.

I need to talk to Henry. He'll know what's going on with me…

Chapter 6: Red Eyes

Bill awoke in a damp medieval-like cell, with scarcely any light save for the nearby torchlight. The floor was dirty and unclean, with mud tracking mixed with residue from a recent struggle. He couldn't see this but felt it with his bare feet. His hands were chained to the walls to make it look like he was surrendering. His hair fell in strands on the tightened bandages wrapped around his eyes, newly applied. Bill's lips had a dark shade to them from the liquid he drank earlier. The taste still lingered in his mouth and when he burped there was a foul aftertaste in his mouth that tasted like bile mixed with rotten milk.

I don't know what that stuff was but for however long I live, I don't want to taste it again.

The door to the entrance of the room opened and the sound of three sets of feet emerged. Bill couldn't see them but recognized one's footsteps as being notably heavier than the other two.

His eyes continued to irritate and hurt him, with the urge to scratch at them increasing with each beat of sweat he began to emit.

Whatever that stuff they gave me is doing to me, it's like it's cooking me alive from the inside.

Bill heard the door to his cage open and felt the intruders eyeing him like a predator about to pounce on a prey.

"Meet your new bunkmate, Devon," the man with the booming voice from before said. Bill didn't catch his name. "Devon, this is Bill. He comes from the same place as you once did. Camp Supernatural. It's almost like a family reunion."

The boy named Devon did not make a sound, but the other one like him seemed to grunt in annoyance.

"Apologies, it seems I've forgotten my manners myself; this is Payne and he has no use for his real name. That right there is a real shame."

The boy who was called Payne also made no sound except for what could be interpreted as someone who is anxious to get on with something.

"Right, yes, so Devon here will be in charge of keeping you company and making sure your stay here is as pleasant as possible," the man declared. "Payne, meanwhile, is in charge of keeping you in line, should you choose to act out for any reason. Keep in mind that he is eager to rip you a new one, so try not to give him a reason."

One of the boys came near Bill, made grunting sounds, and proceeded to knock on the older boy's head like a door. Bill heard a brief scuffle ensue between the two silent boys, which was broken up abruptly by the man.

"Hey, hey, kiddies, fight in your own time. Here you will behave yourself like the little imps you ought to be."

Since Bill couldn't see what was happening in front of him, he had to imagine it. He saw a tall man in-between two boys, one who appeared normal and even friendly, while the other had a more sinister aura to him. Despite their differences it was evident that both boys were in the same league.

I don't know anyone named Devon or Payne.

Bill tried to make words from his mouth, but each puff came like a wheeze from a broken-down engine.

"Don't try having a conversation with either of these gents. They cannot speak and even if they could, nothing they say would be able to help you. So, think of them as boxes in the corner of a room that you won't even notice if you don't look."

Bill grunted, trying to move himself into a better position. He felt his arms straining and the binds on his wrists digging into his skin, making deep imprints. His eyes began to emit a very soft glow and he could see the orange wall in his eyes turning into a bloodied red.

"The good news is if you haven't died from the effects of the liquid yet, then we can rule out another casualty."

Bill's heart stopped at that last word.

"Cathulty?" He uttered the word with a swollen tongue that made it come out in a lisp.

"Yes, that's right. Try not to talk so much either; your tongue is going to be that way for a while. Anyways, the children we captured from your group underwent the same conditions as you, but sadly the results were not favorable."

Bill became anxious, his heart pounding heavily on his chest and his legs moving to find something to make contact with.

"Are they dead?"

"This latest batch was rather new, so as they say in the medical field; sacrifices must be made for progress to happen. Since we don't exactly have a firm grasp on it, we're basically shooting arrows in the dark and hoping we hit a bullseye. Of the recent batch we used, you're the only one who survived. Hooray."

The strength Bill had felt before began to dissipate, while the glare from his eyes was beginning to rage. His throat clenched like a fist, causing him to breathe through his nose in an effort to control his body.

"Why me? Why ith thith happening to me?" Bill asked in a way a person would beg for food.

"I could say the wrong place, the wrong time, but the truth is you were the convenient option. If I had it my way, I had my eye set on another prize. Unfortunately, he got away, so you were plan B since Jacob knows who you're closest to."

Closest to? Who is he talking about? That name. Jacob… What does he have to do with this?

Bill heard hands hitting against something and snapping fingers that were like someone audibly jamming to a beat only they could hear. The man made an exasperated sound and from the way he moved, he kicked up loose dirt from the floor that flew into Bill's face. It made him nearly want to sneeze.

"Devon is insisting that your bandages be changed. When he does this, you'll want to keep your eyes closed. Not so much for his own sake but mainly yours. This new ability you have is new territory and you wouldn't want to blow up your own head I'm sure."

Bill backed against the wall so fast he felt the hard concrete scrape his back. He groaned in pain and listened to the soft footsteps approaching him.

I can use heat vision on him, but what was that about blowing my head up?

He thought about this as Devon began to undo his bandages. It was at this moment when Bill's eyes began to feel even more incredibly itchy and warm. He kept them closed, gritted his teeth, and fought a strong urge to open them. Within seconds, his eyes were bandaged again with a new cloth. This new one was slightly loose on the back.

Wait what? Why is he…?

"Are you done?" the man called out to Devon. "Make sure it's secured because once I close this door you're not coming back in here until tomorrow."

The boy turned and pounded a soft closed palm on his open one. Bill heard this and didn't know what it meant.

"Good boy, now get out of there."

The footsteps belonging to Devon exited the cell and Bill heard the doors clang together, shut, closed.

A new sound began to make its presence known. Bill knew for a fact he had not heard this person enter along with the other three and wondered if they had been in the room the whole time. This person had a dangerous aura to them, something that made the very air in that room feel suddenly engulfed in it, drowning in it.

"What's the prognosis? Is a second opinion needed?" the new person said as if he were reading the words out loud. "Why ask questions when they're more interesting than answers? Who else cares about what a thing wants instead of what it thinks it needs?"

"I didn't hear you come in, Jacob," the man said, indirectly introducing his guest. "This is Bill, you might be familiar with him. He's closest to Lucas, your opposite. Do you recall?"

Even though Bill couldn't see Jacob, he tried to bring back a memory he had of the previous day. He saw a man who looked more like a corpse than a person. Despite the cold, he walked the snowy landscape as if neither the wind nor the snow bothered him. His hair was as silver as the snow itself, and his skin was a pale shade that reminded him of someone else.

It's him! The other telepath who is crazier than Lucas.

"Silence! His thoughts irritate the thoughts in here," Jacob proclaimed, making a scratching, grinding sound with his teeth. His footsteps were more rapid than the others in the room, going back and forth, sideways. He continued this dance for what felt like hours. When he stopped, he spoke once more. "Yes, the opposite values the one we chose, that is good. The ones who speak to me say his value is more in life than death. Though they carry no shapes or forms, they say his purpose will be tested, like a shimmering ocean upon a new wave. It must break to be reformed anew. As with the others, he can experience the joy inside after feeling the pain from oneself."

What does that mean for me? I don't understand anything he just said.

Jacob made an angry gasp and screeched softly, as the man scoffed and nodded.

"To summarize for the uninitiated here, you're saying we should keep him alive and see what his power manifests as." The man seemed to be saying this more for his own benefit than as a direct conversation. "I concur, though I don't have much of a say in the matter." He paused, shifting slightly almost closer. "In the meantime, we'll monitor your progress and make sure your stay here is as cozy as one of those five-star hotels."

The child called Payne defiantly proceeded to use body signals to convey his annoyance. Bill heard his hands flying through the air, his feet pounding the floor, and grunting sounds escaping from his throat.

He sounds like a monkey trying to talk. Even from the way his feet are stamping the ground, as if he's expecting a banana.

"After how you dealt with the last batch of kids we had here, I'm not about to leave you alone with this one," the man remarked. "Either you come willingly, or I'll shish kabob you into a smoldering asphalt." The man began to emit a heat that even from a distance Bill was able to feel as if the flame were in front of him. This flame was stronger than the torch and was akin to the rays the sun gave off on a hot day.

When Bill didn't hear any protests coming from the defiant child, he assumed the matter had been begrudgingly settled.

"Good boy. You could learn a thing or two from Devon here. He gets to have his surname because he doesn't talk back to me. Not in the way you do."

Is that how it works around here? They're punished by having their real names taken from them? What kind of place is this?!

"Proof may be required to show resolve," Jacob proposed. "If need be, be quick about it and only take a morsel. Do not be greedy. Enough to show a valid receipt. Most items can be returned within a thirty-day period, unless otherwise specified."

Bill was reminded of a thought he once had pertaining to Lucas upon learning of his ability.

I used to worry Lucas would be like Jacob; a basket case who by all accounts was crazier than a nuthouse patient. But after meeting Jacob now, I can tell Lucas is sane compared to this guy. He's become my best friend.

Jacob seemed to perk up all of a sudden, as if he heard something that amused him.

"The concept of friends was invented by fools who believed in law and order similar to technological algorithms. When one cannot quantify something, it's explained as a feeling. Feelings lie, they create unexpected emotions that can easily turn one way or another. Better to expel them and not hear of it."

Bill heard his cell door reopening, a terrible fear grasped him and held him in place. The footsteps that came near him confirmed this. There was a protesting grunt, someone fighting silently with an unspoken argument.

"Just one hand, Payne, not both. As our illustrious telepath here says: do not be greedy. Stay on, Devon. Your medical expertise will be needed in a short while."

What are you going to do to me? I need to loosen the cloth on my face.

Bill heard what sounded like a throat clearing as he tried to move his head back and forth. He couldn't explain why but he somehow understood the throat sound.

Don't. He's saying don't.

Bill felt his body shiver, and the muscles in his body stiffened, as Payne came up to him. He buried one fist in Bill's stomach. The older boy grunted in pain, coughing out bits of saliva.

Too much to hope for the black liquid from before.

"Take hold of the left," Jacob instructed.

Payne took hold of Bill's left hand and began his work. Bill thought about his sister, about his girlfriend, and about Camp Supernatural.

Please don't let this be the end. I had so much I wanted to do and say, so much I…ahhh…AHHHHHHHHHHH!!!!!!!

Chapter 7: What If…?

When Lucas entered the camp director's office, he saw that Henry was not there. Instead, to his annoyance, Lucas noticed that Zane was rummaging in Henry's house as if he owned the place. He was going over the casualties list and was skimming through the pages until he noticed Lucas.

"Oh, it's just you. If you're here to see Camp Director James, he's busy doing important stuff, kid," Zane brusquely told Lucas. "Like preparing for the rest of the camper's arrival."

I don't know what I did to get on his bad side but I get a feeling it doesn't take much to do that.

"What are you doing here? This isn't your home," Lucas remarked boldly.

Zane scoffed as he laid down his clipboard delicately and walked over to him.

"True, it's not my home, but it's not yours either. The real question is 'what are *you* doing here?' Or how about 'why are any of us here?' Not to get all existential."

Lucas felt as if his head had been taken off his neck and spun on Henry's table in front of him. He wasn't sure if it was the questions or the way Zane said them that confused him.

He's like a person who mimics other people's behavior. Maybe he does that to make fun of others.

Before long, another person made their presence known.

"What's going on, Zane? Why are you here?" Daniel exclaimed, to Zane's amusement. He steadied himself on the crutches he was using to walk.

"Relax, Danny boy. I was just getting acquainted with Lucy here."

"My name is Lucas," Lucas said angrily.

"Are you sure? Well, if you say so." Zane turned his attention to Daniel. "Anyways, I don't know if you've heard yet, but I'll be training the campers this year. Got any tips for the new guy?"

Daniel glared at Zane and shook his head.

"You know, life was better when you were gone last year, Zane."

"I missed you too, Danny boy," said Zane with a grin. "With Richardson dead someone needs to take charge of the activities in his place. Wasn't that position originally yours? Everyone thought you were a shoo-in because you're the Camp Director's son, but I guess Richardson was more qualified in the end." Zane spoke with little regard to his tone.

When Lucas turned to look at Daniel, his face was seething with rage.

That doesn't even come close to describing how he is feeling, Lucas thought, experiencing the same tension as Daniel.

"I think you should leave. Now, Zane. Before I get really angry."

Lucas thought Daniel looked like a sulking child, with his pouty lips and clenched fists. Zane only scoffed at him and shrugged.

"If one of us has to leave first, let me be the mature one," Zane remarked as he left.

After he was gone, Daniel sighed exhaustingly and turned his attention to Lucas.

"Why are you here anyway, Lucas?" Daniel asked bluntly as he rested himself on the nearest chair.

"I wanted to speak to Henry about something."

Daniel studied Lucas' face with a fixed expression. He turned away after a moment and grimaced in anger.

"I hate it when he calls me 'Danny boy'," Daniel muttered to himself bitterly. "He knows I don't like it, yet he still does it. I don't call him Zaney or Zane-Boy, or Zannoying."

Zannoying? That's actually not bad. I'll just keep that thought to myself.

As Lucas was thinking, Henry entered the room with a plate of three pizzas and gently placed them on his desk while humming a tune. Underneath his left arm, he held a small wooden box, which he slipped into his drawer before anyone could ask about it. Henry looked at both Daniel and Lucas without any hint of surprise, as if he expected them to be there at that moment.

"Hello, Lucas, hello, Daniel. What brings you here on Pizza Day? Would either of you care for a slice?"

Lucas shook his head, and Daniel seemed too occupied with himself to think of food. When Lucas opened his mouth to speak, Daniel cut in.

"Father, Lucas came to talk to you about something, possibly about Bill," Daniel explained as Lucas felt dumbfounded. "What's the plan for rescuing him and the other campers?"

That's not what I wanted to talk about.

Henry did not reply immediately. He took a small bite off the tip of his olive-topped pizza and looked uncomfortably calm for either of Lucas and Daniel's reassurance.

"Are you sure you would not like a slice? The cafeteria will be running out for the day soon and I brought extras with company in mind."

Daniel shook his head, a little too curtly, while Lucas modestly said, "No, thank you."

To be honest, I am a bit hungry, but Daniel is killing my appetite right now. He really isn't hiding those daddy issues he has.

After finishing one slice of pizza, Henry proceeded to explain the plan of action.

"Bill will be returned to us safely," Henry explained indifferently. Both Daniel and Lucas waited for more, but the Camp Director remained silent.

It became evident that Daniel did not like this answer.

What else is new? Better stop thinking before I say something out loud.

"That's it? That's not even a plan. Don't you care about what happens to Bill? He is Lucas' best friend and Vanessa's brother. She won't take this lightly."

While Lucas wanted to appreciate Daniel's comments, he did not enjoy someone speaking for him when he was still in the room.

Please let this go, Daniel. Did I say that? I did say that.

Henry was halfway through his second pizza as he flipped on his small little television. He set the channel to TCM where an old Broadway musical adaptation was playing.

"What would you have me do, Daniel?"

Daniel approached his father and laid his hands on the desk firmly. Henry continued to eat the slice of pizza, his eyes not moving away from the direction of the television screen.

"The final remaining campers return within the hour. When that happens, you'll be making a welcoming announcement and begin the assigning of cabins for the new campers."

When Daniel paused before continuing, Henry finally got the hint and turned to look his son in the eyes.

"Tomorrow morning, before the games start, I'll be holding a council meeting in the Grand Hall. I will propose to send out campers on a mission to rescue Bill and the rest who were taken. I realize our numbers are stretched thin as it is and I take full responsibility for my part in it, but we need to start sending these kids out into the field regardless of their experience. Even first year campers should be able to go on missions.

"You weren't there, father; you didn't see what Alistair and his 'Silent Ones' did to me, the other counselors, and Mike. Do you even care that we almost died? That *I* could have died? That's why we need to do something about it now and not later. Alistair tried to kill me and he would have if it wasn't for the bravery of those we lost."

Lucas read Daniel's mind briefly and saw that he was thinking about Zane.

He doesn't want to admit that Zane had a part to play by indirectly saving him.

"Mike woke up briefly," Daniel revealed. "He didn't say much, but he mentioned the name Jacob before losing consciousness. He couldn't have known him because Jacob has been gone since before the time I was a camper. If he's working with Alistair, then we have two major problems now."

Despite appearing to accept this, Henry still looked unmoved by his son's words.

Jacob and Alistair? Why do I get the feeling this is a lot bigger than even them? Lucas heard himself thinking in a tone he wasn't familiar with.

"It's never the ones you suspect most," Lucas blurted out loud, to his horror. This caused Daniel to quickly shoot him a disapproving look which was only quelled by Henry's interjection.

"Do you have something you wish to add, Lucas? I believe your insight would be most valuable."

Lucas' eyes went from Henry to Daniel, whose expression was so masked with both surprise and anger that even his thoughts made it unclear what he was truly feeling.

I think he's more shocked by my words than even thinking why I said them. Still, maybe I can make this work for me.

It surprised both when Henry seemed to answer for him.

"You wanted to discuss something that is troubling you?"

And there goes that opportunity.

Daniel's eyebrow rose when Lucas nodded. Then the Camp Director turned to his son.

"Leave us, Daniel."

His son was taken aback.

"But father….?"

"Now, Daniel."

Henry didn't shout, but it was firm enough.

He won't repeat himself.

Daniel rose swiftly and flinched when his leg twitched. Lucas got up fast and tried to help him before he fell, but Daniel brushed him off without saying anything. He silently and angrily left Henry's office.

How dare that brat try to help me, Lucas heard Daniel think, *I didn't ask for it, and I…it…need…don't…*

When Daniel was gone, Henry turned off the television, put the leftover pizza he had aside, and beckoned for Lucas to explain what was wrong. Lucas went into detail about his dream; about Bill, and that Alistair had been in the dream. Lucas called him the 'evil man' instead of by name.

I also need to mention that my powers are messing up. But I think that can wait for now.

When he finished explaining the dream, Henry sighed with exertion.

"This is most troubling to hear. We can only hope that Bill is still in good health, but we have no way of knowing that beyond what you claim to have seen. Tell me, when the dream ended and you could no longer see what was happening, could you feel what Bill was experiencing at that moment?"

How did he know that? Am I becoming that obvious with my powers now?

Lucas nodded and went on to explain the burning sensation he felt from his eyes.

"It wasn't just how much my eyes burnt. There was… something else. They made Bill drink something. I've never tasted anything like it before in my life. It was like…"

"… like death," the Camp Director noted blankly. Lucas' eyes were raised so high his forehead creased like a wrinkled parchment. "It's more than just the liquid itself as it is the process."

Process? What process?

Henry changed the subject as Lucas pondered this thought.

"Due to your abilities as a telepath, you are beginning to experience what it is like to see through the eyes of another, and to feel as they do." Henry smiled and put his hands together. "Your emphatic nature makes you a viable source for forming meaningful connections. You continue to amaze me, Lucas."

There was a brief moment of silence between the two, broken by Lucas' abrupt utterance.

"About what's been bothering me…"

"…Yes," said Henry, with a warm smile.

"My powers haven't been working like they should. I mean, I can still read minds, but I can't control them anymore. The thoughts I hear become jumbled and I can't hear the rest of what the other person is thinking. The worst one is that I am saying out loud what I'm thinking. I did that just now when Daniel was here."

Henry nodded unsurprisingly.

"That is perfectly normal. You went through a traumatic experience last year with the accident. Because of the loss of your parents, your abilities are not going to be the same, but they are still maturing. It all comes from here." Henry pointed to his head. "As well as here." Now he pointed at his heart. After that, his mood suddenly shifted. "Something else is troubling you as well. Does it concern your sister?"

Lucas nodded and tried very hard not to think any thoughts about Shelly.

I just need to know this much if nothing else today.

"Forgive me for asking, but Shelly told me that you gave her a choice and that she chose me. What was the choice?"

Henry contemplated the question for a moment, and this made Lucas fearful of a lie or being asked to leave.

"I offered your sister the chance to attend any prestigious college of her choosing. I even provided the means for it." Henry pulled from one of his drawers a check and he handed it to Lucas.

When Lucas took it in his hand, he couldn't believe the numbers he was seeing.

She said no to this?! Is she out of her mind? That's my line, but still. This is a lot of money.

"This is more money than she would need for college," Lucas noted. "In fact, there's even some money that could be used for other things like paying for the house. Why would Shell say no to this?"

Henry shrugged, as Lucas handed him back the check.

"I do not know. It's possible she feared leaving you behind or giving off the impression that she did not wish to be here."

Lucas shook his head stubbornly.

"No way. Shell would never do that to me. Then again, I don't know what she'd do anymore. We… had a fight. I couldn't believe the stuff she told me. She wanted me to tell her about what you did for me, but I didn't, I swear."

Henry looked pleased by this.

"I appreciate that, my child. Truly. I know it cannot be an easy thing to keep from your older sibling. However, I must ask that you keep our conversations private from her and your friends as well."

"Why, Henry? I don't understand."

"I don't need you to understand. You only need to do what I ask of you," Henry said in a voice that sounded sharp and harsh. There was a brief moment of uncomfortable silence before Henry resumed. "Your sister will be participating in tomorrow's game. Please do not share with her any information in regard to it or the role she will play. The point of it is to reveal what her ability is. Just as you were once tested."

Lucas suddenly felt irritated by this. He remembered being thrown into a near-death experience in order to unlock his abilities. The memory of that revelation still nagged in the back of his mind like an irritable itch.

Henry acted like he didn't care. Just like now with Daniel. I can't read his thoughts, but I feel something that's different. Like something that should be there and isn't...

"About what you did for me?" Henry waited for Lucas to continue, but his face began to look displeased. "Can you do that for others?"

"I could," Henry revealed curtly. "But if you are suggesting that I should do this for Mike, then that is entirely out of the question."

Lucas was taken aback by this, as if the Camp Director suggested he didn't care one way or another whether or not Mike would survive his injuries. He began to wonder if Henry even cared about everyone else in camp.

That isn't right. I mean, thinking that isn't right.

"I'm wrong about that right?" Lucas said impulsively, which Henry noted.

"Wrong about what?"

Lucas shook his head and tried to change the subject.

"Shelly doesn't trust you," Lucas admitted. "She's afraid you'll hurt me for some reason. I wish I could make her feel differently about you, but I don't know what to tell her."

Henry shook his head in an irritating manner.

"It doesn't matter what your sister thinks of me. What matters is… wait a moment."

Henry's mood seemed to shift once more as Daniel burst through the door.

Great, just before Henry could say anything more, Lucas thought irritably.

"What is this, Father?" Daniel asked sharply. "I had to hear this from Zane of all people? You're planning to promote me to Camp Activities Director. I cannot accept the position. I refuse."

Henry sighed and shook his head.

"You can, and you will, Daniel. It may be under unfavorable circumstances, but you are ready."

Daniel shook his head, confusing Lucas.

"It was my fault that Mike may never walk again, and my fault that those campers were all taken. I wanted to prove that I could take charge and bring in more campers to help our numbers grow. I know that wasn't an ideal situation for you, but for a while it was convenient. Everything was fine until Alistair came back. That friend of yours is the reason Jane is in critical condition, Richardson is dead, and Alexander is at death's door. Now that Jacob is in the picture, as mentioned before, we can't—"

"Alistair is no friend of mine, and you would do well to remember your place. How I choose to take action will be my decision alone to make."

The tone he took with his son was not only stern but icy cold, like a chilling wind that just entered the room.

Did winter suddenly come in early or is summer ending that quickly?

"Your decisions matter when they affect everyone in camp," Daniel insisted. "For all we know, Bill and the other campers might either be dead or facing torture."

"Bill still lives. Lucas has seen it." Henry noted Daniel's shock and Lucas' discomfort. "I do not know the purpose of the abductions, but the matter will be resolved. There's a pressing disturbance in relation to these events."

Lucas somehow understood this insinuation better than Daniel did.

He means Jacob, but something tells me saying the whole truth wouldn't help right now.

"What I want to know is why is Alistair doing this, why capture Bill, and a group of kids who haven't even set foot in camp yet? What did we do to him? What did *you* do to him, Father?"

Daniel wasn't asking; he was declaring as if common knowledge. Lucas was taken aback by his defiant and aggressive tone.

He's taking all of this harder than he's letting on.

"If he's not your friend anymore, then what happened between the two of you? At least tell me that, father."

Henry looked calm on the outside, but Lucas believed that the Camp Director looked like he could have an outburst at any moment.

"Alistair is a man I used to know," Henry explained cryptically. "He's respected the sanctity of this place for years and operates with a versatile nature. The understanding between us is one that is still in place despite the circumstances of recent events."

Henry's voice trailed off while his son was beginning to lose his patience.

"It doesn't matter why he did what he did. We should rescue Bill and take down Alistair so he'll never think to cross paths with us again. While we're at it, Jacob is another problem you never dealt with. Ever since he left camp, you just assumed he would never come back. Well, as the saying goes, the prodigal son has returned. If the choice were mine, I'd have made sure that any threats against the camp were taken care of no matter what it takes."

Henry rose from his chair, looked Daniel straight in the eyes, and placed a soft gentle hand on his son's shoulder.

"Has enough not been done to place these children in harm's way, my son?" Henry asked Daniel, who looked like someone splashed hot water in his face. "I don't do this with an easy heart. Someday, if you become Camp Director, you may have to make a hard choice such as this, between the life of one camper and the lives of many campers. The questions you'll have to face will come down to which actions carry the most consequence. If you don't know the answer by then, you will not be ready for the responsibilities to follow."

Daniel paused after that and looked to Lucas for support. Lucas ended up nodding in approval of Henry's plan.

"I'm sorry, Daniel, but Henry is right," Lucas noted to Daniel's annoyance.

That was meant to be an inside thought. Lucas felt frustrated with himself.

"Very well, father. The final decision will be made in tomorrow's meeting. Until then, I think everyone in camp has the right to know about Bill, including Shannon and Vanessa," Daniel pointed out bluntly. "Even in my current condition, I'll go with whoever is sent out to make sure that Bill and the other campers are brought home safely."

Lucas felt his heart jump again at the sound of his girlfriend's name.

I don't have a choice now. It will be much worse if Vanessa hears it from Daniel instead of me.

"Keep in mind that if we move without caution, we may cause undue panic. Something that will make rescuing Bill even more difficult," Henry told his son hesitantly. "Our goal now should be attending to our wounded and ensuring they all receive the best medical care possible. Mike is all little Sapphire has. If anything should happen to him, it will be on your conscience."

Daniel's face fell at the thought of all the injured campers in the attack. He thought of Mike and Sapphire, knowing that his father was right.

That's pretty harsh. It's okay to think that, but I wish he hadn't said it.

"I know, father. But I wonder, if the roles were reversed and I had been taken instead of Bill, would you be so quick to take your time saving me?" Daniel asked bitterly.

Henry did not respond and appeared unmoved by his son's question.

"But you were not captured, therefore it does little to contemplate such things. Now then, if that is all, Lucas and I have pressing matters to discuss. Since you know of your promotion, please begin making the necessary preparations for the last of the campers, and see to it that they are arranged in their cabins before the games tomorrow."

Daniel's face suddenly grew twisted and he looked like he'd kill the first person who spoke. Despite this, he sighed and walked out of the room with thoughts that boiled as hot as an erupting volcano.

Every time…Every time…he continues to treat me like…like…nothing…At least I came back…he…he…never did, until it was too…late…ate…

As he slammed the door behind him, Henry smiled warmly at Lucas.

"I know it's not my place to say this, Henry, but some of the stuff you told Daniel was kind of mean," Lucas heard himself admit to the Camp Director. "He's just trying to do what he feels is right, like everyone else is. I just wish you wouldn't make him feel bad for that."

Henry took a moment to respond, seemingly considering Lucas' words.

"You are right, Lucas; it is not your place to speak of such things. Daniel is a grown man who relies heavily on the past to dictate his actions in the present. In a few moments, I must be on my way to address the campers. But first, we were discussing your abilities and how they are not at their full capacity."

Lucas nodded and winced in pain. Sweat was covering his clothed forearms and drenching both freshly made cuts and scabs.

"It's not just that. It's like whatever progress I made last year became destroyed by whatever I'm feeling inside now."

"And what do you feel now?"

"I feel angry, alone, confused, but mostly scared. I'm scared of what happened to me last year, and… I can't talk about the rest."

Henry nodded knowingly.

"What were the circumstances surrounding your parents passing?"

Lucas suddenly felt uncomfortable but tried to hide it as best as he could.

Anyone with eyes could see through me like glass.

"They died of brain aneurysms. Why did you want to know, Henry?"

"It seems odd that such a trauma happened to both your parents at the same time."

At the same time? I never said—

"They must have been under heavy duress," Henry continued. "Do you know of anything or anyone who could have caused that?"

Lucas did not want to talk about this and the very thought of it began to make him feel like the last moment he saw his parents. It took all his willpower to keep himself from scratching at his forearms. Instead, he clamped his teeth together.

I can't. I won't. Talk about this.

"It doesn't matter because they're dead!" Lucas shouted, unable to control himself. "It does little to contemplate such things." He was surprised that Henry's face appeared so unmoved by this. To his slight relief, the Camp Director seemingly took the hint and changed the subject.

"How are you and Vanessa faring? I understand you were quite taken with her last year, so am I to assume that still stands now?"

Lucas, having calmed down, tried to think of how to respond. He thought about saying that things were going great between them but ultimately couldn't find it in his heart to lie.

We've had our differences recently, but we make it work, was a thought Lucas remembered from a romcom Shelly saw with him once. *It's the only line I can remember from that movie.*

"Honestly, I don't know where we stand anymore," Lucas confessed. "I used to think about her all the time last summer. Then, sometime during the fall or winter, I realized I didn't feel that way anymore."

Henry smiled and chuckled.

"Ah yes, young love oftentimes is more conflicted than certain. You will experience love and heartbreak throughout your life many times. Even if things fail between you and Vanessa, you may have other prospects. You're too young to tie yourself to one idea of what love is."

Lucas did not like that idea, even if it meant being true to how he was beginning to feel now.

He makes it sound so easy, like love isn't a feeling but an emotion that can be discarded like a candy wrapper after the sweets have been had.

"That doesn't seem right to me, sir. Would I be a bad person for breaking up with her? Especially right now with everything going on? Can I still be friends with Vanessa even after all that?"

Henry shrugged.

"You're asking the wrong person these questions. You may wish to direct them to your young girlfriend if you want a proper response."

Yeah, I'll get a response, but there won't be anything proper *about it,* Lucas thought in confliction.

Despite trying to smile, he suddenly felt sad.

"Things haven't been great between me and Ashley lately. I don't think she ever liked the fact that I chose Vanessa over her. Still, that doesn't mean we can't be friends, right? I mean, Shelly once told me that guys and girls can be friends, just friends. The only thing that makes it awkward is that I know Ashley liked me before, and I don't know if she still does. I also don't know if I could see her in that way. I wish I knew what the right choice was sometimes."

Something Lucas had been fond of about Henry is that he listened to him intently. Even if it was something like overthinking or ranting, he never once interrupted Lucas or told him to 'deal with it' like his own father had in his lifetime.

The one time I asked my dad about girls, he said to ask my mom. When I asked her, she told me to ask my dad again and I just ended up asking Shell. All she told me was that when a girl says something, it isn't always as it sounds. Which is very confusing for me since I go by what I hear. If Vanessa told me she's not mad, then I would think she isn't. If she said she needs space, I'd give it to her. How else am I supposed to know what not to do, Lucas thought rapidly, his mind piling up thoughts as if he were playing *Tetris* in his head.

Unfortunately, Henry famously changed the subject, which brought Lucas back down to earth.

"On a last matter, we must discuss this issue concerning Bill's well-being."

Lucas did not want to continue talking about this, but complied, nonetheless.

"I hope you understand, Lucas, that Bill's capture presents a complicated situation," Henry explained truthfully. "At the moment, there are only two possibilities: his safe return, or failing to rescue him. Should we succeed in rescuing him and the campers, there will need to be a contingency plan."

The Camp Director studied his eyes as Lucas shifted in his seat uncomfortably.

"I'm not sure I like where this is going," Lucas muttered. Luckily his voice was low enough that Henry hadn't heard what he said.

"Lucas, if we can bring Bill back alive, I want you to erase his mind of everything that has happened up until his capture. That way he will believe whatever story you tell him and he will be content for it. That is the best-case scenario."

Lucas gulped now, dreading this option. For once, he was happy he couldn't read the Camp Director's mind, but an unknown instinct caused Lucas to ask anyway.

"And what about if we can't save him without endangering other lives."

"It means that he knows valuable information about this camp, of our ways, and perhaps how to locate us. Alistair has found the camp before by using others similarly to how he may use Bill. Should any harm come to you or anyone else in camp, Bill's life will be forfeit immediately."

Lucas was completely shocked to hear this. What he heard sounded very cruel and inhumane. Maybe more so than whatever Alistair was putting his former cabin mate through. But it was not just that: Henry was asking Lucas to treat Bill as expendable regardless of the outcome.

That's horrible. I can't do that, even if it's Henry asking. There's just no way.

His thoughts went to Vanessa and he wondered how she would feel about that.

She'd hate me for it and nothing I could ever say would make her feel differently. I admit, I used my powers last year carelessly. Still, I know this is wrong. Henry should not be asking me to do this.

After coming to his senses, Lucas shook his head.

"No, sir, I won't do it."

I know I owe him a debt that can never be repaid, but this isn't the way to do it.

The Camp Director appeared shocked by this, which made Lucas wonder if he really meant it.

"And is that your final answer? What if I tell you this was the payment for healing you last year? If you don't do this, I will return you to the way you were before. Would you carry out this command then?"

Lucas suddenly felt very fearful of this situation.

He can't. Well actually he can, but why? Why is he making this about that?

Lucas tried to study the Camp Director's face for any signs if he's bluffing.

I swear, I have the world's worst poker face and Henry has the best, Lucas thought, trying desperately to keep the thought to himself.

Shaking his numerous thoughts aside, Lucas quickly nodded and felt more confident of himself than ever before.

"Bill is my friend, and Vanessa is my girlfriend. Even if it means being paralyzed again, I won't do it. My powers should not be used this way and it goes against everything I believe in as a person," Lucas said with no hesitation or doubt. "If you want to do it so badly, then do it yourself. You don't have to tell me to go away like you always do. I'll leave this time on my own."

Lucas was about to open the door when Henry called out to him.

"Wait a moment, Lucas. You remember what I told you a year ago about how everything I do is for the benefit of everyone in this camp? Including those who have set foot here before?"

Lucas nodded.

He made it a point also because I was frustrated that he never told me anything. At least I'm not the only one who feels that way.

"There may come a day, a moment, where you will have to make an irrevocable decision. One that will hold dire consequences for yourself and those around you. Your life is no longer tethered to yourself but to the friends whose bonds are becoming deep seated foundations. As your abilities mature with you, your capacity will become greater than anything you can imagine. Do you understand what I am saying, my son?"

Lucas was confused.

I mean, if he's asking what I'll ultimately choose, I stand by my feelings on this. Nothing, not even the threat of losing what I gained last year, would make me change my mind.

"To put your mind at ease, this was a test," Henry revealed. Lucas suddenly felt flabbergasted by this. "Either scenario proved unfavorable and would not be ideal ways of using your abilities."

"Then why ask me if I would do that? You even threatened to make me paralyzed again."

"Even so, you made the choice I had hoped you would make. You value your friends and sister's lives over any promise you made to me, which is the true measure of your character. You should be proud, Lucas. When your mind tries to play tricks on you, always follow your heart's instincts."

Lucas smiled to himself for making the right moral call.

There is no world where I would consider erasing a friend's mind the best option in any scenario. Then again, I can understand why that would need to happen even if it isn't morally right. It won't come to that, because I have the power to make sure it doesn't.

"I believe it is about time for me to prepare for the welcoming ceremony. You should join your friends and enjoy the moments you have with each of them."

But Lucas wasn't ready now to leave. He had one more nagging thought that wouldn't let go.

"Why did you want to know about how my parents died? What difference does it make when there's no one to blame for it?"

Henry took a moment to answer. This moment lasted what felt like hours but was in actuality ten seconds.

"The circumstances by which your parents died is unusual from a medical standpoint. By your previous claim, the reason you left home was because you believed you had attacked your father. Your mind showed you what you thought you saw, when the truth couldn't be far from it. Telepaths have been known to experience personal tragedies when their powers are left unchecked and you were only just beginning to discover yours."

Lucas began to fear the reasoning behind this.

"What are you saying? That *I* killed my parents unknowingly?" Even saying it out loud, confirmed a fear Lucas harbored deep within his subconscious.

This is why I didn't want to talk about it. Because what if…?

"What if it was of a similar nature to your abilities," Henry implied. "That is not to say you would have done it, intentionally or not. Rather what if another like you were capable of this? Few telepaths exist, and few are known. Only one could want misfortune to befall you."

No, that can't be true. I don't even know him and he's already targeting people I love? Then again, it's better than believing it was me. The question becomes; what if it was Jacob…?

Chapter 8: Night of the Blood Moon

Shelly watched as her brother and Henry exited his home, going their separate ways. Her gaze followed the Camp director as he made his way to the main pavilion where Boris tried poorly to entertain the crowd of campers. The Camp Guardian would mix the punchline with an essential part of the joke, making the overall quality feel half-baked at best. She observed Boris's movements which were a mixture of comedic timing along with what can be compared to a magician's sleight of hand.

"Did you hear the one about the zebra who thought he had more stripes than his brothers? It turns out he had the same stripes as his brother, but he didn't know because his reflection was backwards."

Even the way his mouth moved suggested he thought carefully before each move. However, the overall tensions and anxiety everyone felt seemed to be rubbing off on the monster because he began to sweat profusely. When she touched her own brow, Shelly found herself sweating mildly.

Nonetheless, a few campers clapped for his efforts and some even laughed. Shelly wasn't sure how many did this for his benefit or to save face.

There's not as many campers here as Lucas had said there was last year, Shelly noted. She turned and looked to see how many campers were around her. Some ranged from as young as ten to twelve, and the oldest she saw were near her age or a little older. Anyone older than twenty, she assumed, were the camp counselors. At the moment, the only counselors in attendance were Daniel, Zane and Naomi.

Boris stopped himself from telling another joke when he spotted Henry.

"My apologies, Camp Director James," Boris said bashfully. "I just wanted to entertain everyone before the announcements were made."

Henry smiled warmly and patted Boris softly on the back. The Camp Guardian meekly left the stage to join the others in the audience. He gave a quick glance to Shelly and showed her a small smile.

Where did you go Lucas? Shelly looked for her brother in the crowd, but only saw Ashley and Hailey, who were standing on either side of her. She was grateful their eyes were on the pavilion instead of on her.

Shelly noted that Daniel looked displeased, Zane disinterested, and Naomi had a disconcerting look on her face.

Of the three, Daniel looks like he drew the short straw in whatever they have going on behind the scenes.

"Everyone, new and old, welcome to a new summer in Camp Supernatural," Henry said as he greeted everyone humbly. "For those who don't already know me, my name is Henry James. I am the Camp Director of Camp Supernatural and standing here are the camp counselors. I would also like to take this moment to introduce to you all our new Camp Activities Director; my son Daniel Harrison. Please give him a well-deserved hand."

Daniel begrudgingly made his way to his father with his crutches, and Shelly swore he walked like an inmate on death row.

It doesn't look like that job promotion agrees with him, Shelly noted.

"I'm so happy for Daniel," Ashely told Shelly. "He's been wanting to be Camp Activities Director for a while now. I know he's got this."

Shelly nodded without giving a reply.

Once Daniel was near him, Henry came towards his son and wrapped an arm around his shoulder firmly.

"I have complete faith in my son's ability to carry on this incredible responsibility," Henry proclaimed proudly, as Daniel looked like he was on the brink of tears.

He's either very happy or very sad.

As the rest of the campers began to clap more, Shelly finally spotted her brother with his friend Josh. She tried to get his attention, but Lucas' eyes were fixed forward. His arms were crossed while both his hands were softly rubbing against his forearms.

What are you thinking about Lucas? I wish you'd tell me.

Once the cheers and congratulations were done, Henry proceeded with the announcements.

"Because of unforeseen circumstances, we are beginning the summer late, but rest assured, activities and training will commence soon. Tomorrow and Friday will be the Relic competition, which will consist primarily of first years. Due to a shortage of campers this year, I would like to offer an open invitation to anyone who wishes to help their newly joined campers. Any skills will be much welcomed and appreciated."

Daniel whispered something to Henry. The Camp Director nodded approvingly.

"Also important: tomorrow my son will hold a meeting for all cabin leaders, and counselors at 8am on the dot. Please make plans to attend if you are a cabin leader or counselor. I wish you all luck in tomorrow's game and a wonderful summer here in Camp Supernatural. Remember our camp motto: 'control it, so it does not control you'. Without further ado, please turn your attention to the camp staff. They will explain their roles and assign the new campers to cabins."

The campers clapped for Henry as he let himself down from the stage. Daniel's eyes followed his father with an expression that turned sour like spoiled milk. Lucas and Josh were staring at the main pavilion a couple of feet away from where Shelly, Ashley, and Hailey were, but the duo made no effort to join them.

The ceremony continued with the counselors approaching the stage to introduce themselves and explain their roles in the camp. A newcomer arrived and joined the camp counselors. Shelly recognized her as Keira, the girl who was with Daniel earlier. She introduced herself as the new camp's psychiatrist.

"Hello everyone! I'm so excited to be here with you all," Keira exclaimed. "For those of you wondering, my ability helps me to know when a person is telling the truth or lying. I have a speech sound disorder, which made it hard for me to talk when I was younger. I used to be mute and it wasn't because I was shy; my mind couldn't process language normally. Learning how to speak helped me not only to communicate, but to read the intentions of others. The way my mind processes information is the same as hearing and understanding language."

That's really cool. I like her already, Shelly decided.

"The way my ability works is by taking notice of the body language and mannerism of others. The way a person's face contorts when they lie, how they're eyes look away, and how they shake rapidly." Keira explained to the campers. "My hope in being here is to help as many campers as I can to achieve the best outcome for themselves not just in their abilities, but in their growth as people. I'm still working on my degree so I can't prescribe medication at this time. However, I can offer advice so that you can receive whatever will help you to further your growth and health. If any of you need anything, my door is always open to you, so don't be shy like I once was."

Shelly could tell that she was already well liked, because many campers looked at Keira with admiration and respect.

Between her and Daniel, she's definitely the smart and more likeable one of the two.

After Keira finished speaking, Naomi took the stage next and demonstrated her ability to turn an object, based on its mass and using kinetic energy, into an explosive weapon. She demonstrated this by using a golf ball. She gathered enough energy within the ball, threw it up, and it turned from white into a coal color. It exploded like confetti.

That's a really cool ability. I wonder what's more common, physical or mental abilities?

Next, Zane showed off his electrical abilities. Static electricity sparkled his fingertips and he wiggled them as if performing magic on stage. The most impressive thing he managed to do was short circuit a camper's cellphone. Smoke rose from it and the camper looked to be on the verge of tears.

I get a feeling that's not all he can do with that ability of his.

Once introductions were over, Daniel formally took over and began the traditional assigning of the cabins. Shelly didn't hear any of the names being called out, but considering she already knew her Cabin was the Weeping Willow, she figured she didn't need to know. Besides, she was too distracted seeing her brother talking with his friend Josh.

I'm glad he's with his friends. I hope they can reach him…

As Shelly got acquainted with her cabin, Lucas walked into his own, feeling troubled. He didn't notice when Josh asked him what was wrong.

"I may be deaf, but I can tell when something is off," Josh insisted with rapid hand gestures. Lucas tried to distract himself but knew this wouldn't last for long.

Before he could say anything, Vanessa barged into the cabin and cut off his train of thought.

So much for time to figure things out.

"Did you know about the council meeting, Lucas? And where's Bill? I've been asking around and no one wants to tell me anything?" Vanessa asked impatiently. "I asked Shannon about Bill, but she wouldn't tell me either. Did everything go alright for his first mission? What did the Camp Director tell you about him?"

Lucas was at a loss of words. Unable to hold it in any longer, he impulsively confessed the truth. Turning to Josh, Lucas mouthing and signing the same thing as best he could.

If my powers were working like before, I could talk to Josh in his mind. That would save me a lot of trouble for what comes next.

When both understood, they looked at him with fury and horror.

"Bill's been taken?!" Vanessa screeched as she struggled to hold back tears.

Josh tried to keep a calm face but found himself shaking in a fearful manner.

"You knew about this and you kept it from us? From Vanessa?" Josh asked and signed anxiously. His hands were marching up and down, left and right, like a conductor for a band.

Lucas was helpless against their accusations as his girlfriend sided with his friend.

"How could you do this to me, Lucas? We're in a relationship, which means you don't hide things from me. Especially about my brother's safety."

Vanessa was so angry that her bones were making the agitating sounds that began to make him feel nauseous.

Crackling…crackling…crackling….

Ugh! Okay wait. I wasn't trying to hide anything from her. We've barely spoken since she got back. Trying to explain that won't get me very far.

Finally, after trying to resist the urge to scratch himself, Lucas collected his thoughts and tried to amend the situation.

"Look, Henry has a plan. He will save Bill because he said so."

Lucas realized how childish and insecure this sounded.

Maybe if I said it differently it would have been more convincing. Like, 'Henry has a plan, and that plan involves saving Bill at any cost.' What is the cost? Why not, 'because it's the right thing to do.' 'Henry will save Bill because it's the right thing to do.'

"I'm going to be there at tomorrow's meeting and I expect you to side with me in saving Bill from those maniacs who have him. Even if it's a risk, I'm not going to sit by and wait for something worse to happen to him. If you care about me, about our relationship, you *will* be on my side," Vanessa declared sharply.

Unfortunately, Lucas found himself thinking the opposite was more important.

Your way is going to get others killed and Bill wouldn't want that.

"We need to be smart about it, like Henry said," Lucas affirmed. "He doesn't want to put anyone else's life in danger. He's just doing what he thinks is right."

Josh then cut in. "What is the plan anyways? How are we going to save Bill?"

"We'll save Bill by doing what Henry says. Plus, it's not just about Bill." *Be careful.* "There were other campers who were also taken. We don't know how many of them are still alive."

Lucas tried not to sound harsh about it, but realized his outside voice was mixing in with his inside voice.

I don't know if I believe half of what I just said, or if I just don't want to admit that Vanessa might be right. Either way, maybe it would be better to support her since she is my girlfriend.

Before he could say his new thought, Vanessa cut him off as swiftly as a guillotine.

"You're a coward, Lucas Fargo," his girlfriend said, disdainfully. "If you don't want to help us save Bill, then fine. I'll go alone or with some other campers who will help. That's my plan at least; to do something instead of just waiting to be told what to do. That's what you're doing by letting Henry decide what's best."

"Henry is considering the lives of everyone here, not just Bill and the other campers," Lucas said, feeling his nails biting into his palms. "They're saying Jacob is with them and if that's the case, he'll see you all coming before you see him. Just please trust me on this. I'm asking you, Vanessa."

"Don't ask me to do this, Lucas, and don't say to trust you or—"

"I want to save Bill too, Vanessa. Don't think for a second that I'm not considering all the options when it comes to Bill's safe return. All I'm saying is Henry knows the guys who have him and if there's a way we can get both Bill and the other campers back without further harm to anyone else, then why not? Even if it means we play the waiting game and do nothing, it's better than charging in and losing more people than we have to."

Lucas reheard his words in his head like a playback video.

I know I've heard something similar, but those are my words and these are my thoughts. I believe that. It makes sense to me.

To Lucas' surprise, and Josh's, Vanessa did not react badly to what he said. Even though she was still visibly upset, she calmed herself.

"We'll decide with a formal vote tomorrow at the council meeting," his girlfriend declared with a sigh. Vanessa turned her attention to Josh, who appeared to be a third wheel up until now. "What do you think we should do, Josh?"

"I vote for rescuing Bill no matter what," Josh decided without hesitation and sided with Vanessa, much to Lucas' dismay. "Sorry, Luke, but we have powers and we should be out there using our powers for good. It's not about you right now."

Not about me? What's that supposed to mean?

Lucas thought this, hoping Josh would hear it in his mind. Josh didn't seem to as he finished signing and speaking. Vanessa patted Josh's shoulder and turned to look at Lucas again.

"I don't want to make you choose but my brother's life is at stake. You're either with me or against me."

Lucas wanted to, with all his heart. However, logically, he could not.

I won't be held responsible if things go wrong because of her and anyone who thinks she's right. And things will go wrong, especially with Jacob involved. This isn't just about trying to do the right thing; it's about considering what's going to happen if Jacob and that other guy find a way back here. Why did they take Bill anyway?

He regretfully shook his head and Vanessa sighed in disappointment.

"Okay. We'll see how many people agree with this plan in tomorrow's meeting."

With that, Vanessa exited the cabin and left Lucas feeling worse than before.

"That doesn't look like it went well for you, did it?" Josh noted with a dry tone.

Lucas shook his head and looked down at the floor.

"No thanks to you," Lucas muttered, making sure his face was turned away from Josh's. When he spoke next, Lucas made sure Josh was looking at him. "Bill's my friend. Of course I want to do whatever it takes to help him," Lucas tried to explain without sign language. "It's not just about him or even the other campers that were taken. We don't have the numbers to test our luck a second time. Also, what was that about this whole thing not being about me? Where did that come from?"

Josh looked displeased despite only picking up a few words from his cabin mate.

"I know you're trying to do what's right. I believe you when you say that. What worries me is what you think is right? And what I said is because you make things about you," Josh noted with a begrudging tone and conflicted signing. "All you wanted to talk about when we texted was how horrible your life has been since last year, how you're scrapping by. You never asked about me. How I am."

Lucas considered this and realized this was true.

I don't need to see the texts to know he's right. I never asked because I was too busy with my own problems to wonder what his could be.

Lucas shook his head and decided he was done talking for the rest of the day. He returned to his room and imagined his old room from home again. It was nearly as he remembered it except it looked messier than last year. The rug he had looked like it had been through a blender, his ceiling fan was missing another blade, and the hole on his wall was bigger than before. Lucas barely noticed these differences as he drifted to sleep.

That night Lucas saw another vision, but this one wasn't of Bill. He saw a shadowed silhouette sitting in a dark room with lit candles encircling the person. Lucas noticed a giant, blue-lined tattoo etched on the person's bare back. There were lines that went up and to the sides that looked like branches from a tree.

Wait a minute, that is *a tree,* Lucas realized fearfully. *It's dead. There's no leaves, and the branches look like veins.*

The man was breathing heavily, and he was crouched down in a fetal position. Shaking back and forth. His forearms had blue lines intertwining like twin snakes, and his long silver hair fell over his face and back like a veil. He was muttering under his breath so quietly that Lucas could not hear what he was saying. There were other sounds in the room as well, various ones. The words were a mixture of incoherent screams and silent cries.

The silver-haired man's muscles pulsated from his body with each breath he took and sweat drenched him from head to bare chest. His palms were opened and bloody from his sharp fingernails. The soles of his feet were bare. He had something circular sitting in front of him but in the darkness Lucas could not tell what it was.

I think he's in some kind of trance, or maybe he's sleeping. I can't see his face underneath all that hair and shadow.

The silver-haired man turned in Lucas' direction but did not appear to notice him. He continued to mutter, his voice becoming louder and in synchronous with the voices around him. They seemed to be emanating from whatever object was in front of the man.

Something about those sounds are familiar…

"Yes. Yes. Borderline connection," the silver-haired man snarled. "Look below the furnace… to find what is burning… Band together like… birds of a feather… A voice echoes up loudly… dies silently. Few remain… only embers… Too high…below ground, one feels all…"

Lucas could not understand him, but he feared the words. The man's skin was pale, similar to Henry and Alistair's skin tone.

He looks like a vampire, like Dracula or that other one that starts with an N.

The silver-haired man, still staring in Lucas' direction, began to make a low groaning sound as he began to speak. It was a mix of growls and huffs. His body continued to shiver and convulse as the voices around him became silently coherent.

"*Break the chain*...Break the stallion... *find the one*...reach full potential. *It isn't right*...mind broken... *lost now*...shapeless form. *Entering the passage*...similar to the one... *back-alley entryway*...to each their own. *Soon there are two*...to carry the mantle. *Down and out*...A door that opens once... *no longer valid*...does not close the same way. *Wind is free*...come like the seasons... *death is work*...dying is inevitable," the silver-haired man rasped.

Suddenly, Lucas could hear sounds that were not coherent words. They were like echoing sounds that became distorted loops. He heard what sounded like an open telephone line.

I...think...can't....clearly

"**You** are not meant to think clearly," a booming voice suddenly arose. The force of this power caused Lucas to be pushed back by a nonexistent gust of wind. "This moment is not now. Don't be so eager to spin the wheel and see where it lands. Conversations will be had, ideas challenged. This moment has happened, for **you,** it is the first time."

Lucas woke up screaming at the top of his lungs and found himself somewhere unfamiliar.

He was in a larger room than his cabin with a bed on one side and a wide table that appeared worn with etchings carved across it. In a chair sat a gray robed woman whose face was obscured by shadows. All Lucas could see were her green irises which stared at him intently.

This has to be a dream. If it's not, I'm definitely having some kind of a mental breakdown.

"Hello, Lucas, my name is Shanine. I have been wanting to meet you for quite some time," said the green-eyed girl. Her face was still obscured in darkness, but Lucas could see what looked like line slashes going down from each of her eyes down her cheeks.

He tried to pinch himself, feeling nothing there. Where his forearms should have been were gaping holes like Swiss cheese.

"What the heck?! What happened to my arm?!"

Shanine shook her head.

"Your form will be returned to you upon completion of this moment," Shanine said as she got up and walked over to him. He could see more of her features now. She was young-looking, but the scars on her face made her seem older than she might have been. Underneath her hood, her hair appeared purple. "Would you care for a refreshment? You won't taste it but you'll still feel it as your mind allows."

Lucas nodded and gratefully accepted a beverage. He felt something that was cold to the touch. When he examined it, Lucas saw it was some kind of herbal tea that gave off no smell. He pressed the cup to his lips and just as Shanine had told him, the drink had no flavor. She was suddenly illuminated in the moonlight, making her appear like an actress on stage with a spotlight. When she removed her hood, Lucas saw her purple hair that looked too natural to be dyed.

There's something seriously off about her and it isn't just her hair color or those lines running down her eyes.

"How did I get here? Where am I?"

"Jacob was told to send you to me and as to where we are, this is my domain. The place in which my mind goes when I sleep."

Lucas suddenly felt fearful of this person standing in front of him.

She mentioned Jacob by name. Is she with him? What does she mean by domain?

"What do you mean by 'your domain'?" Lucas asked warily.

"You are not capable of this ability yet, but in time you may be," Shanine revealed to Lucas. "Your visit here will be short, so I would prefer to use this moment wisely and observe your character."

Lucas felt curious now.

My character? Why does she want to know me? What ability is she talking about? Ability what about talking she is.

"Why does it matter who I am? What does that have to do with anything? "

"Everything. It has to do with everything," Shanine emphasized with a spirited tone. "Your mind is a pathway leading to many abilities, all tied into the main one. However, you are a casual observer and a careless operator. The door is broken now and won't close the same. This has caused your powers to seek control."

Lucas was even more confused than before but tried to piece her words together in his mind.

Casual observer and careless operator. The door that is broken doesn't close the same. My powers are seeking control, against who and what?

Shanine was silent after this, but her face was working. Her green eyes were scanning Lucas' body movement. It was as if she were a scientist and he was her test subject. When he tried to read her mind, Lucas heard something comparable to the sound of a hard object hitting a solid wall.

Ugh! What was that? I couldn't hear or see or feel anything? It doesn't hurt though; it feels addictive.

"What does he want?" Lucas asked Shanine. "Why is Jacob doing all of this? I just want my friend back and the rest of the campers. Maybe we can work something out."

Even as he said this, Lucas knew it was futile. The look Shanine gave him said this without having to speak it.

"You have nothing to offer Jacob and he has everything to give you. The two of you are within a similar field, but you are both in opposite directions. If you were to land with the same side like the flip of a coin, there would be no difference between what you both can do. Only the execution and intent."

Lucas shook his head in defiance, refusing this conclusion.

"We're nothing alike. I would never hurt anyone the way Jacob has."

"But you have. Your friends, your family, those closest that you claim to love. I speak through Jacob; so much of what you feel can be unfelt if it is what you choose. All that is needed is loss of control."

Lucas continued to shake his head and began to stubbornly try to wake himself.

"Do you think raindrops decide where they will land, or fire how fast it will burn? Jacob had no reflection by which to compare himself with. He was half of a whole that needed filling. Until now. With you, he sees a potential ally and someone to see just as he does."

Lucas was becoming uncomfortable and desperately wanted to awaken from this nightmare.

I won't ever see things the way he does. Not now, not ever. The only thing Jacob should see is a trip to a mental hospital.

"This has been a most disappointing venture," Shanine revealed in resignation. "I had hoped you would be a worthy ally for Jacob, but you seem content on your path. Even so, when we meet again, you will understand. Until then, prepare yourself and those around you for the night of the blood moon."

"Why the blood moon?" Lucas asked hastily, hoping that it would catch Shanine's attention.

She only offered part of the overall answer: "The chance to become his equal."

Shanine swiftly disappeared as if she had never been there. Lucas felt his eyes on the outside flutter open and he was back in his cabin room. He stared at his bare forearms and saw the visible lines decorating them. When he touched them, he winced in pain.

The night of the blood moon?

Chapter 9: Over the Years

Shelly dreamt that night, the same dream she had every night since a year ago. In it, her parents were in the kitchen. Her mom by the stove with eggs burning in the pan, while her father's eyes were glued to the television screen. Nothing was playing that Shelly could see or hear.

She walked up to her mother and touched her shoulder softly. It was like activating a detonator when her mother's face lit up and her breathing began to inhale, exhale quickly.

"Where are you, Lucas?" Shelly's mother said under her breath. "Are you here? Did you come back yet?"

Shelly shook her head and pressed herself against her mom in a warm embrace from behind.

"It's me, mom. I'm here," Shelly said, tears streaking down her eyes. The burnt eggs looked like charcoal. She reached for the burner and turned it off. The smell of smoke didn't seem to bother her parents in the least.

When Shelly turned, her mother put her hands on her shoulders and looked at her face. She looked at Shelly as if seeing through her.

"I'm so sorry, Lucas," she began to say, sobbing into her hands. "We tried. We really tried." Across the kitchen, Shelly heard her father also similarly sobbing. Both were like mirror images of each other; hands on their faces, sobs occupied by rheumy noses and abrupt gasps.

Mom…dad… talk to me…please….

After she sobbed, Shelly's mom looked through her again but this time her expression darkened.

"We don't know you," she said coldly. "What are you doing here?"

Shelly remembered the first time her parents behaved this way. It was when her brother left for Camp Supernatural and they had come out of their daze. Since then, both appeared to be in some form of dementia where their memories relapsed from knowing to obliviousness.

"I'm your daughter Shelly, mom. Lucas isn't here. He left for Camp Supernatural. Don't you remember? Dad, do you remember?"

Neither of her parents reacted to this. As the dream began to fade, Shelly saw her parents sob again. This time they both fell to their knees. Her father slunk from his place on the couch and thumped his knees on the floor. If the pain bothered him, he didn't show it.

Shelly heard their cries and screams as she awoke. Sweat-stained and tear drenched. She was alone in her cabin. Her head was throbbing, the same side as before. It took a few minutes for her to calm herself. Making her way to the bathroom, Shelly brushed her teeth, showered, then dressed for the Relic game that was to take place that morning.

She made her way to the cafeteria where Ashley and Hailey were waiting for her. For breakfast she had bacon with eggs, corn, hash brown, and sausage. Ashley and Hailey talked to each other, while Shelly kept to herself, picking at her food like dissecting a frog.

I'm sorry mom. I'm sorry dad. I don't understand why…?

"Has Lucas told you about the Relic game?" Shelly heard Ashley ask her after the memory of her dream faded.

"No," Shelly answered back abruptly, only to clear her throat and repeat herself. "No, he never told me anything about it."

Ashley and Hailey then proceeded to explain the rules to her, much of which went over her head. Shelly found it harder to focus than usual and wasn't sure if it was because of the dream last night or her own anxiety.

What she was able to catch felt like a series of scattershots.

"It's like capture the flag," was one part she caught. "Each team member has a specific job." "You'll likely be a runner. But there's also—." "Lucas helped me when I wielded the orb." "Since your power isn't known yet, you'll probably be—."

Shelly felt herself in and out of the moment. She struggled to stay engaged, but her mind was drifting back and forth on itself, like a tug of war.

Mom…dad… Why did you leave me?

After the three ate breakfast, Ashley and Hailey accompanied Shelly through the campgrounds. The aroma in camp smelled of recent rain. Despite clouds covering the sky, there wasn't enough to warrant anything more than a light drizzle. The morning sun was thankfully, for the most part, obscured by the clouds. Shelly diverted her thoughts from her parents to her brother.

I wish Lucas would talk to me. I want to trust that he knows what he's doing, but when it comes to Henry, I think his mind is cloudier than the sky right now.

As they neared the training field, Hailey revealed she would be helping the yellow team while Ashley would be going to the Grand Hall as Cabin Leader of the Weeping Willow. After parting ways with Ashley, Shelly and Hailey saw Sapphire whimpering on the ground, crying her eyes out. Some older kids in orange camp shirts encircled her. They were taunting her and calling her 'See-through" because of how her power made her skin appear translucent.

Shelly got so angry that she went up to one of the bullies and screamed at them.

"Hey, leave her alone!" she shouted at the lead tormenter. The girl was heavily built with long curly brown hair. She wore an orange camp shirt and had a small entourage of other campers with her.

Why does there always have to be people like this everywhere in the world?

Shelly got in-between Sapphire and the big girl, who said in annoyance, "And who are you supposed to be? This little See-through's fairy godmother?"

The other campers in the bully's entourage snickered at this, which made Shelly seethe.

"I'm someone you don't want to mess with if you know what's good for you," Shelly said bravely.

What am I doing? I don't know what her power is. I can't just tell her to back off and expect a teacher to come around like they would in school.

"Is that a challenge, Newbie," the curly-haired muscular girl decided.

"It's a promise," Hailey announced, coming to Shelly's aid. She towered over Alexia by a few inches, and it was clear from their body language that the two are familiar foes on the battlefield.

This could get bad fast.

Before an escalation could happen, a camp faculty member came by, but it wasn't any of the counselors. It was Keira. She wore a yellow camp shirt and had her hair tied behind her in a bun.

"Leave the yellow team alone, Alexia. You're not in the games this year, so stop encouraging the orange team to misbehave. Why don't you try being a better role model instead for the younger ones?"

Alexia gave her a nasty look, like the very sight of Keira disgusted her.

"I may not be in the orange team, but I'll still lead them to victory," Alexia declared loudly. "If this is all they have to worry about, it won't even be a challenge." She looked at Shelly when she said this part.

With that, Alexia led her group away, but a few still shot Shelly and Sapphire ugly looks, including a tongue out and one involving the bird.

Nice to know kids here are like kids out there. I get the feeling if it weren't Boris or the camp counselors, some of these kids could be very dangerous.

Keira sighed, turned to Shelly and Sapphire, and offered them a smile.

"It's good to see you again, Shelly," Keira noted. "You too, Sapphire. Are you feeling alright?"

Sapphire shook her head sniffling back fresh tears with the back of her small hands.

"That big meanie girl scared me. I went to where the tag game would be, but that big meanie girl came and made me cry. They called me a see-through." The phrase caused the little girl to start tearing up again, which made Shelly wrap her arms around her.

"I miss Mikey," Sapphire said in-between sobs.

"We were lucky you were around. Thank you, Keira," Shelly thanked her.

"You're very welcome, Shelly. The reason I was coming around is because I'll be supervising your team. They're already assembled and just waiting on you and Hailey."

Acknowledging her presence, Hailey gave Keira a knowing friendly look and wave.

"It's a great honor to have you here," Hailey noted, bashfully.

"The honor is all mine," Keira said in a tone that suggested pride. Shelly recognized this but didn't give it much attention. "Thank you for helping Shelly before I came in. Best of luck to you both out there."

She cleaned Sapphire's tear-stained face and dusted off the little girl's dirtied tie-dye shirt.

"You'll be alright, Sapphy. After the games, we'll celebrate, no matter what happens," Shelly promised her.

The little girl stopped crying and softly nodded back.

"Thank you for the save, Hailey," Shelly mentioned to her taller cabin mate. Hailey nodded with a smile and regarded her with an appreciative look.

When she reached her team, Shelly was given a dark yellow shirt to wear. It was nearly skintight and she felt like the outline of her bra could be viewed if the sunlight hit her. For a weapon, she chose a shield and decided to forgo a sword or spear.

In the olden times, shield bearers fought with nothing but a shield and used them to defend warriors against enemy flankers. Maybe this way my role will be clearer.

Shelly began to flex her muscles. The hand holding the shield twirled sideways, cutting the air like a Frisbee. She breathed, inhaled, exhaled. Her eyes were moving in every which way. Her pupils took in her surroundings; various children of differing ages, a bright sun shrouded by moderate clouds, and an air of anticipation among those in attendance.

She was so focused on her preparation that Shelly didn't notice when Henry came up to her as suddenly as a shadow. His silhouette overcast her physical form, making it seem as if she were engulfed by it.

"Are you prepared for the game, Shelly?" the Camp Director asked in a tone that didn't suggest he cared for her answer. She nodded and equally didn't mean it.

"What exactly am I expected to do," Shelly asked pointedly. "I don't know my power, so how am I going to defend myself?"

"That shield you carry will be most useful," Henry noted. "What talents do you feel you possess based on what your ability may be."

Shelly thought for a moment, considering the list that was assimilating in her mind.

Running, karate, acrobatics when I was in middle school, every subject in school, and I can tell when people are full of it. I don't need a power like Keira's to know for sure.

Instead of saying all of this, Shelly simply mentioned excelling in her classes.

"I noticed your preparation a moment ago. It is related to your photographic memory, an innate talent," Henry revealed. Shelly seemed taken aback by this, knowing full well this wasn't public knowledge.

"What does that have to do with my power? I thought to have one, I needed to have a disability."

"This is true, child, but your gifts are not without their drawbacks. Do you ever experience any forms of pain in your head, similar to a migraine?"

Shelly nodded.

Only my parents knew that, not even Lucas. It doesn't happen often, but lately, it has. Since coming to this place.

"That is an unintended side effect of not using your abilities properly. Think of what you have as a water current. When you restrict it, you cause it to flow improperly. When it builds up too much pressure, then you start to feel agitated and cannot process information fully."

I thought that was just my time of the month, Shelly noted to herself. *If that's how it works, is it that way for everyone here or just me?*

"Now then, as for the games," Henry swiftly changed the subject, "each yellow team member has been assigned their respective duties. Yours will be as defense, with your shield being an ideal weapon of choice. You will run point with your orb wielder and ensure their protection."

Shelly felt off about this, thinking about what Ashley had told her about the orb itself.

'It felt almost alive.' What exactly is the orb and how is it so important in this game?

"If I may, Henry," Shelly said cautiously. "Who will be taking the role of orb wielder? I was just wondering in general."

Henry suddenly looked guarded, as if the question caused him to feel exasperated.

"Your concern is noted but not necessary in this instance," the Camp Director responded coldly. "You'll meet the orb wielder in just a moment along with the other member serving as your defense team."

Shelly did not like the hesitation Henry was giving her. She wasn't sure where it came from or if she was imagining it.

Since meeting him, it seems like there's all these red flags that my body is telling me, and yet my mind is like Lucas'; trying to justify his intentions vs. what I know I feel.

As Shelly pondered this, Henry had departed, with her team suddenly spotting her. She saw the orb wielder who was not at all as she expected. He was a tall lean boy who had an eye patch on his left eye. What surprised Shelly the most (and baffled her) was the teen boy's long blue hair. His eyebrows were blue along with the hairs on his arms.

The eye patch makes him look intimidating, but the blue hair just throws off the picture completely.

The blue-haired teen regarded her with a quick glance using his one good eye, which was yellow, in a way that made her feel judged.

Maybe he's not a people person. I'm pretty sure people ask him more questions about his hair than his eye patch.

The other defense yellow team member was a teen girl with brownish mousy hair with red highlights in a pixie cut. Her face looked feline, with a small nose, thin lips, and deep-set green eyes. On her wrist she wore a set of beads with various colors. Shelly noticed pink, blue, red, and purple on them. She also noticed a few different combinations but was unable to see them fully when the girl's hand shot up as if to tell her to 'halt'.

"I'm Katrina," said the girl amiably. Shelly noticed the girl's sharp nails, which were painted a deep shade of yellow with points to them that looked freshly done. She cautiously shook hands with her fellow yellow team defense member, who gave her an appreciative look. "I know my nails can be intimidating, but I promise they are more for show than anything else," Katrina assured Shelly in what sounded like an attempt to apologize for a future crime.

The way she moved her hand was so fast I'm pretty sure if I was within arm's length, those nails would have cut me. I wonder what her power is. Razor sharp claws?

As the Relic game commenced, Lucas made his way towards the Grand Hall where the council meeting would be taking place. His mind took him to the dream he had of the man he believed to be Jacob. His silver hair, the way he spoke, and the voices he heard which sounded inaudible to Lucas were like some kind of fever dream come to life.

The feeling I can't shake is he wasn't in control at all, Lucas noted to himself. *There was more than one voice in that room, more than one feeling, and I couldn't tell which ones were his. Even the words he spoke came from other thoughts; jumbled together like different fruits in a blender.*

This last part of his thought especially latched itself onto Lucas like a leech and drained away his sense of direction. He nearly ignored Ashley's greetings and didn't notice her when she had joined his pace.

"Why are you walking to the Grand Hall?" Lucas asked, too pointedly. He regretted his tone, although Ashley didn't seem bothered by it.

"I am the Cabin Leader for The Weeping Willow. Hailey didn't want the title and Shelly isn't allowed the option until at least her second year of camp," Ashley explained informally.

Lucas nodded and resumed his thinking.

If Jacob has Bill, he's in more danger than Henry has been letting on. Why are we wasting our time talking about this? Maybe Vanessa is right; maybe we should do something.

He nearly said the thought out loud but stopped himself with a cough. Lucas played it off like he was clearing his throat. It didn't take long after that for Ashley to ask him the question he dreaded.

"Lucas… how have you been? I mean since, you know…"

Her voice sounded strained, like the very effort of asking hurt her as much as it would Lucas to come up with an answer.

The question she means to ask is: 'Hey Lucas, how have you been doing since your parents died' and my response would be 'I've been good, you know, just missing them like crazy, regretting that I was a selfish son to them, and Shelly doesn't say it but I'm pretty sure she blames me for it. Thanks for asking me though.'

Lucas did not want to talk about it, so he changed the subject abruptly.

"What plan of action do you think we should take to help rescue Bill?"

Ashley noticed his curt dismissal of her question but didn't pursue it further.

"I don't know. I just care about bringing him back to camp, that's all. Have you met his girlfriend Shannon? She's a nice person, but right now, and understandably, she's really upset about his capture. I tried saying hi to her at one point, and she just looked at me like I disgusted her or something."

'No, I have not had the pleasure of meeting Bill's girlfriend yet', Lucas rehearsed in his mind.

"No, I haven't," was all Lucas said in response.

Despite feeling agitated, he was happy that it stayed an inside thought. *Bill didn't exactly strike me as the 'boyfriend' type. Then again, I don't think I am either, and I'm dating his sister.*

"What are you planning to say at the meeting?" Ashley asked Lucas, trying to continue their conversation before entering the Grand Hall.

"It doesn't matter," Lucas said, slightly aggressive. "Everyone has their mind made up on what's best, and I'd just sooner go along with whatever the majority wants to do. I'm sick of this." He muttered the last part to himself.

He's sick of what? Ashley thought with concern. *Does he not care what's going on with Bill? I know Lucas has a lot on his mind, but this is about his best friend. Is he really trying…about…it…himself…make...to…*

The sharp pain returned as he winced backwards. Ashley looked at Lucas with concern as he groaned in pain.

"Are you alright, Lucas?"

Impulsively, he swatted her hand away and looked at her accusingly.

"Wait a minute! Sick of what? You think I don't care about Bill's wellbeing?" Lucas snapped back. "And making it about myself? You're the second person to say that about me. What's up with that?"

Ashley's eyes widened and she looked at him in shock.

"You read my mind."

It wasn't a question. Without waiting for a response, Ashley sighed and nodded.

"Yes, it's what I think, because you haven't been yourself since losing your parents. And I understand that, Lucas, I do. I want to help you, but I don't know how."

Everyone wants to help me and no one knows how. What's wrong with making things about myself? I lost my parents and my powers don't work anymore. Who cares what others think? I'll complain until the sun goes down if I want to.

"Why didn't you want to talk to me while we were away from camp?" Lucas asked Ashley in a way that sounded harsher than he intended. "I mean, I had a lot of stuff going on, but I would have made time for you."

Ashley's brows furrowed at this, appearing to focus solely on the way the comment was phrased.

"You made your feelings last year perfectly clear, Lucas. There was nothing more to say on it and there still isn't," Ashley responded with her own harsh tone that matched Lucas'.

"It doesn't matter. What matters now is that I'm always here as your friend, Lucas, and I've always meant that. Shelly is also worried about you. She's tried to talk to you about it, but you've been pushing her away. I know you're close with the Camp Director. Has he told you anything about what he plans to do to help Bill and the other campers? Maybe you can ask him to do something about it regardless of how the meeting turns out."

The situation turned from a semi-friendly conversation to something else entirely. Lucas was seething through his nostrils like a train preparing to depart.

How dare she ask that of me? Who does she think I am? Now she talks about Shelly like they're best friends all of a sudden, he thought angrily. *She has no right to ask that of me. None at all!*

Without thinking twice about it, Lucas heard his voice rise with each word as he stopped walking.

"Don't ask me to do that! If you really want Henry to do more, ask him yourself and see what happens!" Lucas roared in anger as tears began to form in his eyes. The next words came before he could stop himself. "Since you and my sister are cabin mates now, and apparently best friends, has she told you how our parents died? That it was probably my fault? I couldn't control my powers and because of that, they both died of aneurysms. Want to know what else? Get this; do you know the last thing I did before I never saw my parents again? I punched my father, and all through last summer I kept thinking about how I could make things right when I got home. In my head, I played scenarios where maybe they forgave me, or maybe they didn't. At least I would have had closure either way.

"Now, not only will I never get to do that, but I never got to say goodbye to them. I thought I had more time to figure myself out and be better. I wanted them to know I wasn't bad, that they raised me the best they could. Even though they hurt me, they were my parents. I wanted to come back to camp so badly because I missed everyone here. I missed you, Josh, Bill, Mike, Henry, and Vanessa. You all saved me last year and kept me going. I can't lose you all the way I lost my parents. I couldn't live with it… I won't live with that… I…"

Lucas felt his body shake while Ashley slowly walked towards him. His hands became tight fists, his nails digging into his palms, and his shoes were scraping the ground. He suddenly felt lightheaded and composed himself to keep from saying anything more.

Ironically, Ashley was the one who was speechless. The look she gave him was both sadness and regret. She started to sob softly, burying her face in her hands.

Now I've done it…

"I'm sorry, Lucas… I…I had no right to ask that of you. Please, please forgive me," Ashley pleaded tearfully.

Lucas suddenly felt guilty as he approached her. He gently took her hand in his own and brushed the tears from her cheeks with his thumb. As he did this, he began to remember how nurturing she was towards him during his stay at the hospital ward.

She was there for me last year when I needed someone. Not even Vanessa was there for me. She let words I said when I wasn't awake get to her before I had a chance to explain myself. Who's to say she wouldn't do that again?

When Ashley stopped crying, Lucas nodded stiffly.

"You're right about everything, and the truth is I haven't been myself for a while now," Lucas admitted with shame.

Ashley touched his cheek softly and waited for him to continue.

"Lately I just feel like I can't make sense of anything anymore. The only things that have been consistent for me have been this place, you, I mean you all, Henry, and Shelly. I wasn't ready to admit to myself that Bill is in real danger. I wanted to believe that Henry had a plan and was doing all he could to help him. But I honestly think maybe he isn't taking this as seriously as the rest of us are. I'm afraid to ask him anything more because I know what his answer will be. The truth is he's not the man I thought he was. I thought I knew who Henry was, except now, every time I talk to him, I'm becoming more and more scared…"

Lucas forced himself to stop talking. He suddenly felt his shoulders shaking violently and he knew what was coming.

I've held on for so long, because the fall felt like it was still happening inside my head. Now all I want to do is let go and trust that someone will catch me…

As his body began to shake again, Ashley instinctively wrapped her arms around him and held him close to her. His face was buried on her right shoulder, and he pulled her into a similarly affectionate embrace. Lucas began to sob onto her shoulder, first silently, then louder.

Continuing to cry, he felt a small touch on the side of his neck like a kiss. He was beginning to calm down as his eyes met Ashley's.

Their eyes were so connected to each other that Lucas barely noticed how close Ashley's face was to his own. Her lips were so tender and slim that they were suddenly intoxicating. He swore the morning sun's rays were directing their beams at her, illuminating her. He was suddenly reminded by how beautiful she was to him.

I really want to kiss her. I don't know why. Do I want to? No, I can't do this. I have a girlfriend. It isn't right. Not like this.

Luckily for him, he didn't have to. The two eyes disconnected when Vanessa came from the Grand Hall entrance and saw them. She made that bone crunching sound everyone hated.

"We're about to start," Vanessa said in a brief sharp tone.

Ashley and Lucas nodded as they followed her into the building. Lucas could hear the voice of his girlfriend in his mind and knew she was very angry at him. Everything she thought was about how he didn't seem to care for her, and that he was two-timing with Ashley.

The rest of what she's thinking isn't worth mentioning right now, Lucas thought in embarrassment.

This was the first time he had entered the new building which had begun its early life late last year. Lucas glanced left, right, up and down in all directions to see the detail put into it. The Grand Hall was nothing less than spectacular, with the hall itself stretching like the inside of a medieval castle. Lucas had learned by now that in camp things were not at all like they seemed.

On a good day, I'd want to ask Henry about that. Why things are so different here, and how much of it is his doing?

The Grand Hall was indeed grand. The walls lined beautifully with decorations of flowers, freshly lit torches, statues of who Lucas thought must have been great heroes, and at the very end of the hall, where the room suddenly was circular, was the council room. The floors were polished wood with carpeting for guests to walk through like a garden path.

Something notable that caught Lucas' eyes were yearly pictures that decorated the wall to the left with a sign on top reading: **Over the Years.** These pictures featured many campers throughout the years, from the time of the camp's inception, to as recent as last year. Lucas tried to get a good look at them, giving the most attention to the year he thought Jacob would have been in camp. He got distracted by a teen who appeared taller than his fellow campers and had a serious look on his face.

Unless my eyes are mistaken, that looks like Daniel, Lucas noted to himself. Henry was in the picture but at a great distance, as if he were steering clear of the child.

All that time, he had no idea that they were related… Why would Henry do that to him?

Lucas didn't have a chance to give the rest of the wall a thorough look but promised himself he would once the meeting concluded. When they entered the council chambers, the others were already seated in their respective positions. The room was lit by candles in protective glass that encircled the tops of the walls. The table itself stretched like the Knights of the Round Table with each chair having the respective cabin's name. Lucas and Ashley took their places on opposite ends, with their chairs adjusting to their respective sizes and branding their names on the back of the chairs next to the cabin's name.

This is so cool. I wonder how much it cost to make it look real. It also smells really nice here. Like the inside of a new car. Henry really pulled all the stops in making this place feel relaxing. As that old guy says in that one dinosaur movie Shell and I like, he spared no expense.

Vanessa had taken her seat and gave her boyfriend a side-eye-glance as everyone settled in. Zane drank a Monster energy drink and began to burp obscenely. He nibbled the drinking hole of the can like a goat chewing grass, while Naomi giggled and laughed next to her boyfriend Marcus. Across from Marcus sat Shannon, who was wearing her hair backwards, showing her sharp facial features. Her eyes glistened with anger and her hands were clasped in front of her as if she were arm wrestling herself. Lucas saw her pointed nails and noticed all of them were painted black except her thumbs.

Her thumbs look discolored and scarred. She must bite herself there often.

Some other campers were still proceeding to seat themselves. Lucas saw a few he only knew by face and others he knew from last year. Notably, he saw Alexia seated in the far corner indicating her cabin's position in alphabetical order. Ashley was seated next to her, and to Alexia's right was a tanned young boy who looked to be about as old as Sapphire.

I'm not sure that's a boy, Lucas noted to himself. *I made the same mistake with Hailey last year and felt embarrassed about that for a while.*

The Camp Director was seated in the center of the table, staring around idly at the occupants of the room. Once everyone had taken their places, Daniel rose to begin the meeting. He was no longer using crutches but still grunted slightly with each movement.

"Thank you for joining us everyone," he started off as the others turned their attention to him.

Lucas looked around the table to see counselors and campers alike sitting attentively. On the far-left corner, Lucas spotted Alexander for the first time since he was brought back to camp.

He looks very different and not in a good way, Lucas thought pitifully.

Alexander's hair was worn thin and long. His skin looked scorched like a burnt marshmallow. In addition, the camp counselor's eyes were withdrawn and his face was the picture of sadness. He was sitting in a wheelchair, which caused Lucas to feel a sudden surge of discomfort.

Not that… that… not…

Lucas averted his eyes to Daniel, who, unlike his father, appeared to be taking the situation more seriously.

"This meeting will be formal and fair. All opinions and thoughts will be heard, with a final decision to be made by the majority vote. Does anyone have any questions before we commence?"

Shannon began digging her nails into her palms. Her breathing hitched as she tried to calm herself and prevent her claws from retracting and drawing blood.

"When are we going to rescue Bill?" she asked as if the answer were written on a board somewhere.

Henry then got up before Daniel could answer.

"In due time, my dear. Now, to make sure we are all on the same page and have all the facts taken into account: Bill has been taken prisoner by a man named Alistair. However, it is not just Bill's life that is in danger," Henry explained as Shannon looked like she was ready to charge at any given moment. "There are children who never made it to camp who are also being held prisoner. It is my firm belief that acting with haste will bring harm to Bill and the children. While I agree that the goal is to bring them back alive, we must also do so in a way that does not cause further harm to the rest of the campers and counselors here."

I noticed he left out the mention of Jacob, Lucas thought discontentedly.

The counselors and Cabin Leaders began to mutter to themselves and think loudly. Shannon's thoughts seemed to topple over everyone else's, with Lucas hearing her disagreeing tone.

What's he talking about? How does he know this Alistair guy? What does he want with Bill? The Camp Director didn't even answer my question!

We are wasting time. We need to find my brother right now!

Lucas heard Shannon and Vanessa think respectively. He clenched his fist underneath the table, hiding his sudden surge of inner pain. His sharp nails embedded themselves in his palm. He started picking at the hairs on his arms underneath his sleeves and stopped himself.

When Henry raised his hand, the commotion ceased.

"I believe it is time to hear your individual words and thoughts. Let us listen to the counselors first. Those who were in close acquaintance with Bill, please rise."

Out of the six counselors in attendance, only three of them stood. The three counselors were Daniel, Naomi, and Shannon. Henry allowed them each to share their ideas on what plan of action to take.

After Daniel explained his idea, which was identical to Vanessa's own, Naomi began to talk about hers.

"I believe we should have a group consisting of no more than three campers ranging from ages 13 to 16. They'll be led by one of the Camp Counselors, which could be me, Zane, or Marcus. Everyone else, including Daniel, needs to stay to ensure the safety of everyone here."

Most of the attendants seemed to agree with this idea, while Daniel appeared exasperated at the mention of his name in such a way. As they whispered to each other, Naomi turned to look at Lucas.

"I understand you and Bill were close friends, and cabin mates?"

Lucas nodded as the others turned to him.

"Would you agree with my plan if it meant saving Bill as soon as tomorrow?" Naomi asked him.

Lucas found himself in agreement as Naomi sat back down in silent satisfaction.

Before Shannon could explain her plan, Lucas hesitantly stood to speak instead.

"If I may, I would like to share my thoughts already," he announced boldly.

What am I doing? Shannon is going to kill me for that.

Daniel's eyes shot up at Lucas like targeting beacons.

"It's not your turn, Lucas. Shannon must be allowed to—."

Henry cut him off abruptly.

"Allow Lucas to speak, Daniel. I would very much like to hear his thoughts on the matter," his father insisted.

Daniel hesitantly complied but still turned towards Shannon.

"What were you going to propose, Shannon?"

"I don't think it matters right now. The Camp Director wants to hear what Bill's friend has to say. Who am I to argue against our 'benevolent leader'?" The way she phrased the word 'benevolent' had a hint of animosity, as if she were disrespecting him openly.

I'm pretty sure if no one else caught that, Henry did.

With all eyes still on him, Lucas proceeded.

"I do want to rescue Bill and the other kids just as much as the rest of you. It's not right to suggest that one person has a better idea than someone else when it comes to saving lives. Still, I think there's a way we can do this without risking anyone's life."

Lucas thought carefully about what he wanted to say and thought of this scenario like disabling a complex bomb.

If I say the wrong thing, Daniel and Shannon will be on me like a pack of wild wolves. If I don't say this right now, I'll never get another chance.

"We should send out one experienced counselor and one camper. At least that way, they can scout ahead and find out what we are dealing with, and report back swiftly. If nothing else, it will give Camp Director James the time he needs to find a way to avoid any more lives lost."

Some of the counselors and Cabin Leaders were beginning to agree with Lucas, until Daniel rose to speak.

"Can you also mention to everyone here how you've seen Bill in your dreams being held prisoner by Alistair," Daniel said, pointedly. "I've had similar dreams myself, but it looks like our young telepath here hasn't been as open with them as I have. Why don't you tell everyone about what he's been going through and why we cannot waste another second debating about this?" Daniel seemed satisfied when everyone else began to look at Lucas as if he had committed a crime.

The truth struck Vanessa like a sucker punch to the face. She was already angry from before, but this new revelation seemed to infuriate her. Shannon's eyes lit up, and they looked as if a fire were brewing from behind her pupils.

Daniel really knows how to stir the pot in an already tense situation.

"It's true," Lucas admitted with discomfort. "I've seen Bill and what he's going through. But he's alive, and that's all that matters. If he's still breathing, we can assume the same for the campers as well."

Daniel didn't seem pleased by this, as he turned towards Shannon. She offered up no response.

"For now, at least," Alexia blurted out as she stood up to speak out of turn. "This Alistair struck the first blow when he decided to kidnap Bill and the campers. So, we need to strike back. Otherwise, he will continue to attack us."

Alexia spoke with an authoritative tone and rocked the table when she slammed her fist on it.

She gets her point across at least. That warhammer is definitely for show, because her physical strength alone makes me want to keep my mouth shut.

"I like her attitude," said Shannon, admirably. "I wish I could say the same for others." Her eyes pointed to Lucas with a look of both disapproval and tension.

"You will not speak out of turn again, Alexia," Daniel said in anger. "I know you're frustrated, Shannon, but we have to maintain a semblance of order here."

"What's the point," said a gloomy voice from the far corner of the table. "If we fight back, he'll kill us all, like he killed Richardson…" Alexander's voice was shriveled and weary, a far cry from how he sounded a year ago.

While Alexander began to sob, the others ignored him and were beginning to berate each other.

"If we do nothing, then Alistair will have won," Alexia emphasized as she stared around the room.

The meeting began falling apart, as Vanessa delivered the final blow.

"If we do nothing, Bill will die!"

This caused Alexia and Vanessa to start shouting at each other furiously, while other members of the council began arguing with the person next to them. Shannon joined in and was already baring her teeth at the cabin leader next to her.

"Don't you people care about what happens to one of your own?!" Shannon shouted loudly. "Our numbers are dwindling and letting this madman get away with this will only invite more conflict as Alexia pointed out. We can't be weak, and I won't be."

"The word 'I' makes 'it' about you," Zane said pointedly. He discarded the empty soda can and sighed heavily.

Daniel attempted to restore the peace but to no avail.

This is not going according to plan, thought Lucas anxiously. *Right now, everyone's voices are as loud as the voices in my head.*

Finally, Ashley slammed her palm on the table and shouted so loud that Lucas was sure her voice projected itself throughout the whole camp.

"ALL OF YOU STOP THIS RIGHT NOW!"

They all became silent as they turned to her stunned. Even Shannon was surprised by Ashley's booming command.

"You're all behaving like children who don't know better. Bickering won't bring us any closer to rescuing Bill and the other kids."

Wow, I honestly did not expect that from her. She was louder than even Alexia was a while ago. I need to remind myself not to piss off Ashley again in the future.

When order was restored, she turned to Lucas.

"Have you had any more visions about Bill? His whereabouts? Anything to help us find him?"

Lucas said no, but the small-looking child near Alexia said something.

"His heart is beating rapidly, and his nails are cutting into his palms."

What the…? How did…?

Vanessa then glared at Lucas.

"Lucas, tell us right now! What are you hiding?"

Shannon added, "Tell us now, Mind Freak, or I'll bust your head open and see what's inside."

"I'd start singing, kid," mumbled Zane in-between biting the inside of his cheeks.

Why is everyone suddenly ganging up on me? Seriously though, I better start talking, or else my girlfriend, my friend's girlfriend, and Zane will flatten me like roadkill.

"I don't think Alistair is working alone. Last night, I had a vision about a guy with silver hair and a tattoo of a tree on his back. He was talking strangely and I heard voices that were unnatural. He said he needed Bill to lure someone out, and that person is the reason he's back."

Henry was the only member in attendance who knew what Lucas was talking about.

"What you saw, Lucas, was the other telepath before you; Jacob."

The sound of his name seemed to cause a deep panic in nearly everyone in the grand hall, save for Lucas, Shannon, Vanessa, and Zane.

Why does everyone act like he's the biggest baddie there is? There's got to be worse than a loose cannon mind freak. Oh wait… no there isn't.

"Jacob's reappearance is no coincidence," Henry noted. "If he is indeed with Alistair, this may prove an impossible task regardless of the set skills for who we choose to send out. Jacob is a threat not to be taken lightly."

Before Henry could explain more, his son interjected in irritation.

"This meeting concerns the safe return of Bill and the other campers," Daniel insisted sharply. "Besides, there's no guarantee that what Lucas saw was Jacob. He hasn't been seen in years."

"True, but even so, as I was about to say, the risk has become too great," Henry concluded gloomily. "The children are likely no longer as they were and the only reason Bill has not met a similar fate, is because he is still useful to Jacob. No one here is prepared to face him alone if need be."

Lucas suddenly felt bad about the situation altogether.

It's worse than anyone thought. Why now though? Why has Jacob decided that now is the time to do all this?

Vanessa fumed angrily.

"No, we are bringing my brother back home. Even if we have to fight this other mind freak. I refuse to wait any longer!"

Daniel raised his hand.

"Please calm down, Vanessa. I know he's your brother and I want to help him as well. We all do. Many lives are at stake here. It isn't just about Bill. It's about the rest of these kids who are in danger."

"With all due respect to both Camp Director Henry and Counselor Daniel, but I won't stand by as my boyfriend is being tortured by some telepathic psychopath. He's been a captive now for what? Days? How do we know what condition he really is in?" Shannon asked, bluntly. "Maybe Lucas just saw what Jacob wanted him to see if he can manipulate minds also."

I honestly didn't consider that, Lucas realized. *But if Bill was dead, I'm sure I'd sense something.*

Zane, who had been waiting for the room to quiet down, spoke up again.

"I know it's not my turn to speak, but here's what I think: we don't have all the facts to be rushing in through the gates with no way of knowing what's waiting for us. It's starting to sound like anyone we send will either be killed or turned over to Jacob's side. So, I hate to be the one to say it, but I think we should consider cutting our losses. Enough lives have been lost and some of those kids have families back home who will be wondering what happened to them. Does anyone here want to volunteer to be the one to tell them their kids are not coming home?"

This caused everyone to become so silent that Lucas could hear Daniel's soft gulp. Even the Camp Director looked speechless by this, which made Lucas pause.

That's the first smart thing he's said since I've met him. He's absolutely right, and everyone here, including myself, has been missing that point.

"We've all been selfish about this," Lucas muttered to himself. The Grand Hall room was so quiet that everyone heard him. All eyes were immediately on him again like locusts, and Lucas was suddenly annoyed with himself.

"You said it, Lucas," Zane noted, to Lucas's surprise. "Look, I've never been the voice of reason in any given situation. Consider this though; the needs of the many outweigh the needs of the few. Soldiers die every day in war, and make no mistake, Jacob and Alistair have declared war on everyone in this camp. The next time we see them, and it will very likely be soon, they won't take hostages away again."

Who is this guy? Lucas thought in complete bafflement. *Earlier he was acting like a complete jerk, and now he's saying things that a person might think but shouldn't say in front of other people.*

"That's enough, Zane," Daniel exclaimed in annoyance. "You are out of line with this talk of wars and the needs of the many. We are all equally important in this camp, and the purpose of this council was to give everyone a voice, not only a select few. That is why at the end of this meeting we will all vote on what the best course of action is. Regardless of what we know or think we know."

Zane merely shrugged and sighed tirelessly.

"I already know what my vote will be. It's whatever will keep the most lives safe. That's my duty not just as a Camp Counselor, but as what we are. Even so, while we play by the rules, I guarantee that Jacob and Alistair won't. The time may come when we'll all have to break those precious rules we hold dear to us."

Zane got up to leave and proclaimed his vote to be in favor of Henry's plan.

While Lucas wanted to disagree with Zane, he saw the logic in his view.

If no one goes after Bill, he will die. No more lives will be lost. If we go after him we could all die trying and he will still die. The needs of the many, huh? There's some truth to that.

Despite this point in mind, Lucas agreed with Alexia's view as well: If they did nothing, then Alistair would continue to torment them one way or another. Based on the visions that Lucas saw, Bill was undergoing the final stages of whatever Jacob and Alistair had planned for him.

Once that's done, they won't just let him go. He's a loose end at this point for them.

"After hearing most everyone here out, how do you feel about your plan now, father?" Daniel asked Henry while ignoring Lucas' comment.

The Camp Director paused for a moment before answering.

"I still believe we should do whatever is in our power to bring Bill and the other campers home, even if it means doing nothing. However, as Zane suggested, we must also avoid any more innocent lives being lost. Everyone here who has spoken has brought up valid points that are worth considering. Taking all of these facts into account, unless the need calls for it, my role in this will remain neutral."

Vanessa was seething. Her thoughts suggested she wasn't thinking rationally about this.

"I'm sorry, Camp Director James, but I've heard enough. Regardless of what you all vote in favor of, I'm going to save Bill and the rest of those kids," Vanessa declared boldly.

"Not alone," interjected Shannon, "I'm coming with you. If I have to listen to one more argument here, I'll bash someone's head in."

Vanessa nodded and turned to Lucas.

"Are you with me, Lucas, because I need you now more than ever?"

The look his girlfriend gave him was of desperation and also indifference. Lucas knew what the last part meant.

She's leaving here regardless of whatever I say. Still, if the roles were reversed and if it were Shelly in place of Bill, I would probably be exactly like Vanessa. No, I know for sure that I would have done the same stupid thing I did last year, which is what got me into the mess that nobody except me and Henry know about.

"It's not about that," Lucas heard himself admit. Before his girlfriend could respond, he quickly continued. "I can't, Vanessa. I won't abandon Shelly and my friends here in camp."

I did that once and it almost cost me everything, Lucas wished he could have said.

When he spoke, Lucas noticed that he sounded as impassive as the Camp Director himself.

The worst part is, I don't feel bad about it the way I know I would have. I don't know if it's because it's right or because it's the only real choice.

Vanessa looked at Lucas scornfully.

"Bill was wrong about you and so was I," Vanessa declared as she began to march out of the hall. Daniel called out to her and Shannon, stopping both in their tracks.

"If you leave camp, you will not be able to return," Daniel reminded Vanessa and Shannon. "It's one of our most sacred and important rules. Bill wouldn't want this for you."

Vanessa shot a sharp glance at Daniel's direction and ripped off her bracelet with the camp beads on it. The beads fell to the ground like marbles and scattered around.

"Then I won't be back. And don't ever presume to know what Bill would want because he's my family. Come on, Shannon, let's get out of here."

Shannon nodded and followed after Vanessa.

Everyone looked in their direction in surprise. The room became silent until Daniel decided to formally conclude the meeting with the remaining members.

"All in favor for those who want to follow my father's idea."

Lucas' hand launched up, and Ashley's, who thought telepathically, *I hope you know what you're doing, Lucas.*

He wanted to reply, but the pain came again.

Agh!

Lucas felt himself go backwards, nearly losing balance in front of everyone, but reclaimed control of his legs.

Two other counselors also raised their hands and twelve other cabin leaders as well. The opposite vote for Daniel's plan saw all hands that did not rise previously go up, including Naomi, Alexia, and even Alexander voted yes.

"It's what Richardson would have wanted," Alexander explained as he wiped his face clean with a soiled handkerchief.

It was a tie between the sides, since Shannon and Vanessa's votes were technically counted for Daniel's plan. The Camp Director's son sighed in frustration and turned to his father.

"It's officially your decision, father. Do you still think you can resolve this on your own or will you let us help you?"

Henry remained silent. Even from a great distance, Lucas could hear the other campers in the games fighting to win. Lucas thought it was just his imagination but he thought he saw Sapphire wearing armor that might have been too big for her, wielding her shield, while Shelly was using strange defensive moves that appeared choreographed. He wasn't sure if what he saw was happening or if he was imagining it in this moment of great stress.

Based on what I'm seeing, Shelly is doing the same thing I've seen her do when she watches those movies about mixed martial arts and mimicking the way they are fighting. But that's all she did; mimic, not actually fight.

When he made his decision, the Camp Director's melancholy blue eyes looked as solid and hard as giant icicles.

"I vote for Lucas' plan." The decision sent everyone in the Grand Hall into such a wave of shock that Lucas felt as if a meteor from space had come and obliterated them all in one fell swoop. "Only one camper and one counselor will go to retrieve Bill and the other campers. I will make the final preparations for the duo and this will be done at a time when I see fit. With that said, this meeting is adjourned."

The last sound that was made was the echoing of the wooden gravel pounding against the table. It seemed to mirror the heartbeats of all in attendance who both doubted what would happen and were ultimately in agreement with this decision.

As everyone in the Grand hall prepared to leave, Lucas couldn't help but think to himself that the Camp Director's plan wasn't as foolproof as he had hoped.

Whoever Henry sends out, they won't be coming back. This could be a one-way trip for the benefit of everyone in this camp…

Chapter 10: Silence the Dream

Shelly was panting, doing her best to keep a level-head, as two enemy combatants came charging towards her. She dodged one of their attacks, a high punch, while the other attacker tried to swing a blunt sword at her stomach. Shelly wasn't sure how or why, but she recalled moves she saw in one movie involving kung-fu. Her body moved on its own as if possessed. She had always taken great care of herself to the point that she could do back flips and acrobatics without much effort.

Backwards, left side, up, and down, dive, low.

Pushing one of the attacking orange team members backwards, Shelly charged for the one with the blunt sword to her left. Using an open palm, she slapped both sides of the girl's cheeks, disorienting her. Before the enemy combatant could recover, Shelly shot her knee upwards and brought her shield down on her opponents back. Glancing left, right, she dived down low to where she was told to take position previously.

Taking a brief pause to regain herself, Shelly suffered a minor headache.

Ugh! This is what Henry was talking about before. Okay, breathe, calm down.

As she did this, the other orange team member made his way towards her and prepared to attack her legs. Shelly saw this coming, and did a high jump, allowing her to gain the upper hand on her opponent. She leapt behind him and with her elbow hit the teen in the back of his neck, knocking him out.

How did I know that was going to work? Shelly felt bemused.

Her body had suddenly become sore and she had a hard time reorienting her muscle movements from the way she had started off.

Not long after that, Shelly spotted Katerina and the orb wielder returning with a charged yellow orb. Since she did not know his name, Shelly took to calling him Blueberry on account of his naturally blue hair. He displayed no signs of fatigue or slowing down.

He looks like he's running a marathon. I feel like without that hair, he would be plain looking even with the eye patch.

Shelly joined Katerina's side, running with Blueberry as they were being chased by the remaining orange team members.

"Looks like you handled things here, cutie," Katerina noted slyly with a wink in her direction.

Shelly flushed and caught her breath before speaking. "I guess I didn't know my own strength."

"Apparently neither did they," Katerina noted, her sharp-nailed finger pointed at the battered and unconscious orange team members. "Let's hold the line here and give Nathan a chance to win this thing for us." Katerina turned to look at Shelly. "Are you ready for this?

Shelly nodded and prepared to take a battle stance.

"Then let's not keep the enemy waiting."

After the meeting had concluded, Lucas saw Daniel speak with the Camp Director for a brief time. When they had finished talking, the Camp Activities Director brushed past Lucas with a quickened limping pace. He appeared disgruntled and upset by something.

He's sending Lucas and Zane out there? What is my father thinking? Lucas can't control his power and Zane can't control himself, Daniel thought with confliction.

Lucas was about to leave when Henry's expression said he needed to speak with him.

Lucas complied and joined him in his office.

Is it going to be a continuation of our last conversation?

"Do you recall the voices that spoke to Jacob in your dream," Henry asked Lucas.

Lucas tried to think of how they sounded but only came up with the way they were distorted.

"The sounds they made were like this one time when I read the minds of animals," Lucas confessed with uncertainty. "Animals don't think in words; they think in feelings. These voices Jacob was hearing were emotional, raw, and very angry."

Henry studied what Lucas had said for a moment before speaking.

"There is only one entity that fits the explanation you are describing. They go by different names; the First Ones, the Dark Harbingers, but for oversimplification purposes, they are called Shadow People."

The way Henry talked about them, Lucas knew there was more to it than their names and what they were.

I don't know why but their sounds were familiar. Shadow People. That name is also familiar.

"However, until we know more, it would be best to keep this knowledge between ourselves."

Lucas nodded in compliance but felt his stomach twist and a shortness of breath. The secrets were beginning to pile up like dominos.

Add enough to the pile and it will eventually all come down.

"I read Daniel's mind as he was leaving today," Lucas noted. "You're sending me and Zane to rescue Bill?"

Henry nodded.

"You are a telepath and your skills will be useful when it comes to anticipating Jacob's next moves. Zane is seasoned and his powers will benefit you as well."

Lucas nodded stiffly but felt very uncomfortable with this sudden responsibility.

I don't know which idea is worse: sending me out with Zane, just the two of us, or the idea of running into a telepath who is crazier than I am.

"You will leave in three days' time. That is all," Henry announced, intending for Lucas to depart the office.

"I'm sorry for asking this, Henry," Lucas started, suddenly fearing what the answer would be, "but I want to understand who Jacob is. What exactly happened to him that no one in camp will talk about? How did he lose control of his abilities? I thought the point of this place was to help everyone who came here?"

Henry sighed and adjusted his seat calmly.

"Jacob was a rare Alter Child in that he has, like you, telepathic powers which are considered incredibly difficult to master. Can you imagine the difficulties he faced at a young age, unable to control his impulses, and lacking the basic understanding between right and wrong?"

The Camp Director was about to continue when he suddenly stopped. Lucas feared this meant Henry wasn't going to continue. To his relief, he proceeded with an exasperated sigh.

"Perhaps it is best if I show you as a one-time exception. I will allow you access to a specific memory from my mind."

Lucas felt hesitant. He couldn't shake the thoughts of doubt that began to creep into his mind.

Why now? I haven't been able to control my abilities recently. What if it doesn't work? Will I disappoint him?

"I can't," said Lucas hesitantly. "I haven't been able to read minds the way I could last year."

"This does not require you to read my mind, but rather you will observe the memory through my guidance. I will be the mast and you the sails, my child."

Lucas nodded and prepared himself by closing his eyes.

"Remember, this is a memory, and nothing you say or do can change the outcome of it. Mind yourself."

When Lucas opened his eyes once more he was no longer inside the Camp Director's house, nor was he in Camp Supernatural. He was outside an orphanage…

The orphanage looked plainer than Henry thought.

Henry thought?

The sun had just been swallowed up by the clouds, with the last rays of light shining on the front entrance of the building. Henry was joined by Alistair, who looked similarly to how he appeared when he visited the camp last summer.

We may be the first of his kind that he meets, Henry thought. *If it can be controlled, his possibilities will be an asset.*

I can feel what Henry is feeling and thinking. He's afraid, I think. I don't know if it's me that's afraid, or if he is, Lucas thought, doubtfully.

Alistair gave Henry a look of assurance, something which surprised the Camp Director given his friend's propensity for directness rather than conversing.

How far back does this go? Henry looks younger, like maybe his late forties? But Alistair can't be any older than Daniel. How can he still look the same?

"So, what are we dealing with here? I know you didn't bring me out here just because you missed my company. Is the kid going to be that much trouble for you?" Alistair said with a smirk.

"Not at all," Henry stated. "But if the information is correct, then this child is the youngest recorded _____ to have discovered their abilities. And a telepath no less."

Wait, why was that blanked out? I don't know if I missed it or didn't hear.

The smile on Alistair's face died down. He looked at Henry now with a look of both fear and wonder.

"He sounds too far gone based on his age and abilities. Are you sure it's safe to bring him to that camp of yours?"

"That's what we are here to assess. If he is as dangerous as I believe, that's where you will come in."

What exactly was Alistair supposed to do? It looks like something else happened since Alistair is now with Jacob.

Henry and Alistair entered the orphanage, the inside looking even more dreary than the outside. The hallway looked destitute, save for one lady, the receptionist. She was standing in the middle of the room and appeared to be staring at them intensely. After a moment, she came out of her daze and immediately asked them what their business was. Henry noticed that the lady's face appeared transfixed, with her smile looking more like a picture than something moving.

"I am Dr. Harrell," Henry lied, "and this is my assistant Carroll."

Alistair gave Henry a derisive look but quickly turned and smiled at the receptionist.

"You wouldn't believe how many people compare us to Abbott and Costello. He's my Costello and I'm his Abbott of course."

At this, Henry gave Alistair an annoyed look, but the receptionist interrupted them by asking if they were looking to adopt a child.

"We are doing a study on young children who exhibit very strong abilities akin to that of the extraordinary range."

When the receptionist looked confused, Alistair simplified it.

"We're looking for a gifted kid to see just how gifted they really are."

The receptionist clapped her hands as if realizing something for the first time and led them to the rooms where the children were staying.

This is no place fit for children, Lucas heard Henry thinking. *Our numbers are strong and growing every day. This boy will change all of that. When one child exhibits more than extraordinary abilities, it only means one thing: a tip in the scale.*

The hallway they were walking through had doors on all sides, which looked more closet-sized than big enough to house a child.

"We have over fifty children here. Lately though, that number has dwindled somewhat."

"How so, if I may ask?"

"The child you speak of, he's… found much success here and has encouraged the children who remain here to feel as if they have a place to…to…be…long…gone." The lady's mouth notably twitched as she said the last part.

Henry softly nodded and gave Alistair a look of concern. Lucas felt himself reading the receptionist's mind instinctively.

This isn't like when I try to read Henry's mind… This is sound, but the words are scrambled. What she meant to say was 'he's frightened the children here and many have gone missing since his arrival'.

Henry and Alistair spotted a few children in their rooms playing. Many looked like puppies in an animal shelter. Some looked up to see them walking by, with the same unblinking expressions as the receptionist had.

All these young minds… so much pain and solitude. They're trapped in their bodies like fireflies in a jar. Their minds are burning thoughts into their heads and they cannot set them free.

How is that possible? Lucas heard his own voice ponder. *Is Jacob controlling everyone in this place?*

Alistair leaned into Henry's ear as the receptionist began to talk inconsequently about other parts of the facilities.

"Are we adopting anyone else today?" Alistair quipped. "You know, besides the mind freak we're already here for? Some of these kids look right up your alley of desperation."

Henry swatted his companion's comment aside and listened as the receptionist located one of the ladies in charge of the kids.

She was an older-looking lady with short greying hair, wrinkles all over her face, and one leg that looked weaker than the other. When she walked towards them, she did so with a noticeable limp.

"You're here to see Jacob," the lady said, knowingly. "I can take you to him. He's such a good boy. It will be a shame to lose him."

The receptionist walked back to her side of the building, giving Henry and Alistair a pained look in her eyes. That pained animated smile remained crudely drawn on her face.

Henry moved his hand to the side, as if he were swatting away at something, and the older-looking lady stopped walking. Standing still, she began to shake rapidly.

"Are you here to take him away?" the lady asked Henry.

When he nodded, her body went from shaking to shivering as if the temperature in the hallway decreased.

"Please, save us from that boy. I… I don't even remember what I'm doing here! How long have I been here?" Her voice rose with each word she spoke. Her teeth were grinding, her nails biting into her palms, and the veins in her neck were pulsing rhythmically with her rapid heartbeat. The way she behaved became familiar to Lucas.

I can hear her mind and it isn't good… Henry is figuring it out also. She's scared, like really scared of Jacob. All her thoughts are about a daughter that she hasn't seen in months and a husband that she thinks is dead, but her mind keeps convincing her he isn't. What's scaring me more is the way she's acting, like how my parents were before I left home…

Alistair looked about ready to laugh as if she told a joke, but Henry approached the situation seriously. He used the same gesture again. This time, the lady's rapid movement calmed and she appeared to be almost in a trance.

"What has he done? Is he keeping you all here against your will? We can help you if we understand the situation."

"Yes. That's it. Please, kill me. I don't want…He's…node…thi…Nothing," the lady suddenly said, with a similar smile to the receptionist. "He's done absolutely nothing wrong." Her mood even changed as well. She wore a face that betrayed the wrinkles on her skin. "Would you like to see him now? He will be so *happy* to see you." After she said this, her facial expressions appeared fixed and animated, as if she were struggling to say something but couldn't.

Excessive use of mind wiping abilities, Lucas heard the Camp Director thinking. *This woman's mind is no longer her own. It has been commandeered by a stronger presence. Even if I helped her, her mind is already too far gone to be without the control this boy has placed on her. Perhaps this also is the case for everyone else in this orphanage. They are all caught in a spider's web, unable to leave.*

Henry ignored the ladies distress and gestured for Alistair to pay it no mind as well.

"Since when don't you help the common people," Alistair whispered. "Only one of us can afford to not care and that's because you still cling onto that humanity of yours."

This boy has had no guidance or restraint in his abilities… He may be even more powerful than I previously believed.

The lady led the pair to a solitary room, which appeared wider and even fuller than the others. This private room had a notable feature; a label with the word 'Caretaker' on it.

"He's such a sweet child," the lady said, her mouth twitching, and her body sizzling as if she were burning. Her nose began to bleed and tears streamed down her cheeks. Her face remained the same. "Really, you should meet him right now. At this moment. We don't want to lose him. Please don't take him from us."

Henry nodded and looked at Alistair, who also nodded at him.

"Do not worry. We only wish to speak with him," Henry assured the orphanage caretaker.

There is nothing we can do for these people, Henry told himself, as if he were also telling this to someone else.

They entered the room, with Alistair expecting to find a deranged raving child, while Henry saw exactly what he expected. The boy looked no more fragile than a bear cub. His arms and legs were thin, and he looked like he hadn't had a decent meal in days. His long black hair flowed down his back with a collection of split ends.

"Hello," the child said, with a voice so soft that Henry almost didn't hear him.

"Hello, child. We are…"

"Henry James and Alistair Kaine," the child said to the pair's astonishment. "You're here to take me away from this place."

Henry nodded, feeling uneasy now.

He read our minds as if they were thought out-loud…

…Can he hear me? I feel like he's reading my mind.

"Jacob, I come from a place where there are other children like yourself. It's a special place that can help you control your powers. Many others like you have come there and emerged in more control than they had prior."

Jacob turned his attention to Alistair.

"He fears me," Jacob said, pointing to Alistair. "He's afraid because he thinks you cannot help me."

Alistair looked at Henry as if to deny the accusation, but the Camp Director shook his head.

"Can you sense my intentions, child?"

"Stay out of my head, you Mind Freak," Alistair said to the boy's annoyance.

"Don't use that word for me," Jacob said in a louder tone. "The last one who said that word no longer has a head. He cried when a mirror was forced in front of his ugly face. Why is that? This mind cannot stand others who can't keep their thoughts to themselves." Jacob pointed to his own head with a tiny finger.

That is what Henry needed to know.

So that's it… he has no control of his power whatsoever. It acts completely on his impulses, like an unquenchable fire.

"My friend means you no harm, Jacob," Henry promised. "Now, do you believe my intentions to be pure?"

Jacob didn't need to contemplate the thought; he already knew.

"You wish to help me. For what cause? What personal gain?"

Henry gave Jacob a smile and walked over to him.

"No personal gain, but a mutual benefit. You are one of us. A child born with an ability that is adjacent to your disability. A ______. Tell me, are the voices you hear a mixture of your thoughts intertwined with those in this orphanage?"

The blank out happened again.

Jacob nodded stiffly.

"Their voices cry out for deliverance. They long for a sun they will never see again. All that sustains them is the thoughts this mind helps them feel. Without them, they're meat suits left out to rot."

He's aware enough to know what he's doing. It's hard to know if he cares what he's doing or knows how wrong it is.

As Jacob began to look fearful, Henry suddenly sensed something was amiss.

Something isn't right about this… his thoughts do not match his body…

Henry closed his eyes and touched his forehead with his index finger. When he opened his eyes, he saw Jacob for the first time. The child was no longer fragile or thin. He appeared healthy, nourished, and had long silver hair as opposed to the black hair he previously had. He now looked to be a teenager, around the same age as Lucas a year ago.

"You don't look fragile to me," Henry said to Alistair's bewilderment.

"What are you talking about, Henry? The kid looks like he's on death's door."

Henry lifted the mind veil from Alistair, who looked as if he had just awoken from a long nap. The room was luxurious, even more so than the rest of the orphanage. It was apparent from the way it looked that it wasn't a room for children.

This is the main office for the caretaker of this place, Henry realized in horror.

"What have you done, Jacob?" Henry heard himself say, his voice losing the usual composure he had. "Alistair, go check on the children." Alistair rushed out of the room just as the boy dropped his façade.

"It's better than before," said Jacob, speaking now fluently and more loudly. His demeanor made him seem more on edge with his surroundings than Henry thought. "The lady who once took this room was a contemptible individual. The thoughts she had were a persona as fake as the words from her mouth. A husband who perished by his own hand, a daughter who resembled a child from here. They were neither real nor fake. She couldn't be true to herself until this mind arrived. Now, everyone here is truthful."

"You've created a lie to tether everyone here to your mind frame," Henry noted. Despite how calm he sounded, his thoughts portrayed an opposite viewpoint.

What is this feeling? Why is he so angry deep down? Can Jacob sense this?

Alistair returned with a look that confirmed the Camp Director's worst suspicions.

"Those aren't kids anymore, Henry," Alistair said fearfully. His face looked more exposed now than the Camp Director's. "They're all trapped in some kind of trance. This kid is a monster and he needs to be put down like the rabid dog he is." Alistair's hands began to emit fire, which swirled through his fingers.

"Wait, Alistair! Don't—"

It was too late. Suddenly, Alistair's hands began to seethe with a terrible sensation which ran up to his elbows, shoulders, and eventually his whole body.

When the flames in Alistair's hands dissipated, he fell to the floor writhing in pain and gasping for breath. Jacob turned his attention to Henry, intending to use the same ability on him, but the Camp Director appeared unfazed. His face was transfixed, with his body making no motion to move.

"You're different from that one?" Jacob noted, as Henry remained calm while Alistair moaned in pain.

"I am. Now release my companion this instant."

As fast as it started, the pain Alistair felt was gone and he was no longer on the floor. When he recovered, he looked about ready to charge for the child and murder him.

"Stop at once, Alistair," Henry cautioned, as he placed a soft hand on his friend's chest.

"He made me think I was drowning. If you saw what he did to those kids, you'd think twice about bringing him to your camp. He's not worth the air he breathes."

Henry's hand suddenly became firm as Alistair tried to move forward.

"Everyone deserves a chance to be saved, and he still has great potential."

The way the Camp Director said this sounded detached, as if he didn't believe his own words. Lucas knew this couldn't be the case.

I just don't see it, Lucas thought to himself. *He's a clear danger to everyone here. Why Henry? Why did you bring him to Camp Supernatural?*

"When will it be enough? How long do you think you can control this boy, let alone whatever he has inside him?" Alistair asked the Camp Director with much disapproval in his voice.

Henry looked at Jacob with a cold expression. The boy returned his gaze.

"He will prove useful regardless of the outcome. In camp, his abilities will not have the same influence they do here. I will see to that."

The Camp Director turned and extended a hand towards Jacob, who looked at it and Henry with uncertainty.

"Come with me, my child, and I will help you to achieve control unlike anything you can imagine. Your powers will become—."

Before Lucas could hear anymore, the vision began to dissipate and became like an abstract painting.

Abruptly, Lucas was thrust back to the present and found himself near the center of the room just as Jacob had been.

"Lucas, are you well?" asked Henry with concern.

Lucas nodded and rose up stiffly.

"You called him 'my child' at the end."

Henry nodded.

"I did."

Lucas waited for more, but the Camp Director made no effort to continue.

"That's it? I thought I was special to you. I thought…"

"What did you think, Lucas?"

I thought you cared about me, he wanted to say with all his heart. But, for this instance, he was glad his inside thoughts stayed silent.

Henry looked like he was going to say something, but ultimately he sighed and reclined in his seat.

"I care very much about your well-being, Lucas. Along with the other campers who are also here, as I have told you before. Jacob's case was unique due to the nature of his abilities. This camp's purpose is to help all who need it, even when it seems like they are too far gone. Despite this, I did not understand at the time the severity of Jacob's loss for control. Along with another element..."

Henry paused and appeared flustered.

"It is time for you to go. Please leave me now."

Lucas shook his head. He wanted answers, more so than ever before. When Henry's cold eyes turned to notice that he was still there, it was as if he were someone else.

"Why do you still remain, boy?" Henry asked in a cruel harsh tone. "I have nothing more to say on the matter."

"I want to know more about Jacob and how you failed him? What if the same thing happens to me?"

Lucas' choice of words seemed to incite an anger in Henry that he had not witnessed before.

"I did not fail Jacob. He was already too far gone before I could do anything more for him," Henry angrily said. "And if you wish to avoid his fate, you will take your lessons from camp with the utmost seriousness."

His usual calm tone was replaced by one of pure anger, so much so that even Lucas could feel as the Camp Director did.

This anger... it's not just frustration or annoyance... it's something else, something... almost sad.

"You seemed so sure of yourself in the memory; that you could help Jacob to control his abilities and for him to become an important part of the camp. I just want to know when you were sure that he couldn't be helped."

What I really wanted to ask was, 'When were you sure that he couldn't be controlled? Lucas thought as Henry responded.

"Jacob's power manifested in ways no one could have foreseen. Telepathic abilities, as you are aware, are unstable in their nature, and the younger a mind is, the less capable they are of wielding it properly. You were fortunate to have discovered yours when you did, but Jacob had no such luck."

"If you knew what you were getting into with him, why didn't you listen to your former friend when he said that Jacob was more trouble than he was worth? Everyone else could see it but you," Lucas heard himself say the last part out loud. This was meant to be an inside thought.

The Camp Director's previous behavior returned.

"Anything more is irrelevant to this matter. You wanted answers, and you have them. If they are to your dissatisfaction, it is of no concern to me."

Lucas began to feel depressed. He was glad that Henry was willing to give him truths, but now he realized he had gone too far.

I had to push for this, and it took cornering Henry to finally get some answers. I didn't mean to upset him.

Henry sighed and shook his head, calming himself.

"Forgive me, my child," Henry said in a tired voice. "It is unseemly of me to behave in such a manner. I will refrain from doing so in the future. Please accept my sincerest apologies for that outburst."

Lucas nodded, fighting back the urge to say anymore. He had trouble shaking off the feeling of sadness and fear that had suddenly hit him, which Henry seemed to take note of.

"As much as I appreciate your presence, you have overstayed your welcome. Please leave my company."

Lucas wanted to tell Henry that it was alright. He understood what it meant to become suddenly angry, but the emotions he was feeling paralyzed his tongue.

Of all the times for my mind to not speak out, when all I want is to say something reassuring to Henry. 'It's okay. I know what it's like to feel this way. It helps me to know that you're like me in that way. Being in this camp has helped me not feel alone, and it's thanks to you.'

Henry winced, as if he cut himself on something, but when Lucas looked at him before departing, the Camp Director only regarded him with emotionlessly cruel eyes.

After departing from the Camp Director's home, Lucas decided to go visit Shelly in Ashley's cabin. He felt the sting of tears beginning to swell in his eyes, but he fought the urge to cry. Lucas tried not to think about what he saw in the memories and Henry's uncharacteristic outburst.

I think letting me see his memory made him more tired than he let on, Lucas observed. *Usually he is so calm, but I saw a rage in him, an anger that wasn't hate; it was hurt. Unbearable hurt.*

He was about to enter the cabin when Shelly came out laughing with a soda on one hand and her other hand on the cabin doorknob. When Shelly saw Lucas, she looked even more excited. She embraced her brother, spilling some of her soda in the process, but Lucas did not return the hug.

"You should have seen the game, we won, Lucas," his sister remarked ecstatically. "I was told this is the second year in a row that the yellow team has won. There was this guy with blue hair who had the orb and he was able to get it to the main field before the orange team had the chance. They were too busy fighting off me and Katerina. Also, I figured out what my power is. Apparently I know kung fu. If you liked movies you would understand that reference." Shelly noticed Lucas' silence and tried to break it by clearing her throat. "Anyways, want to join us? We're having a small celebration before the bigger one this evening for the yellow team's victory. Ashley and Hailey are inside."

Lucas shook his head in response. Shelly immediately picked up on her brother's uneasy expression. She made sure to close the door behind her and walked a few feet away from the cabin with him.

"Hey, what's going on, Luke?"

Lucas shrugged as Shelly moved closer to him and suddenly she felt worried.

"Look at me, Lucas. What's wrong? Talk to me, please."

Lucas could not stop shaking the rest of his body, with his head being like a bobble-head.

I…I…feel…

"I…..I….."

Lucas heard himself stammer and felt very cold suddenly. Shelly wrapped her arms around him in a loving embrace as he began to sob hard. He could feel the tears coming and Shelly rocking him like a baby. She had a mother's touch. Lucas remembered times in his life when even his own mother rarely showed affection. It scared him to be held in such a way. He forced himself to stop crying when someone approached the two of them.

"Are you alright, Lucas?" Daniel asked as he came over towards the two siblings.

Shelly nodded as Keira followed closely behind her boyfriend.

"He was just sad about home," Shelly answered almost too curtly. Nonetheless, Daniel smiled humbly and introduced himself.

"I don't believe we have had the pleasure. I'm Daniel Harrison, the Camp Director's son and your brother's former trainer in camp."

Shelly smiled back at him but something about him made her uneasy. Maybe it was the way he said, 'your brother's former trainer' like it was some kind of offensive remark reminiscent of what Lucas' teachers would tell her about him.

"You did wonderful out there, Shelly," Keira mentioned when Lucas' sister did not say anything to Daniel. "The counselors in attendance took a notable interest in your abilities. I probably shouldn't tell you this, but I think Naomi will be training you. She expressed an interest in you and your cabin mates, particularly Hailey."

Keira gave off a more amiable presence than Daniel, who began to remind Lucas of Henry in the last moment they spoke.

"It's about that time, dear. I think we should leave them to their business," Daniel told Keira abruptly. He gave Shelly a nod but she did not return the courtesy. The Camp Activities Director looked ready to hurl, with his body tensing up. From the quick mind-read Lucas heard, he knew where they were going.

He's about to fall asleep. His body is tensing up and it's taking everything he has right now to not close his eyes.

When they were gone, Shelly turned back towards him.

"Are you feeling better, Luke?"

Lucas nodded but fought the inside thoughts that said otherwise.

She wouldn't understand what I am feeling even if I told her. The less she knows about it the better.

"Alright. You know you can always talk to me about anything. You used to tell me everything."

Lucas knew this was true, but since last year, nothing had been the same.

It's not just everything that happened; we've both changed in the short time we spent apart.

"So what's going on between you and Ashley? When I asked her about you, she just changed the subject all of a sudden."

It wasn't something he was eager to talk about, but he knew that his sister had good intentions and wanted to help him if possible. He decided to explain the events of last year leading up to his conflicting feelings for Ashley. When he concluded, Shelly shook her head in disappointment.

"I can't believe you, Lucas," said Shelly with a sad expression. "You broke her heart to be with Vanessa. Why would you do something so stupid? Ashley is so sweet and beautiful, while Vanessa is so… don't get me wrong, she's pretty, but she's so… bossy. I just don't think she's good for you."

This comment took Lucas aback.

That's not what she thought before. I thought I knew how Shelly really felt about Vanessa.

It took him a moment to realize that Shelly had been courteous and hid the truth even in her own mind.

I can almost see it now, as if I am reliving that moment; one of the times when we went to the mall, Vanessa kept wanting one thing after another. First it was shoes, then dress shirts, then pants, and something called a promise ring. Shelly had to stop that one because she said I wasn't ready for that. Whatever that is.

"You don't really know Vanessa the way you think you do," Lucas said pointedly. "Just because you've become fast friends with Ashley and Hailey doesn't mean you're up to speed on all my friends."

The tone Lucas said the last sentence was etched in something he felt was similar to something Daniel would say.

Jealousy. What do I have to be jealous of?

Shelly looked hurt by this, and Lucas quickly felt another feeling.

I thought he would have been happy for me, Lucas heard Shelly think. *If anything I was worried I wouldn't fit in here, but his friends have made me feel so welcomed. He has no idea how lucky he is.*

"You have a lot of people here who care about you, Lucas," Shelly finally said to her brother's surprise. "It's almost crazy how everyone here talks about you in such a favorable way. Back home, all I would hear is how you weren't doing well in your classes, you didn't have any friends, while mom and dad were constantly worried about your future. But here in Camp Supernatural, you have genuine friends who like you for the person I've always known you are and I'm very proud of you for that growth. I'm even a bit envious to be honest."

Lucas was surprised by this. Never in a million years did he ever imagine how the roles would have reversed for the both of them.

Envious? What does she have to be envious about? I'm the one who can't keep my head on straight for the life of me. Now she's proud of me.

"How did the council meeting go? What was the decision on saving Bill?"

"Henry wants Zane to go along with another camper to rescue Bill. He thinks fewer numbers will mean fewer casualties."

Shelly gave him a nervous expression.

"I'm guessing the Camp Director wants you to go with Zane."

Lucas shrugged, which made Shelly appear fearful.

"Lucas… I don't trust Henry. I'm sorry but I don't," Shelly confessed regretfully.

This shocked him. Lucas couldn't understand where her hesitation was coming from.

Henry is a good man. He helped me when I thought my life was over. Of course I can't tell anyone about it. But if she knew…?

"Why don't you trust him, Shell?" Lucas asked, defensively. "He's done a lot for everyone here and he's doing what he believes is best to help Bill and the other campers. That should count for something."

Shelly shook her head and appeared unconvinced.

"Be that as it may, I get a feeling his interests are not completely in line with what this camp is supposed to be doing. Ashley also told me a little about this guy named Jacob who, like you, is a telepath, but unlike you, couldn't control his abilities."

As Lucas heard her speak, he thought about the way Henry's behavior shifted after the memory he showed him.

It was like reliving his biggest mistake and having to admit it all over again.

"One mistake doesn't define a lifetime," Lucas said out loud. He didn't understand the words, but the look his sister gave him confirmed she did.

Shelly wanted to trust her brother's intuition and that he wasn't hiding anything more in regards to Henry's motives. Regardless, Lucas could tell she had her doubts, both from reading her face and mind.

What does Lucas see in Henry? I know he's right in saying he made his camp and brought all these kids together. The real question is why? Why make a camp and why is he selective when he invites kids here? I mean, if I was an Alter Child this whole time, why didn't I get an invitation the way Lucas did? Then there's the way he tried to get rid of me…

"Henry wasn't trying to get rid of you," Lucas ended up blurting out to his sister's shock. "He gave you a choice, and you chose to stay with me. Which I appreciate, but maybe you should have done something for yourself for a change. I survived three months without you and I can do it again if I have to."

Lucas couldn't believe his own words. They were in sharp contrast to how he felt a year ago.

It's true though, every word. I managed to make it out with my sanity intact without the one person in the world I thought I needed most. Now, it's like Shell said; I have friends here who care about me. Then there's Henry who, even though I don't always understand why he says or does the things he does, I know he has the best interest of everyone here.

"I'll consider your current feelings right now as a result of all the stress you've been feeling lately," Shelly told her brother in a calm tempered voice. "Now come inside, Lucas. Let's talk about this some other time."

Lucas shook his head abruptly.

"Let's talk about it right now. You've spent your whole life looking out for me and I will always be grateful to you for that. But why would you sacrifice all that money and the chance to do something with your life beyond making sure I'm okay?" Lucas demanded.

I don't need you anymore, Lucas wanted to say next but stopped himself short. He knew those words alone would hurt Shelly more than any apology could fix. *And I wouldn't mean it. Of course I want her to stay. I just don't know how to say that.*

Shelly shook her head and looked disquieted.

"I'm not sacrificing my future for you, Lucas, because you are my future. I'll deny all the money in the world and all the chances if it means knowing you're safe and happy. I've also thought about this and I wonder if you have too, but what if the idea isn't to control your abilities, but rather to find a way to live with them the way you would with your disabilities? You can do so much good for so many people with your powers. You've always been a good person and everyone here knows it. Your abilities are defined by your character and actions, not by how Henry thinks they should be used. That's what I believe at least."

Lucas thought for a moment, and realized his sister had a strong argument.

I never considered that idea about actually doing something more with my abilities beyond learning how to control them. Maybe Shell's right. Maybe this is why I have these powers. Not to control them, but to work with them.

"Henry said that telepaths rarely if ever are able to control their abilities fully," Lucas noted. "Maybe in time I can get close enough to not go crazy like Jacob did. I know I'm not alone like he was because I have you, my friends, and Henry promised to help me as long as I am here."

Shelly shook her head.

"You can't stay here beyond the summer, Lucas. You need to have a future beyond this place, beyond the promises Henry has told you."

I get the feeling he's better at making them than keeping them, Lucas heard Shelly think briefly. He silently winced in pain. She didn't notice.

"I won't make you leave with me, but I also won't leave without you."

Lucas nodded and was about to walk away when Shelly gave him one last plea.

"Just stay for a little bit, Lucas, please. If not for yourself, then do it for me."

He considered this for a moment, before ultimately deciding to put his sister's mind at ease with his own compromise.

I should find out how Mike has been doing.

"I'd like to check on Mike if possible. After that, I'll come back and join the party for a bit. Deal, Shell?"

Shelly nodded and smiled. She threw herself on her brother and the two embraced.

"Even if you don't need me around," Shelly whispered to her brother, "I'll always be here for you. All we have is each other and I won't lose you for anything or anyone."

I know you'll always make the choice you feel is right, Lucas heard Shelly think. He groaned and made it seem like a soft cough.

Lucas turned to walk away and winced in pain. He heard more thoughts directed at him from his sister but could not discern them audibly.

Oury a ogod erpson how edsevres a ogod ifle. Ondt elsl ouyrlefs hsrot dan eliebv het owsdr fo osonme ouy odnt uflyl onkw.

After recovering himself, Lucas walked towards the hospital, as the surrounding campers walked past him and kept to themselves. He saw the Camp Guardian standing dutifully at the entrance to the camp with watchful eyes. Boris seemed so fixated on his duties that he didn't spot Lucas when he waved at him.

I can understand why he's taking his duties so seriously. After what happened with Bill and the other campers, he wants to make sure no one else gets taken. We're really lucky to have him, Lucas thought admirably.

Entering the hospital, Lucas saw Caroline exiting Mike's ward. She had been crying when she spotted him and wiped her eyes with the back of her hand. The eyeliner she wore smeared across her eyelids and made her look like she was weeping black tears. Appearance-wise, Caroline looked slightly different then Lucas remembered. She now wore make-up which looked ruined because of her tears. Her blonde hair had been trimmed slightly but otherwise her only other difference had been her clothing. She wore a baggy yellow camp shirt and shoes that looked stained from grass. She wore her beads bracelet which showed a variety of colors, though from what he could count, she didn't have as much as he did. When she smiled, Lucas noticed that she had a small gap between her front teeth.

I never noticed that last year, Lucas realized. *Then again, I never paid attention to her until now.*

"Hi, Lucas, are you here to visit Mike?" Caroline asked meekly as she sniffled and composed herself.

Lucas nodded and peered behind her.

"Is he awake?"

"He was awake a while ago. He was saying some strange things I didn't understand," Caroline replied with a quivering tone. "He told me to tell you something but I got scared and I can't remember anymore."

Lucas wanted to press for more but decided to ask Mike himself.

I can't understand what she's thinking anyways. It's like when I last read Shelly's mind; the words keep sounding muffled.

"Do you think he'll be okay?" Caroline asked Lucas. He didn't realize he was nearly inside Mike's room when she asked this.

When he turned to look at her, the expression on her face gave the impression of being worried, along with something underneath the surface of that. The next thing she said made him certain of his thoughts.

"Please tell me he'll be okay."

The way she said that reminds me of how Hailey feels about Josh. I wonder if Mike knows and would feel the same if he knew Caroline feels that way about him.

"He'll be fine. I'll make sure of it," Lucas said confidently, although he didn't believe himself. "Shelly told me they're having a celebration tonight for her team's victory. Right now there's a small party in the Weeping Willow. Sapphire is there and it would help her a lot, I think, to see you."

Caroline nodded and smiled timidly at Lucas. He also noticed how mature her face looked compared to the previous year.

"Thank you, Lucas. I'll go over there right now. Please be here for Mike. He's always spoken so fondly of you as a really good friend."

She left feeling more reassured by both Lucas' words and his encouragement.

.I'm glad for that because I see Mike as a great friend too. He tried to stop me from leaving camp and that's a debt I haven't been able to repay yet.

Inside the room, the young boy was covered with bandages and bruises over most of his body, just as he had been before. What got Lucas' attention though was Mike's leg and his left arm. His leg was wrapped in a tight dull cast that masked the grievous wound where an arrow had pierced him. His arm was also in a cast with Mike's right wrist in a restraint of some kind.

Lucas sat on a chair near the bed and saw to his delight that Mike was awake. He was staring up at the ceiling with his eyes transfixed on the light bulbs.

"Hey there, Luke, I'm really glad to see you," wheezed Mike, in-between breaths. "Caroline was just here." When he noticed Lucas staring at his arm, his eyes turned in that direction. "It's not that bad. Hurts more than it looks I'll say. Anyways, how's Sapphire doing? Is she enjoying camp so far? "

"She's doing good. Great actually. She participated in the Tag game and I heard she loved it. You would have been so proud of her, Mike. Shelly's been taking care of her for you."

Lucas tried to sound cheerful, but seeing the empty look Mike had made him feel gloomy. He wasn't fond of the hospital ward, but based on how his friend was feeling, it seemed he shared this feeling.

"I can't stand being here… it reminds me too much of when… Sapphy… I'm so proud of her. I hope she's having fun here. Is she?"

Lucas nodded, doing his best to smile sincerely, knowing full well how perceptive Mike could be.

What was he saying before? He cut off for some reason only to circle back.

"They told me… ouch…I might have lost my leg if we…ugh… hadn't teleported back here when we did. I might have…argh… trouble walking for a while, if not…forever," Mike explained sorrowfully. "I need to get out… of here I mean. This place… doesn't feel good for me."

This was how I must have felt last year after my accident: sad, alone, until Henry healed me. Mike of all people does not deserve to be in this situation.

Before Lucas could contemplate further, another thought replaced his concern for Mike.

He knows firsthand what happened with Bill and the campers who were taken.

"I'm sorry this happened to you, Mike. I promise to help you in any way I can, but I need to know why Bill and the other campers were taken. Henry wants to send me and Zane to rescue them and I don't know what we'll be walking into."

Lucas knew he was asking for a lot, but it was necessary to know. Mike groaned and shook his head softly.

"I can't… remember, Lucas. It isn't coming… right now… Please don't make me think of it," Mike begged weakly. "Hospital rooms… IV's…blood… needles… What comes before five? Four? How much does it take to make a dollar? Four quarters."

Lucas could tell Mike wasn't going to be able to explain further in his current state.

He's saying his thoughts out loud like I've been doing.

Making sure no one was around, Lucas decided to do the only other thing he thought could help.

"Please stay calm, Mike. I'm going to try and see if I can view your memories."

"No, Lucas, wait!"

As he did though, something very ominous happened. Lucas heard what could only be described as a collective voice. Something so interconnected with each other that the words it said were not of interest. Mike's eyes became black, and his body became as limp as stone. The only part of it that moved was his mouth.

"Can you hear me?" Mike said in a voice Lucas wasn't familiar with. "Can you see me? Do you feel this?" Mike moved his cast left arm as much as he could. Lucas felt his arm become numb suddenly. "Does this hurt?" Mike bit the inside of his mouth. Lucas could taste blood. "This is what it means to unlock the mind's full potential. Right now, your vision is distorted by the broken mirror. Once you see the one, you'll know and understand."

Lucas tried to use his mind control to subdue Mike, but the stinging pain he felt became even more excruciating than before.

"Do you want to know what I told the one before you? What sent her into tears?"

Lucas waited for something to happen. Then he saw it in a flash…

Mike's eyes opened wide and for a brief moment he didn't know where he was. He tried to remember the last thing that happened to him before this time.

Where am I? How did I get here? Where's Bill and Connors? They were taken. By that man with silver hair and the man with golden hair…

Mike's eyes adjusted themselves to the room he was in. He turned to the right and saw a young female camper who he recognized from the year before. When she noticed he was awake, she nearly fell from her seat.

I'm in a hospital… HOSPITAL!... No… I can't be here!... This place isn't safe for me… I'm not safe… Going up the wall, climbing down the hall, better to wear mittens, in order to save kittens.

She was so pretty to him with her slightly trimmed blonde hair, small bits of make-up, and a shirt that was far too big for her. Her name is Caroline, Mike knew. He breathed and calmed himself.

Caroline smiled happily at him and exclaimed with joy, "You're awake. I'm so happy to see you, Mike." She touched her hand to his softly but quickly withdrew it when Mike smiled weakly back at her. Her face blushed an intense red.

"I'm sorry, forgive me. I forgot you don't like when people touch your hand," Caroline said, turning away from Mike.

He shook his head and tried to reach for her, but his right wrist was restrained to the bed while his left arm was in a cast.

"How…are you?" Mike wheezed as best he could.

"I'm doing a lot better now that you're awake," Caroline admitted, the gap in her teeth was notable through her wide smile. Mike liked that about her, though he didn't want her to know he felt that way.

This is different than before, another voice thought in his head. *I don't remember how this went… where was I when this happened?*

"I'll go tell Sapphire," Caroline said. She was about to get up to leave when Mike called out to her. She went back into the room and sat down in the chair near his bed.

"You won't understand what I am about to say," Mike began, with Caroline listening intently. "This moment has already happened for me, but for you, it will be the first and only time. This place, this camp, isn't about saving everyone here. You don't build a house without sacrificing a lot of pieces to make it. It takes a lot of work, patience, and planning before its true intentions can be revealed. Once it's given fertile ground and legs to stand with, it's just a matter of how long it will last. Some will fall faster than others, just as some trees bend before they break. When I touched Jacob's ankle, I felt something. I can now see what he sees and know what he knows. There's a reason he doesn't kill those he controls. They don't want him to. They want to set us free from the confines of our shackles. The ones that someone else placed on us all."

Caroline was shaking fearfully as Mike spoke these words, and by the end she was in tears at not knowing how to help him. She wanted to say something, but Mike cut her off with a final sentence.

"Tell Lucas, Jacob's goal is not to understand the purpose of the dream; it's to silence the dream forever…"

Chapter 11: Sweet Jane

Jane lay on the hospital bed, with ventilators and an IV attached to her, remembering her first day in Camp Supernatural. She was thirteen and had just discovered her ability to create wood from both her body and to absorb it from trees. Her disability was having a tree nut allergy and once her ability manifested, she was invited to the camp.

She was taken to camp by a skeletal cab driver named Katie, who spent the whole trip talking about her death and complaining that Henry didn't give the cab drivers life insurance. Instead, he worked them to the bone.

I remember she was joking around a lot, Jane reminisced to herself. *She mentioned some guy named Francis who she had a bone to pick with. I didn't get it.*

Upon arriving in camp, like most of the kids who first enter, she feared the Camp Guardian. However, she was quick to find a group of campers to call friends. The first friend she made was Naomi who, like her, was a first-year camper. She was then assigned to the same cabin as her, the Swan Song. The next day she was designated to the ill-fated yellow team and through there met Daniel Harrison. He was the same age as her and was also there for his first year. Jane developed an instant infatuation with the young boy at first sight.

He was tall, had striking features that Jane likened to an actor she had a crush on at the time, and his mismatched eyes made him appear even more unlike anyone she had ever seen. Daniel was very welcoming to her and while he explained the rules of the Relic game to her, she spent the whole time thinking about questions to ask him.

What's your favorite color? Do you have a girlfriend? What's your favorite movie? Do you like girls with long or short hair? What's your favorite food? Do you like fat or skinny girls?

The yellow team did their best but ultimately lost to the orange team. The opposing team had a camper named Zane, aged fourteen, who was able to force his way to the finish line with some kind of electrical field he created. He zipped through the forest like a speeding bullet and threw a blowing raspberry in Daniel's direction.

Despite their loss, the yellow team had a gathering that night, and Jane found herself within close proximity to Daniel. He was with Naomi and another girl Jane hadn't seen earlier. This girl was pretty looking, with long brunette hair that fell into ringlets across her shoulders. She, like Jane, also seemed to have an interest in Daniel.

"Here's to a crazy second day of Camp Supernatural," Daniel exclaimed, as he and those around him lifted up their soda cans like goblets. Taking a sip, tasting it, Jane found herself fluttering from the memory. Her eyes were adjusting themselves to the room she was in again.

She turned to the side, tried to speak, but something was covering her mouth, and she could not feel the right side of her face. When she tried to look at her right arm, Jane saw bandages wrapped around it like a Christmas gift. She suddenly noticed Daniel in the room. He was still using crutches to support himself, but he otherwise looked to be improving from their attack. Daniel gave her a weak smile and she could tell why.

I can't feel my arm… I can't feel my face… I can't see with my right eye…

"Hi, Jane," Daniel said, softly. "I came by to check on you. How are you feeling?"

Jane wanted to answer him back so badly but only puffed out the words she meant to say.

"I…uh can't…feel…ah anything…"

Daniel nodded and appeared sad now.

"Jane, the doctors here are doing everything they can to help you, but the burns were severe. You suffered fourth degree burns on your right arm, part of your face, and shoulder. They said you might not be able to use your powers anymore."

The female counselor shook her head, trying very hard not to burst into tears in front of the man she loved.

"I…uh can…do…it…"

Daniel shook his head, as Jane tried feebly to manipulate the pieces of wood from the empty chair next to her bed. It remained unmoving even when she used her good hand.

Why did this have to happen to me? I thought I was getting stronger. Strong enough for him to notice me.

"We'll do everything we can to help you, Jane," Daniel reassured her. "We had our first council meeting about an hour ago. A decision has been made to rescue Bill and the other campers. Our numbers are smaller now and we have to find replacements for counselors. We lost Richardson, Alexander is in no shape to help anyone, and… The point is we need to start training a new group of counselors to take their place."

Jane knew Daniel was going to say: *And take your place.* She shook her head furiously, with her heartbeat rising. He looked apologetic and did his best to remain calm.

"What you did was beyond brave, Jane. You saved us all, and I'll always appreciate the wonderful, amazing person that you are. I'm sorry this happened to you. I really truly am."

He was about to leave when she called out to him.

"Daniel…please…ah don't…ow go."

Daniel hesitated and looked as if staring at her were more of a painful reminder of his mistakes rather than selflessly comforting a fallen comrade.

"It's my fault this happened to you," Daniel admitted. "I wanted to prove to my father that I could handle a charge. I wanted him to see me use my powers in a way that made him proud of how far I've come. Sometimes I think I should have spent more time appreciating the friends I made here, like you, instead of wanting something my father is incapable of giving me."

Jane nodded, her face swelling up with tears streaming down both her normal cheek and her burnt one.

I want to say it now. If I don't, I won't ever.

"Daniel…be…uh with…meh me."

She tried to say more, but her throat tightened. Breathing for her right now was like having a mouthful of food blocking her windpipe. The Camp Director cautioned her from speaking further, but Jane persisted.

"I've…ah always…loved…uh you…"

Daniel's expression suddenly changed. He went from looking at Jane with sympathy to looking at her with pity. She couldn't tell what he was feeling beyond the way his face quickly turned from hers. His body began to shake and the female counselor swore she saw something bright glisten down from his cheeks.

A moment later, another person entered the room. It was Daniel's girlfriend, Keira. She wore her hair back today, had a brown camp shirt, and wore a skirt over black leggings. When she noticed her boyfriend's distress, she went to Daniel and comforted him. The sight of the two embracing made Jane's heart rate level race again. She couldn't stop staring at them with her good eye.

He was never mine. I loved him, but I knew he wasn't for me. I want him to be happy.

"Be…gah good…for…he him…" were Jane's last words before her heart began to flutter faster than she could stop herself. She felt her body seize and take on a mind of its own. As this happened, nurses rushed into the ward and instructed both Keira and Daniel to leave immediately. Jane's mind was suddenly overtaken by a memory she had long forgotten. She was with Naomi, who she knew was close with Daniel, and sought advice to learn about him through her.

"You like Daniel?" Naomi had asked her playfully. Jane remembered blushing so much that she couldn't contain herself. She started asking Naomi all the questions she wanted to ask her crush.

"What's his favorite color? Blue. What's his favorite movie? Gladiator. What's his favorite food? Lasagna, and he only likes it home cooked, not store bought."

Jane had purposefully left out the other half of her questions.

I remember not wanting to say so much and yet what I learned only made me want to know more. I wanted to know his hopes, his dreams, his passions, and what he wanted to be five years from now.

They spent the rest of that afternoon by the lake gossiping about the camp. Naomi revealed how Zane pranked Daniel by causing the light bulbs in his cabin to short circuit. When Jane asked her friend why the two didn't like each other, she was surprised by the answer.

"Zane has a juvenile record," Naomi revealed. "He's not a bad person, but his history makes everyone here feel on edge around him. For some reason, Daniel doesn't like him because of this. I can't say why, only that the two, despite being similar, butt heads more than they shake hands."

Jane didn't know Zane very well. She only knew how competitive he was and that he took a kind of pleasure in making Daniel upset. Jane thought, by default, this meant she needed to dislike him but found she couldn't.

I feel like people are so quick to judge what they don't understand. Like me, I was scared people would be afraid of my power even though I can control it, mostly. But this is the first place I've felt like myself. That I can like who I become here.

The next memories that came flooding into her mind were speed-runs of her time in camp. From obtaining her first couple of beads, emphasis on the colors pink and red, to befriending more campers, and participating in the survivalist activity. She ended up helping her team win and because of her kindness, earned the nickname 'Sweet Jane'. After this, she had returned to her mundane life back in the real world, just bidding her time until camp the following summer. Thanks to Naomi, she was even able to get Daniel's phone number and email. Even so, the two hadn't kept in touch as often as she had wanted. Their correspondence led to nothing more than a few emails exchanged here and there. The next years in camp involved Jane honing her abilities and going on missions. She went with Margot and Lucinda to find another location for the camp to settle in. They chose a beach-like area where the island was far enough away to remain unnoticed by anyone living in Mississippi.

Another mission Jane went on, with her same teammates, was to locate past campers who were now living ordinary lives. One was a man in his mid-twenties named Luther, who had the ability to use X-Ray vision and was working as a security guard at an airport. On the side, he was also using his abilities to steal belongings from people and sell them off online under a false name. Jane and her group provided an anonymous tip which caused him to be arrested, with some of the stolen items procured and returned to their rightful owners.

Jane spent her final year as a camper trying to muster the courage to tell Daniel how she felt about him. She imagined telling him that the times they spent together talking on the phone, hearing about his day, and sharing with him her dreams were the happiest moments of her life.

I wanted to be a neurosurgeon, Jane remembered. *I didn't realize how demanding the job field was and that it meant I wouldn't be able to stay on as a counselor. When Daniel told me he wanted to be a Camp Counselor, I wanted to be where he was…*

During their time in camp, Daniel began to date Keira, but Jane never held any bad feelings towards her and spoke favorably of her to her friends.

I always liked Keira and considered her a friend just as much as Naomi. If I couldn't have Daniel, at least she could.

Jane's vision became blurry on her last good eye, and all she could hear around her were the sounds of many voices. Some she knew and others she didn't. They were at first ravenous, then calming. She found herself in the ocean, a child now.

Remembering her childhood, Jane thought about her mother, who passed away when she was born, and her twin sister as well, who would have been named June. She felt her death but not her mothers. Raised by her father, the young girl was given all the love a child could want. It was during this time when she developed her first fear, water. This happened, she felt, as a result of her birth in which she was nearly unable to make it out of her mother's womb. She believed the sister named June might have saved her, but in doing so, caused herself to remain in the womb; unable to experience life.

In contrast to her home life, Jane's school life was troubled. She had a hard time fitting in among her peers and could not be near plants or trees without feeling a strange foreign sensation akin to magnetism. Before controlling her powers, roots would upheave themselves around her, leading her to believe what she had was incurable.

In her last dream, Jane could not feel the soil underneath her feet; only the pressure of each ounce of seawater, and the beatings she took. Therefore, she decided to do the one thing no one had ever told her to do: back paddle. She calmly lay herself against the ocean, even as it fought against her, and she let herself be taken by it. The last wave that hit her didn't make her cry out or cause her pain. It was as soothing as a kiss on the forehead.

I wanted a family. I wanted to marry Daniel and to have his kids. I wanted my mommy to look down from the skies and be proud of me. I wanted my daddy to be happy. But most of all, I wanted to be selfish, just once. Not just Sweet Jane, but to take what I wanted. Maybe if I had told Daniel how I felt sooner, maybe…

The heart monitor suddenly went into a ringing silence, with Jane's fluttering heart coming to a halt. Her last thought before she let herself drift was: *I wish for all the happiness in the world for you, Daniel. If there is a place in the skies for me, maybe I'll see my mom and the sister I never knew there. At least now, I can be whole again…*

Chapter 12: The Escape

Henry sat in his room, trying to concentrate on what he was writing. It always changed shape, never staying the same for long. He knew something was interfering but didn't know what.

No matter how much he tried to get ahead of that twisted telepath, Henry was still far behind and the losses the camp suffered these last few days were still being felt. Around this time, he received a small package from his old friend Alistair. It came through one of the many fake addresses he kept for filing purposes.

See you soon, old master, Henry read on the small card along with Bill's name written crudely.

He closed his eyes and tried to imagine the words in his mind he wanted on paper.

Mind. Dream. Silence. Shadows. Threat.

Henry began to write sentences with these words but soon lost his concentration.

Feeling he needed to get fresh air, Henry decided to leave his home and walk around the campgrounds. He spotted Lucas leaving the hospital, looking as if he had just witnessed a terrible crime take place.

There was an urge he felt to walk towards Lucas, but it was quickly dashed away when another thought entered his mind. This one wasn't his own.

Come and see for yourself what I showed him, Henry heard both his mind's voice and another voice intermixed with it. He made his way to the hospital and his steps took him to Mike's room. The small boy was in his bed, looking dazed and weary. He noticed the Camp Director and weakly greeted him.

"Hello, Mike," Henry said, making sure the door was closed and no one else was around. "How are you feeling?"

Mike shrugged and mentioned Lucas' recent arrival.

"That is good. I'm glad he came to visit you. I require something of you, Mike."

Before Mike had a chance to question him, Henry closed his eyes and thought about Jacob.

When he opened them, Mike began to speak with a voice that wasn't his own.

"Old master, it has been long," Mike's voice said. Henry knew who the voice belonged to and did his best not to show the discomfort he felt deep down. "For you time isn't the same, is it?"

Henry shook his head.

"You must leave this boy alone, Jacob," Henry told Mike. The small boy's eyes were black and his body, although still in recovery, acted like he could lurch out of bed at any moment.

"He is merely the messenger. Once the message is delivered, I will have no more use for him." Mike paused, his black eyes like pools of tar, and spoke once more. "I would like to meet my opposite one. He is like me and can become greater should he choose. A choice must be given. Do you agree?"

Henry was close to doing something rash but knew it could harm Mike.

"No, Jacob, I do not. That choice will be given, but not by you."

Mike's head shook and a smile crept through his lips. A smile that wasn't his.

"The truth surfaces like a message in a bottle. You cannot hide from what is to come, and what will be. They have seen it, they have written it. What you once believed has taken on a new face and shape. I should thank you, old master, for showing me this way. Because now I will show others what I know. That is my message."

With that, Mike's head fell backwards and he was breathing rapidly. His eyes fluttered closed and he was fast asleep.

Henry left without anyone noticing he had come and when he returned to his office, he began to write more.

What was the last thing Mike told Caroline? Jacob doesn't want to understand the dream, but to silence it for good? What does that mean? Lucas pondered this as he walked outside of the hospital.

Lucas tried to remember the way Mike behaved before he left. Mike was very to himself and confused, like he had woken up from a dream he couldn't remember.

Someone else was speaking through him and thinking for him. That's why when he was done he had nothing more to say.

Lucas was so distracted that he did not hear when Zane was calling out to him. The camp counselor was wearing a faded vest over a red camp shirt, with torn jeans and converse high tops.

He looks like a rock star, Lucas thought in annoyance.

"Sure is a nice day today, don't you think?" Zane said in a manner that suggested someone talking down to another person. Lucas was neither amused nor did he appreciate it.

"What do you want?" was all Lucas could say. Zane seemed to respect the sudden promptness of the question.

"I was hoping we could talk. There's an important question I've been wanting to ask you about your abilities."

Lucas rolled his eyes, sighed.

"What is it?"

"When you read minds, do you ever hear people talk bad about you? Because I feel like that would make you regret hearing their thoughts, am I right? I mean it's great to know what people really think of you, but doesn't that make it hard to keep friends?"

Lucas shook his head.

"I'm doing fine keeping the friends I have and if anyone thinks anything bad of me, why should I care?"

Zane shrugged at this response.

"Why should you? After all, the energy you give is the energy you get back, so they say."

Lucas was preparing to walk away when Zane got in front of him.

"Cutting to the chase, got it. Okay here's the thing; I know your privy to more things than a camper ought to be and it's not just because of your abilities. You have Henry's ear in a way that nobody else does. He only tells the counselors so much and he shares absolutely nothing with Daniel. Not even a last name apparently."

I'm very tempted to use my powers on him to make him move, Lucas thought in annoyance. *Then again, he could probably zap me to death faster than I could think of the word 'move'.*

"Your silence could make screams in space loud, you know that? Alright, here's why I'm talking to you right now. As per Henry's orders, you and I will be going on the mission to rescue Bill."

Anticipating this, Lucas responded accordingly.

"I know, and that is a horrible idea." *It's not a bad idea, but I'm not going to say that.* "My powers haven't been working the way they used to. Why is Henry sending me out there?" *And with you of all people?*

"Correction, he's sending 'us' out there and my job is to keep an eye on you for any signs that you might be going cuckoo. Also, you're the only mind reader we have here so you're the only one of us who can evade Jacob's notice. Of course that is assuming you can get a handle on your powers by then."

Lucas couldn't understand why Zane was telling him this until he read his mind.

Henry wants me to babysit him anyways, so now… isth illw akem ti oemr ikley ot ese…

Lucas' head began to hurt now, something Zane took notice of.

"Looks like your powers really are not agreeing with you these days," noted the Camp Counselor. "Don't worry, you won't have to do any heavy lifting. That's what I'm for. Think of yourself as a backup plan, or if you prefer, a lucky charm."

Lucas knew exactly what Zane meant by this but kept the annoyance to himself.

After they parted, Lucas spotted Alexander in a wheelchair near the stage area, looking up at the sky. The sight of that chair reminded Lucas of his time using it the summer before, and it made him feel like running away from his skin.

Lucas read his mind and saw the memory he was thinking about. It was the first day he met Richardson. Alexander had come from a broken home with his parents' divorce wrecking what childhood he had left while Richardson came from a good upbringing. The two became acquainted during the relic game and were inseparable ever since.

As close as brothers and they loved each other more deeply than just friends…

Lucas also learned that Alexander never had a girlfriend for very long, while Richardson met the mother of his child while the two attended camp.

His son will never know his father because of those monsters. They'll pay for Richardson and all the lives ruined by them.

Both thoughts from Alexander broke Lucas' heart. He wondered how fast gossip traveled in camp and if Richardson's girlfriend knew the truth.

If she doesn't know now, she will soon.

Lucas walked over to Alexander, trying his best to not seem direct. Alexander noticed him almost instantly but didn't turn to acknowledge him from his wheelchair.

Up close Alexander looked like he had aged considerably. His skin was pasty like an elderly man, his brown hair had streaks of grey, and his furrowed brows looked even more twisted at the sight of Lucas. His limp legs were covered by worn jeans and his feet were bare and colorless.

He can't be any older than his twenties, but right now he looks like his mid-fifties to early sixties.

"What do you want, boy? Are you here to mock me? Some of the other children already beat you to it," he rasped bitterly.

Lucas shook his head. In annoyance, Alexander lifted his jeans and started scratching at his limp legs. They also had small cuts on them, like the marks decorating Lucas' chest and forearms. The sight made him shiver.

Why is he doing that to himself? He can't feel it, so why do it?

"Stop staring at them," Alexander screeched, pulling his pants legs back down like a skirt. "I can't feel anything on my legs, which is just as well since it's nothing compared to what I feel here." Alexander gestured to his heart with a trembling hand. "Now what do you want?"

"I just wanted to offer my condolences for Richardson," Lucas said sincerely. "He was a good Camp Activities Director."

Despite the sincerity, Alexander did not believe him.

"Don't act like you knew Richardson, kid. He was a *great* Camp Activities Director and a wonderful friend. He deserved better than what this place had to offer, that's for sure. I only stayed here because of him, you know. He thought we could help other kids have a chance and look where that got him."

After he said this, he began shaking hard and pulled from his shirt pocket some painkillers. He swallowed more than a handful.

Always thinking of others, never himself, Lucas heard Alexander think sorrowfully. Lucas tried to hide the sharp pain he felt from the disabled camp counselor. *I wish I was as strong as him, but I can't do it. Poor Little Theodore. He'll never love...as...him...did...I...*

"Is Theodore Richardson's son?" Lucas asked impulsively.

I thought his name was Teddy. Then again, I don't know any president they call Teddy.

Alexander turned to look at him and gave him a scowl.

"Are you still here? Leave me alone!" he growled, nearly dropping the pill container in his rage. "You wouldn't understand how I feel anyways. What it's like to lose someone and never get to say goodbye to them properly? We don't even have a body to bury!"

Stubbornly, Lucas was seized by an urge he couldn't help and did not leave.

"I wish you were right. I wish with all my heart you were right. But I know what this feels like. It isn't just my power that lets me feel this. I...I lost my parents last year..."

He didn't know why he was telling this to Alexander. Shockingly, Alexander put the pills he had away and looked up at him with attentive eyes.

This is the most I've spoken to Alexander and it's about my parents. About me. Why do my feelings matter compared to what he's feeling? I wish I knew how to say this better. How to say, 'it's going to be okay', 'time will heal all wounds', and 'life will be worth living again.' I wouldn't believe anyone who told me that. My mom and my dad, I didn't...

"...I didn't even get to say goodbye to them," Lucas said out loud, as he felt his throat become tight and his eyes watery. "You were with Richardson when he died. He wasn't alone because his best friend was there with him. It sucks that you weren't able to get his body back, but he wouldn't want anyone's lives to be put at risk for him. Everyone did what they could; YOU did what you could. One day, you can tell Theodore the kind of man his father was."

Lucas expected Alexander to tell him to leave. Instead, Alexander sighed and stared up at the sky as if looking for a shooting star.

"He wouldn't have wanted anyone's lives to be put at risk for him," Alexander repeated Lucas' words sorrowfully. "That madman cut Richardson down and no one is doing anything about it. If I could, I'd go after him and get revenge and justice for Richardson. As it is, I can't even… I can…"

Alexander began to stammer. He dropped his pill container and began to shake violently. Lucas rushed to his side and watched in horror as he clutched his chest in agony. His dead legs wiggled like a fish out of water. Boris, who had been stationed to the front, caught sight of the trouble and darted to his aid. He lifted Alexander from the wheelchair to the hospital ward as the Camp Counselor dug his nails into his chest gasping for air.

He's dying, Lucas realized horrifically. *I can feel it. It's like he's drowning from the inside, unable to move, or breathe.*

As Lucas watched in horror Alexander's struggle to live, he heard his thoughts, as coherently as if he were saying them aloud.

I'll see you soon, Richard… I'm sorry, but I can't do this… I can't be broken and alone…

It's okay, Alexander, Lucas thought in silent response, as the sharpness of the pain he felt almost made him stagger backwards. He recovered his footing and finished his thoughts. *When you see Richardson, let him know that we will make things right and get justice for you both. But for now, go in peace and rest…*

Lucas watched as the camp became lively with campers and staff alike, all their attention on the hospital ward. No one else was permitted inside after the Camp Guardian left him there. Lucas picked up the pill container and noted the fact that there were only a few pills left in them. When he read the label, he realized Alexander had overdosed since he took more than what was prescribed.

I saw him take a handful. Why didn't I say anything? I knew what he was doing, right? That it was wrong? Maybe I was too focused on what I was feeling that I couldn't hear what he was planning…

With little choice, Lucas decided to leave Alexander's fate in the hands of the camp doctors and decided, before checking on Vanessa, to enlist Josh's help.

That was crazy. I know he just lost his best friend, but that doesn't mean he should kill himself just to be with him. Losing my parents didn't make me want to do that. I still have Shelly to think of. She's the only family I have and the only person who matters to me now. Still, I'd be lying if I didn't admit that… no, forget it.

Entering his cabin, he found Josh sitting by the couch reading a book. Josh's eyes were so fixated on his book that he hadn't noticed Lucas' presence until Lucas was standing in front of him.

"Hey, Lucas," Josh signed and said with a concentrated tone. "How did the meeting go? Did you see Mike yet?"

Lucas nodded and heard the restroom toilet go off. When the person came out, to his delight, it was Gary. He looked like puberty had hit him in the year since Lucas had last seen him. Gary had grown out his hair, wore a red camp shirt, and had a new pair of sneakers similar to the ones from a year ago.

He must really like shoes. Personally, I like shirts more.

"It's good to see you, Lucas," Gary exclaimed. He walked over to Lucas and the two fist bumped, clasped hands, and gave each other a half-hug. Josh looked at the two like they had spoken a foreign language in front of him.

"Since when did you two become friends?" Josh asked and signed in astonishment.

"Don't act so surprised, Joshua," Gary said to Josh's annoyance. "It turns out Lucas is the reason I came back here. Thanks to him, I'm planning to take my training seriously, and I've got some new tricks I can't wait to show you all once that part of the summer starts."

I wonder how much of that Josh picked up. When Lucas looked at his friend's blank facial expression and felt his thoughts, he got his answer.

"How's Mike doing?" Gary asked Lucas as Josh resumed reading. "Have you gone to visit him yet?"

Lucas nodded and was about to say what happened but decided to only mention part of it.

"I only talked to him for a bit, but then I had to leave because he needed to rest," Lucas heard himself lie. He felt bad doing this but knew Gary wouldn't understand what had happened.

The less anyone knows, the better.

"I hope he recovers soon. I need to go visit him before training starts. How've you been doing with… you know?"

Lucas knew what Gary was thinking without having to read his mind. He simply shook his head.

"As well as can be expected. I'm glad to be back though, and I'm happy you're here also. I was worried we'd have too many new faces here with Bill gone and Mike in the hospital."

Before Gary could properly respond, Josh interjected so fast and suddenly it was like someone had snuck up from behind the two campers.

"What's the word on Bill's rescue?" Josh bellowed in his usual loud tone. Lucas noted a small rumble in his friend's throat, similarly to when his powers activate. It subsided seconds later.

I've never noticed that before.

"A team is going to be sent to rescue him" Lucas both said out loud and signed to the best of his ability. Josh easily picked up the lip movement without needing the poor attempt at sign language.

"Who's going to be on the team? Not you because that would be obvious," Josh noted with some sarcasm in the way he signed.

For a guy who's deaf, he hears truths better than people with two working ears.

"It doesn't matter. What matters is rescuing Bill and those kids," Lucas reaffirmed. Gary nodded in agreement, and Josh sighed in disappointment.

"I'm not sure if you've heard but we might be short a camper or two this year," Gary noted to Lucas. "Attendance isn't as high as it was last year from what I heard, and Mike might not be able to be here if he spends all summer in the hospital ward. Bill is out, of course, because he's a counselor now. I hope everything works out with the upcoming rescue mission. I was really looking forward to this summer in camp."

Lucas nodded and had felt similarly to his cabin mate.

You and me both, Gary. I hate how all of this happened. First Bill was captured, then Mike started acting weird, and now I'm going on some crazy possibly suicidal mission to meet another crazy telepath. What can go wrong?

"It was really great to see you both, but I need to talk to my girlfriend before she becomes my ex," Lucas told both Gary and Josh, making sure that Josh was looking at him as he said this.

What was that about an ex? Did they break up already, Lucas felt Josh think in a witty thought.

Lucas pondered this thought to himself as he made his way to Vanessa's cabin. He also thought about what happened in the Grand Hall.

I don't get how this relationship works. Even when she's wrong, I'm supposed to support her? I'm supposed to lie and make her think she's right when she isn't? How do I make what I feel known then? When is it my turn to be right for once?

To his dismay, when Lucas entered his girlfriend's cabin, he found her packing her backpack full of essentials for traveling such as food, water bottles, and clothing.

"What are you doing, Vanessa?" Lucas asked nervously.

It occurred to him that she wasn't aware of the camp's announcement when it came to the rescue mission's commencement. When Vanessa glared at him, Lucas could see in her eyes the betrayal and contempt she felt for him.

"What do you care? It's not like you helped back me up when I needed you most," Vanessa snarled at him. "I thought you were my boyfriend..."

Lucas heard the past tense and sensed how she felt at the moment.

Looks like Josh was right. .

"I *am* your boyfriend. How can you say otherwise?"

Vanessa shrugged in annoyance.

"Oh I don't know. How about when you almost kissed Ashley? I saw how close you two were and I can't imagine it was to smell her breath."

Lucas knew she got him there, but he also feared breaking up with her now that she was vulnerable and lonely.

If I do that now she'll definitely take off without any concern as to whether she will be allowed back in camp or not. Plus, if anything happens to her, rescuing Bill will be the least of our problems since he won't be a happy camper.

"You know what? I don't even care. If you want to be with Ashley now then go ahead. I don't need you to rescue Bill. I don't need anyone's approval," Vanessa said with a shaky voice.

"You can't save Bill alone."

"Who says I'm going alone? Shannon's going with me. Bill's her boyfriend and she's sticking by him, unlike his supposed 'best friend'."

Lucas sighed, knowing that her mind was made up. Not knowing what else to do, he decided to share with her the council's decision along with information he tried to keep to himself from Zane.

"Henry has approved the quest, and I'll be going with Zane to rescue Bill and the other kids," said Lucas, half-hoping he sounded convincing enough for the truth.

When Vanessa looked at him, although she was still suspicious, she momentarily stopped packing.

"Can I come with you?"

"They want to keep the group small to avoid anyone else getting hurt. I think it's a really good plan, Vanessa... but if I can't stop you maybe you could come with us. I know you hate me right now, but I don't want you to get hurt."

Vanessa seemed disappointed by this response.

"When is this happening?"

"Soon, like probably in a few days soon."

Vanessa sighed and threw her backpack aside. To Lucas' sudden surprise, his (ex) girlfriend wrapped her arms around him and sighed happily.

"I thought I lost you. Promise you won't leave without me."

Lucas nodded stiffly.

I don't get it. One minute she wanted to break up with me, and now she's all over me again… Are all girls like this? Lucas thought with a sigh.

Just then, Lucas felt his heart rate accelerate at a dangerous level. His eyes began to twitch violently as the world turned into a swirling vortex in his eyes. He collapsed to the floor hard and was out cold. His mind traveled elsewhere, as Vanessa attempted to frantically revive him.

When his eyes opened, he was no longer beside his girlfriend or in Camp Supernatural. He was back in that white room where he first met the two enigmatic creatures.

Oh no, not this again…

In the background Lucas heard music playing. He didn't know what the song was. The only sounds that came to him were guitar, drum, and bass to provide ambiance. When he looked around, Lucas spotted the two birds which had been only a memory until now.

The Crow was the first to cackle at the sight of Lucas. Then entered the Eagle, who followed his brother's insane laughter exuberantly. Both birds were monstrously huge, with the Eagle larger, and despite appearing ordinary, their mouths moved like human lips.

"Look, brother. He has returned, yes. Is he dead this time?" the crow asked sinisterly.

The Eagle shook his head and raised his beak up high as if to stab someone with it. When he did this, the music increased its volume and the drums pounded steadily, firmly.

"His eyes reveal potential, but remain closed like before, yes. This does not help."

Lucas looked at both creatures, as their cold eyes staring blankly at him.

"Why do I keep coming here? Is this real or am I going crazy?"

The Crow did not speak. He only flew over to Lucas and pecked at his shoulder. Lucas winced in pain.

"Ow! Why did you do that?"

"Is that real enough for you, boy, or should I carve out your heart and see if it still beats outside your chest?"

The Eagle roared and the Crow flew away, grumbling.

"Your blind boy," said the majestic Eagle, tensely. "Your eyes remain closed to what is in front of you. Your mind is perforated, with no new occupants staying for long. You fear a shadow in place of a man."

Lucas had no idea what the Eagle was babbling about until the scenery began to shift. When this happened like before, he started to hear loud sounds. This one sounded like an air raid and in the background, Lucas heard what sounded like gunshots. He flinched and felt bits of soot fall on him. He couldn't touch it, but it landed on his body, nonetheless.

"The truth illuminates all. We will show you how cloudy your vision really is. Only then can you awaken your true powers and defeat the one whose eyes are of vermilion. Once you do, a boon from you we shall require."

Before Lucas could speak, they were standing above a cliff with the soot turning into rain that poured down hard on him. He recognized the cliff; it was the same one from his nightmares. Lucas looked down at the never-ending abyss.

No... not this place again... Not here...

Suddenly he clutched his chest where his heart nested and grasped it as if he meant to rip it out with his bare hands. He felt his long nails dig into his shirt, then skin, and nestle on it.

I can't be here. Take me back, please.

"What are we doing here? This isn't real. You're not real," Lucas cried meekly as his nails continued to burrow themselves like a mole with dirt.

Even in the dream he felt the sting of his fingernails clawing at him and winced when a drop of blood trickled down his chest and through his shirt. The Crow groaned a terrible raspy sound and perched on his shoulder again. The Eagle soon did the same and both birds were on either side of Lucas' shoulders. Their clawed feet dug into his sides like clenching fists.

"This is your mind, boy. Your innermost fears come to life. The powers you seek to wield will not function unless you see the lies in truth," the Eagle said as his head turned to look behind Lucas.

"Your opposite uses the fear of those around him to round them to him like cattle. You must conquer your fear in order to awaken that which still remains," the Crow said as he took flight with the Eagle following at his heels. "He has set a time and day, when the Shadows are at their most prominence, during the blood moon's reign."

Blood moon's reign? What does that mean and how does it connect with Jacob and the Shadow People?

Lucas called out to the two birds, but it was too late; they were already gone. When he turned to look behind him, he found the same ominous figure staring back at him with cold malevolent eyes and golden hair that burned away the darkness like fire. The fear suddenly came, as if his own heart was turning against him, when the shadowy figure smiled at him and spoke incoherently.

Lucas kept muttering, "I don't want to die, I don't want to die, I don't want to die..."

It wasn't until he heard the voices of the Eagle and Crow when he stopped muttering to himself.

"Look at him, boy. See the man behind the shadows. Look at his eyes, and you will see the truth. Hear his voice and you will hear the lies. Open your mind and you will be whole again. That which is yours," the Crow rasped.

The fear was strong, as Lucas found himself plunging into the dark abyss, still sobbing and clasping his chest. He fell until the only thing he could hear was the disappointing sighs from both creatures.

"He is not ready," Lucas heard the Crow complain angrily.

"Not now, perhaps he will try again later," promised the Eagle, malevolently. "Beware the eyes of Vermilion, boy. His desire is not connection but separation."

The new place Lucas saw was a black gloomy prison, with Bill slouching by the wall of his cell. It had been almost two weeks since his captivity, but judging by how he looked, Bill felt he had been held captive for much longer than that. Now he was bare-chested, his pants were torn from the knees down, he was barefoot and still had the wool cloth around his eyes. Physically Bill had lost a lot of weight, so much so that the skin had retreated to reveal his bones more plainly. His face was hollow, with his cheekbones showing themselves like bumps on the sides of his face. Bill also had stubbles all over his face that formed the shadow of what would be a black beard. His hands were chained behind him, along with his ankles, and Lucas could feel the chains that held them in place.

I've almost got it, Bill thought to himself erratically. *I just need to feel for the keyhole.*

He's trying to break out, Lucas consciously thought.

Bill was sweating profusely as he fumbled with the pin. The sweat from his hair was drenching his face like a wet towel, wetting the cloth, and irritating him.

At some point, Bill felt he had found the keyhole, but the pin suddenly fell at the sound of the cell door opening.

When the door closed, someone entered. Even though Bill could not see what the child looked like, Lucas could as if seeing with foggy glasses. The young boy had sandy hair and grey eyes that looked as gloomy as rain clouds. The boy did not look as menacing and appeared rather small for his age. He carried a plate of food, which consisted of a loaf of bread, beans, and water in a bottle. When Lucas attempted to read the child's mind, he realized this was futile. Suddenly, Lucas felt a sharp stinging pain similar to the one he got when he tried to read Henry or Alistair's mind. The words that he was able to hear were incoherent and scrambled.

His words are like an incomplete jigsaw puzzle and the images are mashed together.

The silent child approached Bill and placed the meal carefully close to him. Bill heard the boy move and immediately shuddered. "Which one is it? Are you the bad one?" he asked in fear.

After reaching him, the boy touched the left side of Bill's face, which seemed to calm him down.

"Oh, it's you, Devon, thank goodness," Bill said in relief. "Have you heard anything about Henry coming to rescue me?"

The boy touched the left side of Bill's cheek again and he sighed in disappointment.

"Are you sure?" This time the Silent One touched Bill's right cheek and he knew what the boy was telling him.

That is an interesting way of talking. I'm guessing left means no, right means yes.

While he spoke, Bill had picked up the pin and finally got it into the keyhole which undid his bindings. The Silent One appeared to notice what was happening. He placed the food to the ground and reached for Bill's cloth as if to tighten it.

He's going to stop Bill and tell Jacob what he's doing, Lucas thought in horror. He was preparing to try stopping him telepathically, when Bill made a motion to put his hands up.

"If we do this, Jacob won't stop until he's killed both of us. Are you sure this is what you want?"

Devon tapped Bill's right side. Bill nodded stiffly and took a firm hold of the cloth.

What's he talking about? Is that kid helping him? Why are my eyes suddenly burning…again…ARGH!!!

When the small child undid Bill's restraints on his ankles and wrists, Bill began to flex his hands. He felt the absence of his fingertip joints when he looked down to see three stumps in place of where his fingernails should be.

"I'm moving back. Tell me when to stop," Bill instructed Devon. When he walked, his legs gave out on him. He would have hit the floor hard but the small child was so fast in catching him it was like a pitcher capturing a baseball. They both backed up enough so that Devon tapped the middle back of Bill's head.

With shaky hands, deep breath, Bill ripped the cloth from his eyes and slowly opened them. His eyelids fluttered open rapidly like the wings of a butterfly and a large energy beam emitted from Bill's eyes to destroy the room's inner brick wall. The wall crumbled before him, with bricks flying all across in the opposite direction.

What in the world! When did he learn to do that? That's a HUGE improvement from his popcorn heat vision.

Bill screamed as he did this, falling to his knees. Devon scooped up the cloth and wrapped it tightly around Bill's eyes. There was a sizzle sound like burnt meat and Lucas could briefly see what looked like smoke projecting from the cloth.

Even in darkness, Lucas vaguely saw scorch marks on the cloth and faint ones on Devon's palms.

That kid has nerves of steel, Lucas admired. *And a high tolerance for pain to boot.*

Suddenly, there was a loud banging on the door, and the knob began to wiggle with a life of its own. Before anyone could get in, Bill took a daring leap through the still crumbling rubble and managed to avoid any debris. He gestured for Devon to join him. The small child nearly said no but decided to jump swiftly as if he were jumping between buildings.

Bill and Devon both made their way outside of the cell they were in, their bare feet scraping against dirt and grass.

When the other Silent Ones finally opened the door to the cell room, it was already too late. Alistair pushed them aside to find the cell empty. He looked up and saw Bill skittering away with Devon the Silent One.

"Well, what are you all waiting for? Go after him, or Jacob will burst those tiny brains of yours!" Alistair snarled angrily.

Without a moment's hesitation, they sprang from the open wound of the wall like wild animals and chased after Bill and Devon.

I can't keep running like this, Lucas heard Bill think. *I should have had Devon pack me some shoes but sadly there's no shoe stores nearby.*

At this point, Bill was running on pure adrenaline and an uncharacteristically show of force when it came to his survival instincts. Meanwhile Devon was outpacing him and if his bare feet bothered him, he wasn't showing it. Running was proving to be a real challenge for Bill. Because of how much he sat or slouched during the day, his legs were immobile and the idea of running felt more like a dream than anything else. The way his legs moved made him feel like a baby bird trying to take flight. Sweat coated his face so much that it threatened to undo the cloth Devon had wrapped for him. He pressed his hands firmly on the back of the cloth but felt his closed eyes attempting to emit the beam again through his lids.

Groaning in pain, Bill made an effort to focus all his energy on not tripping over anything or himself. Devon slowed his pace to evenly match him but made tapping sounds like his knees that sounded urgent. Bill seemed to understand.

All Lucas could do now was watch and hope that his friend made it out of this alive. He couldn't feel his physical body, but every sensation Bill felt became a feeling for him. It was like both shared the same body and the pain to go with it.

Clenching his teeth hard, Bill let out a soft groan of pain and resisted the urge to scratch at his eyes. His hands flew to his face, mere inches from where the cloth was. In the moonlight Lucas could see what looked like tiny scorch marks.

He must have made that mistake before, Lucas noted. *I get the feeling if he doesn't let those beams out, he's going to burn his insides out.*

Lucas clenched his fists and felt his own eyes fluttering between being open and closed.

I can't wake up yet. Not until I know he's safe.

Without thinking clearly, Bill shielded his eyes with his hand.

Big mistake.

His hand began to heat up rapidly as if he were touching a hot stove. Bill removed them and Lucas could see with the faint moonlight that he added scorch marks on his palms.

Argh! That was not a good idea, Bill, thought Lucas, irritably. *Why did you do that?*

Devon took Bill by the hand and led him towards the right hand side of what looked like tall trees and lots of rocks. Lucas wasn't sure where they were, but wherever it was, there didn't look to be other people nearby. Bill sighed and the burning sensation in his eyes subsided momentarily.

That's why he did that; it's like an itch he needs to scratch.

Even in the dimness of the night, Lucas managed to see the Silent Ones who were trailing after Bill and Devon. They were armed and looked like hunters preparing for a kill.

He won't be taken prisoner again if he's captured, Lucas realized in horror. *This can't be how it ends. We were about to rescue you, Bill! Why couldn't you just wait another day or two?!*

Bill stopped running when Devon stopped leading him. He walked forward, hands flying everywhere, and touched what felt like wet walls. He felt water falling down like melting ice and smelt the faint aroma of mold mixed with clay. Bill let out a small hum and heard it echo slightly. He sighed in relief as Devon tapped his forearms in what seemed like a playful manner.

Why is he acting like that's a celebration? Lucas thought irritably. *A cave is a bad hiding spot. It won't take long for the rest of those crazy kids to find them…*

Bill breathed a heavy sigh of relief, giving himself over to relaxation as his body slumped on the ground next to Devon. He patted the small child in the shoulder and thanked him. The small child gave him a tiny smile.

Without warning, Lucas saw something come upon Bill and Devon. Its shadow engulfed around them, wrapping itself around the two boys, and pulled both backwards like a giant snake. In seconds, Bill and Devon disappeared into a purple portal that looked like a bonfire.

What's happening to me? Let go of me! No, stop! Help me…!

The Silent Ones never found the cave. They circled past it as if it were never there to begin with and were eventually forced to return empty handed. Lucas could neither see nor hear Bill's thoughts anymore.

What was that?! Bill, where are you? Bill!

With a large gasp, Lucas awoke in the hospital ward. Vanessa saw him awake and exclaimed happily, "Lucas, you're awake! I was so worried about you!" His girlfriend wrapped herself around him and breathed a happy sigh on his shoulder.

Ashley, Josh, Shelly and Hailey were there as well. Ashley looked happy that he was awake, but also sad. Lucas tried to speak and felt a lump in his throat that made it hard to say anything at first. Taking in his surroundings, he would have nearly suffered a panic attack if he hadn't noticed Henry's presence as well.

"You collapsed, do you recall?" asked Henry, his form eclipsed those around him.

Lucas took a moment to find his voice.

"Vanessa…" he said weakly. She took his hands in hers and nodded with a soft smile.

"I am here, baby. What's wrong?"

As she got closer, Lucas' voice returned to him.

"I saw Bill escape. He made it out, but then… he… was gone… Bill's gone…"

Chapter 13: Silent Endgame

No! Please! No! I'm sorry! I didn't mean it!

Their cries, their pleas, their suffering.

Don't do this! You don't have to do this!

Why are you making me do this?! Why did you have to say that?!

Help me! Mommy! Mommy! Daddy! I'm sorry I wasn't good enough! Please don't leave me!

Grimaced and twisted, hands burying in scalp, fingernails digging into head, teeth grinding and threatening to undo each other's infrastructures.

Ywh nowt ti otps? Ew usjt natw ot og omeh. Anwt I og ot omhe. Leasp.

As nails scratched against scalp, there was no pain; only the tingling of razor fingernails burrowing in-between hair follicles like angry beavers.

Kill them! Silence them forever! Did you know that if you have forty pennies, a quarter, five nickels, and six dimes, your life would still make less sense than it does an attempt to change? No use for it, identity is given, salvation is taken, put a price on lies, while truths are free. Eating kills you, starving kills you. Voices speak with no form to take.

This last thought caused such anger and irritation that when feet entered, the sharp nails nearly struck out against the unwelcomed guest. The person who entered abruptly was Shanine. The prophet was dressed in a red robe and wore her hood up. When she drew near, she uncovered her hood, her purple hair flowing down her shoulders, and gave a thin smile.

"You've hurt yourself once more, my beloved," Shanine said softly. "Come, let me tend to your wounds, Jacob."

Jacob sat down and murmured compulsively, continuing to scratch head, but Shanine laid a gentle hand on top of Jacob's hand. Biting into mouth, tasting a salty liquid against the inside cheeks, a tooth loose and squirming like a chicken in an egg.

Shanine examined Jacob. Facial features betrayed bitter cognition. Bloodshot golden eyes followed the prophet like a bloodhound ready to pounce at the given command. She lay a pale hand on bare shoulders and there was no reaction from the touch, tender, careful, as it was.

"Do you love me?"

"Be quiet, woman," Jacob repeated.

"I love you."

Jacob began to shake, tremble.

"Ugly toad with disproportionate limbs."

"Are you happy with me?"

Fists clenched, lips quivered.

"Air is wasted on deflated bagpipe lungs."

"I just want to hear you say it."

The muscles in Jacob's throat tightened and the loose tooth wiggled defiantly.

"It's not worth the trouble it took to create life for something that can never look the part."

The words came out like a choked gasp.

Shanine trembled and began to cry. Jacob also felt tears streaming down cheeks, body shaking, muscles loosening. There was no emotion, only reaction.

A voice entered her mind which wasn't her own, and Jacob made sure it was all she could hear. Jacob pushed Shanine aside, fiercely, without care. She cried into a small bottle, making sure her tears filled it to a drinkable measure. She felt a small burning sensation and stifled a whimper while each tear rolled down the etched lines of her face. When this was over, she put a soft cap on top and handed it to Jacob. The bottle was taken, drunken, swished around the mouth. The loose tooth reattached itself, ligaments meeting gum. Its shape and position were not the same. With some leftovers, Jacob slid the remaining towards Shanine. She took it and sprinkled the remains on Jacob's frostbitten feet and bleeding scalp.

"I know you can't feel this," Shanine said, with some sadness in her tone. "You've been hurting yourself more often than before, my love."

Jacob shook head and forced scratching hands down, grinding newly healed teeth that remained crooked. Each tooth was like broken glass. Picking at fingers and forearms, etching new scars from similar a.

"Thank you for the voice. It always helps," Shanine admitted softly, making sure no tear drop was wasted as she resealed what remained of the bottle she had given Jacob for later use. She placed it with a group of other bottles that were similarly filled.

"Don't do that again," Jacob rasped. Shanine hesitated, knowing what Jacob meant. "What power was given can be taken away. Do not test that."

Shanine nodded and took a moment before speaking.

"I spoke to the boy Lucas."

This seemed to interest Jacob, whose full attention was on Shanine. The scratches on scalp were still healing, the frostbite from feet appeared fully gone now.

"Lucas still believes in Henry's promises. His powers are no longer functioning at their fullest capacity. He's vulnerable now. Easy prey, or easy ally."

Neither is one; No equality without opposite to provide proper adversary.

Jacob nodded, teeth grinding together like cogs in a machine. The crookedness caused the inside of mouth to begin blistering with small cuts.

"I wish I could see further, but they're like a canvas, with the paint brush being inconsistent each time. The Gods in their infinite wisdom only grant me possibilities rather than the clearer pictures Henry's son seems to have more convenient."

When the building collapses, no one blames the foundations, but the builders get lynched on the streets.

Shanine observed the room they were in was damp and small like a prison cell. She knew this was the kind of comfort Jacob preferred. In many ways, Jacob reminded her of a nocturnal beast who preferred to be unseen and yet the presence absorbed all that was in the room.

"He's like me." Jacob pointed finger at self. "Lucas feels the enormity that is lacking in the vessel. Too much inside, not enough outside."

Shanine nodded and looked intensely at Jacob's face. Jacob felt her stare and did not return her gaze.

"Leave now, woman," Jacob commanded angrily. "Your presence is unwarranted."

Shanine looked hurt by this, but it wasn't the first time Jacob had spoken to her in this way.

When she left, Jacob read her mind briefly and saw the words she felt.

Even as the voice continues to taunt and hurt me, the tears I have now are not for them, but for my beloved.

Jacob's hands impulsively returned to scalp and began to undo the healing that Shanine had just done. Before tearing a new wound, the voices began again.

It's not my fault, it's not my fault, I tried to be good, please don't be mad at me… lphe em teg hourght ihts…

Jacob groaned and moaned, rocking back and forth, nails dug into arms, and began to etch red lines that complemented each other.

The past was recollected in Jacob's mind, a moment in time that sometimes felt nearer than it was, recalling the moment Camp Director James and Alistair both appeared to the child similarly to divine figures.

Henry had been younger in years, appearing to Jacob like the prospective fathers who came to select a child to adopt, and of course none of them ever chose damaged goods, because why would they? Alistair, on the other hand, surprised Jacob, he hid himself underneath a fiery presence, but there was something with a key component that was missing, which allowed him an advantage that Henry did not have.

As soon as they walked into the room, Jacob knew everything about them; he knew Henry was there to take him to a camp for children like him, and he knew Alistair was there in case there was trouble, when this was happening, he started to hear something in his mind that he had heard before, not like this, with this sound similar to intense feelings that made Jacob agitated, with something else, this became especially stronger when head turned to meet one way.

"Why do you want to help me? What am I to you?"

When Jacob asked this, the sounds that were heard in head took on a voice that sounded like someone speaking through a microphone.

A means to an end. A way to achieve the best possible outcome. Lies hidden in crumpets of truths.

Though the words confused Jacob, attention shifted to Alistair rather than Henry. The fiery man regarded Jacob with eyes that did not betray any malicious intention.

"I seek no personal gain, but a mutual benefit. Your birth is an unnatural phenomenon as we have yet not seen in quite some time. Telepaths such as yourselves are exceedingly rare and must be trained at a young age in order to properly control their abilities. You cannot be allowed to run rampant on your own as you have."

By control, he means caged like a dog, not allowed to go on walks for any longer than how far the ropes goes. Bark! Bark! Hark! Hark! I won't be chained to a post and forgotten to be given water and food, tossed in a nameless grave to be eaten by maggots and mice.

Alistair looked at Jacob with interest. It was like both were on similar levels of staring at each other from a great distance, with tumults of lava raging in-between them.

Your powers do not need to be controlled; they need to flourish, Jacob heard the voice say. *Henry would have you tagged and bagged. We would set you free to destroy what lives and breathes.*

Jacob was grinding teeth, tongue stubbornly beating against loose tooth, at one point, the tongue was injured and felt no pain, feeling the taste of blood run down throat, and licking cracked dry lips.

"These voices call out for a sun they will never see again, by exposing them to the truths they cannot face, there will be no cage, only one who is in control."

Jacob heard the words and thought that they were better hearing than in keeping to oneself.

Fools who can't think for themselves are like broken toys that nobody wants. Discarded with no name to claim an allegiance.

Jacob did not know if this thought was in self's mind or if it was the other voice, using tongue to beat against the loose tooth, causing it to fall, swallowing it, could taste the blood that swam in mouth, with a tingle that came from the absent tooth, no tears, no grimace of pain, no worry.

After a moment, Henry lifted the mind veil Jacob had in place and Alistair saw Jacob's appearance for how it was. Despite having the image of repulsion, Jacob sensed that Henry was intrigued by the deception.

They see you now, it can't be put away, and your truths will be seen as lies, if you want to survive, listen, if you want to become stronger, learn, if you want to be free, supplant the one who is yet to come.

Suddenly, a wave of images came flooding into Jacob's mind like a moving picture, children who are similar and the way they harnessed their powers under Henry's supervision, the moving picture had one of these images, Jacob visualized seeing faces in place of the blank ones from the orphanage, faces with smiles, frowns, and most of all, openness, can't close again, revoking an unwarranted invitation, only from a safe distance to allow for a vantage point, with enough foresight to escape when ready.

Attack! Strike while the iron is hot. That way it will seem like your idea, when really it isn't. The arrow won't strike without fingers to give permission.

Alistair went to check on the other children, as instructed by Henry, and when he returned, prepared to attack Jacob. Deciding a demonstration was in order, Jacob sent the feeling of pain into Alistair's mind, sending him into a state of agony. He writhed on the floor and was gasping for air. His mind convinced him he was drowning, and his lungs acted accordingly.

This power is yours, the pain others feel will not be, only when the minds of others are free to think for themselves will they be allowed to see what is true, when the awaken chooses the dream, silence becomes the solution.

Jacob undid the mind control, with Alistair appearing like someone who has just arisen from the sea, gasping for air. Henry looked beside himself and appeared angered by this.

"This behavior will not stand, you will only be as useful as you make yourself, to be any less is to fail that purpose. Camp Supernatural will condition your mind to see beyond what it believes. I will ensure that your abilities remain in check which will protect those around you and yourself."

Jacob turned his gaze at Alistair, who regarded him with deep interest.

An enemy today is an ally tomorrow, goals intertwining, unknown, listen well now, plot later.

While Henry spoke of the benefits his camp offered children like Jacob, the telepath thought about what Alistair was feeling, a feeling where the people around him suffered more than accept what he gave them, a hard truth to swallow, when he was no longer a child. In days long gone, Jacob discovered that people buried themselves so deeply in their traumas that the truth was apt to cause more harm than good, and because of this, there was more comfort in what they kept in vs. what they gave out, seeing through their view, distorting and warping it, to make them both better than they were, and easier to manage.

"You will never gain full control of your abilities, that is not your purpose," Henry revealed to Jacob, "you are a bridge that will create an obstacle for others to follow. The voices you hear are part of the conflict but not the endgame."

Jacob heard the words, intermixed with his thoughts.

"Never gain full control of abilities," *You will*, "Not your purpose," *That is yours*, "A bridge that will create to follow," *You are an obstacle for others*, "The voices are part of the conflict, not the end," *You are being prepared for the game.*

Jacob heard something more, something that couldn't be discerned at the time, and this caused the choice to be made to accept Henry's offer and join Camp Supernatural. The memory was occupied when a sound came from the door to his room. Unlike Shanine, this person failed to announce themselves, and Jacob slew the person where they stood, slicing their throat open. The child fell backwards, eyes open wide, and stared up at a darkened ceiling, as others like him came to see the commotion.

Once subsided, Shanine made her way past the silent fearful children, not sparing a glance for the fallen boy, and informed Jacob of something.

"We've lost Bill and the boy with him," Shanine explained to Jacob. "He escaped and we have not been able to find him. My vision cannot see where he's gone, only the moment which has passed."

Jacob pounded the floor with bare feet, hard enough to threaten the very earth itself. Looking around, snarling like a rabid dog, beginning to calm when the voices began to speak.

No longer needed, no assembly required, all sales final, return back to sender.

After nodding, Jacob turned to Shanine and the other children who were huddled around the dead Silent One.

"Take that body away," Jacob commanded, "the darkness needs its nourishment, preparations will begin to be made for an attack sooner instead of later. Are the new ones ready?"

Shanine nodded, glancing backwards at a room that Jacob knew housed the captive children who never made it to camp and who were captured by Alistair.

"Old master gives lies with open eyes, while truths are spoken in silence, even in light, there is always darkness, always shadows lurking in the corner, where one needs only to extinguish the established quota, to allow for nothing more to remain…"

Chapter 14: Nailed It

News spread around camp as fast as wildfire regarding Bill's escape from Alistair and Jacob, along with his mysterious disappearance. When Henry made a formal announcement to the camp, he seemed very calm about it.

Henry left out the part about the portal Bill and that kid were sucked into, Lucas mused to himself. *Maybe he doesn't want to cause a panic or assume anything.*

Henry closed the announcements by mentioning that training would commence the next day, giving everyone a day to prepare.

Lucas had to believe Bill was alive because when he saw Shannon receive the news, there was a glimmer of hope in her eyes. Vanessa also looked happy enough to hear of Bill's well-being, but her attempt to share this comfort with Shannon was met with a quick dismissal.

"We don't know all the facts yet," she said with dissatisfaction, "just that Bill is alive. That's not enough to go on yet."

Vanessa seemed hurt by this and it was clear to Lucas that this wasn't the first time their interaction unfolded this way.

I was so happy for Bill when he told me he had a girlfriend, Vanessa was thinking. *But Shannon was always mean to me. Even before they started dating. I know she isn't trying to be; it's because of that wolf side of hers. That doesn't mean her words hurt any less.*

The sharp stinging pain Lucas had become accustomed to came back with a fury, driving invisible needles to the sides of Lucas's head.

I need to figure out what those birds said. There's got to be a reason for why this is happening to me. My powers haven't been the same since…

Later that afternoon, Lucas decided to hang out in his cabin with Josh. The two hadn't spent much time together since the beginning of the summer and Lucas hoped to remedy that. They talked about Josh's new attire. Josh claimed the idea came from an anime he was fond of and hoped that Kendall would take more notice of him since she herself enjoyed anime. This last piece of information was news to Lucas, who didn't figure Kendall was into that sort of entertainment.

I knew people in school who were into that. I feel like it's just to make expensive toys and shirts for people to buy. It's a phase as Shell would say.

While Josh began to jump between different topics which ranged from his overall year to his crush on Kendall, and his anticipation for training this year, Lucas pondered who could have saved Bill and the Silent One named Devon.

Why, and more importantly, how? There was something odd about that portal. It was too dark to see anything except what looked like shadows extending arms.

After the news of his escape, the mission to rescue Bill was replaced with another mission: to save the campers Jacob still had. It

Because of his coma last year, Lucas missed out on seeing who went on missions and what they were like. He didn't think about them for long before Bill's return crept back in his mind.

He knew that boy Devon right? Was he among the kids who were taken? I saw the way the other children behaved when Bill escaped, like they were blindly obedient and fearful without showing it. What made him different from the rest?

Lucas found himself walking the campgrounds after leaving Josh in their cabin, not really having any destination in mind. To his dismay, he spotted Sapphire outside the hospital ward with Shelly, who had a worried look on her face. Seeing him, Shelly nudged Sapphire with her, who in turn took Twinkle by her arms abruptly. The small dog softly yelped in surprise.

"They're saying we can't visit Mike until Henry says so," Shelly told Lucas. Sapphire gave Lucas a pouty look like she was demanding a new toy.

"I want to see Mikey," Sapphire demanded. "Why can't I, Lukie?"

Lukie, I mean, Lucas shook his head, slightly annoyed by the nickname, but let it stick.

That nickname means she's ready to start crying soon, Lucas noted.

Right on cue, the small little girl was beginning to get teary eyed and at this point, more harm would come from silence than an answer.

"They want to make sure that whatever he has isn't contagious," Lucas heard himself lie in the most terribly unelaborate way he imagined. "He was somewhere cold and when people don't get warm fast enough, they get sick."

What do you mean contagious? You make him sound like he was bitten by a zombie or something. Calm down.

Sapphire looked confused, while Shelly looked doubtful.

What's really going on, Luke, Shelly thought and hoped her brother was listening.

When Lucas winced softly and pinched his nose, Shelly got the affirmation she wanted.

Mike acted strange the last time I saw him, Lucas revealed telepathically to Shelly. Each thought was followed by a rumbling noise like the vibration of a phone. When he finished, a sharp BEEP sound came on as if a car horn went off. It took all the consciousness Lucas had to avoid staggering and falling over.

Twinkle began barking abruptly, causing Lucas to regain his senses momentarily. Shelly turned her attention to Sapphire, who was trying to calm down the puppy.

"We won't be able to visit Mike for a little bit." Her voice steady like someone preparing to disarm a bomb. "But it won't take long for them to do what they need to do. You don't want to be around the doctors when they run their tests. It's really boring."

The small girl considered this and appeared to be more comfortable now.

That'll buy you a day or two at most. Make it count, Lucas heard Shelly think.

When they departed, Lucas made his way towards Ashley's cabin. Some instinct grasped at Lucas and he suddenly wanted to speak to her. To his shock, Lucas spotted Ashley speaking with another camper.

A boy!

He knew the boy from last year. His muscles rippled in his camp tank top tee, he wore jeans that looked worn out, and his light brown hair was slicked back to reveal a broad forehead.

That's the guy who worked in the camp store. I forgot his name. James something?

James something was talking to Ashley, while she looked to be having a good time in his company. She smiled shyly at some of his remarks and at one point brushed her hair behind her ear.

Shelly once told me that's a sign a girl likes a boy, Lucas thought in irritation. His body began to tense up and he felt like a soda can about to burst. When Ashley noticed him, she waved at him and James something looked over at Lucas and regarded him like an unwanted guest.

In what looked like a few seconds, Ashley was in front of Lucas and took a soft tumble near him. Before Lucas could catch her, Ashley fell against his shoulder and Lucas had his hands on her hips.

How did my hands get there? What should I do?

Ashley backed away softly but did not thank Lucas for helping her. Lucas expected James something to make his way to them. Instead, he walked away.

He definitely recognizes me from last year and he isn't happy to see me either. I think I know why.

"What are you doing here, Lucas?" Ashley asked him with a tone that was similar to James something's demeanor.

"I go to this camp," Lucas tried not to sound sarcastic but felt on edge. "What were you doing talking to James something?"

Did I really say that? Why should I care? I have a girlfriend.

Ashley was confused by this until she shook her head.

"His name is Jeremy and you know him from last year. We were just talking about our time away from camp."

"What about your time away from camp? You never did tell me?"

"You never asked," Ashley countered.

Even Shelly asked me how my time away from camp was, Lucas heard Ashley think. He groaned in pain and tried to hide it as having stood on the wrong leg for too long. Before she could question it, Lucas cut her off.

"I'm asking now. How was your time away from camp?"

"It was alright. I didn't really do much except go to school and during December, my family took me to see my grandparents in California."

Lucas nodded but found himself not paying attention. His mind went back to Jeremy and why Ashley looked shy around him.

Is it because I broke her heart last year? If she can't be with me, she'll be with him instead? She'll be with him instead, if she can't be with me?

"What does he have that I don't?" Lucas said out loud. He clapped a hand to his mouth but it was too late. Ashley's face went from being lively to looking like someone splashed cold water on her.

"Why does that matter to you? You made your feelings on me very clear last year and you never tried to message me much during the time we were away from camp. So if I want to talk to someone else, even if it's just talking, I damn well can."

Ashley said this last part in a very unapologetic way that Lucas felt dumbfounded. He knew he had stepped on a land mine just now and tried to think of possible ways around this.

"I know it's none of my business and I wouldn't have said anything had I not seen it," Lucas tried to sound more convincing than he felt. "He just doesn't seem like your type."

This further upset Ashley, who looked about ready to use her power to run through Lucas like a blade. "And just what do you know about my type? What gives you authority over my happiness?"

What indeed? She's got us there. I mean she's got me there.

"Look, Lucas, just drop it before you say anything more damaging," Ashley said abruptly, not giving him a chance to properly respond. "You said you saw Bill get taken by some kind of portal right? What could have done that?"

Lucas noted how Ashley changed the subject on him just as he had done with her many times and felt a stinging irony in that.

"Maybe he did it to himself. Everyone seems to think that Jacob is behind all this bad stuff that's been happening lately, but what if he isn't?"

He wasn't sure if this thought was meant to be in his head or said out loud, but now that it was spoken, he waited for Ashley's response. She actually seemed to consider this thought.

"Are you saying he's working for someone else that is worse, or something else?"

Lucas wanted to nod, to confirm that suspicion if only to have someone else to share it with. Nonetheless, he took a neutral stance and shrugged instead.

"Who can say? Anyways, whatever happened to Bill it's beyond our control now. Even Daniel doesn't know what happened to him and I sure don't. Now we can focus on the other kids who were taken."

The tone Lucas spoke in was one he didn't recognize. He felt how even his heartbeat was and the way each word felt easier to say than the last. It was like he rehearsed this speech before speaking it.

"Nothing's felt right since last year," Ashley said out loud. Lucas wasn't sure if she meant to say that or think it, because both happened simultaneously. "We have to assume for the moment that whatever happened to Bill is not going to be explained anytime soon. If we're lucky he'll turn out somewhere soon. If not, I don't even want to think about it."

But she did, and Lucas could see it.

She's imagining Vanessa's rage, Shannon's rampage, and what will likely become a sharp division around the camp if Bill isn't returned safely.

"I'm going to head off and see if I can find Hailey and Shelly," Ashley announced, once Lucas stopped thinking. He wanted her to stay, had more he wanted to say. He tried to give this impression without saying it, but she didn't seem to notice. "You can talk to me, Lucas. You always could have. Just do me a favor and don't make your sister worry so much. She has done so much for you and you're all she talks about. It's actually kind of funny; she was all you talked about last year and now that Shelly is here, you're all she wants to talk about at every moment. You're lucky to have a sister like her."

Lucas knew this to be true but didn't respond. Instead, he kept what he really wanted to say to himself.

I'm sorry I chose Vanessa over you last year. I'm sorry we didn't get to go to the dance together. I'm sorry I never asked you about your time away from camp. Mostly I'm sorry that I've been a bad friend lately.

These thoughts and similar swam in the ocean of Lucas' thoughts, as Ashley turned and darted away. He felt himself mouth one thought before putting it away forever. "Don't go yet."

After a moment, Lucas sighed and went back to his cabin. That night, the yellow team's victory party commenced and Lucas attended to be with his sister. Looking around, he spotted Shelly with a circle of people surrounding her, including Ashley and Hailey. Little Sapphy was there as well, Twinkle barking happily as he was playing with other children who were patting him.

Shelly looked so happy that Lucas felt his presence would only bring her down. So instead he watched from a distance, like someone in a dream.

He was joined by Josh and Gary, who spotted him and brought him a soda can.

"Your sister is becoming quite the celebrity," Gary noted. Josh made a similar remark.

"She looks very beautiful tonight for some reason," Josh said with a smirk. "Has she asked about me yet?"

Lucas shook his head and turned away, his eyes darting from Shelly to Ashley. She looked radiant in the firelight. Her blonde hair was tied back in a ponytail, her pink camp shirt was drenched in sweat, outlining her chest, and she wore sweatpants with dirty sneakers.

I wish I was there with them. I know I can be but it wouldn't feel right. This is Shelly's night, not mine.

A tallish girl walked over to Shelly and swung an arm around her shoulder. She gave her a rather flirtatious look and Lucas read her mind.

That power of hers is wild. I wonder what else she can mimic.

Even though he wasn't as fluent in reading lips as Josh was, Lucas made educational guesses as to the exchange between the two.

"You did good out there," the tallish girl told Shelly. "Want another soda?"

Shelly shook her head and thanked her. "You weren't so bad yourself out there. I wouldn't have known what to do without you."

The tallish girl made an 'awe shucks' gesture and patted Shelly's shoulder.

"We helped each other, that's what we do around here. If you have any questions or anything about camp I can always point you in the right direction."

Lucas noted that his sister seemed to catch the innuendo and softly shrugged off the arm.

"I'm not really interested in that right now. But thank you for the offer."

"That's a shame; I think it's boring when a person goes in only one-way."

Lucas was completely lost at this point, trying to wrap his mind around what he just thought happened between the tallish girl and Shelly.

She was either offering to guide her around camp, or something else? Maybe she was offering to be her friend?

The rest of the night went by slower, and Lucas couldn't help picking at his forearms every chance he could get. He felt the urge to scratch himself, to grit his teeth, and tap his fingers against his knees. Part of this was to calm his nerves, while other parts made him hope someone was watching.

Then I'll know if it's real. If then it's real I'll know.

He made the excuse to turn in for the night, startling both Josh and Gary, who were expecting him to stay awhile longer. Before he could leave, Shelly made her way to her brother. Her small group of newly formed friends had all stayed behind where they were as if they didn't notice her absence.

"Where are you going, Lucas?" Shelly asked. "Want to come with me? We can eat marshmallows by the campfire and I can read a story for Sapphire and the other kids."

Lucas shook his head, feeling his head throbbing now. His arms were crossed and he began to scratch at the edges discreetly.

She won't understand. Look at her. How she looks at you. You're nothing to her right now. She has new friends. New family.

Scratching, Lucas winced in pain and took a step backward, startling Shelly. She noticed his nails and exhaled a soft gasp.

"Come with me right now," Shelly insisted, grabbing at Lucas' right wrist. Lucas did not protest, though he wanted to. It wasn't long before he was led into his own cabin with Shelly pulling him like a dog on a leash.

She sat him down in his cabin room which appeared plain at the moment. Lucas willed his entire might to avoid conjuring up his home's bedroom. Bits of it snuck through though like a leaking bag. Small details such as the missing blade fan, the shadow of a hole in the wall, and what looked like silhouettes of figures on his shelves. He hoped Shelly's attention on his forearms would keep her from noticing.

This turned out to be far worse because when Shelly saw Lucas' forearms, she let out a terrible gasp which made her tremble. His skin was open in various places, and he had scars that were both freshly made while others looked older. The newly imprinted wounds didn't seem to bother Lucas at this moment. His mind was racing back and forth between this moment and where he was a moment ago.

"Why are you doing this to yourself, Lucas?" Shelly asked, tears beginning to form in her eyes. Her brother gave her a blank look, his eyes were dry with no forecast in sight. He glanced down at his forearms, then back to Shelly impassively.

"I can't stop myself," he finally muttered. "I can't help myself. It's what helps me stop feeling this way."

"What way?"

Lucas shook his head, not wanting to say it out loud. He swallowed hard and tried to pull away from his sister. Shelly grabbed his wrists, not hard, but enough to keep him from making a run for it.

"Please don't do this to yourself, Lucas. This isn't good for you. Do you understand what this is doing to you?"

He tried to listen to her words, tried not to read her mind. All he felt in this moment was an urge to scream, to dart out of here, to let the world implode in upon itself.

I'm not hurting anyone by doing this to myself. I don't even feel it. That's why I keep doing it.

"It's the only way I can feel anything," Lucas insists. "It's my punishment for what I did to mom and dad. I'm the reason they're gone, and even before that, I was the reason they were never happy. I was better off… better off…"

He choked on the word he wanted to say. Shelly knew instantly what he meant and shook her head furiously. If her head wasn't attached to her skull, it would have flown away like an aero prop flying plane toy.

"I want you to listen to me right now. Lucas, you were not the reason mom and dad died. You were not the reason they were unhappy. Not everything is about you. Mom and dad loved you so much. It destroyed them to see you gone."

Shelly hesitated, wanting to say more, but restrained herself. Lucas heard the rest in his mind.

They never recovered after that. They withered away and I was left alone.

The sharp stinging pain came, but Lucas did not react to it. He only sighed and sat on his bed.

"Don't move. I'll get some bandages and medicine for those cuts."

Shelly got up to leave and saw that her brother was slumped up against the bed. His back against the wall. She sighed and walked over to him.

"Tell me what's really going on or I'll tell someone at the hospital ward what you've been doing to yourself. This isn't right, Lucas, and it needs to stop."

He shook his head again, his mind telling him not to listen to her.

She's trying to confuse you. Look where you are. What you can do? Do it. You know it's the only way.

Lucas buried his hands on his scalp, his nails digging in. The pain he felt caused him to cry out. Shelly took his hands softly, cradling them delicately between hers.

"At least let me cut these," Shelly insisted. Lucas hesitated for a moment and finally relented. When he imagined nail clippers, Shelly took them and did not question their sudden appearance. She began clipping at his nails as best she could, even when his fingers silently protested. Lucas's mind kept angrily protesting this moment, trying to make him take action. Instead, he sighed heavily, feeling the sharpened nails becoming lighter with each *click, click, click…*

"There, you're all done," Shelly exhaled, putting the nail clippers to the side. She didn't notice their disappearance. She rubbed her brother's newly cut nails, which looked as trim and smooth as polished stone. When Shelly looked into her brother's eyes, she saw the first strands of tears begin to form there. Wrapping her arms around Lucas' neck, he began to sob into her shoulder, his hands falling behind her back, the two rocking back and forth with each other.

"It's okay. I promise it's going to be okay, Lucas," Shelly tells him, stroking his long shaggy hair. He doesn't hear her completely but imagines that's what she would have said.

Better than believing your imaging this all right? Make her leave now. Keep to your own thoughts.

After calming down and letting go of his sister's embrace, Lucas admired his newly cut fingers. He couldn't remember the last time they looked this way, but admitted they were becoming as hard to manage as his hair when the heat covered him in sweat.

"I am always here if you need to talk about anything. Don't ever think I won't be there for you, Lucas. Just promise me you'll stop this." She pointed at his forearms, rolling up his sleeves like she was hiding evidence. "Can you promise me that?"

Lucas softly nodded, though he felt the urge to scratch come to him immediately not long after she was gone. When his newly cut nails didn't make so much as a scratch, he began biting his lower lip. Shaking off this impulse immediately, Lucas threw his head upon the pillow and fell fast asleep. No dreams tonight.

Training commenced the following day in what would mark the second week of summer camp. Awakening from what felt like a huge stupor, he was informed by Josh that Zane was expecting them in the training field.

As opposed to his tent? Lucas noted. He brushed his teeth, tried to comb his hair, took a quick shower, and grabbed a grey long sleeve to wear underneath a blue camp shirt.

Both Lucas and Josh had a quick breakfast in the cafeteria. Lucas noted that the young cafeteria lady, the mother of Richardson's son, was nowhere to be seen.

I wonder if she knows… She must, right?

The two friends ate in silence, with Lucas chowing down a small bowl of cereal with sausages and hash browns on the side. Josh, meanwhile, devoured two eggs over easy with bacon, three waffles and drank orange juice. He noticed the look his cabin mate gave him and gestured to his own plate.

"It's called a buffet for a reason," Josh signed and said out loud. Lucas shook his head.

No it's not.

He half-hoped his friend didn't hear that. When they were finished eating, both made their way to the training field where the rest of their group was already receiving a lecture from Zane. This included Ashley, Vanessa, Hailey, Caroline, Gary, and Shelly.

It's pretty much the same group as last year, except Mike... now I'm depressed again.

"Well, it looks like the late bird came down first. Stellar timing young mind-boy," Zane told Lucas with a hint of sarcasm. "Nice of you to fit us into your 'busy' schedule."

Lucas was in no mood for Zane's sardonic humor, but tolerated him, nonetheless. Shelly noticed her brother and gave him a look of concern. He pretended not to notice.

Let's just get through today and see if tonight any dreams happen with Bill in them.

Zane looked around at the small group of kids and clapped his hands together as electricity emitted itself through like a web. He quickly discharged the energy.

"Ok, now for introductions, or in this case reintroductions for the late ones."

Zane paused for a moment and let out a small burp.

"Great, now that that's out of the way, in case you don't already know, my name is Zane and I will be your trainer for this summer session. You're all my trainees so that makes you my responsibility. The best thing you all can do is not make my job any harder than it already is. The worst thing... well I don't have to tell you all, do I?"

Lucas was waiting for someone, anyone to ask.

I'll reinforce the question, if someone asks, he promised himself. *Quiet, no I won't!*

No one asked.

"I don't care who has what power. I am not Danny the Nanny. You won't see me picking the sharpest straw out of you all, but I do expect at least a few of you to have more than one power mastered at this point. If not, well we will just have to wait and see I suppose. You should all know yourselves well by now, since you all were together last year, so we won't bother with introductions or anything. Any questions?"

He didn't wait for an answer.

"Now then, I already know you all have been here since last year, except for you, Lucas's sister, so go ahead. Show us what you can do? That'll be your introduction."

Shelly sighed and stepped forward.

She looks like she really wants to say something to Zane, I hope she doesn't, Lucas thought fearfully.

Instead, Shelly took a deep breath and charged towards Zane. She went full karate mode on the electric counselor, who defended himself exceptionally. Lucas knew a lot of the moves she was using, and thought they were very accurate to the real thing.

She doesn't just watch the videos online; she actually practices them with exercise to the point where it's like a mirror image of the moves.

When she was done with her demonstration she turned to see everyone shocked by her wild moves. Ashley broke the silence by clapping.

"Wow, Shelly, you are so cool," Ashley said breathlessly.

Hailey nodded in agreement.

"Yeah, I can mimic any move I see performed. The movements and stances just clinked inside me like a beat to dance," Shelly explained while catching her breath. Her hand flew to her head and she exhaled a soft groan.

It's also why she was the most athletically active person in our school. I used to think it was just because she had that thing called photographic memory? Maybe it is something similar to that.

"That's impressive indeed, but your powers have limitations. You can only do what your physical stamina allows you to, correct?"

Shelly nodded.

"And based on that little groan you just did, your condition is something that gives you mild headaches. Isn't that right, Lucas' sister?"

Again, Shelly nodded and took her place back with the other campers.

"My name is Shelly, not Lucas' sister."

"Of course it is," said Zane, with a smirk. "Moving on, who here has developed a new power as of recently?"

Out of the eight campers, only three raised their hands. They were Josh, Ashley, and Lucas. Lucas turned to Josh surprised.

"You have a new power?"

Josh nodded once he understood what Lucas said and pointed towards the Grand Hall. Once he was on the roof, Josh pulled from his backpack a flight suit with Angel-like wings.

I really want to laugh, but I feel like that would be one of the wrong things Zane mentioned would upset him.

Josh fitted the wings onto his back as the others looked at him in confusion.

"What is he doing, trying to fly?" Lucas asked Ashley.

She grinned as Josh finished fastening the straps around his chest.

"Just watch. I saw him do this back home. You'll love it."

Zane climbed up to level with Josh and helped him make sure the wings were securely fastened on him.

"I don't know what the plan is here, but don't get yourself killed this way," Zane said. "The camp's insurance doesn't cover kids dying from falling off rooftops." Josh wasn't looking at Zane when he said this and just nodded his head as if he understood what he said.

I wonder what he would have thought if he knew what Zane actually said.

Suddenly, Josh jumped from the building and let out a huge scream of energy waves that lifted his body high above the ground. He was flying like a paper airplane across the sky, cutting through the air like scissors. Lucas and the others were in awe. Even Zane was impressed.

"I take it back; he's got a unique talent that goes beyond his ability to talk all the time. He'll be very useful in the recon missions next month," Zane acknowledged. "The only thing is his disability may be a hindrance since he can't exactly hear the sounds of commands."

Josh can read hand signs and lip movement, Lucas wanted to say, *and I can telepathically project words onto him,* but he held his tongue back, knowing that Zane would just brush him off.

As Josh maneuvered his wings to land down, he seemed to spot something in the forest. Before he could notice it more, he suddenly began losing his angle and was falling faster than anticipated. Josh tried screaming, but his sound waves weren't strong enough to keep him from falling.

He's falling… falling…

Lucas felt dizzy and started feeling the uneasiness and heavy breathing that usually occurred in his nightmares. He was grateful when no one seemed to notice, with all eyes on his falling friend.

In a split second, Hailey caught Josh a moment before he would have been as flat as dough.

"Whoa, for a second there, I thought I was going to end up like a pancake," Josh said hysterically as Hailey put him down gently.

Pancake? Why did he have to say it like that? Lucas thought, trying to hide a stifled laugh.

Josh thanked Hailey and reported what he saw to the others.

"I saw something in the air. I mean, down from the air. A little that way. Just come on." The furious gestures Josh made were like a mime trying to act without speaking.

Zane and the rest of the group followed him.

As they neared the place, Josh frantically looked around.

"It was right here. I saw it," Josh shouted so loud that his sonic waves began to project through his mouth like an echo. "Now it works." He slapped his forehead in annoyance.

Zane studied the tracks on the ground and noticed that it was abnormal.

"Someone was here. Look at these tracks. They are still fresh."

He looked in the opposite direction and pointed.

"Whoever is here is nearby. That way."

The others looked at him astonished as he shrugged it off.

"I admit I'm not a bad sight, but do you all want to stare at me all day or figure out the answer to this new mystery?" Zane bellowed out with his sarcastic tone.

As they followed the tracks, Lucas got the feeling it could be Bill trying to find his way to camp but couldn't be sure.

That's wishful thinking. Whatever grabbed him wouldn't just dump him here out of convenience, would it?

Lucas was about to bring this to Zane's attention when they finally found the source of their exploration.

Huddled together like conjoined twins were two boys, one who appeared young and incredibly malnourished, while the other was older, similarly in poor condition. Both were unconscious and completely unaware of their surroundings. They had shadows that marked their bodies sharply than any Lucas had ever seen.

It's like they're on the dark side of the moon? Wait, why did I just think that?

Before Lucas could examine Bill further, Zane briefly moved him to the side to identify both the wounded counselor and child. Bill's body was bruised, tattered everywhere, and appearing wounded. His skin was also tanned as the sun cooked him like meat on a grill. The cloth was still wrapped around his eyes and his wrists were bruised heavily. The soles of his feet were bruised with blisters forming on the bare skin. The child, meanwhile, looked like a homeless person. His long curly black hair was baked in sweat and his pale skin was beginning to redden in the morning sun's rays.

He's the one who helped Bill escape, but I don't recognize him.

Vanessa scrambled forward, pushing Lucas aside, while Zane moved hurriedly to examine the child. She wrapped her arms around Bill and cried heavily into his shoulder.

"You're alive! Thank the Gods! You came home, Bill!" Vanessa exclaimed with a muffled voice. She refused to lift her face from Bill's shoulder, even as her arms tightened and the bones in her body made that ear-crushing crunch that annoyed those in attendance.

"It looks like he didn't need rescuing after all," the Camp Counselor said a little too casually. Vanessa glared at him loathingly.

"No thanks to you."

He just shrugged it off and lifted the frail boy.

"I'll take John Doe here to the Ward to see if we can identify him. Early release day, everyone. Go find something else to do."

Lucas lifted Bill and swung his arm over him. Vanessa did the same with the other arm and the two walked Bill back to the camp. Vanessa was sobbing as she reached over to clasp Lucas' free hand.

"I love you, Lucas," she suddenly said, squeezing his palm as if she meant to yank it off from the wrist.

It had been the first time in their relationship that Vanessa said those three words. Ashley pretended not to notice, but Shelly could tell she was uncomfortable about it.

Lucas did not reply and instead pretended not to have heard her. His only focus was on Bill's well-being.

This can't be real. Bill's back, he's actually back in camp. I guess whatever took him actually saved him. Is that what happened?

The whole camp immediately stopped whatever they were doing and ran to aid Bill. Daniel, who was chatting with Keira, caught sight of them and ran to the hospital to get their attention. Shannon abandoned her group of trainees to assist Lucas and Vanessa with Bill. She wasn't sobbing like Vanessa, but her face looked like it was about to when she saw the cloth on his face and the way his left hand looked.

"What happened to his hand?! Why is he wearing a cloth on his eyes? What did they do to him?!" Shannon demanded as her fingers moved to pry it off her boyfriend's face.

As her fingers fumbled to remove the bandages, she felt a burning sensation run through her hand and winced in pain as if she just burnt herself.

"Let the nurses take a look at Bill," said Lucas to Shannon, "they'll know what to do." She gave him a begrudging nod of approval.

The nurses came through, took Bill from them, and strapped him to a gurney.

"Will he be okay?" Vanessa asked helplessly.

They did not reply as they attached a breathing mask to his face and wheeled him inside. Zane put the small boy Devon onto a lone gurney. He also was escorted into the ward by a small cluster of nurses. The Camp Counselor muttered something to one of the nurses and she nodded.

Vanessa was the only one allowed inside to be with Bill because she was family. Shannon tried to fight her way inside, but she ended up wounding two nurses before Boris subdued her. Lucas turned to look at his group of friends in shock at the sight of Bill's broken state. Shelly was the only one who saw through her brother's false ignorance.

"Lucas, what happened to his eyes? Do you know about it?" Shelly asked him softly.

He shrugged, looking away from the hospital as much as his body would allow.

"I think it has to do with his powers. Not as they were before but as they are now."

Shelly nodded, appreciating the honesty her brother gave her. They both noticed Henry's grand appearance due to the notable commotion surrounding the camp. The Camp Director spotted Shannon struggling against Boris' tight grasp and instructed the monster to release her and allow her to visit Bill. She did so without showing gratitude or acknowledgement to him.

"I don't understand her frustration. I thought she'd be happy that Bill has been returned to us," said the monster with a hint of confusion.

Henry shrugged and made his way to the ward, ignoring Lucas' presence.

Deciding he needed a break from all the excitement, Lucas returned to his cabin to sleep the rest of the day away. He was happy for once that the attention was on somebody else other than him. Even more so that Bill was seemingly back for good.

I still don't understand what that portal was and why it dumped Bill and that kid here. Of all places? What's that old saying? Don't look a horse in the mouth with a gift? Something like that.

As he slept, the nightmare of falling returned with a rage. When he opened his eyes, Lucas fell through the endless abyss, clutching himself as if to roll into a ball of protection. He sobbed and begged for it to stop, as the shadow's sinister sneer stared down at him with satisfaction at the deed. Their dark arms grasped at him, as if to pull him up, or to strangle him in midair.

Lucas was ripping at his bed sheets as Josh broke into his room. He frantically shook his cabin mate awake. Lucas looked around at his bed in horror, sweat covered him from head to chest, and his lower lip had a small indentation from his teeth.

"Are you good, Lucas?" Josh asked with concern. "Your lip is bleeding."

Lucas nodded and gestured to the broken door. Josh made a face when he turned to look at it.

"You started it. Just imagine a new door. Make it metal so that I don't break it down next time," Josh joked as he translated part of it into sign language.

Lucas rolled his eyes and shuffled upwards from his bed, dusting away his sheets and bits of torn fabric.

"How did you know I was having a bad dream?" Lucas asked suspiciously.

Lucas realized that Josh hadn't understood what he said when his friend looked at him blankly. After repeating himself both in sign language and outspoken, Josh pointed to his head.

"Your voice was in my head again. Believe me when I say if I could hear with both ears, you're screaming and shouting probably would have made me deaf anyways."

Lucas laughed at that but felt sweat brushing against his cuts. Luckily it wasn't a lot of pain but he did wince. He let it out in a louder tone than usual, making sure that Josh wasn't looking at him.

After a few moments of silence, Josh didn't leave as Lucas had hoped.

"Do you think Bill is fine? He looked like he lost a big fight against someone, well big, but I want him to be fine."

That was Josh's way of trying to lighten the mood. Sadly, Lucas did not respond or laugh.

"Come on, man, what's going on with you," Josh demanded irritably.

Lucas shrugged and leaned his back against the bed.

"I want to see Bill, and find out if he's alright," Lucas muttered to himself so fast that Josh didn't catch what he said.

"You want to see how Bill is?" Josh blurted out, without realizing that's *exactly* what Lucas wanted.

Lucas nodded but was met with derision when Josh turned his attention to their kitchen.

"You want me to imagine some pizzas or chili hot dogs? Maybe both?"

Lucas shook his head and made a disgusted face.

"Why are you wearing long sleeves in doors? It's hot in here."

Lucas shrugged, with the subject being dropped with his shoulders.

Ultimately, Josh chose the chili hotdog and ate ten of them before falling asleep. One thing Lucas hadn't learned soon enough about Josh was his overabundant appetite, which, according to him, was like a 'black hole' in his stomach.

Lucas imagined himself a small plate of pasta and ate it all before he could finish drinking his soda. He remembered the way his father made pasta, and found himself missing it, as much as he missed the man he could vaguely picture. In contrast, his mother loved to make macaroni and cheese, which was Shelly's favorite meal.

She always loved the ones in different shapes; she didn't like the plain ones. She was heartbroken when they discontinued the one with the blue dog on it.

Lucas had a picture of his parents, but it was an old one. It was the day they got married. They looked happy and youthful in the picture: His father wore an elegant white suit with a black tie that seemed to come together on its own, and his mother looked radiant in her white wedding dress. She bore a strong resemblance to Shelly in her youth. They even had the same smile and dimples. When Lucas thought about it, he concluded that he had nothing in common with his father.

The only thing that he had in common with his father was the last name and possibly the way he frowned.

But anyone could mimic a frown right? Lucas wondered silently to himself, but after receiving no confirmation, he yawned and fell asleep, with no further visions disturbing him…

Chapter 15: Jealousy

Bill remained in the hospital for a few days, during which time Lucas trained vigorously with Zane and the others. Josh never got tired of showing off his Screaming Flight, his self-proclaimed new ability, but found himself losing balance often. Zane assumed this was due to the sonic frequencies not being aimed with concentration.

Either that or Zane has no real idea why Josh keeps falling and is just making stuff up.

It started to rain heavily the next day, so Zane hurriedly excused his campers from training. The group joined the others at the cafeteria for Pizza Day. Henry had already gotten his plate and decided for a special (and rare) occasion to dine with the campers.

When the pizza ran out, he gave a slice from his own plate to Sapphire and his last two to some friends of hers, who thanked him with smiles and hugs.

He really is the heart and soul of this camp, thought Lucas, admirably. *If I ever get old, I hope I become like him.*

Twinkle barked happily as the elderly Camp Director patted the canine's head softly. Henry's eyes looked sad as he did this.

The next thing he did baffled everyone in attendance; Henry decided to help the cafeteria staff by taking food to the campers so everyone got enough food. He even helped to make more pizza and brought beverages consisting of milk, water and sodas from his home.

One of the cafeteria workers told Lucas that Henry never stayed in the cafeteria except for when everyone else had already left or before the children arrived. "He is always the first person to enter and first to leave."

Why now? What's changed to make him do something so out of character? Maybe it's how much it's raining outside. I feel bad that Boris always stays outside even when the weather is like this. Maybe I can offer him some food.

As if beating him to the punch line, Henry scurried out of the cafeteria with a plate of food for the Camp Guardian. He made no attempt to cover the food or himself as the rain poured down hard. When he returned, there was not a drop of rainwater on the Camp Director's person or clothing.

Maybe he's like Ashley; he runs really fast, or rainwater is scared of him?

When everyone finished eating, they all gathered around as Henry began to tell stories about the places he had been to in his lifetime. He claimed to have seen five out of the Seven Wonders of the World. The two he was unable to see were the Great Wall of China and The Statue of One.

A child raised his hand and asked softly, "What's the Statue of One?"

Henry smiled at this and prepared to talk about it after taking a good sip from his water bottle.

"The Statue of One is a symbolism of humanity's enduring spirit in the form of the most important person to come from our own history. He had many names: Bringer of Light, Torchbearer, Son of All, but he was often called "The Father of One."

Everyone softly muttered to themselves and looked at one another in awe at Henry's revelations.

"Many of my counselors here know the tale but this one being is responsible for our purposes in life. The first of our kind to bestow these incredible gifts and burdens we bear. It was through him that others came, such as famous historical figures who were also afflicted with disabilities."

An example he noted was the ill-fated King Tut, whose affliction weakened him and made him unable to walk without the use of the cane. But some documents suggested his mind transcended beyond his body post-death.

That sounds too similar to those mummy horror movies Shell likes. Maybe there's more truth to those movies than I thought.

After that story, Henry decided to tell a new story which he promised would delight the younger campers. It was a story about a man named Jorath and his unicorn friend Albus whose magical horn had, according to the Camp Director, the ability to cure any illness and could even bring the dying back to life as if they were never sick.

"Jorath and Albus went on many adventures and fought against many evils together throughout their years. One day, however, Albus was lured away from Jorath and slain for his horn by vile creatures. All unicorn horns are said to have magical properties and if a unicorn horn were to fall into the wrong hands, it could cause misfortunes beyond mortal comprehension. Thankfully, when our hero managed to find Albus before he passed, the unicorn bestowed his horn to Jorath as a final gift. Jorath wanted to use the horn on his friend but its healing properties were not meant to save their own kind. So, in honor of his fallen friend and comrade, Jorath turned the horn into a lance and used it to continue fighting on behalf of humanity for the rest of his days."

Henry turned his attention to Sapphire.

"I know you must have something to say about unicorns," The Camp Director encouraged with a warm smile.

Sapphire nodded eagerly and got up to speak.

"Can a unicorn's sharp horn bring my mommy and daddy back?"

The cafeteria fell silent. All eyes on Henry, who ruefully smiled down on the young child.

"The horn can only heal what is living, not what is already gone, my child," Henry said softly.

Sapphire looked down sadly as Twinkle licked her face.

"But know this little one: As long as I live, you will always have someone to look after you and your brother. I won't ever leave your side. The same goes for you all. I care for each of you as if you were my own children. In some ways, you all are."

This made Sapphire smile as Henry patted her on the head. All the campers, even the older ones, looked pleased by the Camp Director's answer, although some still looked disinterested in his approval.

I get it. Not everyone was happy with the way he handled Bill's capture. I just hope Shannon isn't trying to start something stupid. We just got Bill back. The last thing we need are more problems.

Despite this, the good-natured air Lucas could feel was enough to keep the rest of the uncertainty both he and other older campers felt at bay. Lucas thought that he was too old for story time but decided this would be an exception.

I bet he has so many amazing stories to tell, not just about others, but himself. I wish he would share some of those stories with me though.

The next story the Camp Director mentioned was more for the older campers. It was of Bainton, a legendary Alter Child, who was nicknamed The Lost Lord. He was famous for assembling a group of Alter Children and other species of beings for heroic deeds.

"Bainton was a young man with extraordinary abilities, known for his enigmatic nature and possessed innate charisma worthy of a renowned hero. He bore a greatsword which emitted light based on the strength of the soul wielding it. There are oral tales of his encounters with supernatural creatures such as Wraiths, Sprites, Trolls, and even Dragons. Particularly, how he slew them by wielding his greatsword as if it were a paperweight."

Dragons?! That can't be true. Those are all fairy tale creatures. Also, what makes his sword great? Is it bigger than other swords?

"With each creature slain, Bainton's notoriety grew and he amassed a following of Et-Alter Children all ranging in different abilities, but most notably those with the ability of prophecy and clairvoyance. Those specific followers in his group received visions of dangers near and far and informed Lord Bainton where the threats were most prominent. The origins of Bainton, as you all may have guessed, goes back to a time when Alter Children were not as well documented as they are now. However, his exploits inspired others to begin documenting instances of Alter Children, leading to the discovery of many throughout the years. Moreover, his sword is most notably famous, and similar to the Statue of One, has many names. For the purposes of today's explanation, it's commonly known as Luciastrum which means 'Wielder of Light' in the first language."

First language? Of what?

"During one of his adventures, Bainton became lost and his last known whereabouts were among the deepest depths of the Dark Realm. His followers prophesied that his time to return would come when the Shadows resurfaced."

When the stories were over, the rain outside began to disperse while the little campers ran out to play in the mud puddles. Sapphire joined her cabin mates in doing this but also seemed hesitant in the activity. Henry walked by her, patting her head, and she was suddenly excited to be part of the group. In contrast, the older campers went to their cabins or the training field. Some of the older campers who lingered talked to each other about both the stories and how odd it was for the Camp Director to be with them for as long as he was.

Something is definitely off about all this, Lucas thought, conflicted. The remaining drizzle hitting him suddenly felt like hail with the sharp pain he got.

Making up his mind, Lucas decided to go visit Bill, and hoped they would let him in. The only person who had been by his side the whole time was Vanessa, who had not been that way towards her boyfriend despite their relationship. He entered the hospital and turned to the nearest nurse who had been shuffling through the ward anxiously. It was the same nurse that treated Lucas and Josh last year when they contracted indigestion and poison ivy respectively. She did not seem to recognize him, however.

"Hi, can you please help me find Bill Cooper," Lucas asked, then hesitated when he thought of someone else. "Actually, can you take me to see Counselor Alexander first?"

The nurse's face suddenly dropped at the sound of his name.

"I'm sorry to have to tell you, young man, but he passed away earlier this morning…."

Lucas felt his heart stop, and the whole world freeze with it. He hadn't known the camp counselor very well, but it didn't make the shock any less painful.

How? Why? When? Did he… take the easy way out, were among the many questions Lucas would have wanted to ask.

He composed himself the best he could and followed the nurse to Bill.

"Does Camp Director James know about Alexander?" Lucas asked instead.

The nurse nodded stiffly.

"He was the last person to come and visit the counselor before his passing…" the nurse noted grimly. "He wanted to wait until late in the afternoon to announce it. The kids were having so much fun in the rain and when he was telling stories. I guess he also wanted to lighten the mood after what happened to Counselor Bill and former Camp Activities Director Richardson."

Lucas understood but also wished he had known, because now he felt worse than before.

Henry may have been the last person to see him, but I was the last person to have heard his thoughts. I hope I helped him find peace.

Without trying, he heard the nurse's voice in his head, and realized she was friends with Alexander, and had fond memories of him. He saw one where both Richardson and Alexander made her feel welcomed on her first day as a camper.

They really were inseparable, Lucas thought, ignoring the pain that came with using his powers. He started biting his lower lip then forced himself to stop.

On the outside, the nurse put on a brave front, but on the inside, she was sobbing and breaking down hard.

It doesn't hurt as much as mind-reading does, but feeling other people's pain isn't fun either.

He entered the room to find Vanessa asleep on a nearby chair. The nurse left the two alone as Lucas softly shook her awake. When I saw him, she smiled happily.

"Hey, Lucas, they let you in?" Vanessa asked in a relieved tone.

Lucas realized that she had been in the room the whole time, never once leaving Bill's side.

That should make me jealous, but right now it doesn't.

He went towards Bill, who was still asleep, and saw in dread how his friend looked in the clear light. His cheeks were bruised, like someone had hit him with great force several times. His hair was very long, unkempt, like a wet mop on his head. Bill was also painfully thin, his cheekbones were showing like hollow bumps, and his arms were bruised, both fresh and ones that were still healing. His eyes were the only things that Lucas could not see though because they were newly wrapped in tighter bandages.

I hope no one got burned trying to take off the old ones.

Lucas looked up at the ceiling and saw no scorch marks of any kind, which made him sigh with relief.

"The doctors say that he would not have survived a few more days the way he is now," Vanessa explained sorrowfully. "Why did this happen to my brother? What did Jacob and Alistair do to him?"

As she said this, Vanessa fought the anger and tears that were building up. Lucas wrapped himself around her as she sobbed hard against his shoulder. He stared at Bill while his heart raced with a sadness of his own. He remembered Henry's words.

Bill will never be the same if he is returned alive. Did he know about this? That this would happen to him?

This knowledge alone made Lucas sad for his friend, as he realized the life Bill once had before was over. It would take a long time before he recovered physically and mentally was another endeavor. But Lucas also understood the pain, and the hardships to come.

I wish there was something Henry could do, like when he healed me. I know that was a one-time deal but still…

"You never said 'I love you' back," his girlfriend said suddenly when Lucas returned to the present.

He turned to look at Vanessa and saw the confusion in her eyes.

"Why didn't you say, 'I love you' back?"

He innocently shrugged.

"Can we talk about this later?"

Vanessa shook her head and looked upset.

"Sure, whatever. My brother is not going anywhere, and neither am I," Vanessa said bitterly, as she took her place back in her chair.

Lucas wanted to profess his love for her. *The love that isn't there anymore. It might never have been at all.* But he wasn't even sure if she loved him. *It's probably one of those heats of the moment things that people say but don't mean. Like when they're angry. Either way, it's not a big deal.*

Suddenly remembering the young boy, Devon, Lucas asked Vanessa where he was.

"He's in Zane's tent, I think."

Maybe if I get a chance later on, I can try to see what's going on there, Lucas pondered to himself.

After leaving Bill's room, Lucas made his way to Henry's house to ask about the boy named Devon and Alexander's passing. It was during this time that he spotted James something again with Ashley. Both were talking and laughing almost at the same time.

What are they laughing about?

He concentrated, more so than he usually did when reading minds, and heard their conversation as if he were merely a few feet from them.

"That was a really cool thing you did earlier, Ashley, with the way you ran from the camp lake to the entrance of the camp so fast."

"Yeah, my speed is getting faster now, less stumbling like last year. The only problem is I'm going through shoes now faster than before. I had to bring a couple pairs with me this summer."

Both were laughing now, and Lucas felt himself seething with jealousy.

"What are you doing tomorrow morning? We can get something to eat before heading off for training?"

Sure, I'd love that. Maybe I can invite Lucas also so he can see what he's missing out on.

Okay, I'm sorry, that last part isn't what she said. Lucas let out a long sigh.

The two parted ways but glanced at each other as they made their way to their respective cabins.

Lucas shook his head rapidly, as if trying to purge the memory of what he just saw. Sighing in exertion, he continued to head towards the Camp Directors home.

Lucas' mind had a brief blackout where he was opening the door to Henry's house, before finding himself in the Camp Director's office, listening to him speak.

"Bill can no longer be a counselor," Henry declared to Lucas' sudden shock.

A camper cannot become a counselor if they are unable to control their own ability. That's 101 around here.

Henry nodded silently when Lucas repeated his thoughts to him.

"When Bill wakes up, we must be prepared for the worst possible outcome."

Lucas did not understand what he meant until he elaborated.

"Bill has been through immense trauma, and I imagine he will not be mobile for quite some time," Henry clarified. "He will have many difficulties ahead of him, and I fear we will have little in terms of assurances we can give him."

While Lucas listened, he thought about Alexander ruefully.

"Alexander is dead. They told me when I went to visit Bill today," Lucas said in a low voice.

He fought the tears as a lump formed in his throat at the thought of the sad lonely counselor.

He was fine a few days ago.

Henry nodded in response.

"Yes, I was beside him in his passing," Henry said. "He wanted to die, Lucas. Alexander wanted to be with Richardson."

For most of his life, Lucas had conflicted feelings about taking his own life. He had a different perspective now after his talk with Alexander. The Camp Counselor had died the moment his close friend did.

Would I feel the same without Shelly? With my parents gone, I would be all alone without her. Sometimes I can't help but think that maybe she is the reason why I am still trying to live. If my powers worked the way they should, life would be easier.

"I will be announcing his passing in a moment to the whole camp. I would very much appreciate it if you would kindly help in bringing everyone together immediately."

Lucas complied and prepared to leave. Before he did, he was reminded about Devon.

"Who is that kid that Bill brought with him? Do you know?"

Henry shook his head, not considering the question at all.

"He never made it to camp and has therefore been with Jacob for… how long I couldn't say. But do not trouble yourself with him though. We will figure out what is necessary when the time is right."

Lucas nodded and was about to leave when Henry called out to him.

"Lucas… I am very proud of you, my son."

Suddenly, Henry did something Lucas was not expecting. He rose from his desk and walked over to him. Lucas was unsure of the gesture as the Camp Director came near him.

What is he doing? What is this?

When they were close enough, Henry wrapped his arms around him like a soft blanket and held Lucas there in the gentlest embrace he ever felt. His mind raced with thoughts, many of which ranged from disbelief to astonishment.

My parents never hugged me on a regular basis, though they hugged Shelly often. No, this is something else. Like all the hugs I never got in my life combined with hugs I never knew I missed.

Suddenly, Lucas began to shiver. At first, he wasn't sure if it was his anxiety or surprise at the Camp Director's embrace. Regaining himself, Lucas began to feel a sudden sensation of coldness coming from Henry. Even so Lucas swore that it was one of the best hugs he ever received from anyone.

Besides Shell of course.

It only lasted a few seconds, but to Lucas it felt longer than that. Afterwards, Henry composed himself and dismissed Lucas. He nodded and exited the house, feeling both confused, and strangely elated, without really understanding why.

After he was gone, Henry collapsed on his chair and cupped his hands to his face. He suddenly began sobbing as his hands muffled the sounds of his sorrow.

"What have I done…? What have I done…?" Henry repeated ruefully. His voice sounded like the pain a person feels when they realize they did something wrong.

Unexpectedly, Daniel hurried in after Lucas had departed and, for a brief moment, saw his father crying. When Henry's eyes met his sons, he wiped the remaining tears away and rose from his seat.

"Hello Daniel… I will be out in a moment," his father said calmly as he walked over to the door and closed it shut inches away from his son's face.

He couldn't see Daniel's face, but instead he saw the child he once was. So full of hope and happiness at being in the camp. Henry remembered the day he told Daniel that he was his father. Daniel had been seventeen and was about to become a Camp Counselor. He looked so much like Lucas; looking at Henry with such reverence it was like he could do no wrong in his eyes. But that revelation caused the smile on Daniel's face to twist into something else.

Something that has now become a permanent reminder of all he has sacrificed and sought to do.

"When the time comes, I hope you understand," Henry told himself as if telling Daniel, who had already departed the Camp Director's home in both confusion and hurt. "I wish I could have done more, but this will have to suffice as the fruits of my labor…"

Chapter 16: Best Friend

It was the beginning of the third week of June and Lucas couldn't wait for July to arrive.

After everything that has happened this summer, some time out of camp would be good for me too.

Lucas had no problem with gathering campers; everyone was seemingly already prepared to hear what Henry was about to announce. He spotted his friends and sister in the crowd but made no movement to join or make his presence known to them.

When Henry took the stage, he kept his words short and to the point. He appeared more tired than when Lucas last saw him.

"I have called your attention to address an unfortunate predicament that happened early this morning," the Camp Director began as everyone's attention was on him. Even Boris was taking a break from his guarding duties to observe the announcements.

Well, that didn't take long for things to go back to business as usual, Lucas thought in a similar feeling to those around him.

"Two beloved members of our staff have passed away: Camp Counselor Alexander Lewis and Camp Counselor Jane Serra."

The campers began muttering to each other with some who seemed impassive about it while others appeared genuinely saddened by the news. The only members among the counselors who seemed stricken were Keira, Lucinda, Margot, and Daniel. He appeared to look uncomfortable at the sound of her name. Meanwhile, Keira's eyes were on two people. Lucas immediately recognized them as Richardson's girlfriend and son, both were in a corner. Her eyes were tear drenched and the baby was also crying.

Her son is crying for the both of them, Lucas thought, looking at the face Richardson's girlfriend was putting up. He knew they weren't married, but her thoughts told a different story.

We were going to get married this fall… I didn't want anyone to know until… oh Gods… I can't do this right now!

She turned away from the crowd with the crying baby in her arms.

"Alexander will be missed dearly, as will Jane. She was a beautiful soul who gave much to this camp, and they were the finest to become counselors in this camp since its formation," Henry said with such sincerity that Lucas believed every word of it. "To brighter news: Bill is alive and in our care now. For those of you who wish to visit him, visiting hours are from now until nine. We will also be holding a wake in the Grand Hall for Jane, Alexander, and Richardson, until the same time as well. Please come and pay your respects to them; they gave their lives valiantly for this camp."

"That's a lie!" a voice suddenly called out from the crowd. Richardson's girlfriend returned, tears streaming down her face. She suddenly looked older than she had a few minutes ago. "They were killed because of your friend! What kind of man are you if those are the sort of people you call your friends? Please, Camp Director James, tell us I'm wrong. Tell us the truth of why the father of my son, his best friend, and sweet Jane had to die!"

The silence that engulfed the camp was like a meteor crashed and destroyed the earth in an instant. Everyone was too afraid to say anything, make any kind of sound; even swallowing felt like a deathtrap.

Meanwhile, Henry's calm composure looked to be reaching its limit.

He looks like he did before that outburst with me…

"Yes, Alistair was an old acquaintance of mine," the Camp Director revealed, which caused not only Richardson's girlfriend to cry out in frustration, but other campers to feel both fear and uncertainty. "I do not condone his actions, they are of his own volition. However, I have done all I can to ensure the safety of everyone in this camp. What happens outside of it is another matter entirely."

This wasn't the answer a lot of the people in attendance were looking for.

This isn't good. Everyone was already on edge before. But now… I can feel their anger… their rage… their…

"And what about Bill?" another voice suddenly called out. This time it was none other than Shannon. After she spoke, it was as if all those near her were suddenly dispersed and tossed aside because no one dared be in close proximity to her. Lucas saw the determination both in her eyes and the way she spoke.

I hope you're ready Boris, just in case, Lucas thought, hoping Henry would be thinking the same thing.

"Does Bill's life mean any less than the lives lost? He's also a counselor like they were. He had JUST become one and was then sent out on a mission; when you knew that there was a crazy lunatic out there with a personal grudge against you! Did I miss anything, Director?"

Henry's composure was beginning to betray him. He looked like Lucas did before he was about to faint, or like a fuse before it reached its destination.

"While, you are absolutely correct, young Shannon," Henry said in a shriveling tone. "Bill was sent out on a mission knowing full well of the dangers that were out there. Moreover, my dear, he will no longer be able to hold the title of Camp Counselor."

This was news to everyone it seemed, and Shannon most of all looked to be furious to hear it.

"Do you have any idea how hard he worked to become a counselor? It's all he ever dreamed of. He admires and respects both you and your son so much that he wants to work for you and help others like him!" In a rare instance, Shannon began to tear up, a sight Lucas was sorry he had to witness. "Are you going to tell me that means nothing to you? When was this decision made? What right do you have to decide he isn't fit for it anymore?"

"This discussion is best taken in private, my dear, if you please—"

"No! Tell everyone here the truth. We all deserve to know, because if it's that easy to lose something, whether that's our lives or our place here, why do we even come to this camp? What's the point of it all?"

Shannon's words were beginning to do more harm than good. With tensions rising, Boris was beginning to motion himself towards Shannon, but one look from Henry caused him to stop where he was.

Is Henry really confident he can talk her down in front of everyone? I just don't see that happening.

"Bill's power is now unstable," the Camp Director revealed. "A Camp Counselor who cannot control their abilities is no longer fit to teach others to control theirs. He will receive proper care and in time a new purpose will be bestowed upon him. All I ask for is patience from all of you. I realize this is a bold request, but it must be done. As for why you are all here, it's quite simple; you all possess the capability to do great good or great evil with your unique abilities. What you choose to do with them I cannot decide for you. I can only guide you all in the necessary steps to becoming your ideal selves. I have failed many though, just as I have also aided those who worked for it."

Lucas understood the middle ground the Camp Director was fighting for. He wasn't trying to sell his earlier pitch but reinforce it.

Something about the way he talks rallies people to him, similarly to how I felt during one of those activities I did last year. But there's something different about the way he's talking right now.

Lucas was grateful when Shannon didn't pick this up. Instead, she looked to be calming down and wiped the tears from her eyes.

"I understand that sir," she said, almost meekly. "Of course I understand. What made Bill's power unstable? What did that mind freak do to him?"

Before the Camp Director could say anything, Daniel took it upon himself to say something.

"We don't know what caused his abilities to become unstable. The boy who came with Bill might have those answers. When he awakens, I plan to interrogate him and find out exactly what he knows. Do you concur, father?"

Quite the contrary, Henry looked about ready to plunge at his son with all he had but stopped himself with a long heavy sigh.

"Indeed, questioning the boy is our next step. Please resume regular activities and should any new information resurface, it will be shared," Henry assured everyone.

The crowd of campers dispersed as the Camp Director turned his gaze on his son.

"What is the meaning of this, Daniel?" the Camp Director whispered to his son. Henry's tone sounded uncharacteristically sharp like the slash of a knife.

"You're welcome, father. I just did you a favor," Daniel whispered back. "Do you realize how close Shannon was to convincing every one of your inactions in all this? At the rate she was going, she almost convinced me."

"Is that so? Why do you still remain then?"

The words hurt Daniel more than he showed, but he kept his resolve.

"There is much work to do in order to ensure the rest of the summer goes smoothly. That starts with finding out what Jacob and Alistair are up to. Bill may not be able to tell us much, but that kid can. That's why I mentioned him. Can't you see it was the right thing to do?"

His father's disapproval still lingered, but after a moment, like the crowd, it dispersed.

"It is, my son, but not this way. You should have trusted me to make this choice of my own accord. It was not yours to make in front of everyone."

"Was it your choice to leave me and my mother all those years ago?" Daniel asked, which only made his father shake his head and walk off. "Yeah, that's always the answer you give me, isn't it?"

Henry turned back, giving his son the hardest look Daniel had ever seen in his father. His eyes were like a raging ocean with waves beating against lone ships before dragging them down into the depths beneath.

"You would do well to put these childish insecurities behind you. A person in your position has little use for petty squabbles. Should this prove difficult for you, I can always give your job to another."

When Henry said this, he glanced at Zane, who was idly walking a couple feet away and eating an apple. Daniel noticed the brief look and felt a shudder go through him.

"You wouldn't… you couldn't…?"

The Camp Director prepared to part ways with his son and said the final words that would stay with both of them well into that night. "Don't presume what I can or will do. You may be my son, but I would sooner see you leave this camp than remain if you prove to become a liability."

Henry walked away, his feet stamping on the damp earth, while Daniel stood there motionless. His face fixed into a sharp expression that was only quelled by the openness of their discussion. To save face, he headed back to his tent, hoping to be alone for the rest of the day. It was at that moment when he felt the rush of sleep come to him…

When the fiasco in the stadium finally died down, all of Lucas' friends, including Shelly, went to visit Bill before attending the wake. Wanting to be alone and apart from people he knew for a bit, Lucas decided to pay his respects to the fallen counselors.

That was by far the scariest I've seen Henry get. I know it took everything he had not to lose his cool back there. I wish I knew what he was thinking at the time. When he talked to Daniel just now, he looked so upset despite being calm…

Just as he was nearing the small gathering at the Grand Hall, Lucas was intercepted by Zane.

"Why aren't you with the rest of your friends? Aren't they all visiting Bill?" Zane asked, still eating the apple he had had earlier.

Lucas nodded.

"Yeah, but I wanted to pay my respects to Alexander, Richardson, and Jane first."

"Why? You didn't really know them, did you? I knew them for a lot longer and even I didn't like them very much. Richardson sure but Alexander. The guy was a drill sergeant who enjoyed tormenting young campers. If you ask me, that isn't someone to revere even if they're dead. Jane, sure she was as 'sweet' as people love to say, but she had some sort of fixation on Daniel and that was never going to end well."

Lucas did not appreciate Zane bad mouthing the dead.

Isn't that disrespectful? You're not supposed to speak badly of the dead, no matter how true it is.

"That doesn't mean I can't still show respect to them. No matter how they were, they were a part of this camp and gave their lives trying to protect everyone."

"Correction; Richardson gave his life, only to abandon that girlfriend of his and their kid. Jane, I would also agree because her burns constitute the credit. Alexander took another way out and from what I heard you were there with him. Is that true?"

I don't want to talk about that. It isn't his business, Lucas insisted.

"He didn't know what he was doing," Lucas admitted to Zane's shocked silence. "He lost his best friend, and I could feel his pain like when I… No, I don't want to talk about this. Not to you."

Zane sighed and finished eating the apple. He tossed the core aside and shrugged.

"You definitely need to talk to someone. Take my advice though; don't talk to Daniel's girlfriend. She's more likely to spill those beans to Danny Boy the first chance she gets. She's not exactly licensed, you know. In any case, I should go check on that kid and see if he's conscious yet. Give the dead my best regards."

When Lucas entered the Grand Hall, he observed only ten campers in attendance for the memorial. Richardson's girlfriend sat in the far corner of the room, cradling her son. He also saw Margot and Lucinda next to her, comforting her. Lucas could feel they wanted to cry but were trying to be strong for their friend's loss.

It's not fair to them though, Lucas thought with sadness.

Lucas observed that the few campers in attendance weren't being respectful; they were sitting on top of the table used for the council meeting and laughing. Some were even playing cards and acted like they were in study hall.

Why aren't they treating this like the memorial it should be?

Lucas wondered why Margot and Lucinda didn't try to maintain order, but when he looked at them again, they had finally allowed themselves to begin crying.

Suddenly, a fist boomed on the table, causing the cards to jump up and scatter all over the floor like broken glass. The person who did this was Alexia, who gave the kids playing around a look of disapproval so sharp it could cut them to pieces.

If she had her warhammer with her, she could probably pound them in like nails.

"What is this?! Is this a social gathering or a memorial?" Alexia asked loudly. When the kids who were playing didn't offer a reply, she spoke up. "It's a memorial and if you can't be respectful here, then get out and don't let me see your faces again or they'll be facing the end of a toilet."

The kids hurried away, not picking up after themselves, and bolted through the doors of the Grand Hall. Some of Alexia's friends saw her do this and, not completely in on the situation, let out approving laughter.

It took her a few seconds after this to notice Lucas' presence. When Alexia did, she walked over to him with surprise.

"What are you doing here, Fargo? Shouldn't you be checking on Bill with the rest of your friends?" Alexia asked, irritably.

"I wanted to pay my respects. I promise I'll just be a moment."

The Camp Bully nodded but gestured to her friends.

"That's nice of you, but don't stay too long. They're not exactly happy to see you."

Lucas wasn't sure why Alexia said this until she realized who the group of kids were.

The orange team that we beat last year. Oh look, those are the ones who lost their hair because of Josh's sticky grenades. Their hair grew back but they still haven't forgotten.

Nodding, Lucas walked with Alexia to the front of the vigil that was set up for the fallen counselors. There were two separate pictures of the three deceased counselors. Richardson wore a striped T-shirt with long wavy hair while Alexander wore a suit and had neatly combed black hair. The two were teens in their picture with Richardson looking happy while Alexander had a solemn and unsmiling face. His eyes looked happy though to be by his friend's side. Jane looked beautiful with her long brunette hair in braids. Her smile displayed braces on her teeth, and in the picture, she wore glasses.

Is this the thanks these three counselors get for all they did? A nearly empty memorial and disrespectful campers?

"I can't speak for Jane because I didn't know her well," Alexia began, "but Richardson and Alexander. Even though they were mean, they got the job done. Do you remember last year when Richardson stopped me from pounding you right after you bumped into me?"

Lucas nodded, grimacing slightly, smiling at the memory.

I'm surprised she remembers that. The way she speaks about it is like a fond memory. I'm probably reading into that wrong. Despite this, he sensed nothing but sincerity from the Camp Bully.

"I spoke to him before he died, Alexander I mean," Lucas confessed as Alexia turned to look at him in disbelief. "I saw him take the pills. I didn't think he'd take enough to kill himself. I guess I should have told Henry."

Alexia gave Lucas a confused look.

"What do you mean? Are you trying to say he took a lot of pills on purpose?"

Lucas shrugged.

"I don't know for sure, but it looked that way," Lucas admitted. "Richardson and Alexander really were best friends. Inseparable, like mac and cheese."

Alexia let out a small giggle, which had been the first time Lucas had ever heard her laugh. She quickly turned this into a scoff as her friends turned to look at her.

"That is the lamest comparison I have ever heard of," Alexia berated loudly. "Alistair did this, didn't he?" the Camp Bully asked, returning to a whisper. "I know you don't want to hear it, Fargo, but Shannon is right. Not about Henry, but about him being friends with that monster. I hope I'm wrong, but if they're friends, what does that say about the rest of us? Would he betray Alistair for us? One way or another he will pay though. I'll make sure to get revenge for Richardson, Alexander, and Jane.

Lucas felt uncomfortable with that promise, not so much its validity, which he didn't doubt, but its ultimate resolve.

I don't know if that's a promise she will be able to keep. He isn't just a low-level thug that will be scared off by that huge hammer of hers like most people. He can light people on fire! That should count for some fear on anyone's part.

"What's been going on with you and Vanessa?" Alexia asked curiously, changing the subject. "She seems to be leaning more towards other people's sides than yours these days. In that last council meeting, you two didn't exactly see eye-to-eye with each other's ideas on how to save Bill. Are you guys having problems?"

Lucas shook his head and sighed. "It's complicated," he said, with hesitation and exertion. "Even though Bill is back, she still acts like he isn't, and she was ready to leave the camp to save him. I don't know what I would have done if she had.

"I would hope that you'd go after her, like a good boyfriend. So, are you two going to break up?" Alexia asked, almost eagerly.

Lucas did not want to answer this question, so he decided to change the subject abruptly.

"What do you think about that kid Bill brought back? I know he was with Jacob, but no one else here seems to recognize him."

Alexia considered this for a moment.

"It's suspicious. If you ask me, Bill should have let that kid stay where he was, even if he did help him escape, and that's based on what you saw right? Because I assume your abilities are somehow more accurate than Daniel's now."

This answer shocked Lucas, who realized just how intuitive Alexia was.

Stay inside inside thought; but I always believed Alexia was all about her big hammer and less about, well, people in general. Looks like I was way off.

The two were silent for a minute before Alexia said something.

"Either way, it doesn't help to be making up theories or ideas until we know more. For now, I say we hear what the kid has to say and go from there."

Lucas was surprised at how reasonable Alexia sounded. He almost forgot she was the Camp Bully.

"Do you believe in an afterlife?"

Lucas was shocked by this question. *And this entire conversation.* He thought about it for a moment, then shrugged and admitted to never giving it much thought.

"My parents are religious, but I never embraced the idea of people being good and going up above while the evil were cast down in a Lake of Fire," Alexia confessed. "I think if there is an afterlife, we are all doomed because none of us are pure enough to live together in peace. However, if it ends up being reincarnation, what does that say when we keep making the same stupid mistakes?"

Lucas continued to be surprised by her perspective on things.

It's strange to think that all this time, she had real thoughts about real problems. Even though I've read her mind before, and heard her thoughts, even now, she's saying more here than she's ever said even inside her own head.

"This place is amazing," Alexia said with a sigh. When Lucas looked at her, he saw small glistening tears forming in her eyes. "I never want to leave or grow old enough to be a counselor. The real world isn't exactly the best place for people like us. You can imagine not everyone makes it out there, even those Henry claims to have helped."

Lucas nodded, understanding this better than Alexia might believe.

She's showing a vulnerability I've never seen before. I can feel her emotions too, which is good because I don't want to read her mind. Let her keep her thoughts to herself. Her emotions say all I need to know.

"Well, as nice as this has been, I better get back to my friends. May you find peace and joy wherever you are, Mr. Richardson, Mr. Alexander, and Ms. Jane."

After she said this, Alexia strolled back to her friends and called out to Lucas in a boisterous voice.

"I hope you'll think twice before you mess with me, *Mind Freak*!" to which her friends burst into even more laughter like a chorus.

Thanks, Alexia, I needed this more than you know.

Lucas turned to look at Richardson's girlfriend while the two counselors finally decided to try and get the kids in attendance to behave. He imagined what he would say to her but didn't believe his words would do the feeling justice.

I can hear her thoughts and feel what she is feeling; it's too much for me. Too much conflict and sadness.

Lucas walked up to her and offered his condolences.

"I'm very sorry for your loss, ma'am," he said.

Richardson's girlfriend regarded him with a simple nod, and he expected that to be the end of it. Before he could leave, she called out to him.

"Your name is Lucas, right?"

Lucas turned around and nodded.

"Alexander told me about you. When he was lucid enough to talk that is. He said how you came and offered your condolences for Richardson to him. Thank you for that."

Lucas smiled and nodded.

"You've spoken with the Camp Director in private?"

The question made him uncomfortable.

What is she implying? Why ask me that here and now?

"What do you want to know?" Lucas heard himself say suspiciously.

Of all the times for an inside thought to…!

"Just… the next time you talk to him, please tell the Camp Director to not let their deaths be in vain. I don't want any more lives lost because of him."

Lucas nodded but wasn't sure if she meant Alistair or Henry in that last instance.

Maybe I heard her wrong.

Leaving the Grand Hall, Lucas began making his way to the hospital ward. Just as he was about to enter, Josh emerged with a shocked expression.

"Lucas, Bill is awake and is asking for you!" he exclaimed without signing.

Lucas rushed with him to the ward and entered with hesitation. Other campers were gathered around, as if something big were about to happen.

It looks like the whole camp is here.

When Josh and Lucas entered Bill's room, their former cabin mate was sitting up on his bed. Vanessa and Shannon were beside him when they both noticed the newcomers. Vanessa gave Lucas a concerned look.

You shouldn't be here, Lucas, Vanessa thought in fear.

Bill turned his head to the side and pressed his upper lip on his blistered lower lip when he heard someone enter the room.

"Lucas, is that you?" Bill croaked, his voice sounded like someone who has spent hours screaming. "How did I get here? Are the other kids here also?"

Lucas walked over to his friend. He observed the bandages on Bill's eyes, how they held back the red beams that appeared to be an upgraded version of his original heat vision. Bill's left hand was bandaged and the tips of three of his fingers appeared shorter than they should be. This was the hand he used to scratch at the cloth covering his eyes.

"I don't know," Lucas admitted for both answers, "but I can honestly say I'm so happy you're back. We were going to get you. We had a meeting about it and—"

"Vanessa told me," Bill croaked, his head turning in his sister's direction. One of his hands was clasped in hers, and the other hand was in Shannon's. "Why did this happen to me, Lucas? All those kids and they said I was the only one who survived..."

That was when a particular question hit Lucas' mind. It flew out of his mouth so fast he didn't even think it clearly before it was out in the open.

"Did you tell them anything?" Lucas said. The question seemed to offend Bill, who raised his head to the sound of Lucas' voice.

"Did I tell them anything? That's a really stupid question. I didn't get to do much talking when they were shoving a drink down my throat," Bill was near screaming. He swatted Vanessa's other hand away when she tried to touch his shoulder. "All I know is they wanted you, so this happened because of *you*!"

Lucas began to hear his former cabin mate's thoughts in his head. They were beating against the inside of his skull like hammers.

His mind is very loud right now, Lucas noted painfully. He read the most coherent of the rapid thoughts.

They wanted him, not me! They did this to me because of him. Why did this happen to me?!

Behind the others, Daniel watched in case the situation escalated.

"Alistair wanted you, Lucas. *You*," Bill repeated in an agonized tone. "I don't know what you did to piss him off, but *I* had to pay for it. I never did *anything* to him. My only crime was being your *best friend*!"

Josh only understood the words '*best friend*' and raised his hand in objection.

"Hey, get in line pal. *I'm* his best friend ��, Josh remarked in an attempt to be humorous.

Bill was anything but amused.

"Not according to the other Mind Freak, Deaf Boy."

When Josh understood the '*Deaf Boy*' part, he retreated and kept his mouth shut the rest of the time.

That was a low blow, even for Bill, Lucas thought.

Lucas was speechless. He tried thinking about what was happening and how he could turn it around.

I get it; Bill's mad at me and rightfully so. But it isn't like we were going to leave him behind. What about what Henry said? The whole wiping his mind? Can I actually do it? I said I wouldn't but…

Lucas shook his head, trying to chase the thought and impulse away. He knew in his heart it was wrong and stood by that feeling. Taking the high road became the only option.

"I don't know what to say," Lucas finally said with regret.

Bill's teeth clenched as hard as a fist, with his voice booming like the sound of thunder.

"You could say 'I'm sorry', and I could say 'Go to hell'!"

This caused Vanessa to slap Bill hard on the cheek.

"How *dare* you, Bill! He is my boyfriend, and he was worried sick about you. We all were."

When Bill didn't reply, Vanessa continued. "We voted to go save you. Lucas and Zane were going to go. I would have gone if they hadn't let me. My point is that you're angry at the wrong person."

Shannon glared at Vanessa for the slap, but when her gaze returned to her boyfriend, it softened considerably.

"Do you need something for the pain, Bill?" Shannon asked, as she called out for a nurse to come in.

Bill quickly shook his head.

"No, no more medicine. Please. I'll be fine." His head turned around instinctively, as if he were trying to get home in on a specific location. "Where's Devon?"

Most of the occupants in the room didn't seem to know who he meant except Lucas and Daniel.

"He's the kid I came in with. He helped me escape. If it wasn't for him… Where is he?"

"He's being monitored for suspicious behavior," Daniel spoke up. "The boy was with Jacob for quite some time, and we want to make sure his mind is still his own."

Bill perked up slightly at the sound of Daniel's voice.

"Please, I want to talk to him, Daniel," Bill pleaded in a soft voice. "He isn't like the rest of those children. He wasn't being mind controlled."

"How can you know that?" Daniel asked Bill. Lucas thought the same question but kept it to himself.

Coming from him will sound a lot better in this situation.

"Because he told me."

"Told you what?"

Bill's face turned in Lucas' direction. Even though he couldn't see, he still seemed to be able to see in a different sense.

"Not with him here," Bill announced. Lucas felt all eyes on him, and Daniel got in between the two.

"Everyone else will need to leave as well," Daniel announced. The rest of the campers scurried off, with Lucas following behind Shelly.

Why is he blaming me? We tried to help him. We wanted to. He should be grateful. I hate that he said those things about me. They're not true; none of it is. None is not true; they're not of it.

He felt anger building up inside of him. It didn't take long for Lucas to catch the attention of his sister, who laid a soft hand on his shoulder. He quickly swatted it away, but she persisted.

"It wasn't your fault, Lucas. Bill was upset even before you got there. I told Josh to tell you not to come, but he didn't understand me.

Lucas shook his head.

"He's not wrong; I am the reason that happened to him. I saw what they did to him, when they fed him that liquid he mentioned. Maybe if I had more control of my abilities. I could have done something. Maybe I should have wiped his memory of…"

Shelly spun her brother around and stared him straight in the eyes.

"No, don't you *dare* finish that sentence, Lucas!" Shelly shouted as she struggled to fight back the tears that were forming. Lucas was stunned into silence.

"You are not that person. Your abilities are not for that. You have this incredible gift, Lucas. Even before your abilities became a part of you, you always could make people feel seen just by being near them. I think the reason you never saw that was because you pushed others away."

Lucas was about to protest, recalling his memories of his youth; these consisted of his peers bullying him and his teachers thinking the worst of him before he could mess up. Shelly continued speaking.

"You're a good person who focused too much on the bad from people around you. It wasn't until you came to this camp that you started seeing the good as well. There's so much good out there, Lucas, and once you embrace what you can do, I promise, you'll find your crowd."

My crowd? I've never had that. I never thought I wanted that. But I do. I want to belong.

Lucas nodded, embraced Shelly and apologized. He kept thinking about the word 'crowd' when Ashley and Hailey approached the two of them.

"I'll see you later, Luke," Shelly told him. Lucas nodded as the three of them walked off.

Lucas sighed and walked off towards his cabin. He was about to enter when he saw something that caused him to pause in his tracks. At first, he thought his eyes were playing tricks on him and that he was seeing an apparition. However, what started as a shadowed form slowly began to materialize in front of him. The new being had a scalp full of bright white hair and a thin calculating sneer, but what really shook Lucas was its eyes. Eyes which glowed a menacing red hue.

Lucas' concentration broke and he decided he needed sleep. That night he had no dreams.

The next day he saw something that took him by surprise and made him forget his appetite for lunch altogether.

What are they doing together?!

Chapter 17: The Weeping Willow

Early that next morning, Ashley walked with Jeremy towards their planned destination. She thought about turning down his offer to get something to eat, thinking it would seem like a date when it wasn't what she wanted. Both Hailey and Shelly had encouraged her to give him a chance.

"He's really handsome and all the girls here like him" Hailey insisted, giving off a slight look of envy as she said this. "He's not as cute as Josh though, but he's definitely in the top two."

Shelly nodded in agreement about Jeremy, while also bringing up something Ashley thought about often.

"My brother will be so jealous to see you move on from him," Shelly said playfully. "In all seriousness, you deserve to be someone's first choice and Jeremy asked you out. So, I say give him a chance."

Relenting, Ashley went along with the date hoping it wouldn't take up too much time. She wanted to discuss the encounter with Bill to Lucas, knowing he would be feeling upset about it.

I wish I could have said something then, but I know it wouldn't have helped, she noted to herself. She glanced at Jeremy who was walking at a steady pace. He wore a blue flannel over a purple camp shirt. His cabin's words were embroiled on the front, and his hair was combed backwards to show a broad forehead. Ashley thought he looked slightly older for his age.

I know he's around my age, but he looks more like someone who just graduated from high school.

Jeremy seemed to notice the silence and brief glance, giving Ashley a brief smile.

"Thank you for agreeing to this time alone," Jeremy said with gratitude. In the time they walked, he made no effort to brush her hand or touch her shoulder.

I can always move faster than the time it takes him to put one finger on me.

She stared down at her shoes and noted their worn-out appearance. These were the third pair she had replaced since coming to camp and a new pair would need to be called upon soon.

"Yeah, thanks for the invite." Ashley was preparing to make her way to the cafeteria, when Jeremy walked past it as if it wasn't there. "I thought we were eating in the cafeteria for lunch?"

Jeremy shook his head.

"I never said there. There's a spot where the forge is that I think is a bit more private."

Ashley began to get a bad feeling. More than butterflies in her stomach, but the feeling of being alone with a boy who was known for 'playing the field'. Not wanting to make her uncomfortable feeling known, she sighed and silently went along with it.

For some reason, Ashley felt watched, like something was looming in the background. Her eyes darted as fast as her speed towards a corner where a shadow apparition was attempting to take on a clumsy form. This looked like someone she knew, and she couldn't shake the feeling that this person was closer to her than she wanted to admit.

I'm not thinking about him right now. Why would I see that and think of him?

She wasn't sure if it was her speed at work or attention span, but either way she was at the spot Jeremy mentioned and as advertised, it was indeed private. It was similar to an outdoors restaurant, complete with a small fence, benches, and lamps to illuminate the occasion.

"This was an idea I had last year that Henry finally did," Jeremy admitted when he gestured for Ashley to take a seat opposite him. "I mostly wanted it as a place to relax after a hard day of forging, and I also thought it would be cool for occasions like this."

"Like what?" Ashley asked, bemused.

"Like getting to know each other," Jeremy revealed. He brought out what looked like a picnic basket which contained various foods from the cafeteria. It was like he raided the kitchens and brought leftovers as well. "I didn't know what you'd like so I got you a bit of everything. Are you allergic to any foods?"

Ashley nodded. "Tomatoes. I can't eat anything with tomatoes."

This revelation caused Jeremy to frown when he looked at some of the foods he had that contained tomatoes in them.

It's a very mild allergy, but I spotted some pizza slices and burgers in there, Ashley thought to herself, smiling slightly.

"That's okay. We've got some stuff with cheese, milk, and corn. Are those alright?"

Ashley nodded again, not wanting to overplay her hand. As Jeremy began to set down some food, consisting of a cheese sandwich, tatter tots, and corn on the cob for Ashley, she glanced once more at the corner where she saw the familiar apparition. This time the form looked more materialized and less unfocused. This person had long shaggy hair that appeared like the heads of trees. He was crouching in a corner with a fixed expression in his eyes.

That can't be… No way… Is that…?

Before she could finish the thought, her eyes went to Jeremy's plate which included a steak burger, two tacos, and mixed fruits.

"I hope you're hungry, because there's more where this came from," Jeremy noted with a smile as he brought out plastic utensils. He handed Ashley hers and his fingers briefly brushed against hers. She recoiled faster than she had intended. If he noticed, he didn't call attention to it.

"For drinks I have soda, water, and carbonated water. What's your poison?"

"My what?"

Jeremy shook his head and pulled out one of each.

"I'll have these out and you can get what you want." He said this with a hint of annoyance in his tone. It didn't take long for him to appear regretful. "I'm sorry, I know this is a different setting than where everyone usually is and I get it if you're not completely comfortable with me. The truth is I really like you and want to date you."

Ashley felt herself flush at this, not from shyness but more from a place of shock.

"You want to date me? When you can date any girl in this camp?"

Jeremy nodded and appeared surprised by this question.

"I like that you're not like those girls. When we've talked, I can tell you're not just admiring the muscles on my body or the shape of my chin. I had one girl tell me my chin looked like that old actor in the *Evil Dead* movies. Bruce something, I forget his last name."

Ashley chuckled and shook her head.

"I don't see it."

"The chin? Yeah me neither."

"No, I mean you liking me like that. I just keep to myself and that's how I prefer it."

"What about with that guy Lucas? He's clearly got a lot of issues going on and needs to figure himself out before he can be with anyone."

Ashley felt herself flush again, this time from annoyance at his name and the last comment in particular.

"Lucas has been through a lot and is still growing as a person," Ashley said defensively. "He's my friend and someone I care a lot about. I just wish he'd see me the way I see him."

Ashley caught herself and dropped her eyes in embarrassment. However, when she looked up, she saw the understanding in Jeremy's eyes. She imagined how that revelation must have made him feel.

He's probably thinking, 'she's still in love with him. How long does it take to get over someone? Maybe I don't really like her after all.'

"If he doesn't see you the way you want after everything you've done for him, forgive me for saying so, then he doesn't deserve you," Jeremy admitted. He had finished his meal and was beginning to get more food. "Do you want more food? You already finished what you had."

Ashley was surprised to notice that she had eaten all her food in the time it took her to think her last thoughts. She was either very hungry or eating her feelings.

I'd say a bit of both since Lucas is making me want to bite down on a chicken bone right now.

She tried wiping her mouth, but her arm moved downwards instead of to her lips. Ashley nearly spilled her drink but regained her composure.

"So what do you think? Would you be interested in dating?" Jeremy asked Ashley again. He gave her a patient look but she could tell that he was putting on the kind of smile someone saving face would wear. Instead of giving him a direct answer, Ashley decided to redirect the conversation.

"What's your condition and how does it go with your ability?"

Jeremy noticed the quickness in the shift but regardless obliged her wishes.

"I have osteoporosis. It's because I suffer from low vitamin D. Do I get enough sunlight? Sure I do, but I need to be careful because my bones are delicate. The cool thing is my ability works in different ways."

Jeremy began to explain this in great detail to the point where Ashley only retained the main parts: "The sun gives me strength, and can heal most wounds, except broken bones. It also makes me immune to fire which is why the Forge is a perfect place for me. Of course all that is during the daytime hours. No nightshifts for me."

He let out a mild chuckle, which Ashley returned with a half-hearted one.

"But yeah, I've suffered four fractures since before coming to camp. One happened when I fell off my bike. Another happened after I got into a fight with some guy at school. Hence the chin and jaw." Ashley noticed now how his chin did look like that Bruce actor he mentioned. "The third time was when I fell down the stairs at home. The fourth time, ironically, was last year here in Camp when I ended up hitting my hand with my forging hammer."

Jeremy brought up his plain looking hand which had a purplish look to it.

"It healed but the bruise never went away. Now it looks like a grape. It does make for a funny story though, don't you think?"

Ashley's attention was back on their uninvited guest.

"Excuse me, I need to use the facilities," Ashley abruptly said. She crawled away from her place on the bench and moved so fast that the person she ran towards jumped backwards at her arrival. "What are you doing here, Lucas?"

Lucas looked up at Ashley who appeared very annoyed at him.

"I heard a noise nearby and thought I should check it out," Lucas told Ashley. "It just so happens I also saw you and James something there together. What is that? A date?"

Ashley frowned, crossing her arms against her chest.

"Not that it's any of your business but yes, *Jeremy* asked me out and we were having lunch together. Is that a problem for you?"

Lucas threw up his hands defensively, as if surrendering to an enemy foe.

"Hey, what you do in your free time is your business."

"You got that right. Now what were you looking at?"

When Lucas didn't understand the question, Ashley rephrased it.

"You said you heard a noise nearby. Did you see something also?"

Hesitantly, Lucas nodded and mentioned the shadow figure that appeared like a combination of more than one thing.

It's like the one I saw just a moment ago. Are they the same or different?

"Are you alright, Lucas?"

"Yeah I'm fine. How about you? Don't let me keep you from that guy over there," Lucas added in a sulky way.

Why can't he just talk to me? I know something is bothering him and it isn't just the circumstances, Ashley thought sorrowfully.

"Alright yeah, I should go back. I'm always here if you want to talk, Lucas. I mean it."

She was about to turn and speed back towards Jeremy when her peripheral vision noticed that Lucas was shaking. He appeared to be sweating as well and looked like he would begin melting like ice.

"What's wrong, Lucas? Do you want me to get your sister? We can go to my cabin and I'll just let Jeremy know I had to leave for something else."

Lucas shook his head and began panting as if he had been running for miles. The rest of the words Ashley said became incoherent to him.

"No… It need to sleep. I mean *I* need sleep."

Suddenly, the daytime sky darkened. A giant overhead cloud covered the sun, and a giant fireball soared down towards the camp. It made contact near where the tents were. One burst into flames instantly. Naomi cried out and ran towards it. She cried out to her boyfriend, Marcus, who was last seen in the tent.

Another fireball impacted nearby where the forge was. Jeremy was thrown backwards, with one of the benches landing on top of his legs, crushing them both. He cried out in pain and tried to lift the bench on his own.

The sun's covered; he can't use his powers, Ashley noted. She speeded towards Jeremy and lifted the bench off his legs. Indeed they looked like mashed potatoes. Ashley lifted him up and looked around, searching for Lucas. He was still in the same corner as where he had been earlier. His face was turned away from her and looking at something in the darkness of that spot. She noticed the sudden darkness that was engulfing the camp. Shadows were more pronounced here and began to slither on the ground like snakes.

Screams followed while Henry rushed outside with Boris and the surviving counselors in an attempt to find the source of the attack. More fireballs began to rain down on them as if a dragon was attacking from above. Ashley saw Henry's eyes dart in all directions. She was the one who found the source of the attack; it was a figure similar to the one Lucas mentioned. It had no physical form, only a mishmash of other parts that made it look like a collage.

"Everyone take cover!" Henry shouted as another attack came from above the cloudy darkened skies. The fireball was heading towards a group of frightened young campers, so fast it would be impossible to dodge it in time.

No. I need to do something.

Ashley took a deep breath, stamped her shoes to the ground, with Jeremy on her side, and deposited him swiftly with another group of campers who were helping each other move. He was whimpering and crying out in pain as they led him to his cabin. The latest fireball was so close to the younger campers that when Ashley moved to save them, the impact blast sent her and the other four children rolling on the field as if they were bowling balls. When she came to, her shoes were scorched at the soles of her feet.

There goes that pair.

When another fireball fell down, Boris threw himself in front of the fireball, shielding a group of younger campers, and was burned in the back badly. He wailed in pain and dropped to one knee while pressing a hand firmly on the ground. The children below him ran away fearfully, but the Camp Guardian appeared to be balancing himself between the act of staying awake and falling unconscious.

Henry rushed to the monster's side and instructed the counselors to assist in getting the rest of the campers to safety. Naomi was forced to compose herself as she led the young campers towards one side of the camp that was away from the flames and burning tents. Zane did his best to help as well but found the raucous wails of the children to be too much for him. He groaned and shot a bolt of lightning in the direction where shadows were forming what looked like a dust devil. They seemed to recoil a little bit due to the flash of the lighting strike but quickly returned and began to take more ground in the camp.

What is happening? Who's shooting those fireballs? Where did those clouds come from?

The monster whimpered and had his eyes closed the whole time as his back sizzled like a burning barbecue pit. Henry did his best to tend to the wounds but it was clear the damage was extensive. Ashley looked back and forth now, trying to locate Lucas. When she saw him, he wasn't himself…

In all the commotion, Lucas' eyes were fixated on the shadowy figure that appeared to be a canvas with various crude brushstrokes.

It's him again…I can't move. No, not again, please, not again, I…I don't want to die…

He heard a voice speak inside his head; it wasn't singular but felt like multiple sounds talking at once.

It's like this one. Abomination written all over it. Unconsciously aware of surroundings. Look forward but don't look back. Ni ighlt heter si kardensse. Control it, so it doesn't control you.

In a flash, Lucas found himself with someone's arms wrapped around him. Together, they were hurling away from what appeared to be another fireball. He had heard a few of these but none had come close to his location. The person holding him was Ashley and both of them staggered upwards. When Lucas tried to rise, his right ear rang like the end of a telephone line and his eyes twitched as he struggled to keep them open. Dazedly, his eyes saw the shadowed figure disappear with a final word from his sponsor: *We'll meet again soon, when the blood moon rises.*

Ashley acted fast and helped Lucas up towards her cabin. It all happened so fast; his mind was spinning like a merry-go-round, as he tried to grasp the situation and keep himself from losing his balance.

Wha…what's happening to me, I…I can't feel anything. No… wait… I feel everything… too much now… much too now… chum oto won…

When they were safely inside her cabin, Ashley barred the door and peered outside to see the screams and sobbing of the campers. Some were barricaded inside their cabins and others were with the remaining counselors.

Finally, when Lucas composed himself, he realized what cabin they were in. This was the first time he had ever been inside The Weeping Willow. There were five beds, all within inches from each other. Their TV room and kitchen were adjacent to each other to the back of the cabin, with a back door for their bathroom. The perks of the cabin was a small little willow tree which was planted in the center where the beds were spread out. It seemed to pass on a sort of aroma inside the cabin. It was a calm feeling that Lucas began to feel, but something was off.

His mind was racing faster than a hamster on a wheel and he had trouble distinguishing reality from the dysfunction inside his head. He saw images of his father and mother, both happy, with Shelly smiling beside them.

But I'm not in this picture, Lucas realized as his figure became as dark as a shadow. *Where am I? Is this before or after? What happened to then and now? Right and wrong? Girth dan grown.*

He also saw Henry, as he appeared the previous year, animated and lively, but now fragile and elderly. Daniel cast a black shadow that seemed to illuminate his father's figure, while Jacob and Alistair cast larger shadows that threatened to swallow everyone in Lucas' view.

One sun rises so another can fall. Easy prey or easy ally.

Meanwhile, Ashley didn't seem to notice his distress and blushed since this was the first time he came to her cabin.

"This is my cabin, The Weeping Willow. I guess I should show you around since you're already here."

Ashley pointed to one of the beds that was closest to the window of the cabin.

"Your sister's bunk is next to that one. Mine is near the window and Hailey's is over here. The other side is where Valerie and Lily sleep. You can sleep on my bed if you want. I'll take Shelly's for right now. Hopefully things will settle down now that it looks like it's getting calmer."

Unbeknownst to Ashley, Lucas was not hearing a word she said.

Leave now. We don't want you here anymore. You're disgusting. Monster! A mistake just waiting to happen. Wasted potential. Use your abilities to get what you want.

Ashley's voice became incoherent to his ears, as if she spoke another language.

One less thing for him to worry about. Just know this is for him.

Lucas was still covered in dirt and pieces of grass, while his right ear continued to ring. It stung like an open wound.

Oh yes brother, we will both *be there when this one dies, yes indeed.*

His heart was pumping at a dangerous rate and his hands began to tremble violently.

Ugh… Ach… Agh…!

He *feeds you promises like food. You eat it up. Guzzle guzzle. Yum yum. Think for yourself! Live in the moment. It drifts away and ignores all in attendance. Laughing at the pain of others before one's own is understood. Can a mirror reveal more than what the eyes can see?*

Lucas' moods erratically changed from panic, to angry, to dreary. He began sobbing one moment, and another laughing manically. Ashley took his hand in hers and stroked his fingers.

"Are you alright, Lucas? Please, tell me what's wrong. What's happening to you?"

After a moment of shaking and shivering, he finally stopped.

What's happening to me? I can't feel my body, my legs, my arms…Wh…Wha….No...not you! Please don't hurt me! Get away from me you monster!

Lucas became unresponsive, his eyes unblinking and his face still. Ashley put a hand on his shoulder, feeling the warmth his body radiated like a heater in full blast.

"Lucas, please talk to me. Lucas…"

Suddenly, Alistair appeared in front of Lucas. The shadow he saw earlier took form to reveal the golden haired man reflecting in his eyes. Without thinking clearly, he lurched forward, tackled Alistair to the ground and pounded all his emotions on his face.

At first the hits were mild but became more and more aggressive as the memory of falling and the smiling shadow came back to him.

GAH! AH! STOP! NO PLEASE! LEAVE ME ALONE! I don't want to die! I don't want to die!

"I DON'T WANT TO DIE!"

He felt his knuckles beating against Alistair's defenseless face as he continued to smile and laugh maniacally. He turned from cheek to cheek as Lucas' knuckles punched one, then another, and another.

It lasted for what seemed like a long period of time until he suddenly regained his senses and realized to his horror what he had done. His knuckles were bruised and he was sweating as if he had just finished jogging. It wasn't Alistair's face beaten down below him; it was Ashley's. She lay there, unresponsive. Her face was unrecognizable. Lucas cried loudly as he clasped his own face and muffled a scream.

Done I have what?... I have done what?!

A banging at the door came abruptly as Daniel and the others broke down the door to her cabin. They heard Lucas' agonized scream and rushed to find the source of the commotion. When Lucas and Ashley were in sight, everyone stared at the two in complete horror. Hailey shrieked in terror at the sight of her best friend lying on the ground motionless. Shelly saw the horror and stared at her brother in terror. The Camp Director looked neither shocked nor horrified. Lucas shivered and appeared like a rabid animal. The cabin's entrance was filled with a mixture of confliction, as Lucas muttered in-between babbles "I didn't mean to. Please, I didn't mean to."

Henry uttered only four single words in response.

"What have you done…?"

Chapter 18: Consequences

Foolish **boy***. Knows not what he wants.*

That night, Lucas was detained and locked up inside of his cabin, as the remaining counselors and Henry discussed the course of action for his assault on Ashley. These were the facts, while the Camp recovered from the fireballs and shadowy presence, Lucas underwent a spiral of emotions that ultimately led him to nearly beating the life out of his friend Ashley. She was now in the hands of the emergency staff at the ward and he was not allowed anywhere near her. The voices in his head were as loud as megaphones and he had a harder time than usual ignoring them.

Injure the cause, join the revolt. Like black stains on a white shirt, it's now there for others to see. Can't keep it to yourself.

That's not me saying or thinking these things. Who is it and why? Why?!

Boris was stationed in front of his cabin despite his injuries. He was covered in bandages and soot, his stature appearing not to show any discomfort. Lucas couldn't see the Camp Guardian's face but read his emotions, which were both conflicted and angry.

"Why did you do it, Lucas? What could have made you do such a horrible thing to someone as good and kind as Ashley," Boris asked him bitterly.

Lucas could not justify himself as he stood at the doorway to the cabin, with Boris's back against the door like a brick wall.

"I didn't mean to hurt her. Please, Boris, you have to believe me."

Boris didn't like the word choice and did not respond after that. When it didn't seem like the Camp Guardian was going to talk anymore, Lucas finally gave up and huddled near a corner, rocking himself while beginning to sob. He looked at his hands, which were shaking, while his knuckles were heavily bruised.

A big reason Boris was bitter towards Lucas about Ashley's condition is because the Camp Guardian himself was the one who carried the wounded camper to the ward and did all that he could to soothe her pain. As he led her there, she begged for Lucas to stop hitting her.

Boris told me that she was barely conscious. But she kept saying my name, and what I did to her… what did I to Ashley…

Meanwhile, in the Grand Hall, Henry took Lucas' side, knowing of his severe form of bi-polar, but Daniel was firmly against letting Lucas go without punishment.

"Father, Lucas did an unforgivable crime," Daniel declared furiously, "he must be punished. You cannot just wipe the slate clean! Not this time!"

The other two counselors were inactive on the issue: Naomi was still grieving for Marcus. There was nobody from the wreckage of the tent, but she knew that he had been inside when it went ablaze. Zane, on the other hand, had no quarrel against Lucas. He would no sooner condemn him for his actions but voicing this opinion wouldn't do any good. So he kept the thought to himself and fidgeted with a hole in his jeans. It was up to Shelly and a few other cabin leaders to defend Lucas' case.

I'm technically not a cabin leader, but since Ashley can't be here, I was allowed to take her place.

"My brother has a history of violent mood-swings, this is true, but he would never intentionally hurt anyone," Shelly revealed as she thought about the memory of when she saw her father after Lucas ran away.

She hadn't seen her brother strike at their father, but she saw how he looked after Lucas was gone. How he sobbed afterwards, asking where he went in what seemed like complete confusion.

Lucas didn't even hit him, thought Shelly. *Dad was more confused than upset, like he had been abruptly awakened from a deep sleep. They wanted to go out and search for my brother, but I didn't want to mislead them. They never left the house after that…*

"Before my brother left home for camp, he assaulted our father," Shelly heard herself reveal, but just as quickly she continued. "But he didn't hurt him badly. It was just a mild hit. What you're describing, how he attacked Ashley, isn't like anything he's capable of doing without thinking clearly. Something must have triggered him. You all should be trying to help my brother instead of condemning him!" Shelly insisted stubbornly. "I thought that's what this place was all about, or am I wrong?

Daniel was unmoved.

"We've given him many chances to come forward about any problems he may have. I understand the loss of your parents was overwhelming to both of you, but that is no excuse for his actions now. We can't pretend what happened to Ashley was an accident because that would be far from the truth!

For all we know, maybe Lucas is crazier than anyone here cares to admit. You said it yourself just now; he attacked his own father without provocation."

Daniels' tone was rising as he continued.

"No, that's not it at all. Please let me explain—"

"Explain? How do you explain an assault on a fellow camper, a close friend of yours, at the hands of your brother?" Daniel asked angrily. "Ashley means a lot to me and she is my responsibility. I was the one who invited her to come to camp, and this incident is my fault for not doing something sooner about Lucas. No, the time for understanding is over. Now it's time to do something that should have been done a long time ago. Father, the decision ultimately must be unanimous, this is what I believe must be done: Lucas should be banished from Camp Supernatural, effective immediately. In the real world, he would be arrested on assault charges. But given his place here, the only suitable punishment is banishment. I consider that a mercy to what he did to Ashley and anything less than this consequence I won't stand for."

Shannon spoke next up.

"I don't know Lucas as well as the rest of you, but I don't think he's the sort of person who'd hurt anyone on purpose, let alone Ashley. It's clear based on their interactions that they are on good terms and it's more likely that she was attacked by someone else. There was a lot of confusion out there and we can't know all the facts since Ashley isn't awake right now."

Daniel scoffed at the attempt to defend Lucas and glared at her.

"You probably didn't notice but he looked as freaked out by Ashley's appearance as the rest of us. Not to mention his knuckles were bruised, so he must have attacked her," Daniel asserted defiantly. "You can't expect me to believe that he is innocent simply because it's what everyone wants him to be."

"I would never call Lucas a friend," Alexia's voice boomed, to the surprise of everyone in the Grand Hall. "But he was there for the Camp Counselor's wake earlier. Alexander, Richardson, and Jane all gave their lives for this camp. Everybody else was too busy with themselves or visiting Bill. Even you, Camp Activities Director Harrison, weren't there. Maybe Richardson and Alexander weren't the most liked counselors in camp, and maybe Jane was as sweet as everyone loves to say. The fact is Lucas took time to go and pay his respects, even when others who were there didn't take the loss seriously. I know he also tried to comfort Alexander before his death. That's more than anyone else here or in camp can say. We all just turned a blind eye to his pain. Just like

Lucas' pain was ignored. He cares about people, and someone like that couldn't have done what you say he did."

She's the girl who was picking on Sapphire before. I thought she hated Lucas. Wonders never cease, Shelly thought with a faint smile.

The Camp Activities Director looked unconvinced still.

"I mourn for them, along with Marcus now. I wish I could have known them better as friends instead of just co-workers, but we don't have the luxury of time here. I only want to see Lucas punished as he deserves to be and to make sure that no further harm comes to Ashley or anyone in camp for that matter. If he's capable of this, who's to say anyone else is safe with him around. It's Jacob all over again, father."

Henry did not look like the last part rubbed off on him well. Shelly could tell that the words awakened a dormant feeling that up until this point was like a distant sound, nearly forgotten.

Daniel really knows what buttons to press when it comes to his father.

"That is enough, Daniel," commanded his father, coldly, "I understand your position in this perfectly. You care deeply for Ashley, but our duty is to help all who come to this place. Even someone as lost as Jacob isn't always beyond hope. Regardless of all that, Lucas is a good person and capable of being saved. That is my promise. I will see to it that this does not happen again."

Daniel shook his head in disbelief and bit his lip.

"Father, why do you care so much about him? He's not your son. *I'm* your son. You're supposed to support *me*! Instead you defend a camper who is clearly guilty. If it were anyone else we wouldn't even be having this debate. You talk about helping other campers? What about those in the infirmary, or those who are six feet under?"

Henry softly shook his head.

"You don't know what you're talking about, Daniel. If there is nothing more to discuss, we can begin deliberation on helping Lucas regain control of himself," Henry said with a cold distant voice.

The Camp Activities Director felt as if he were being humiliated again, only this time there was an audience around. Henry only looked at him with those ocean blue eyes as the waves in them seemed to almost ripple with tension.

His eyes are old. Maybe older than the man himself.

Daniel looked conflicted at first, his face a contortion of muscles that were working against each other. It took a moment for him to compose himself, which is when he asked his father a question that appalled Shelly.

"How was Lucas injured last year, father?" Daniel asked with a more relaxed fixed tone.

Henry looked back at Daniel with uncertainty as all eyes in attendance became transfixed on them.

"He fell from a cliff," his father responded with a calm demeanor. Shelly remembered her brother telling her about it.

Lucas told me he got lost on his way back from training because of the rain. 'I woke up back in camp. That's all I remember.' I wanted to believe that, but I knew, somehow I knew, he lied.

The others nodded in agreement but Daniel was unconvinced.

"Why, father? Why would he be out there unless he tried to run away? It just so happens that the cliff and the Forest of Time are adjacent to each other."

The council considered this for a moment as Henry sat passively, with his long face appearing uninterested.

"Who said anything about my brother running away," Shelly interjected. "He told me that it was raining and he got lost on his way back to camp. What reason would Lucas have for wanting to leave camp?"

"To get back to you. It was all he talked about during his time here last year," Daniel revealed nonchalantly. "Keira, is my *father* lying about Lucas' accident??"

Keira fixed her gaze on the Camp Director.

"Did Lucas try to run away from camp the day he fell from the cliff?"

The Camp Director's expression was just as fixed as hers when he answered.

"He found himself away from the camp when his accident occurred. The circumstances of his accident are still not definitively known to me."

After a few seconds, Keira shook her head.

"He's… telling the truth," she responded uneasily.

Henry's gaze never left Daniels.

"What do you believe happened?"

"I believe Lucas tried to run away, he fell and you healed him somehow. Because whatever you did made him whole again," Daniel concluded. "He was broken beyond repair. He should never have been able to walk, let alone leave that bed ever again. Whatever you can do, it's capable of helping so many people in this camp better than even the best nurses and staff can."

Henry was silent. All eyes were suddenly on the Camp Director, waiting for his defense. With a sigh he relented.

"Yes, Daniel. I healed Lucas. Indeed, this power is very much a means to save many lives, but nothing is without consequence. Do you believe I should have done otherwise?"

Daniel shook his head.

"You used your powers on him, when you could have used them on Bill, Mike, and everyone else your 'friend' has ruined. What made their lives any less than Lucas'? You can't tell me after what he did to Ashley that he can just be allowed to go about his business as usual."

Henry nodded. His son bit his lower lip and twisted his head slowly, turning his attention to Shelly.

"I understand completely that he's had a difficult year. I am truly sorry, Shelly, for the loss you both suffered. It's a pain I am familiar with. Regardless, your brother broke the rules, and now, because he was allowed to stay, his actions almost cost the life of a beloved camper. I may be responsible for Ashley being here, but you're responsible for Lucas' place here, Father. If you had banished him a year ago, this wouldn't have happened at all. Alistair never came to camp until Lucas' arrived. Why is that? It seems like both of you have a particular interest in him all of a sudden."

Henry did not look at his son now and did his best to calm both himself and those in the Grand Hall who were beginning to see Daniel's point. Shelly feared what this meant for her brother's place in camp.

It doesn't sound like anyone want's what's best for Lucas but what they think is best for him.

"I know, Daniel," was the only response Henry offered.

Shelly could see the conflict in Daniel's eyes, reading the way his body was rocking itself back and forth. It was similar to how Lucas coped with anxiety.

"We need to restore morale in camp after this attack, and Lucas being around is too much of a risk for everyone here. If he had killed Ashley, I would—"

"But he didn't," Henry affirmed.

"But he *could* have! And who's to say he won't hurt someone else. He can't control his abilities. He's a danger to himself, and more importantly everyone here. He can't be trusted no matter how much you want him to stay."

"If Lucas goes, I go too," Shelly insisted to the disagreement of everyone in the Grand Hall. "He's my brother and I won't abandon him."

"I don't want you to go, Shelly," Daniel said, with true sympathy in his tone. "You've become a welcome addition to this camp and everyone here has nothing but high praise for you. Even so, your brother cannot stay; once that decision is made it will be final. If you choose to leave with him, you won't be able to return either."

Shelly nodded, understanding, and turned to look at the Camp Director.

"Is that really true? Did he try to run away because of me?" Shelly asked with a shaky tone. "He holds such reverence for you, Henry. I have to believe on some level you know that and have his best interests at heart."

Shelly turned her attention to Daniel.

"Truthfully, if the decision had been solely mine, we would have stayed home, I promise you that, Daniel. But Lucas has made so much progress as a person since coming here. This school year alone, he worked so hard to catch up on what he missed and passed all his classes with the credits he needed. I know he still has a lot inside that he doesn't talk about and I could have done more to help him. I accept full responsibility for that consequence. I knew what he was going through but I trusted that my brother could handle it and come to me for help if he needed it. My vote is that Lucas be provided the help that he should have received before. That offer you gave us before, Keira, does it still stand?"

She nodded and looked to Daniel for confirmation.
"I would be more than happy to counsel Lucas, Shelly," Keira said, trying to appease her boyfriend. Daniel continued to look persistent in his conviction, which is when she spoke once more. "Give me two weeks to work with him, and after that, when the missions begin for second year campers, he can go out for the remainder of the summer. That way Shelly can also continue her training and we can begin private sessions as well." Keira gave a quick wink in Shelly's direction and she nodded in gratitude.

"That seems most reasonable to me," Henry said, appearing more comfortable with the idea than Daniel liked.

"Counseling and going off on a mission is not a fit punishment for the crime he committed, father," the Camp Activities Director insisted. "What about Bill and Ashley? What are you going to do for them?"

"We will do all that we can for Ashley and Bill. Until then we must attend to Lucas and get him the necessary help he requires," Henry finally concluded. "Keira's plan is sufficient enough that Lucas will continue to receive help in both his training and well-being. It allows both siblings to stay here for the remainder of the summer."

Before Daniel could say anything in response, Zane raised his hand.

"If I may interject for a moment." Zane's hand was up in the air as if he were in a classroom.

"You may not, now—" Daniel tried to say.

"What is it you wish to add, Zane?" Henry said, his hand going up as if to tell Daniel to be quiet. His son complied but looked less than pleased with the abruptness of it.

"I understand Danny Boy's concerns over what Lucky Luke did to the Fast Girl," Zane started, to the annoyance of Daniel, "and I understand the concerns of his martial arts sister and the scary bully. But I speak for myself in this regard. He's a kid who hasn't exactly had the best stuff coming his way lately, and I'm not saying what he did wasn't his fault. We're all responsible for how we learn to control our own abilities. Correct me if I'm wrong, Henry, but you made this camp to help and protect ALL Alter Children, even those who seem like they are beyond help. I believe in that promise, and I know everyone else here does, too. Before anyone can beat me to it, I hereby volunteer myself to watch over him for the remainder of the summer. He will be my sole responsibility. If he gets out of line again, I will formally resign my position, and yes Danny, that's forever."

This last part seemed to give Daniel a mixed expression. Shelly imagined it was something appealing while also the closest thing to a compromise that may be reached at the moment.

"I believe that is worth consideration, don't you agree, my son?" Henry said, turning his attention towards Daniel.

After he finished contemplating the idea in his head, Daniel reluctantly nodded.

"Let's begin the vote. All in favor of Lucas being banished, raise your hands?"

Daniel raised his hand and was surprised that no one else in the council was raising theirs. He looked at Keira and gave her a hard look. She eventually relented but looked regretful about raising her hand.

"All in favor of my plan over Danny's," Zane said, raising his own hand. The rest of the council raised their hands, with Henry remaining neutral on both votes.

"You have to vote, father, otherwise it can't be a majority vote," Daniel insisted, half-hoping Henry would disagree. Instead the Camp Director raised his hand and thanked Zane.

"Lucas will remain in camp for the duration of the summer. Meanwhile, he will receive counseling sessions with Keira, and be monitored by Zane, who will lead him on a mission outside of camp."

The others agreed, as Daniel stood in that candle-lightened hall. He fought the tears that were forming as he walked out of the building, with his pride shattered like broken glass. Keira walked after him, but he shrugged her off. She continued to follow but from a safe distance.

Why did you do it Lucas? Why do you have to be the way you are? Why can't you just be…normal?

Josh entered the cabin where Lucas was staying with a plate full of the lunch from the cafeteria. Lucas quickly cleaned his face before his cabin mate could see he had been crying. .

"They said you can't leave, never said you can't eat," Josh remarked as he handed the plate to Lucas.

It was a cheeseburger with fries on the side and small pebbles of corn. Lucas wolfed it down like a wild animal as Josh stood in the doorway and watched in silence. He drank the whole can of soda in just ten seconds and coughed roughly.

"Take it easy, dude," Josh said and signed. Lucas brushed off his concern. "I also brought you these." Josh put down bandages and medicine for Lucas' bruised knuckles. He shook his head and continued to eat.

"Why did you do it?"

Lucas looked at his friend and saw the confusion in his eyes. Josh 'heard', because he couldn't hear in the traditional sense, the perception of sound that Lucas projected in his mind: *Josh, please listen to me…*

Josh cut him off with the wave of his hands like swatting a fly.

"No! If you are going to confess then sign it, or lip movement. Don't do that mind thing on me," Josh said irritably.

"I didn't mean to hurt Ashley. I would never do anything like that."

Josh nodded hesitantly.

He doesn't completely believe me and why should he?

"I know you would not, but she's in very bad shape. Daniel is convinced that you should be punished," Josh signed and said with concern. "The whole camp is turning against you thanks to him. Hailey is really pissed. I would steer clear from her <u>forever</u>."

He's thinking about emphasizing that last word under a line.

Lucas did not understand everything Josh said as he used sign language for certain words and phrases, but the point across was made that Daniel had it out for him.

It's no secret by this point that Daniel has had it out for me since I've been here, Lucas reflected. *I never did anything to him except get his father's attention.*

"Is Ashley alright?" Lucas asked in a concerned tone.

Josh nodded.

"She'll live, but you're not going to be able to see her again," signed Josh.

Lucas knew this to be true already, but his expression suggested perhaps the intent was misleading.

"What's going to happen to me?"

Josh shrugged.

"The whole camp is talking about it. Daniel wants to kick you out, but Henry wants you to stay. My money is on Henry."

Lucas knew that Daniel's word did not carry the same power as the Camp Director himself. If Henry said he could stay, then he could, with or without Daniel's satisfaction.

I'm grateful for that much at least.

It was then when a surprise visitor came; the Camp Director himself.

"Camp Director James sir," Josh fumbled with the wordings.

"Hello, Josh. May I have a moment alone with Lucas, please?" Henry asked with a warm smile. Josh retreated to his room while the Camp Director sat across from where Lucas was seated on the couch. A minute passed between them before Henry spoke.

"Lucas, why did you attack Ashley?" The Camp Director asked firmly.

He was about to answer when Henry asked another question.

"Or rather, what were you doing in her cabin in the first place?"

Lucas went on to explain how during the haze of the shadows movements and the fireballs, Ashley had saved him from being roasted alive and that they took safety inside of her cabin. He couldn't recall anything after that, only seeing Ashley's unconscious body, and his bruised knuckles.

"What's going to happen to me, Henry?" Lucas asked.

"It took some persuasion, but you will remain in Camp Supernatural under the express supervision of Counselor Zane. I believe you are familiar with him." Lucas was. *Unfortunately.* "It was the best accord we could reach. Daniel wanted to see you banished from camp, and he already strongly suspects that you tried to leave camp the previous year. I would suggest you keep your distance from him as well for the foreseeable future."

Lucas felt a lump in his throat, and an aching in his chest. It was like he wanted to throw up but couldn't.

Best case scenario, at least for now.

"Thank you, Henry, really. Is Zane going to be watching me all summer?"

"I'm afraid it is the only way you will be allowed to remain here. In addition, you will not be allowed to be alone with other campers with the exception of your sister. Beyond that, I ask that you respect these rules and follow them to the best of your ability."

Lucas nodded and felt his left eye becoming teary. He stopped himself from crying again and felt a small sense of relief.

"Sir, you have to know I would never hurt Ashley, ever. I don't know what came over me, but it wasn't me."

"As it stands, Lucas, you are guilty of what you have done, regardless of what the cause might have been."

I don't know why but that sounded colder than usual.

Lucas had no explanation. He hoped that Henry could just take his word for it. After a moment, the Camp Director confirmed his belief in Lucas' innocence.

"I understand that you had a lapse in judgment. Perhaps it was a manifestation of some level of trauma you are feeling, but Ashley has suffered for your lack of restraint. I fear that I have been too lenient on you, and that must end. Even so, I believe that you will benefit more from help here than you would in the world out there."

This made Lucas happy, until Henry's face grew darker.

"You must attend mandatory counseling sessions with Keira. I know that you will be on your best behavior, but I must insist. One day, my son may be Camp Director if that is what he desires, but I fear he will still lack the humility and compassion needed to inspire loyalty in others."

On this, Lucas agreed.

The apple has definitely fallen far from that tree.

"Thank you for everything, Henry," Lucas said meekly. "I'll do my best to make sure your efforts weren't for nothing."

"You're welcome, my child. I appreciate that but know that this chance will not come again. If you cannot control this conflict you feel, I will no longer be able to vouch for you."

With that said, Henry departed, leaving Lucas feeling bittersweet.

I can stay in camp, but I'm basically going to be watched and whatever time I hoped to spend with everyone else is not going to happen now…

In the solace of his cabin, Lucas brooded on his situation: He was to be confined to his cabin, with no contact outside, or at least unsupervised. Lucas has known for a while now that Daniel wanted him out of camp. He made it so painfully obvious that even Josh noticed it. What he couldn't understand was why.

Last year he seemed less like he is now. I don't know what to think, much less say to him. First he appears nice, friendly, then he becomes jealous of me for something I can't help. It's bad enough that I talk with Henry probably more than he does, but hurting Ashley was the last straw for him.

As he tried to find some outlet, some way to distract himself, Lucas began to scratch his head as if he had fleas. He also bit the sides of his fingers since his nails were still outgrowing their last trim. When this annoyed him, Lucas went back and forth between walking to the kitchen, walking back to where the TV was, and fell on the couch backwards.

I could watch something on the TV but I probably won't pay attention to it, Lucas mused.

By the afternoon he had received a visitor. It was Kendall, Vanessa's cabin mate. She looked very radiant to Lucas with her long chestnut hair that nestled on the sides of her shoulders. Her hair was fringed with stripes of light yellow that contrasted with how dark her hair looked. While she wore simple attire of a camp shirt and shorts, what attracted Lucas' attention was her use of make-up. She had dark eye shadow as well as eye liner making her eyes pop and her lips were a light shade of red, it was hard to tell whether that was her regular lip color or lipstick.

She definitely looks like a model.

"Hi Lucas, my name is Kendall. I don't believe we have met properly," she said courteously.

In truth, this was the first time Lucas and Kendall ever once spoke. While he had seen her around camp a few times last year, the two never had any form of greetings up until now. Lucas suddenly felt himself blush inside, but after a moment he made himself presentable.

"Yeah, hi, I'm Josh's friend," Lucas replied impulsively.

He was suddenly embarrassed.

Wow, and here I thought I was getting better at talking to girls.

"Is it okay for you to be here?" Lucas asked, wondering if Zane was outside the cabin.

"Yes, the Camp Guardian is outside. He said if I needed him I should just scream as loud as I can."

Lucas nodded, understanding.

"I want to ask you something and if I ask you this question, will you be completely honest with me?" Kendall asked uncertainty.

Lucas nodded. Something in Kendall's tone told him that she wasn't entirely trusting of him, at least not at the moment.

He read her mind just to be sure and heard her think, *I want to believe he's innocent, but all signs point to him. Ashley doesn't deserve this and I hope everyone is wrong about him.*

He felt the sharp stinging pain as Kendall asked her question.

"Did you really hurt Ashley on purpose?"

Lucas immediately shook his head and grimaced silently. Kendall did not notice. He explained to her how his abilities were becoming unstable due in part to his mood swings and increasing flare-ups. With every word he uttered, she would nod and listen intently without so much as interrupting. When he concluded she paused for a moment to consider what he had confessed.

"You really mean it don't you? Despite everything everyone is saying about you, I believe what you're saying."

Lucas was grateful to her for being one of the few to believe him.

I may have gained her trust, but I know that I will have a long way to go before everyone else in camp feels the same.

"Yes I do. I just wish I could see her, and tell her how I really feel about her…"

Lucas suddenly trailed off as he said this, but Kendall understood already, better than even he did.

"If you feel that way about her, then why haven't you told her?" Kendall inquired curiously.

Lucas shrugged.

"Last year, the only girl I wanted to be with was Vanessa," Lucas confessed. "I fell for her the moment I met her, but I never thought she'd want to date someone like me. You know." Lucas gestured to himself as if he were highlighting himself. Kendall nodded as he continued. "It wasn't until the accident and I saw how Ashley was there for me. That's when I realized I made the wrong choice."

Kendall let out a small giggle, which puzzled Lucas.

Why is she laughing at me? Is there something on my face?

"Boys are so unsure of themselves. Don't worry you're not the only one. I swear, one day you love a girl with all your heart, then the next day you'll break her heart because you can't figure out if you like her or love her or none of the above."

Her words cut through Lucas like a knife. He found himself agreeing with Kendall, though he didn't mean to be unsure.

I don't need her to like me back. I just want Ashley to know that I am sorry. I'd do anything to make things right.

"Do you think it could ever work, even after what happened?" Lucas asked her.

He almost expected her to say "no", or "not in your life", but instead she shrugged.

"If you feel something for Ashley, and you know it's real, just tell her. I believe she will forgive you, if she hasn't already. She's a very sweet person and the nicest person I know here. Vanessa isn't bad either. I think she just feels intimidated by how Ashley is true to herself and isn't sure how to be that way. But she's my best friend and I'd always have her back regardless."

After a minute of silence, Kendall got up to leave.

"That was all I wanted to ask, just to know if you meant to hurt Ashley or not. For what it's worth, I'm glad you didn't mean to and that you intend to do right by her."

Before she could walk away, Lucas blurted out something.

"Josh has a crush on you. I mean it's none of my business but anyone with eyes could see how he looks at you."

Lucas didn't know if he was doing the right thing, but knew Josh wasn't making a move, and a girl like Kendall couldn't stay single forever.

I'd be surprised if she didn't already have a boyfriend.

To his surprise, she just smiled at Lucas and nodded.

"I know. Girls are smarter than boys think. We know when a guy likes us. But I want to get to know him first before anything happens and see where it goes from there."

Lucas nodded as she promised to visit again if possible.

It was close to nine at night, when Josh came into the cabin. He looked elated by something, but Lucas decided to just ask instead of reading his mind.

"What are you so happy about, Josh?" Lucas asked intuitively.

He had to repeat himself, but Josh only got the "happy" part of the question.

"Kendall and I were talking. Nothing to brag about but she smelled so nice. Like strawberries. It's my new favorite food."

He smiled so wide that Lucas was afraid that Josh would scream out loud and destroy the cabin.

"Oh man you should have seen the look on all those faces. The guys who passed by us made faces at me and gave me ugly eyes. Jealous they are." Josh's signing towards the end became so fast and complex that Lucas interpreted the words based on how they appeared to him.

He smiled and patted his cabin mate's shoulder.

"Good for you. How about we celebrate you sniffing the hair of your future wife?"

Lucas meant for this to be a joke, not really intending for Josh to become ecstatic by it. Surprisingly he only understood the last part of the joke.

"You really think so? I can almost see it now: Kendall Tucker has a nice ring to it."

Lucas rolled his eyes as Josh was getting a little ahead of his years, but for the moment he let his friend relish the idea. Josh rummaged through the refrigerator and asked Lucas for his menu of choice. Lucas allowed his cabin mate the honor of choosing the menu for the night.

"I'm thinking of chili hot dogs, with pickles. Everyone loves pickles."

Lucas complied, if only to spare Josh the heartache of telling him how gross the combination is.

"Yeah…that sounds like a *real* appetizer."

Josh made the chili hot dogs and baked them in the microwave to make them extra hot. He even added hot sauce and bits of garlic, while Lucas only used mustard for his hot dog.

As they ate in silence, Josh imagined some mayonnaise and dipped the pickles in them. Lucas could not hide his disgust from Josh's strange appetite. He noticed the look immediately and wiped his lips clean.

"I used to do this to gross out my parents when they would invite their rich friends home. Turns out it really tastes awesome. You should try some."

Lucas shook his head as Josh offered it to him.

He also has a naturally high tolerance to certain foods. I can tell that just by feeling his reactions to what he eats. It's like how dog food tastes gross for people, but to Josh, certain foods are more heightened and less disgusting.

After they finished eating, Lucas thought about what was to come: July was new terrain for him. He had missed out on it last year and realized he may miss it again this summer.

At least I have my first mission to look forward to. Whatever that is, and wherever it is.

Lucas spent the whole night worried about Ashley. The Camp Guardian was very subtle about his exits from the front of Lucas' cabin when patrolling the camp. Sometimes he would be gone only to reappear in the blink of an eye as if he was a phantom.

And that's why he's Camp Guardian.

When he looked at Josh's very skinny physique and flat stomach, he wondered how his cabin mate could eat five chili dogs, with about the same amount of soda to wash it down and not be overweight. These thoughts, and many more urgent ones, plagued his mind that night…

Chapter 19: Forgiveness

Part of Lucas' road to recovery was to begin immediate counseling sessions with Keira, which he quickly disliked. It wasn't so much her questions or the way she looked at him like he was about to lie at any moment that made him uncomfortable. Rather, he felt like a science experiment.

She's just waiting for me to give her a reason to believe every word Daniel says, he thought knowingly.

"Lucas, do you know why you're here?" Keira asked him when he zoned out.

Lucas composed himself and shrugged. He ultimately decided to go along with the therapy, hoping it would end soon.

"I'm a basket case with uncontrollable anger problems connected to my bi-polar side," Lucas said, casually.

Keira nodded and scribbled something into her notebook.

"Ok… tell me about the first day you noticed the flare ups. How did you feel?"

Lucas tried to remember. It had been a long time ago, but he couldn't quite remember when it had been exactly. The memory then clicked in his mind as he remembered when his parents were both yelling at him rhythmically and it made his heart pump like a machine. After he fled from his parents' bitter words, Lucas remembered punching the wooden wall hard and breaking through it.

The weirdest part of that was I didn't feel any pain, not even after the adrenaline or whatever made me punch the wall wore off. I just remember going inside of myself for the first time when I was nine years old, and it was like I began to repress myself before I even knew what I had.

Recalling that feeling of going inside scared him, and he tried not to show it. Lucas remembered his parents telling him before he was medically diagnosed that he would grow out of this feeling on his own, because he was just acting out for attention.

That was their theory on why I was 'dysfunctional'.

He recalled a moment in time when he got bullied with taps on his arms, his head, and shoulders. It was so much of a trigger that even someone touching his shoulder just to get his attention caused him to go on the defense.

I was like that for a while at least, not so much since coming here.

He told all this to Keira, who wrote it down as he spoke. She promised to keep everything between them, but Lucas knew she was planning on sharing the information with Daniel.

I don't need to read her mind to know that.

"When I get angry, it feels like a soda when you shake it. The fizz is building up. Then someone opens the can and it explodes," Lucas described using peculiar objects as analogies.

Nonetheless, Keira understood.

"I see." Keira finished scribbling in her little notebook and set it aside. "Tell me how we can stop this from happening. To stop the fizz from building up and exploding."

Lucas shrugged.

"I usually sleep or do something to take my mind off things. It works most of the time. If not, some meds help also. I used to take something with an A at the beginning and an L also. I don't remember what they are called but they sometimes helped."

Emphasis on 'sometimes.'

Keira reached in and pulled from her bag a small little pill container, similar to the one Alexander had before his fatal stroke. She handed it to Lucas, who read the label to see the word *Clozapine.*

Is this the same thing Alexander took? If it is, I don't want it.

"I talked to one of the doctors at the hospital. They went over your medical history and talked to your sister to know what medication you are on. She was quite thorough. The doctors think it's best to shift gears after... well current events... and have decided to make you a prescription for these. We can't force you to take them but at least consider it."

Lucas looked at the pills and quickly shook his head.

"Is this the same medicine Alexander took?"

Lucas remembered the way the counselor's body had shut off after he had overdosed.

At the time I thought he had done it by accident, but now I'm not so sure…

Keira shook her head.

"Like I said, once you can, consider giving them a try. We can talk more about it in your next session."

As she was leaving, Lucas called out to Keira and asked something impulsive.

"Did Daniel tell you to give these to me?"

He already knew the answer, but he wanted to see if she would admit it.

Keira turned to look at him and sighed.

"He's worried about you. He's too proud to admit it but I know he cares about you."

Really, because I didn't notice.

"Do you want to talk about the cuts?"

Lucas' face felt cold as the goosebumps crept upon his skin.

How did she notice them?

Instead of pressing the issue, she gave him a sentimental smile and answered his question.

"You're wearing long sleeves in-doors when the temperature is near a hundred degrees and throughout the session you've been scratching at your arms. I'm glad to see that you're at least cutting your nails now."

When Lucas did not answer back she opened the door to take her leave.

After a short nap, a Camp Counselor came to Lucas' cabin. It was Naomi. She studied him as she entered the cabin and had a hollow appearance, like losing Marcus took out all the color from her skin.

"Hi, Lucas, do you remember me?" she asked plainly.

He just looked at her with a blank expression.

"You're a camp counselor. I've seen you around a couple of times," Lucas said, rubbing the sleep from his eyes. Naomi nodded. "Are you here to ask if I meant to hurt Ashley? Do you blame me for the death of your boyfriend Marcus?"

She shook her head calmly.

"No I do not and no that's not why I'm here. I'm here because what's happening to you is wrong. It's another example of why this camp is failing. It's becoming more about passing judgment before understanding all the facts," Naomi answered sorrowfully.

He could sense her sadness, not only through her words, but how audible her thoughts were to him.

Losing Marcus is a huge part of what she's feeling. But I can feel something underneath that loss, like a secret that is bothering her. If I try to read that part of her, it's definitely going to hurt more than surface-level mind reading, and that isn't exactly my biggest fan right now.

"How long were you two together?" Lucas asked curiously.

She suddenly flushed but stopped herself as if others were watching.

"Since High School. Why do you ask? Can't you just read my mind?"

Lucas felt a bit offended by this even if it was true. Before he could voice this thought, Naomi apologized.

"I'm sorry, that wasn't nice to say. I appreciate that you genuinely want to know." She paused, then continued. "Marcus had a crush on me since we first met, but I never really noticed him that way until… Well, I'll just put it this way; I took a chance on him and never regretted it. He was always such a sweetheart, always trying to make others happy even if he couldn't help himself…"

Lucas in a way could sympathize with Marcus.

I remember talking to him last year and he seemed so much more down to Earth than Daniel. I never felt any bad vibes from him, so what Naomi is saying and feeling adds up.

"You both had something special, I think. I really can't say I know what that feels like," Lucas confessed sincerely.

"You're young, Lucas. You have your whole life ahead of you. Besides, that girl Ashley seems to be fond of you. I know you didn't mean to do what you did to her, so don't beat yourself up for it any more than you already have. She wouldn't want that for you."

He nodded, feeling the shame all the same.

"It's what I deserve though. I don't deserve her friendship. I doubt anything more can come of it after what I did to her."

Naomi shook her head.

"If she really cares about you, then it won't change anything. But you also need to do your part and tell her how you feel. Even with your powers, you can't always know what a person is really thinking and feeling until you ask the right questions."

Lucas thought about this and realized Naomi was right.

I'm starting to realize women know guys a lot better than guys know themselves.

After she got up to leave, Naomi said, "You know, you remind me a lot of Marcus. He told me that you two talked last year and he took a liking to you. Something about you, he said, gave him a positive feeling. I feel the same way about you as well."

Lucas put up a small smile and nodded.

Sitting there alone in his cabin, Lucas pondered the words of both Kendall and Naomi. Both in relation to his conflicted feelings for Ashley.

If you feel something true for Ashley, then just tell her. If she really cares about you, it won't change anything.

Lucas realized that he did feel something for Ashley, and it wasn't just a friendship.

"I haven't wanted to admit it to myself because I didn't want to lose our friendship or hurt her," Lucas whispered to himself.

Then he realized how much he *did* hurt her and knew he had to make it right.

I don't know how and I don't care if everyone in camp still hates me. As long as I know Ashley doesn't hate me, I'll be okay.

A few minutes later, Josh came in with lunch. The menu consisted of Pizza for Wednesday with corn on the side and a fruit cup. In between crunching his food, Lucas seized the moment and made sure his cabin mate was looking directly at him as he spoke.

"Josh, I need a favor," Lucas asked.

Josh only understood the word 'favor' and immediately shook his head.

"No way. You're already in trouble. You're not dragging me down. I know my rights," Josh signed and said with exaggeration.

Lucas rolled his eyes.

He's not going to be coaxed easily. Or will he?

He suddenly had a light bulb idea.

Ding.

Lucas instantly reached for a paper and pen and started writing down his favor. He showed it to Josh, who had a hard time reading it due to Lucas messing up on a few words.

"Your penmanship could use some work. Besides that, you want me to help you *kidnap* Ashley?" Josh signed in shock. His exaggerated tone persisted.

Lucas shook his head frantically and fixed it up to say: *'help me see her'*.

"Oh, you want me to help you see Ashley," Josh noted with clarification. "Well that's nice, but can I ask? Have you gone crazy?!" Josh blurted out so loudly his sonic waves mildly vibrated the cabin like the buzzing of a phone. "Hailey will murder you if she catches you anywhere near Ashley. I thought I made that loud and clear last time."

Lucas shook his head.

"That's where you come in. You'll be distracting her with your charms." Lucas did his best sign language impression he could, adding emphasis on the last word. He moved his hand to make a 'C', and touched his chin, clicking off his two fingers like he was trying to scratch himself there.

I saw how to do that in Josh's mind, but it doesn't feel completely right.

Josh did not understand him, so Lucas repeated it and made sure he understood his lip movement.

"No chance. I may be deaf but I understand the difference between a dumb idea and a stupid one," Josh asserted.

What? Never mind, alright plan B: use Kendall's name.

Lucas then revealed Kendall's mutual crush on him, and how he'd see about getting them together if he helped him. Although reluctant, Josh finally relented.

"Fine, but if we get caught I'll say you mind controlled me again."

Lucas nodded in compliance.

With the way my luck has been lately, he's likely to be taken more seriously for that kind of claim. I better not press my luck.

They imagined themselves a top exit and made their way through it.

I'll never get tired of that, Lucas thought gratefully.

Boris was standing in front of the cabin like a sentry as his eyes were fixated on a mockingbird.

Big guy has a thing for birds, Lucas heard Josh think.

He also has a thing for punishing kids who don't follow the rules.

While Lucas didn't think the Camp Guardian would hurt him, he was not about to take a chance that Henry would let more than one strike go.

They got down from the cabin and tiptoed as quiet as a feather across the cabins. They took a while, navigating the eyes and ears of those around them, but finally made it to Ashley's cabin without being spotted. They hugged the back of the cabin next to hers and Josh gestured for Lucas to run as soon as he made the distraction. He nodded as Josh walked towards Hailey. She was standing outside of the cabin similar to Boris and had her arms crossed against her wide chest. Her feet were tapping against the ground.

She looks like she's waiting for something.

"Hey Josh, are you here to see Ashley?" Hailey asked with a warm smile when she spotted him. Lucas tiptoed fast and made his way to the back of the cabin.

Josh shook his head.

"Actually, I'm here to see *you*," Josh signed playfully.

This caused Hailey to look around her and to make sure no one else was around. She quickly seized the opportunity to talk to him.

Meanwhile, Lucas observed a small window behind the cabin which led into the Weeping Willow's bathroom. He became troubled by its size.

Maybe if I was thinner, like a twig, I could fit like a key. Why did I think of that word?

He began stacking up small boxes that were lying around and carefully leveled himself upwards to reach the window. Lucas overheard Josh and Hailey's conversation.

More like Hailey's.

She was going on about a boy who likes another girl in camp but is too shy to ask her out. Even though, according to her, the girl likes him a lot. The gossip annoyed Josh, who pretended to listen, but in his mind he was saying, *boring* to everything Hailey said.

Why's he complaining? It's not like he can hear her or anything.

In truth, Josh had no clue what Hailey was saying, and did not bother to read her lips, or look at the hand gestures she was using.

Hurry up already, Luke! Josh thought loudly.

His thoughts are as loud as his voice.

Lucas finally got high enough to reach the window and squeezed himself through, but felt very claustrophobic as he tried his best not to fall hard or get stuck in-between. The space between the window was small but luckily Lucas slipped through as easily as if he were a fish.

After a few seconds, he fell down flat on his face, not hard enough to knock himself out. He was surprised to find the floor was very soft like a fluffy pillow, making it easy for him to not make any noise.

Lucas looked around the room and noted that the cabin's bathroom was very small, consisting of only a sink, toilet, and one shower. He noticed the vast amounts of shampoo with each having their own aroma respectively and how the five girls used the same type of toothpaste: minty green freshness.

I always thought Shelly was the only one who liked that brand, Lucas thought humorously.

He understood how serious a violation against their privacy it was to even be in the bathroom alone. Even so, at least for now, Lucas decided he didn't care for rules or formality. Peering through the door, he could no longer hear Hailey and Josh talking, but heard Josh in his mind.

Blah blah blah. Times like this make me happy I'm deaf. Now if only Lucas could hurry up, and get me a date with Kendall, I'll be happier.

Hold out for a few more minutes and it'll be dinner and a show for you two, Lucas thought, tensely.

Deal.

Lucas opened the door slightly to the bathroom and saw that the doctor still remained. It was the same one who treated Lucas before during his stay in the hospital ward. He was a young looking man, but his eyes made him look older.

"Alright, you're looking better today. Just take these pills twice a day after you eat, and you can start training with Counselor Zane tomorrow," said the camp's doctor in an unconcerned tone.

Lucas could not see how Ashley looked but heard her struggling in an agonized tone.

"You expect me to train like this?"

Ashley's voice sounded swollen, like she had food in her mouth.

The doctor sighed and walked out of the cabin without another word.

When he was gone, Ashley broke down on the bed and began to sob. After a few seconds, Lucas approached her cautiously. She did not scream, nor panic like he expected. She wiped her face clean and turned away from him. Her body began to shake with her hands moving to her lap.

"Ashley…… I am so *so* sorry, please *please* forgive me…"

Truth be told, Lucas had only apologies for Ashley. Anything else was only guilt and sorrow when he walked closer to see the damage he had done. She hesitated at first, but after a while, she turned to look at him and his own face suddenly became pale.

She had two black eyes, both cheeks were swollen like balloons, and her nose was broken. Ashley's jaw had wires that still allowed her to speak, but Lucas could tell that she felt immense pain from talking. He couldn't look at her eyes, even as hers searched for his. He tried to hide the discomfort her face brought him to no avail. Her face dropped after a moment and Lucas wanted to say something but didn't know what.

Nothing I say will ever take back what I've done.

When he didn't say anything else, Ashley decided to speak.

"It wasn't you, Lucas," she said to his relief. "I know because you would never do anything like that to me, right?" Lucas nodded and was about to say something but Ashley continued. "I also knew when I looked into your eyes…you have an unsure look, like you don't know yourself. But you also have a kind look, like Daniel. You're a good person and that's why I can forgive you."

Lucas felt himself quiver as he listened to every word she said. He clenched his fists until his thin nails etched themselves onto his palms.

I can't cry in front of her. She's the one who's hurt and it's my fault. Would a good person do what I did to her? No, they'd have more control over their abilities, Lucas thought bitterly.

Sitting there in silence, Ashley opened the pill container, and popped one into her mouth. Lucas read the label and realized it was a painkiller, and that it was the same one Alexander took before he died.

She hasn't eaten yet. The doctor said she has to eat before taking those pills.

"Shouldn't you eat first before taking those?" Lucas asked with concern.

Ashley shook her head and smiled thinly.

"What's the worst that can happen?"

You can overdose.

"You can overdose," Lucas heard himself say out loud frantically.

This made Ashley frown and look uncomfortable at the same time.

"I…I'm sorry. I shouldn't have said that."

"It's okay. I'll eat before taking the next one. I promise."

Lucas nodded in reassurance and took an empty seat closer to her bed. She flinched a little bit, but composed herself as best she could. When he motioned to move back to where he was, Ashley reached out and brushed her hand against his wrist.

"Please, stay. Just right there." The words still sounded painful, but the way she felt made Lucas think that his presence was doing more good than bad.

"Okay, I will. I never thanked you for staying with me in the hospital last year."

Ashley nodded softly.

"You don't have to thank me. I know you were grateful."

"*Are* grateful and I want to thank you," Lucas corrected her softly. "So, thank you, Ashley, for being there."

Ashley managed a thin smile and turned slightly away from Lucas' face. If it wasn't for the fact that her face was delicate right now, he would have wanted to touch her cheek and turn her back to him. At the moment he feared any contact might cause her to flinch in fear again.

That's going to be with her for a while… because of me.

Lucas looked around the cabin and noticed how distinctive her bunk was. Her bed had a purple mattress, a few magazines that he knew belonged to Shelly, and hand lotion that smelled of lavender.

Shell's turning this into her home, Lucas thought with a smile.

He also noticed the flower, *Ashley's Willow,* right next to her bed with a vase underneath. It had been a rare flower he discovered last year in the nature walk activity and named it after her. It looked so bright in the sunlight. The red ovaries inside shone like the sun and the outside yellow petals seemed to dance in the sun's rays.

I feel like if I look at it too long I'll go blind.

"You still have the flower I gave you?" Lucas asked, hoping to lighten the mood.

Ashley nodded stiffly and turned her head towards it. She groaned as she did.

"It's named after me. I may as well keep it as a momentum of our victory from last year. Plus it makes Vanessa jealous whenever she passes by the cabin and sees it on the window."

The two laughed for a moment, but Ashley was the first to stop. She winced in pain and clasped her face as if it were about to break. Lucas motioned to help her, but she extended a handout towards him.

"You'd better go, Lucas, before Hailey comes back."

Ashley coughed hoarsely and drank water from the cup near her painkillers. Lucas nodded, but decided to ask about her and Jeremy.

"""Did you like your date with Jeremy?" Lucas said out loud, when he meant to keep the question to himself.

Ashley's expression was hard to discern from the injuries she had. It was either a frown or grimace.

"I wouldn't call it a date but it was still nice."

At least it was cut short, Lucas thought to himself, grateful it stayed in his mind.

"Good to know. So is he your boyfriend now?"

Ashley shook her head slowly.

"I don't feel that way about him."

Lucas nodded, gratefully. He was about to leave when he heard her voice in his head.

If only he could see what is plainly in front of him, Ashley thought ruefully.

The pain that had been coming from his mind reading came suddenly, as fast as a whip, but he hid it well.

"I'll stay for another minute. Let Hailey beat me up. I don't care."

Of course I care!

Lucas sounded bolder than he felt as he resumed his place on the bed. Ashley inched closer to him, but still appeared guarded.

"Do you love Vanessa, Lucas?" Ashley finally asked awkwardly.

It had been one of the thoughts Lucas heard in her mind, but hearing it out loud made him think of an answer. With no hesitation, he shook his head.

"No. I mean I *liked* her before, but now, I don't know… I just want to make her happy. At least until Bill gets better, then I'll break up with her."

From the way Lucas sounded it was almost as if he didn't care at all about Vanessa. In reality he did.

And that's what hurts. Knowing that she cares more for me than I do for her.

With what seemed like great effort, Ashley took Lucas' hands in hers and ran her fingers against his.

"This calmed you down before when you lost control of yourself."

Lucas remembered vaguely, but had trouble recalling anything after the fireballs began to rain down on them. The only thing he recalled was seeing Ashley on the ground moments before the others found him.

That memory, along with waking up paralyzed in the hospital bed, will haunt me until the day I die, Lucas thought grimly. *I wish I could forget everything bad that has happened to me: the golden haired man in my nightmares, being broken, the crow and eagle, hurting Ashley, my parents dying. Why is this all happening to me? Why did my parents have to die? I didn't even get to say goodbye. I didn't even get to apologize for the misunderstanding. I didn't…*

He was so immersed in his own thinking that he did not notice when Ashley's hand moved to his wrist. By the time he noticed, she had already discovered in horror the self-inflicted marks that decorated his wrist.

"Lucas, why do you have cuts on your wrist?" Ashley asked in horror.

Before he could protest, she yanked both his sleeves and saw more cuts and even bruises on his forearm, one scrape was new and it showed plainly. Lucas began to sweat from anxiety, causing the cut on his chest to begin burning like being in an oven. Ashley noticed and swiftly lifted up his shirt. She saw the small scrapes and cuts that decorated his chest, including the one encircling his heart. The wound itself consisted of small uneven lines that looked as if Lucas was trying to cut out his own heart with his fingernails. Its scar would look like a broken circle.

Why did I have to do it so much? Lucas thought regretfully.

Ashley looked at Lucas with distraught eyes, as he turned his face away from hers. He did not want to tell her why his body was covered in self-inflicted wounds. He especially did not want to talk about the dreams of the golden-haired madman and the two maniacal creatures that haunted him since the day of the accident.

Oh yes, brother, we will both be there when this one dies, yes indeed.

The memory played itself in his mind as Lucas struggled to hold back the tears. He sniffled and quivered as she grasped his hand and with the other caressed his right cheek.

"Oh Lucas, what have you done to yourself?"

He shook his head shamefully and pulled away from her.

"Don't make me talk about it, Ashley, please…"

She decided not to pursue it any further, despite her strong desire for an answer.

"You know, boys can be so blind to what's right in front of them," Ashley teased. "You want what you don't have or can never have. Then once you have it you don't know what to do with it."

While Lucas did not quite understand the insinuation, he realized she was building up to something.

What's she talking about? I don't know what I want, so how can I get it if I don't even know what it is?

"What's your excuse, Lucas?" Ashley continued. "You can read people's minds, control them, and know their whole life story in a matter of seconds. What does it take for you to finally open your eyes and realize when someone really truly cares about you? Do you have to lose people in order to appreciate them, or do you just have to be told the truth upfront?"

Her voice began to rise as her jaw flared with pain. She paused for a moment before speaking again. Unfortunately, Lucas couldn't contain himself.

"Okay, what are you trying to tell me, Ashley, because right now I'm really beginning to…"

Before he could continue, her voice echoed in his mind with the exact words corresponding from her lips.

"I'm in love with you, Lucas. Since last year," Ashley revealed, with a voice full of hurt and truth. None of the previous shyness remained, and despite how red her face became, she was looking straight at him through her swollen bruised eyes. It was especially discomforting to hear her confession as she struggled through the pain of her jaw.

"It was more of a crush at first, but after seeing you in the hospital and getting to know you better, I realized that I wanted more than a friendship from you. You're the bravest, most compassionate, and sincere person I've ever met. I adore you so much."

Ashley took Lucas' other hand in hers and placed her free hand on his face again.

"When you attacked me, you said the name Alistair. He's the guy who captured Bill and the other campers." Ashley noted. "Why did you say his name?"

Lucas' face fell, as her warm soft hand rubbed against his cheek. He shook his head and tried to take her hand from his face, until her finger pushed his chin upwards, forcing him to meet his face with her own.

I can't keep this up, this lie anymore. I have to tell someone.

"I don't know how or why but I think he tried to kill me last year," Lucas confessed as memory crept into his mind and he began to shake erratically while breathing heavily. "I was in the Forest of Time after I left camp, and he must have found me... and... fell... no... I... can't..."

Lucas was shaking. He feared losing control of himself again.

No, please don't. I can't, not again. Again, can't I not.

Ashley's body shook in a similar fashion to Lucas, but she pressed on and pushed his face to her shoulder. He let out a hurricane and folded his arms around her back. As she held him, Lucas felt safe, like no one, not even Alistair and Jacob, could tear them apart. It was like the times when Shelly would hold him. Their bodies so close to each other, Lucas realized something important.

I do love her, too, Lucas thought sorrowfully. *But I can't be with her, not now, maybe not ever. I need to get better. I can't be like this to her.*

After he finished sobbing, Lucas cleaned his face up with the sleeve of his shirt and composed himself.

"I can't right now, Ashley. After what I did to you, I need to focus on getting better so I don't hurt anyone ever again. I'll do whatever it takes to control this."

Lucas could not bear the thought of hurting her again, but in a way Ashley was not disappointed. In fact, he read her mind and realized that she already expected the answer.

"I just wanted you to know, Lucas. I'm not asking anything more from you."

On the contrary, Ashley sounded like she had hoped he would reciprocate her feelings on the spot. Even after they stopped hugging, for a moment, their hands still held each other.

"Would you date me, even like this?" Ashley asked jokingly as she moved her free hand around her beaten face.

Lucas smiled and kissed her forehead gently. The shaking returned, but it became like the feeling of melting ice.

"There's nothing about you I wouldn't say no to."

Ashley smiled brightly but had to stop after a while when the pain became too much.

"You should tell Henry about this. About Alistair trying to kill you, I mean."

"I think he knows, but I don't know why he wouldn't tell me," said Lucas, uncertainly. "Nothing makes sense anymore. Maybe he..."

Just then, the voices outside grew louder. Lucas realized it was time to go.

"Thank you for coming, Lucas. Whatever happens, Henry will protect you from Alistair and Jacob, of that I know," said Ashley with a warm smile.

Lucas nodded and swiftly exited the way he had entered.

He had barely squeezed himself through the small window of the bathroom when Hailey entered the cabin. Josh was waiting for him a few cabins away. As they walked back to their own cabin, Josh could not help boasting where he would like to treat Kendall for their first date.

While ignoring Josh's babbling, Lucas felt a small sense of joy for talking with Ashley, but also bad because now he realized it could not wait any longer. The one thing he kept pushing back and knew now he had to do.

I have to break up with Vanessa before the summer ends…

Chapter 20: Josh Date

Josh looked at himself over in the mirror again, again, and again. He combed his hair, which he ordinarily didn't like to do. Even though his hair wasn't as unruly and shaggy like his best friend, Lucas Fargo, Josh still felt insecure about how orange it was.

It's not like a carrot, but it's not like an orange either, he mused to himself.

He was trying on various clothing to make sure he had something that was at least semi-formal considering this was his first date with Kendall. Josh recalled the moment he mustered the courage to ask her out.

It was the day after Lucas spoke with Ashley in her cabin. A few campers still lingered in the cafeteria after lunch ended. To his delight, Kendall was sitting alone at her usual cabin table. Josh made his way to her, pretending to be as cool as he saw actors behave in movies.

Act like you don't care, don't be too nice, always end with, "whatever", and smile a lot.

Josh had practiced in the mirror lip movements and hand gestures he had seen both from movies and other guys around camp who had girlfriends.

He set his plate next to Kendall's. Josh had chicken strips with parmesan, sides of corn mac and cheese, and a diet cola. Kendall had a salad with chicken soup and water. She looked like she hadn't touched her food, which gave Josh an odd feeling.

I know she can go through things like a ghost, but maybe she doesn't like to do that in front of others.

Kendall smiled at him and waved at him. Josh waved back and began to move his lips as if practicing what he wanted to say.

"Hey, Kendall, you're looking really beautiful today. That isn't to say you don't look beautiful other days because you're always beautiful. I mean, whatever. Don't listen to me."

Josh got as far as "beautiful today" when Kendall surprised him. She began to make motions with her hands that at first looked like charades, which caught Josh off guard. After a few seconds, Josh realized Kendall was signing with him. She used the sign with her hand to her chin to say, "thank you" and made a circle on her lips for "compliment."

As if struck by a love arrow, Josh slammed his hand on the table. He felt the vibrations traveling from both the table and his own hands impact like a drill. He also used a bit of sign language as well to communicate, but admitted that he was better at reading lips.

"I have nice lips," Josh said out loud, both unintentionally and purposefully. The sounds he made were met with silence.

Kendall made a giggling face and it was in moments like that when Josh felt that ache in his heart.

"Want to go out with me or whatever." Josh tried to behave the way he saw actors in movies behave without knowing exactly what their voice pitch was like. Based on their lips and posture, he felt it was like the word sarcasm or uncaring.

Kendall nodded with a smile.

She also said other things as well but Josh was too happy with himself to catch everything she said.

"Where do you want to go out?" was all he managed to see her say.

He thought for a moment, remembering Lucas' promise for a paid date.

How can I make my best friend pay?

The idea came to him like a light bulb, and he made his way to the Majestic Meadow cabin. They were usually the ones who were technologically gifted and for movie night they set up the movie projectors and speaker sound systems for Camp Director James's announcements. He spoke to Lester Conway, the head of the cabin.

Lester was a wiry boy of thirteen with short cropped brown hair. He fancied himself as being a film aficionado and often asked people randomly what their favorite movies were. He did this today with Josh, who had a hard time understanding him because of his lisp. When he spoke, Lester's tongue waggled against his teeth like a dog's tail in excitement.

Once he understood Lester's question, Josh tried to think of the first movie that came to mind.

What's a movie everybody likes?

"*Star Wars*," was Josh's abrupt answer. Lester gave him a quizzical look which suggested that Josh's answer was inadequate. Even so, his mannerism seemed to shift back into a weariness of compliance since he asked Josh, using both his lisp and writing stuff down, what he needed help with.

"Movie date night with food," Josh said and signed. Lester nodded, and entered his cabin briefly to show him the stuff he had for the proposed date night. Josh rarely visited other cabins and appreciated the chance to see the inside of the Majestic Meadow.

Looking up and down, sideways, backwards, Josh saw piles of discarded equipment that looked like trash. He remembered the saying: 'One person's trash aside was another person's treasure lot.' He spotted Lester's cabin mates but didn't bother with names. Josh often had to think of nicknames like Luke and Bill was just Bill.

If I called him 'Billy the Kid' he'd melt my face off.

Lester showed Josh what he needed to make movie night happen. The tech savvy boy's mouth began to gallop like a racehorse. Josh had a hard time catching everything he said. Most words were lost in the drumming of the boy's tongue, his lips moving in a slurping manner, and his facial expressions did not seem to match whatever his tone might be.

"Ith not hard," Lester insisted. It was all Josh picked up on. Looking at the equipment reminded him of what he had in his room.

Dad calls them speakers. They don't do anything for me but they look cool on the walls.

Using various hand motions Lester tried to explain to Josh how they worked. It didn't take him long to notice that Josh was not registering any of the information, even as he did his best to replicate his idea of sign language.

He said some things rapidly, but when Josh didn't catch any of it, Lester wrote it down on a notepad: "Bring back stuff or there will be hell to pay."

Josh nodded and left the cabin just as fast as he had entered.

Making his way to the Imaginarium Illusion, Josh began to assemble the equipment for movie night. Once put together it appeared to be a crude film projector which would have looked more at home in a classroom than something to use outdoors. Recalling Lester's advice Josh made his way to the pavilion area, which was right now free of campers and counselors. He found a place to set up a medium sized screen, courteous of Lester. It appeared dusty and had bits of sand on it, but was otherwise in good usable condition.

Putting the finishing touches to both the film projector and the screen, Josh went back to his cabin and imagined some popcorn, pickles, hot dogs, butter, and a few cans of soda. He asked Lucas to make sure they had the pavilion to themselves (courtesy of the favor he was owed) by talking to the Camp Guardian about it. Josh's best friend promised begrudgingly as Josh dressed for the occasion. He went through the clothes he wore for the summer, and settled on some newer ones he hadn't yet worn. These included khaki shorts, and a red dress shirt with his camp tee underneath. A pair of sports shoes adorned his feet, which sadly were his only pair he had thought to pack.

If I had known this year would be the time I get a date, I would have brought the good stuff.

Josh recalled what both his parents said about a potential girlfriend. His mother: "Be kind, sweet, gentle, and sincere." His father: "Women only know what they want when they don't have it. Once they have it, they don't want it anymore."

He tried to recall the words to the best of his abilities, but even as good as he was at lip reading, often the words got mixed up and he would have to fill in the blanks and intentions.

Tapping his feet on the ground, watching, heart hammering, Josh began to fear he was being stood up. He set the food aside and was about to dig into the popcorn when he smelt the most incredible scent to enter his nostrils. It was a sweet fragrance that reminded him of the garden his mother planted at their home. He identified various scents from lavender to roses intermixed with both Kendall's natural scent and what she was wearing. When his eyes beheld her, his heart began to thump against his chest rapidly and his face contorted like someone who just tasted the best candy ever.

Kendall was radiant in the night sky. She had her hair done up to show her whole face which was heart shaped. She wore a long sleeve pink shirt which had the camp words embroiled on the front and back. Josh expected her to dress up more appropriately for a date (he had seen in movies the women wearing dresses and handling big purses over their shoulders) but Kendall looked like she was going for a jog later with her lounge pants and sneakers.

She began to speak, her mouth moving as softly as her voice might sound. Josh thought he would give anything to hear her. He couldn't stop the rhythmic beating of his heart, and tried to focus his eyes on Kendall rather than the outline of her shirt which was skintight, he noticed.

"You good," Josh mouthed and felt the vibrations his both emanated at the words. He knew they fled from his mouth before he could stop himself. Clasping his mouth in shame, Kendall made her way towards him and extended her hands as if to touch him. She hesitated, her own mouth suddenly appearing immobile.

"I mean you look good," he finally corrected himself. The vibrations came out with more surety and force than before, causing him to still his body and regulate his breathing. He wanted to say 'whatever' also but hesitated. Kendall smiled at him and from her lips he could tell her words were in gratitude. She began to sign the next part which Josh both caught and had to ask for clarification on.

"You look handsome and dashing," Kendall signed and said. Josh blushed and suddenly felt self-conscious about the food he had with him. "Is that for us?"

Josh nodded and gestured for her to take a seat on the blanket he was hurriedly readying for them. It occurred to him that in his preparations for the movie and snacks, he didn't get Kendall flowers. Suddenly he wished he had the speed of Ashley.

What kind of flowers does she like? If Lucas were here he'd know.

He was preparing to set up the movie when Kendall tapped his shoulder to get his attention.

"What are we seeing?" Kendall asked, although her mouth moved more than the words Josh caught. He looked through the small case of discs that Lester had handed to him along with the equipment. They were labeled with **Film #2, Film #5, Film #7.**

Josh groaned, not knowing what those numbers meant. Not wanting to look unsure in front of Kendall, he grabbed the second disc, and prayed to the silent gods that it wouldn't be anything weird or bad.

To both their delight, it was an animated musical that both had seen and enjoyed. As the movie played, Josh offered the bulk of the snacks to Kendall, who appeared nervous around the temptation. She softly nodded and took the soda and some popcorn. Using napkins she placed the popcorn on there and delicately took them as if she were trying not to hurt herself.

The movie played and got to a musical part where the lead character confessed his feelings for the girl he loved through a song. Josh read the subtitles and closed captions which described the emotions and actions of both actors. He slowly motioned himself to Kendall, his eyes constantly darting to her as if to make sure she was still there. She, in turn, glanced at him a couple of times, and both were inching nearer each other like mirror images. He wanted so badly to take her hands in his, to look in her eyes and face without just trying to figure out what she was saying.

"I'm happy," Josh said aloud. He meant to say more, but purposefully left it at that. He wasn't sure if Kendall heard this or not. All he felt was his head and hers touching each other, and he felt vibrations coming from Kendall which were similar to the way the actors performed in the film they were watching. When he looked at her, it was like a spotlight was being shone in their direction, and it took all he had, in all the times he spoke to women to trust that they both felt the same.

Josh braved his hand to move forward as the film was beginning to reach its conclusion. His hand slid across the carpet like a worm itching towards its destination. He feared that she would outright reject him or use her power to avoid touching his hand. In the movie, as the couple held hands, Kendall reached out and grasped Josh's hand. Her skin was smooth and warm against his. He was so overwhelmed with both shock and happiness that he felt the sudden urge to scream.

Don't scream! Don't you dare scream! Calm, calm down. Anchovies. Worst Pizza topping. Anchovies and olives.

Sighing and collecting himself, Josh peered at Kendall, who was looking at him now instead of the movie. When the movie ended, Josh offered the remaining snacks to Kendall to share with her cabin mates and she nodded with gratitude.

He was ready to walk back to the Majestic Meadows cabin and return the borrowed equipment when Kendall gave Josh the greatest gift of the night. Besides his first true date, he also received his first kiss ever on the lips. This time he did scream.

Chapter 21: These Scars

The 4th of July celebration was commencing that very evening. Luckily for Lucas, Henry and the council decided to allow him to participate in the festivities and, most importantly, enjoy the company of his friends, with the exception of Ashley; he was still not allowed to be anywhere near her.

With the festivities underway, everyone gathered around the main pavilion area where Henry set up a projector to show a movie. Attendees brought in bowls of popcorn and drinking sodas from big cups that required two hands to keep from spilling. A few campers had soda drinking hats that were being sold for three dollars at the camp store. It didn't surprise Lucas when Josh appeared with one on his head.

That thing looks ridiculous, he thought with a snort. *I better make sure he can't read my words in my expression.*

When they took their seats on the ground, Lucas saw Ashley with Hailey and Shelly, but did not dare look too long. He briefly saw Ashley smile at him for a half-second before her eyes darted back towards the front. She thought about him immensely, and even though they were only a few feet away from each other, there was a barrier of campers in between them.

I wish we could talk more. Maybe if we talked I could sort out these feelings she has for me. These feelings that we have for each other?

He was still conflicted by his feelings for Ashley, even as he insisted that she was nothing more than a friend to him. With this in mind, Lucas' main concern was on how to break up with Vanessa, to let her down easy.

She does like me, Lucas knew. *She even said she loves me, but can we still be friends… maybe if I don't mention Ashley?*

Then the most unexpected thing happened; Bill was seen for the first time outside of the ward with Vanessa leading him by one arm and Shannon was by the other. Everyone's attention went from the movie projector screen to Bill. He was beginning to look like himself again. His hair looked recently trimmed and his physique appeared livelier. Lucas' eyes immediately went to Bill's bandaged left hand which was missing the tips of three fingers, while his thumb and pinky were intact.

Bill still had the cloth wrapped around his eyes, making him seem more intimidating than Lucas knew his friend to be.

Vanessa left the company of her brother and Shannon to join Lucas' side of the group of gathered campers for the movie screening.

"Hey, babe, are you happy to see me?"

She moved in to kiss him on the lips but Lucas didn't kiss her back.

"What's wrong?"

The projector was still being set up when Lucas decided to pull her to the side of her cabin, the Kruel Kingdom.

"We need to talk," he said, tensely.

When they were a good distance away from everyone else, *including Bill*, Lucas decided to be as straightforward as possible.

"I think we need to break up, Vanessa," said Lucas a little *too* bluntly.

He figured there was no easy way to break up, but his words sounded more insensitive than he intended.

I should have said: 'We need some time apart, see other people maybe. But can we still be friends.' I mean we can.

Vanessa's eyes suddenly looked stricken with pain as if she had been struck by a stray arrow.

"What? Why, Lucas? Did I do something wrong? I know I haven't been a good girlfriend lately. But I'm trying. I really am."

She sounded like every word was fighting its way out and this made Lucas very uncomfortable.

Please don't make a scene, please don't make a scene.

"I know, but it's too much right now, Vanessa and I haven't been completely honest with you."

He paused to think of something, but when he saw Vanessa's face he knew she was going to make a scene any moment.

"I don't feel the way I did before. I don't like you anymore."

He tried not to sound so cold, but he had no other way of putting it besides the hard truth.

Yeah, this is really the first time I've broken up with a girl, and I thought it wouldn't feel so bad. It feels terrible.

Lucas was shaking, and he felt himself breathing rapidly as Vanessa began to sob. Thankfully, she didn't cry loud enough to draw attention to them. Not only did he sense her thoughts; he felt her pain.

It's like someone tore out my heart and crushed it in front of me. I really messed up, Lucas thought.

After she finished crying, Vanessa wiped her tears away and didn't look at him for a short period.

She had her back turned to him when she asked, "It's because of *her* isn't it?"

Lucas didn't answer back, but she knew the answer already.

"I can't deal with this right now. I just got my brother back and he doesn't need to worry about me."

Neither do you, Lucas heard Vanessa think.

Before he could say anything, Vanessa had already run into her cabin. She shut herself off from the rest of the camp with a bang from her cabin door.

That was not the best way to have broken up with her. Then again, is there such a thing as a breakup where both boy and girl remain friends? Probably not.

After taking a deep breath and putting Vanessa's thoughts aside, he rejoined Josh as the movie began to play. Lucas saw the Camp Director seated a few feet away from the projector. He had a bucket of popcorn on his lap, and a drinking hat just like the one Josh was wearing.

And I said it looked ridiculous… At least I didn't say it out loud.

When Henry sipped from it cautiously, a few drops stained his beard. He chuckled softly to himself and turned his head to where Boris sat. The Camp Guardian appeared as immense as a tree even when seated.

"I remember when they had video tapes rather than discs," he told the Camp Guardian cheerfully. "It confounds me to no end how easily it is to break one of those contraptions."

Boris chuckled softly and nodded.

"My fingers are too big to put in the middle of them. I miss the discs that were large enough for me to hold without feeling like it would shatter in my hands."

Lucas overheard their exchange and smiled to himself.

I wish I could sit by them. They'd make better company than friends who want nothing to do with me.

Giving brief sideways glances at Ashley, Lucas' mind was on rush hour trying to get from one point to the other.

She was always there for me, even when I was at my worst. Vanessa never connected with me on a personal level; I was just her tissue paper when she needed to cry. She was someone I wanted to be with, but didn't know how to handle her once she was with me. Oh gods, Ashley was right about me and guys in general.

Distracted by his own thoughts, Lucas didn't feel the hand that clasped his shoulder. When he turned around he saw Bill standing above him. Shannon was beside him and gave Lucas an ugly stare.

"Hey, Luke, have you seen Vanessa? She said she was going to talk to you about something."

Lucas felt his heartbeat racing and was thankful that Josh was not paying attention to them (his eyes were glued to the screen) and that Bill's eyes were bandaged.

I don't have a poker face to save my life.

Shannon's nose began to sniff as if catching a powerful aroma. Lucas tried to calm himself, thinking about Ashley before the accident and how beautiful her dimples looked when she smiled.

Her freckles, how they complement each other like sparkling sand in ocean water.

"Okay, well, if you see her before I do, just tell her she doesn't need to worry about me. That I'll be okay."

That's too ironic coming from him.

Bill was about to walk away when Lucas called out to him.

"Wait, Bill. I wanted to apologize for my part in what happened to you."

The attention of every camper and staff was still on the movie, so no one noticed the way Bill's bandaged face turned towards Lucas with a feeling like a bomb that was about to go off.

"I know you didn't ask for what happened to you and I'm glad you're alive and home. But my only part was Alistair wanting to take me instead. I don't know how I know him but something about him scares me. He and Jacob both terrify me and all I want to do is make sure neither of them hurts anyone else. I'm mostly sorry that they hurt you and Mike because you both mean a lot to me. You were the first friend I made last year and I'm sorry I never said that before."

Lucas felt tears welling in his eyes. He tried not to cry out or make a scene, but Bill laid two hands softly on Lucas' shoulders.

"They won't. That's the same promise I'm making; they won't hurt anyone ever again. In the morning I'm going to visit Devon along with the Camp Director and Daniel. That's what I wanted Vanessa to tell you so that you can join us."

Lucas nodded, before saying yes out loud. His heart still sank and he knew any moment now he was going to cry more from his friend not knowing about the breakup than by the breakup itself.

The movie lasted until eleven, after which the fireworks began. The counselors tried their best to get some good fireworks but the recent events had shortened their mobile access. Marcus had been good at procuring things. Richardson was also known to obtain supplies at a fast rate. Alexander could always pull anything out from seemingly nowhere like a rabbit from a magician's hat. Now all three counselors were dead, and the camp was suffering for it. Despite this, those who remained made the best of things and Lucas felt that here and now everyone was united upon a common banner.

Where the Counselors memorial and Bill's return divided us, Fourth of July brought us all together.

The next day, before training sessions, there was an announcement about missions being distributed earlier than in previous years. In addition, any first year camper above the age of 13 can take part in missions as long as their ability is stable. Lucas heard Zane being mentioned, which made him wonder what that meant for his watcher.

Maybe I'll get early parole for good behavior? I can dream at least.

Later that day, while training sessions were taking place with Naomi's group, Daniel came across them on his way to his father's house. Lucas noted the Camp Activities Director appeared more tired than usual. The dark circles under his eyes looked more like bruises than bags. Lucas watched as Daniel made his way to Naomi's group.

"Hi, Naomi. Maybe have them split up into groups based on their abilities. You know that's how I did it when I used to train campers."

The group Naomi had appeared more interested in learning more about this than she did herself.

"Good to know. Thank you, Daniel, for passing through," Naomi said with gritted teeth.

Hearing a scoff in the distance, all eyes turned to Zane, whose smirk looked specifically designed for Daniel. Lucas felt his hand slap his forehead.

I wish my power was to disappear right now.

"You always have the answers to everything right, Danny Boy?" Zane said aloud, which caused the younger campers to chuckle, and Naomi suppressed a giggle. Lucas saw Daniel seethe and moved his shoulder up to purposefully bump against Zane. He saw him coming and moved out of the way, instead giving Daniel a firm pat on the shoulder. "Watch yourself on those footfalls. Those bags under your eyes look like you walked into a wall."

Lucas couldn't help feeling bad for Daniel, but knew the story between him and Zane was probably more complicated than either let on. He thought about that as Zane led him towards Henry's home where Bill and Devon would be. Daniel walked behind them from a distance.

When the three of them entered Henry's home, Lucas saw Devon, who looked to be around the same age as Sapphire if not slightly older. His hair was dark brown and fell over the top of his eyelids and covered his ears. His green eyes were bloodshot similarly to Jacobs and the look he now gave Lucas was both knowing and uninterested. Although his attention shifted more towards Daniel, his appearance seemed transfixed and unemotional.

He looks like someone who is doped up on medicine; more in their heads than out, Lucas noted uneasily.

"Thank you all for coming here," Henry noted. His own attention was shifting between everyone in the room. His eyes darted past each of them like a pinball machine. First at Devon, then Bill, Lucas, Daniel, and finally Zane.

Devon mumbled wordlessly to himself. His knuckles cracked and he clicked his tongue a couple of times.

"What's wrong with Devon?" Bill asked Henry. It was like he was barely noticing his new companion's inactive state.

"He is still feeling the effects of his separation from Jacob's proximity," Henry noted, as if instructing a classroom full of students.

In other words, Devon is going through some kind of withdrawal. Why isn't that happening with Bill?

"If that's the case, how can we know whether Bill is feeling those same effects in a different way," Zane noted.

Bill tensed at this but said nothing. His thoughts told Lucas the comment hurt him more than he showed.

"We cannot know for certain," Henry responded pragmatically. "But there are other matters of grave importance we must all discuss going forward."

When no one said anything else, Henry continued.

"I gathered the five of you here because there are a couple of things that must be addressed."

Lucas saw how Bill trembled and appeared anxious as if already anticipating the worst.

"First off, there is no easy way for me to say this, but, Bill, you can no longer be a camp counselor," Henry said impassively as Bill's heart sank. "We are short staffed so you may assist the counselors with their training, but you will be a camper for the remainder of your time here. I am truly sorry."

Bill started to shake compulsively and he fell to his knees, looking nearly as immobile as Devon.

No…No…All I ever wanted was to be a counselor, to help others, to be like Daniel…

Lucas heard Bill rant angrily inside his mind. Daniel calmly took hold of him and took him to the nearest seat. He cried so hard that the cloth began to melt with the tears streaming down like ice. A glow began to emit itself from his bandages.

"Everything's going to be alright, you said so yourself last night, Bill," Lucas noted. His former cabin mate looked up and his mouth made a snarling gesture similar to Shannon's.

'Shut up, Lucas!" Bill shouted out loud angrily. "You broke my sister's heart. When were you going to tell me about that?!"

Zane began to emit electricity from his fingertips when Bill's eyes were becoming visible through the cloth. He adjusted his bandages clumsily and threw up his misshapen left hand palm up.

"Please, Camp Director James, there has to be a way I can still be a counselor. I'll do whatever it takes," Bill pleaded as he rose from his seat and tried to find Henry's desk.

Why does he sound so much like I did when I woke up from my accident?

When he found Henry's desk, Bill laid his palms on it firmly.

"I never did anything I wasn't supposed to do. My training here, helping people, and now you can't even try to help me? After everything Lucas has done, you still want him around?"

Lucas felt his own heart sinking as Henry shook his head firmly.

"I am sorry, Bill, but there is nothing I can do. My decision is final."

When he said this, Daniel looked at his father and his eyes glanced at Lucas then back to the Camp Director.

"What about what you did for Lucas? Why can't you do that for Bill?" Daniel asked sharply.

"It's not possible, Daniel. This is a power. It's something that can never be altered."

Daniel did not respond. He only glared at Lucas with contempt.

"Funny, that's what we call ourselves right? Alter Children?" Zane noted. "Yet our power cannot be altered once it's been a certain way. Is that how it is?"

"In a manner of speaking, yes," Henry noted.

"So you can't help Bill the way you healed me?"

The Camp Director gave Lucas a sharp look and he realized the thought was spoken out loud.

That's not good at all.

Bill didn't know this part and looked about ready to unleash his volatile energy beams.

"Wait, what? So *that's* why you weren't paralyzed anymore?!"

If my voice were legs, I'd win every race there is.

Bill's face grew tight and his fists clenched. He was about to lunge at Lucas when Zane intercepted him and placed his hands under Bill's armpits. The counselor's fingers interlaced behind his neck, with a small static charge coming up.

"Quit while you're ahead," Zane cautioned, his grip tightening as Bill's arms flailed up and down like a dog's tail.

"You got your body back. I want my power back. I want my *life* back!" Bill shouted. He groaned at the burning tears, as the fight in him dissipated.

"This isn't right," Daniel admitted. "There has to be something that can be done. What if we understood how it was done? That could make a difference."

Henry looked like he gave this some thought but didn't seem to be making a motion to give those thoughts the light of day. After Zane released Bill, he calmed down and began to explain what happened to him.

"I was strapped to something hard and wooden," Bill remembered in anguish. "They made me drink something that was like slime and tasted like… death. One minute I could see fine. Then my eyes began to burn really badly. When I opened them again, that's when the beams came out. I could never do that before."

Henry understood instantly.

"You would have eventually. Powers are like any other muscle in your body; they must be exercised and mastered in order to reach their full potential," Henry explained, "but I fear what has been done to you has not only halted any further advancement in your abilities. It has also evolved into something that may prove to be potentially fatal in time."

The whole room became cold and all but Devon seemed to feel this.

"You mean this will eventually kill me?" Bill asked tensely.

Henry nodded calmly in response.

He probably should not have told him that. This could get ugly fast.

"There must be a way to prevent that from happening," Daniel insisted. "What if he doesn't use his beams too often? That way it won't hurt him."

Henry shook his head, just as Devon seemingly ended up perking up to that. The small boy made a shaking motion that was eerily similar to the Camp Director.

"The best we can hope for is assisting Bill to master the ability as it is now. At the moment, it is still young just as a newly discovered ability would be. It won't be long before it will require a more concrete way of preventing the beams from emitting themselves. Those bandages will not help and to suppress them would be ill-advised. "

Bill's face turned in the direction of Henry.

"How long do I have?" he muttered with fear.

"I cannot say. It could be years before your powers manifest strong enough to cause you more harm, but its acceleration is alarming to be sure."

The small boy made a motion around his eyes with his hands, as if trying to zoom in on something. He made grunting sounds like a monkey, and it took all of Lucas' impulsiveness not to laugh out loud at the charade-like behavior.

"Can someone translate what the kid is saying," Zane asked in annoyance. "I always hated charades."

Why doesn't he just say what he wants to say? Lucas wondered in a similar feeling to Zane.

Bill lowered himself to a knee so his face and Devon's were inches from each other. The small boy patted his shoulders, nose, neck, and forehead.

Bill nodded and rose back up.

"He mentioned something about glasses I could wear," Bill said to the astonishment of the room.

"You got all that from some tapping on your body parts?" Zane asked in disbelief.

"It's hard to explain but it's how Devon communicates and he does it in a random way so that his mind can't be read by telepaths like Jacob."

Out of curiosity, Lucas decided to put that to the test and read Devon's mind. What he got back was a series of sounds that were like static at the end of a dead radio. There were other sounds as well such as bubble popping, hiccupping, and vibrations. The pain that occupied mind reading hit Lucas' head like a belt.

Ugh, that felt more like hitting a wall headfirst.

When he was finished, Devon gave Lucas a direct look as if knowing what had just happened. He touched Bill's elbow rapidly, then tapped the bridge of his own nose.

"He says he knows what you just did, Lucas," Bill said, "and to not do that again."

Lucas frowned as Zane let out a soft chuckle.

"Somehow I understood that without explanation."

"I do not believe all Silent Ones are of a similar caliber to young Devon here," Henry noted.

"What's a Silent One?" Lucas asked Henry.

"They are children who are under Jacob's control and cannot speak because of something he does to their minds. That is all I can say at this time."

Devon looked in Henry's direction and gave the Camp Director a similarly knowing look. He tapped the desk a few times, knocking one side, then another. When he was satisfied, he began to tap rapidly on it. It didn't take long for all but Lucas to realize what those tapping sounds were.

"What is he saying, Bill? It sounds like Morse code."

"He's going too fast. Devon, slow down."

The small boy did not slow down and instead kept going rapidly, until he began to appear lightheaded. His eyelids were closing up and down similarly to the tapping he just did. Then he found a chair and slouched down with a silent sigh.

"That was quite the display," Henry noted, appearing unmoved and unaffected by Devon's display. While the small child attempted to regain himself, the Camp Director moved on to the next order of business.

"The other reason I wanted you all here is because Lucas will be going on his first mission and he will be accompanied by Zane and Devon. This mission will take place by the end of the week, so you have time to select two more campers to join you three as well, Lucas."

Wait what? A mission? Already? So soon?

Daniel looked like he wanted to protest, but a look from his father silenced him completely.

"You will be in charge of training the campers in Zane's group, Daniel, after this week. Please make sure to complete your other tasks as well."

Daniel nodded and looked even more displeased than he had initially. Turning his attention back to Lucas and Zane, Henry continued.

"This mission will be different from ones we ordinarily send others on," Henry noted. "Zane will lead this mission with Lucas and two other campers joining him."

Devon opened his mouth as if to say something. Instead, he just yawned and shook his head.

"I'll escort him back to the ward," Daniel declared. Henry raised his hand in protest.

"That won't be necessary, Daniel. Devon will be placed in the Imaginarium Illusion along with Bill, who will be rejoining the cabin for the duration of the summer."

Bill's face fell and it took all he had to not say or do anything. All he did was lift Devon to his feet and walk him out of Henry's home silently. Daniel walked after to help Bill since he couldn't see, but Bill insisted he knew the way.

When the meeting was finished, Zane made a coughing sound as if he had something stuck in his throat.

"If there's nothing else, I'd like to talk with Lucas about the mission."

Henry nodded, appearing exhausted suddenly. He didn't say another word as Lucas and Zane left his home.

What does he really want to talk about? Lucas wondered. He tried to keep pace with Zane but found it harder than he initially thought.

When they neared the training field, Zane sighed and immediately took a firm hold on Lucas' forearm. For a moment Lucas thought he was going to zap him to death or carry him off.

Instead Zane pulled back Lucas' sleeves to reveal the cuts and marks around his wrist down to his elbow. He also lifted Lucas' shirt, revealing the nail-mark scars, and lines that encircled him. Lucas didn't even fight back when he did this, and looked at the wounds and small scars impassively.

"You stupid, idiotic boy. So it is true," Zane said with disdain. "That girlfriend of yours is worried sick about you, and not the one that you just recently broke up with. The blonde-haired re-bound. She told me about these little marks of shame. I didn't think much of it but I guess I gave you too much credit."

Lucas did not say anything back. He only rolled up his sleeves and swatted Zane's hand away. Zane shook his head and sighed.

"Can I at least ask why you're doing this to yourself? I'll show you mine if you tell me yours?"

Lucas felt reluctant to say anything, but from the way Zane's eyes looked at him, he knew no response would only get him into more trouble.

Lucas also read Zane's mind and heard him think: *If you don't tell me, I will report this to Henry and tell him that you are a danger to yourself. You'll be put in a nuttier box than your cabin.*

Before Lucas could respond, Zane looked around the training field and rolled up his long sleeves to show small lines across his arms from his wrist to his elbow. He also lifted his shirt up, revealing a surgical heart scar, an appendix scar, and a burn mark on his right hip.

All those scars tell a different story.

After showing them, Zane covered the scars and spoke with a soft tone.

"I've been through worse, kid. Worse than anything you possibly have, but believe me when I say it does not get easier, not in our line of business," Zane said sympathetically. "Scars don't lie though. They are a reminder of the small little things you did wrong in your life. Since we'll be going on a mission together, I want to know what you did wrong to give yourself those scars."

Lucas revealed hesitantly the nightmares of falling and the dreams about Jacob that he still had. Zane's face grew even more twisted and sour, so much so that Lucas swore he had never seen the counselor look this way before.

He looks like my dad used to when he was about to hit me or my mom.

In an instant, Zane's fist flew into the air, but he did not strike Lucas. Instead he laid his palm very calmly but heavily on Lucas' shoulder, while sighing with similar emphasis.

"You are a real handful, you know that?" said Zane with a hint of sympathy. "Why can't you be like half the kids in this camp? Not a care in the world or worry. I'll let you in on a little secret; stop me if you've heard this one: You want to hurt your enemies? Live. You want to make your loved ones happy? Live. You want to do something worth doing? Live. Death is easy, but life is hard. Nothing worth doing is ever easy, and for however hard life can be, there's more possibilities in it than in death."

Lucas swore that Zane acted very empathetic, like he somehow *cared* about him.

And the sky will fall before I believe that.

The very thought made him want to laugh, but not in front of Zane.

"Also it might not be any of my business but I feel someone needs to tell you this. That girl, Ashley, is one of a kind," Zane noted to Lucas. "I'm on the side of the fence that believes you did not hurt her purposefully, because if you did I'd punch you out before Daniel had the chance. Regardless, you need to make things right with her before we go on this mission. I'm not saying buy her flowers or chocolates or anything, but show her you care. Just don't treat her like a rebound because no one deserves that, least of all her. If you're willing to do some growing up, she's the best person to do it with."

Lucas raised an eyebrow and was about to insist she was just a friend when he hesitated.

No, she's not just a friend.

"There's not a lot of girls in this world who would put up with crazy and you, kid, are certifiable." Zane didn't say this with any malice in his tone and when Lucas looked at the counselor, he had a grin on his face that made him look younger.

"Thanks I guess," Lucas said in a dry tone.

"Sure, kid. Anytime. Now then, as you no doubt are aware, we will be going on a mission soon," Zane stated. "I figured since you and I didn't get to do the last mission to rescue Bill, this can be a nice redemption arc for both of us. When it comes to the last two team members, I'll leave that choice to you."

While Lucas wanted to be more excited about the upcoming mission, he felt annoyed that it would be with Zane. The circumstances also felt like a way to get rid of him after what happened with Ashley. Despite this, Lucas hoped by the time he returned he could talk to her more about her feelings for him before the end of summer.

Just her feelings? What about mine? I'm still not sure how to feel…

"Who do you think should join us on this mission?"

Zane shook his head.

"That's for you to decide since you'll be team leader this time. You'll still answer to me, but whoever you pick answers to you. Like I said last time, your sister is welcome to join us. She shows promise with that ability of hers and Henry said first year campers can go on missions if they have a good grasp of their power. If you choose her, all we need is one more team member."

Just not Josh, Lucas heard Zane think. *For a kid who's deaf, he sure talks more than a person who can hear themselves.*

He was about to walk away when Lucas called out to him.

"Why me? What makes me leadership material?"

Zane turned to look at him and gave him a grin with a shrug.

"Absolutely nothing. But you need the training, and something to do, don't you? The way I see it, you're still under my watchful eye, so you coming along will continue your house arrest on the road," Zane replied ironically. Lucas frowned, feeling disappointed he expected any other kind of answer.

In the solitude of his cabin, Lucas thought about who he should take with him. He thought about Josh despite Zane's apprehensive thoughts, but besides him the only person who came to mind was Bill. Sadly, his former cabin mate was less likely to go than anyone else he could think of.

I should visit Ashley and Mike before the week is over. If Hailey will let me go as far as the door that is.

Nearing the Weeping Willow, Lucas spotted Jeremy and Ashley talking near the entrance of the cabin. It was the first time Lucas had seen him since the last attack on camp. Even though Jeremy was in a wheelchair with his legs in casts, he otherwise looked to be in good health. His face said he was confused by what he was hearing while Ashley looked firm in her words.

"I don't understand," Jeremy said, his voice sounding less confident than usual. "I was hoping you'd be up for another date since the last one was cut short."

"I'm sorry, but I don't think of you in that way, Jeremy," Ashley insisted. "I'd like us to be friends if you're open to that."

He seemed to consider this before glancing in Lucas' direction.

He definitely noticed me.

"I get it. Someone beat me to it already right?" Jeremy's voice sounded like he was defeated but that aura of confidence reemerged. "You'll be the first girl in this camp to reject a second date. Is that weird if it impresses me more than upsets me?"

Lucas heard Ashley chuckle and the two parted ways after that with Jeremy wheeling himself away.

Is that how people break up? That is a far cry from how Vanessa and I broke up.

With Ashley alone again, Lucas expected Hailey to turn him away. Instead, she allowed him to see Ashley, but she stayed near the entrance and appeared as vigilant as Boris.

"You're going on a mission? Already? What kind is it?" Ashley asked through clenched teeth. She appeared to be doing slightly better. Her face was returning to how it used to be and despite still speaking with difficulty, she was healing at a remarkable rate. The damage wasn't as bad as Lucas had feared, but Ashley would need to recover for the rest of the summer.

"I'm not sure. I just know that it's going to be with Zane and I can pick two more people. I would pick you but…"

He could feel Hailey's glare by the door, as if she were honing in on him with laser beams.

"I heard about you and Vanessa. I'm really sorry," said Ashley, sympathetically.

No she's not.

"It's okay. I'm okay. How about you and Jeremy? Are you going on a second date after all?"

Ashley seemed surprised by this question and gave Lucas a quizzical look.

"Apparently I'm the first girl in camp to deny him a second date," Ashley admitted with a tone that suggested sadness. "Which is a shame because he's really a nice guy."

Nicer than me? Is that what she's saying? He also has more muscles than me. She forgot to mention that.

"His loss, even though I know he would have if you wanted. I don't know why I said that." Lucas tried to recover but decided to own his fumble. He appreciated it when Ashley gave him a soft smile.

"Anyways, when I get back from this mission you'll be the first to know."

Ashley nodded and smiled at him.

"Actually, *I'll* be the first to know. Then Ashley," Hailey corrected him sharply.

She's not going to make things easier for me. Great. Hailey in camp, and Zane on the road, why does everyone always hate me?

"I'm going to visit Mike also just to see if anything has improved for him."

Ashley nodded and thanked Lucas for visiting her. He was about to leave when he remembered what Zane told him.

"Hey, Ashley?"

She looked up at him expectantly and her smile never wavered.

"You're pretty awesome." Lucas shook his head and rephrased the word. "You're amazing. Pretty amazing. I just wanted you to know I think that of you."

He considered saying more but bit his tongue, knowing Hailey's impatience.

"You're incredible, Lucas," he heard her say from behind him. "I meant every word I said before. Come back safely, please."

Lucas nodded and made his way to the hospital ward.

To Lucas' relief, Mike was awake and appeared calmer than the last time they spoke. His arm was no longer in a cast and looked pale, but was otherwise fine. Lucas could also see Mike's leg, which despite still appearing injured, did not seem in the least bit to bother his friend.

"Hey, Luke, it's good to see you again," Mike said weakly.

He closed his eyes and concentrated on some words and images.

Pears and apples are good for you, and provide lots of nourishment. Banana and bread can be combined like cherry and pie. What do you do?

Mike sighed and turned his attention back on Lucas.

"I'm guessing you heard that?" Mike asked Lucas.

He nodded.

"It helps to calm me down and the voices I've been hearing in my head since I got back. I'm not sure what to think of that."

"Do you remember anything, Mike?" Lucas asked, changing the subject. "I don't know if anyone has told you but Bill's back."

Mike nodded, his face making a twitching gesture like he ate something sour.

"Bill came by to visit me not that long ago."

That's good, I wonder what they talked about.

"Do you still feel Jacob's mind control? How are you feeling?"

Mike shrugged, his fingers beginning to scratch themselves. Lucas began to feel uncomfortable and turned his eyes away from the sight.

"I felt him, Luke," Mike revealed. "He didn't use mind control on me. He didn't have to. All he needed was to plant something inside me. A feeling mixed with a thought. Jacob did that when I grabbed his ankle. My new ability lets me see things about someone when I touch them. It's why I need to wear gloves now, not just because of the sensation I get from touching stuff."

Lucas wasn't sure he understood until Mike continued.

"When that moment of contact happened between me and Jacob, something went wrong. He did something to me, because instead of seeing one of his memories, he made it where I couldn't think of anything else except that one moment in time where... He made me remember the hospital where…" He couldn't get the words out to say what he wanted, so he let his mind do it for him.

Where my sister spent much of his life and where my parents lost their lives.

Lucas felt the sadness seep into him like a cool wave, looking at Mike's expressionless face that concealed so much pain from that memory. It was too much that he didn't notice his own pain because Mike's was more prominent.

"He made it so it was all I could see. I was so afraid that it was all I could do to try and stop it. The crazy thing is I'm not afraid anymore. Look at me. I'm in a hospital and I'm not afraid."

Mike closed his eyes again and recited more words in a specific way.

Strength in numbers. The more the merrier. United we stand, together we fall. No wait! It's divided. I need to start all over again! Strength in numbers. The more the…

Mike let out an exhaled groan and tried to calm himself.

"I need to tell you something, Luke. It's about what I saw Jacob do with his abilities." Mike paused, collecting himself. "He doesn't just control people; he breaks people down from within. Their fears, hopes, doubts, and insecurities. He forces a mirror in front of them so it's all they see. He magnifies that image until it's all a person hears. When he does that, he plants thoughts into a person's head. Only they're not typical commands but rather ideas that feel as natural as love and hate. I don't know how else to explain it except that it feels right. Like something I was missing my whole life and Jacob helped me see it without even trying."

Mike said this last part in such a dreamlike state that Lucas began to feel even more unsettled.

"He's not the monster everyone in camp has made him out to be and he's not about hurting people; Jacob is about helping others to see themselves in order to be free."

This part in particular interested Lucas.

"Free from what?"

"From control…"

Before he could say more, Mike sighed and turned away from Lucas.

"I need to sleep now, Luke. When you can, have Shelly bring Sapphire by."

Lucas made his way towards the exit of the room. Suddenly, a thought entered his mind in both Mike's voice and intermingled with his own. He wasn't sure if this was his thought or Mike's.

Mom…Dad…she'll be home soon…we both will…

The pain that Lucas felt from this was like being pricked with a needle in the back of the neck. It took all he had to keep it to himself when he spotted one of his cabin mates coming towards him.

Gary was hard to miss with the red camp cap on his head. He was also holding an open box of Whoppers.

"Hey, Luke," Gary said mid crunch. "How's Mike doing? I was just about to check on him."

"He seems to be doing better," Lucas lied, "and asked that someone look after Sapphire since he'll probably be here the rest of the summer."

There was a conflict in Gary's face that told a different story. Lucas knew without having to read his cabin mate's mind that he didn't completely believe him, but accepted the explanation regardless.

"Best of luck to whoever gets that gig," Gary said, before offering Lucas some Whoppers. Lucas politely declined and the two parted ways with Gary wishing Lucas luck on his first mission. "You got this, Lucky Luke."

Before he left the hospital, Lucas picked up the pills Keira prescribed him and decided he would take them the night before the mission.

After Lucas visited his two friends, the rest of the week flew by. He took his meals with Zane a distance away from him, did a few more sessions with Keira, and attended his training but was excluded from the rest of the campers. At the end of each day, he was told to report directly to his cabin. As time went on, Lucas was liking house arrest a lot less than how it was advertised.

I'll ask Shelly if she wants to come, and I guess Josh can be the second person.

Asking Shelly didn't go how Lucas expected.

"Who's going to take care of Sapphire while I'm away?" Shelly has responded. He sighed in frustration at the oversight. The little girl was sitting in the corner of the Weeping Willow playing with Twinkle and her stuffed doll. She didn't seem to notice they were talking about her.

"Maybe Keira can look after Sapphire?" Lucas thought, remembering that Sapphire liked Keira. "We won't be gone that long. Plus with Mike awake, Sapphire can go visit him more often now."

Shelly seemed to consider this idea with some thought.

"I can ask her and if she says yes then I'm in. You said the group is going to consist of you, me, and Zane. Who else is coming?"

Lucas mentioned Josh, which made his sister frown.

"I know he's your friend, but he keeps trying to flirt with me every time I see him. It was cute at first, but now it feels annoying. Isn't he dating that girl Kendall?"

Lucas didn't hear more. He was focusing on the fact that Josh was hitting on his sister, something which clearly annoyed her.

"I'll talk to him and see if he can stop doing that. If he does, he can be the last member of our group."

His sister seemed satisfied and the two parted so Shelly could make arrangements with Keira to watch over Sapphire in her stead.

Convincing Josh for the mission ended up being easier than getting him to admit to flirting with Shelly.

"She told me you're dating Kendall now?"

Josh shrugged.

"We kissed but that doesn't always mean anything," Josh responded with signing and speaking. The way he said it did not sound convincing.

He's definitely head over heels for her and I don't need to read his mind to know that.

"Are you going to be cool if you join us on this mission?" Lucas asked, making sure Josh's face was looking at him 100% of the time. Josh looked like he was going to joke at first, until he saw the seriousness in Lucas' eyes.

"Fine, I'll be on my best behavior."

With his group assembled, all that needed to happen now was the day itself. Lucas took the pills he received from the hospital and made sure to read the prescription first. Taking the pills helped not only calm his nerves, but helped him sleep peacefully that night.

Back in the Camp Director's home, Henry's mind wandered away that night. When he was alone, the Camp Director began to sob silently, and found himself on the floor weeping.

"What have I done? What have I done?" Henry repeated, each time with more pain than the last.

Daniel made his way towards his father's home, intent on talking to him about sharing the load of his tasks with the remaining counselors, only to find Henry in tears. This was the second time Daniel found his father in a troubling state and he began to worry.

"Are you alright, father?" Daniel asked with concern, the previous resolve he had just felt was being replaced by genuine concern.

Henry noticed him and tried to compose himself helplessly.

"I am fine, son. Thank you," the Camp Director responded amid the tears that kept coming.

Daniel heard the word 'son' and felt a bit of happiness at the sound. Nonetheless, he offered to help him up, but Henry rebuffed him softly. When he wiped his eyes clean, the Camp Director sighed deep and hard.

"So Lucas leaves tomorrow if I am not mistaken," Henry said calmly.

Daniel nodded.

"Yes, father. He will be with Zane. He is… in adequate hands."

As he said this, Daniel questioned his own words. A part of him wished to be the one to lead the group, even if it meant spending time with Lucas. Still, anything had to be better than all the responsibility that was now expected of him. Henry felt new tears begin to surface, until he wiped them in their infancy.

"The reason I came here tonight was because I wanted to see if some of the tasks you mentioned could be—"

Henry didn't look at Daniel as he interrupted him.

"The day you were born I never left the room," said Henry softly. "I stayed there with your mother the whole time, holding her hand as she brought you into the world. All the time thinking what a cruel thing I was doing…"

As he spoke, Daniel listened to his father intently but did not understand the last part.

"She was a beautiful person, your mother. The love of my life," Henry added sorrowfully as the tears streamed from his eyes down. "She wanted a child, more than anything…"

"Then why did you leave us, father?" Daniel asked bitterly. "You left us alone. You left *me* alone, your only son."

Henry shook his head.

"I never meant to abandon you or your mother. I never belonged in the world that your mother welcomed me to. It was through her that I became the man I am now, but you. You have made me see the fruits of my labor."

The Camp Director broke down and buried his face with his right palm. Daniel relented and held his tongue for what he really wanted to say.

"I am so sorry. I'm sorry for everything I ever did…I couldn't save them… I tried. Oh I tried. With all my heart. There was no other way… it was the only way…" Henry confessed in deep regret.

Most of the time, Henry's words and appearance seemed cold and distant, but at this moment he was very vulnerable, very human. Daniel shook his head and put his hand on Henry's shoulder.

"You helped me when I came here. I didn't know you as my father, but I knew you as a Camp Director who helped me and everyone else who has come before and after. That's what's important. I am proud to call you my father."

Finally, Henry calmed himself and wiped his eyes clean. The room was silent, the only sound that was in it was their breathing as Henry stopped sobbing and Daniel held back the urge to say more.

"I need rest. I must gather my thoughts."

The Camp Director rose from the floor and walked over to his desk. Daniel found a blanket for him and eased him to comfort. He wrapped the blanket around his father as gently as a mother would for their child.

After Daniel tucked him in, Henry smiled thinly with his eyes closed.

"Are you having a good time in camp this year?"

Daniel nodded and cast a dark shadow above his father's own.

"It's been hard, but I appreciate the responsibilities you've given me. I really do, father. I just wish it wasn't all on me sometimes. I have to remind myself how strong you are though. For all you do and the greatness that comes with it." Henry said nothing to this. "Keira and I are doing great though. She is the greatest thing in my life. The reason I can get up in the morning and the person I see a future with."

The Camp Director smiled and exhaled.

"In fact, I wanted to tell you this sooner but I guess now is as good a time as any. I'm going to ask Keira to marry me and I'd like for you to be the one to initiate the marriage. Here in Camp Supernatural. Can you imagine? The first wedding here?"

Henry did not respond.

"I know we've had our differences, father, and that it isn't easy for you to talk to me about my mother. I miss her so much and all I want is to know her the way you did. Sometimes I can't even remember what she looked like… except in the end… But I want to change, and I will for you. I want to let go of the past and for us to become closer. I want to be the son you deserve," Daniel asserted with pride.

Henry smiled with one last tear trickling down his closed right eye. Daniel patted his father's hand softly and got up to depart.

"I will come back in the morning to check on you. Thank you for everything you do and I will trust in your judgment going forward. Sleep well, father."

Henry nodded and finally spoke up before drifting to sleep.

"That's great… I'm so proud of you, Lucas…"

Daniel stopped dead in his tracks the moment he heard the name. He turned to look at his father who was sound asleep.

Suddenly, it felt like time had frozen on him. Nothing else mattered, as he stood there motionlessly staring at his father, half-hoping for him to wake up and correct himself.

He was supposed to say Daniel, not Lucas. Why is it always Lucas? Lucas this, Lucas that. I'm his son, me, not Lucas, me! Daniel thought in a fit of rage as he left the room and returned to his tent.

He was relieved when he saw Keira was asleep. Daniel walked outside and sat in the front of his tent. Rocking back and forth, he clasped his hands to his head as if he were trying to keep his head attached to his shoulders.

I'm Henry's son, his only son. He should love me, only me. He never loved me. He never loved my mother. Only me, there is only me.

He began to cry, thinking about his mother and how much he missed her. He remembered how she made him feel seen in a way few people ever did. When meeting his father, he hoped to feel the same way, but at every turn, Henry ignored and belittled him.

He hates me. He can't stand me. I'm a bad son. I'm not good enough. I'll never measure up to his expectations. I'm just a reject compared to Lucas…

Chapter 22: Memory Has No Color

Bright and early on that July morning, Lucas was the first to arrive at the camp's entrance. Today he and his group would be setting out for his first mission.

Zane isn't *here, which doesn't set a good example for the rest of us,* Lucas noted. *He probably overslept or forgot to set his alarm clock.*

Josh came running up to Lucas as he was thinking this. He had a backpack slung over his regular attire and his hair was all unruly this morning. It seemed both cabin mates were sporting similar hairstyles.

"What do you think?" Josh asked. Lucas wasn't sure if he meant about the hair or something else. So he took a wild guess.

"Not bad, not original but alright."

This answer didn't seem to satisfy Josh, who looked disappointed.

"And I thought I was the deaf one." He shook his head and turned his back to Lucas. During this time, other campers were gathering around other parts of the camp to prepare for their own separate missions.

I wonder if they'll be like our mission or different, somehow. Maybe? Big maybe.

Shelly arrived next. She looked restless, like she hadn't slept the night before. Lucas noticed bags underneath her eyes and the way she walked like someone who was coming down a hill. She gave her brother a small smile and Josh a polite but cautious one.

"Nice to see you, Shelly," Josh said out loud and signed. It looked like he wanted to say more, but Lucas nudged him on the shoulder. "I'm sorry for making you uncomfortable with how I talk."

Not sure if that's how he said that part but it's close enough.

Lucas' sister nodded and appreciated Josh's attempt at making amends.

"You really do look nice in orange," Josh noted, giving particular attention to the orange camp shirt Shelly was wearing. She sighed and shook her head amiably.

I think things are going to be fine.

A few minutes after the initial group arrived, Zane finally showed up with Devon by his side. The small boy regarded the group with shrewd eyes that told more than his expression did.

What's Devon doing here? No one said anything about him coming along?

Zane had a biker's jacket on, sunglasses hanging from his shirt collar, and ripped jeans with holes he kept fidgeting with. He didn't look like he was going on a mission that was camp related.

He definitely just woke up. His hair is as unruly as uncut grass.

"What time is it?" Zane asked, looking at his watch and tapping it with a yawn.

"Time for us to go on a mission," Lucas responded irritably. He gave Zane an annoyed look, which Zane returned with one of his own.

"Alright, in that case, let's get some rules out of the way before we leave." He made sure all eyes were on him. The only one who didn't seem to be paying attention was Devon, but Zane didn't appear annoyed by this in the least. "Rule #1: I'm in charge, meaning what I say goes. I tell you to jump, you don't ask how high. You do it. I say use your ability on that guy, use it. No questions, no hesitation. Rule #2: This isn't a field trip so we are not bringing back souvenirs and we do not need dead weight. So I suggest you empty your packs and take only what is needed to survive such as food, water, and an extra pair of clothing. This won't be a long trip but still, just in case. Last rule #3: This mission is top secret and when we return none of you are to talk about it. That's the last one, simple and straight to the point. Any questions?"

Josh raised his hand but Zane ignored him.

"Onwards boys and Lucas' sister."

Shelly sighed as the five of them departed from the campgrounds. Lucas looked around as the environment began to change around them. This wasn't like the previous times where he left or entered camp. This felt like stepping into a new car which felt familiar but wasn't.

"Keep your shoes on at all times during the ride," Zane noted when they departed the bright summer feel of Camp Supernatural. The new landscape was the same as what Lucas saw before, which was the misty humidity. What was different from before were gulls encircling the skies around them.

It smells like the beach here. It didn't smell that way before. Also recent rain.

When Zane saw the group's surprised expressions, he grinned to himself.

"If you think that's impressive, you're going to enjoy this. Stand back." Zane lifted his hand up to the sky and began to make a circle with his index finger. The clouds began to mash together like a blending machine and bits of electricity were creating small sparks.

How is he able to do that? I thought the electricity came from his body. He doesn't say the whole truth apparently.

After a moment, Zane stopped and looked around with a sigh.

"Well the good news is we shouldn't be expecting any scattered showers or storms. I was barely able to make that light show for you all. The bad news is this fog isn't dissipating as fast as it should."

Zane pointed towards the heavy fog in front of the group which looked too thick to see beyond. Lucas was worried that walking too close to it would result in hitting an invisible wall.

"Isn't the fog supposed to be thick though?" Lucas noted. Zane gave him a disapproving look.

"Sure, when it needs to be, but it doesn't in this case. Now if we're done talking, we need to figure out a way out of this. Does anyone have any ideas?"

When no one responded, Zane seemed disappointed by this.

"Don't all volunteer at once. No need to be shy when one of you is deaf and the other is mute. What's your excuse?" Zane pointed to Lucas and Shelly.

"I don't know much about regular fog, much less supernatural fog like this," Shelly admitted. "What we need more is a compass or some kind of navigational device that takes us out of this fog."

Zane gave Lucas a knowing look.

"Maybe I should give your job to your sister. She seems to be giving this problem more thought."

Lucas grimaced and sighed, trying to think of a way they could navigate the fog.

Each of our abilities; telepathy, mimicry, screaming loudly, not sure what Devon can do yet, and electricity. Actually, wait.

"Doesn't Josh's ability allow him to read sonar? Vibrations on the Earth, that sort of thing?" Lucas asked. Zane looked intrigued, like he knew this answer but hoped Lucas would come to the same conclusion.

He definitely did.

"That's a good point but it will only help us so far as knowing where we are, not what to do once we figure that part out. There is a simpler version though." Zane pointed upwards towards the gulls. "We could just follow them."

Lucas realized this had been a test and they all failed spectacularly.

"It's great that you're thinking of using your abilities to get out of jams," Zane noted to Lucas, "but always remember your other senses too. The biggest one is common sense." He patted Lucas' shoulder hard and walked ahead of him.

He got me there, okay I'll admit that one.

"Why is this different from when we last came through here?" Shelly asked Zane. She gestured to herself and Lucas.

"The Camp's location is always changing," he noted. "You don't think we have one permanent residence do you? We'd invite all sorts of fellows that way. Not sure how Alistair found the camp last time though. For now, worry about those gulls. In this location they take us where we need to go."

Lucas and the others nodded (with Josh and Devon keeping to themselves) as they continued to walk through the fog.

Trying to pick up his pace a bit, Lucas reached into his pack to get some water and found a small piece of paper that was carefully wrapped. When he showed it to Shelly she regarded it knowingly.

"I put it there," Shelly admitted to her brother's surprise. "Read it to yourself."

Lucas reluctantly unfolded it and read it as Shelly joined Josh, Devon, and Zane forward.

"Dear Lucas, we have known each other for a year now. I have seen you at your very best and worst of days, but never once have I blamed you or wanted to push you away.

So please do not blame yourself for what happened. It wasn't your fault no matter what you tell yourself. I will always be your friend and I will always believe in the best of you. Love, Ashley

After reading it a few more times, Lucas also noticed a small sentence at the bottom.

"P.S. Don't be mad at Hailey, she is only looking out for me. Please come back safely."

Once Lucas finished the letter, he put it back inside his backpack, while Zane continued to use the electricity from the clouds overhead to call the gull's attention.

"We should be near water by now. Those birds are definitely playing us somehow," Zane noted in irritation. "Did anyone bring any food with them? Something to munch on like crackers or gum?"

The four companions shook their heads simultaneously which caused Zane to groan in annoyance.

"This is definitely not where I would have parked the camp unless there was some kind of rest stop nearby."

Zane took a quick breath and set himself on the ground to rest.

Lucas approached him and asked, "What exactly is our mission and why did we bring him?" He gestured towards Devon, who looked uninterested by his surroundings.

Zane scoffed.

"Do you really want me to spoil the surprise, kid?"

Lucas nodded.

"Alright. So originally, we didn't really have a lot of information on Jacob or his plans. Even with those weird dreams of yours, there was only so much information you could give us. Keeping that in mind, no pun intended, when we found out that Bill escaped and that he brought along his own pet Silent One, well, we pretty much hit the jack pot. While Devon over there isn't exactly a chatterbox, Bill was able to get him to open up. We found that Devon has a more personal connection with Jacob than the other Silent Ones. And that there is something big going down soon that can be prevented by going to

Domeworld. The bottom line is we need to go there and track someone down who has what we need. Capisce."

Domeworld? What kind of idiot came up with that name?

Lucas felt eerie about that. The fact that Devon didn't talk and Zane didn't seem concerned about all this made him wonder who was playing who?

"Do you trust him?" Lucas whispered to Zane. He gave Lucas a doubtful look and shrugged.

"He could be leading us to a trap. That's a possibility. We don't know. What we do know is he saved Bill's life and as far as I can tell he hasn't been to camp before. He might be one of those kids who got grabbed by Jacob early on and never made it."

Lucas got a chilling feeling, and thought about what this meant for the other kids who were with Bill that didn't come back.

I don't think finding them would help since they've been with Jacob now for too long. Then again, if Devon isn't as affected, there has to be a reason why.

"Okay so why do we need Devon? I get he knows stuff but who is he to the person we are meeting?"

Zane threw a finger up and made a tsk sound.

"That's enough spoilers. This is a need to know mission and right now that's all you need to know," Zane told Lucas, to his annoyance. "Focus on the task at hand and that is getting out of here. Once we do, you can ask me again."

Lucas sighed and followed along the same path as the gulls. He made sure to pace himself with Josh as well, who finally began to talk up a storm with him.

"So what's the deal with the kid?" Josh signed and asked, gesturing towards Devon.

"He's helping us, I think he is," Lucas signed but knew he had fumbled. Regardless, Josh nodded. "He knows where Jacob might be." Lucas said this part aloud but mostly mouthed it so neither Devon nor Shelly would hear.

"Is he taking us there or not?"

Lucas shrugged.

"Wait here."

Josh fell back a few steps and matched Devon's pace. The height difference between the two was noticeable. Devon went up to Josh's stomach and he didn't seem to notice an interruption to his thoughts until Josh tapped him on the shoulder. This caused Devon's head to shoot upwards, as if he were a bolt from a crossbow, and level his eyes in Josh's direction. The two began to communicate through a series of hand gestures although Devon's was notably different from Josh's.

It's like they're speaking an unknown language that only they understand.

Josh was speaking using both his voice and hands, while Devon's hands were both mimicking Josh and doing their own form of communication. In one instance, the small boy tapped Josh's knees one after the other, and to Lucas it looked like a kiddie version of Patty Cake. Josh seemed to understand the implication though, and responded accordingly.

Something in the way Devon moved his hands and his facial expression made Lucas feel uneasy. His eyes showed a boy whose field of vision wasn't concrete and interchanging depending on the circumstances. Trying to read his mind before did not yield any results, but this time Lucas picked up things he didn't before.

Right Yes, Left No, Below Tap Watch, Upper Tap Sky. Two taps Listen. One tap Simple. It's not a super accurate cheat code but it's enough.

Devon is tapping on his leg, he's clapping upwards, clapping his hands together once, and he keeps tapping his right shoulder. I don't get it but Josh is thinking, 'He's a little brother. We're going to see his big brother. His big brother says Devon is not very smart. He keeps insisting that he knows where he's going even though he can't say.'

Lucas was scratching his head as Josh and Devon continued to communicate with each other. He didn't notice Shelly walking up to him.

"I wanted to introduce him to Sapphire," she noted with a playful tone. "I feel like she'd be a good friend for him. She isn't getting along with all the girls in her cabin."

Lucas didn't know this because he rarely spoke to Sapphire or asked how she was doing.

I should. Josh was right about me; I tend to make things about myself more than I'd like.

"How are you holding up?" Shelly asked her brother cautiously. "We haven't really talked a lot since the whole, you know."

Since I almost beat a close friend and possible romantic interest to death? I'm doing greaaaaat. Thanks for asking.

"I'm fine," Lucas said simply. "We worked it out and everything is good between us now."

Shelly seemed doubtful of this but didn't pursue the topic further.

She knows about Ashley's feelings towards me. There's something more there but if I dig too deep, the pain will come and she'll know I read her mind.

He tried to keep to himself, hoping the conversation would die down, but Shelly seemed to have something else bothering her.

"I've been having a lot of dreams recently about mom and dad."

Lucas didn't reply. He tried not to read her mind even at a surface level for fear of what he'd find. When he didn't say anything, Shelly continued.

"I didn't tell you everything about what happened. Not because I didn't want to but because I don't remember a lot of it." Shelly paused and made sure it was just the two of them. Devon and Josh were still talking through a mix of sign language. Zane seemed to keep to himself but looked like he was near becoming impatient. He fidgeted with his watch and looked at the gulls with squinting eyes as if he meant to zap them down.

"It doesn't matter, Shell. You said so yourself."

"I know I did, but I was wrong. You deserve to know the whole truth."

Even though Lucas swore to himself he didn't want the whole truth, he had to admit the knowledge was gnawing at him like an itchy scab. He knew if he picked at it too much it would cause a new wound to open up where the old one had barely healed. On the other hand, he also knew not knowing now could cause him to begin self-harming himself again.

"What's the whole truth?"

"I'll tell you but first, you need to look into my mind, Luke. No matter how painful it is for you. We'll do this together."

Shelly was back in their parents' house in Austin. The walls had no color or pictures, only frames. Newspapers and book covers were blotted out as if with invisible ink. Every step she took made her feel like she was wearing noise canceling headphones. Looking around the living room, she spotted her parents, both immobile and unkempt.

Both their parents were sitting in the living room muttering to themselves. Their dad was crushing an empty beer can while staring down at a blank paper in his lap. Shelly's steps carried her close enough to her parents that she felt something off about their presence. It wasn't just the way everything felt, sounded, and looked to her. There was something very wrong with this recollection of her memory.

It feels like an old silent horror movie.

She extended arms as stringy as spaghetti strands and wrapped them around behind her mother. Shelly begged her mother to stop muttering to herself and to come back. Being in such close proximity made her behave exactly as her mother. She too began to mutter: "What have I done? What have I done? What have I done?"

Shelly's father said something different but in the same monotone as both mother and daughter.

"I don't want to die. I don't want to die. I don't want to die."

The room began to tremble and ethereal chimes began to play along to the rhythm of all three occupants' rapid hearts beating. Shelly held onto her mother for dear life. She tried to silence herself, covering her mouth, but she kept saying 'What have I done? What have I done? What have I done?' She squeezed her mother from behind until she was sure she'd suffocate her.

She wasn't sure if this was a good idea but hoped that if it was a dream she would wake up to find her parents incoherent instead of in this nightmare-like state.

Her mother made a gagging sound, as did her father. Both began to mutter something else now.

"**He is the one**," Shelly heard both her parents say at the exact same time. "**He will confront the darkness. He is the opposite of the one who came before him. One's destiny is written, the other must be made to see. Shrouded now because of pain that is to come. The path is there, only one must walk it. When the blood moon rises and the eyes of vermilion set on him. Once he knows, he will see, he will understand**."

The vision continued to become hazy and Shelly could hear Lucas' agonized screams in the background. His tears and his blood running down his nose at all these revelations. Shelly was no longer holding her mother from behind but Lucas. Her arms were wrapped around his chest and he was in a bear hug. He wasn't struggling, but he also was muttering, "I don't want to die. I don't want to die. I don't want to die."

Face this, Shelly thought and projected this to Lucas. *Lucas, you need to face this. You need to face mom and dad!*

Lucas opened his closed eyes and stopped muttering. The two of them were staring at silhouettes of their parents. Shelly wasn't sure what this meant, but when they shifted places, it looked like their backs were turned to them.

"I can't do it!" Lucas cried out. "I'm sorry, Mom! I'm sorry, Dad! I can't see you!"

The memory began to vanish and Shelly found herself on her knees with Lucas' head on her shoulder. Both were tear-drenched and covered in humidity. Zane, Devon, and Josh surrounded them and had concerned looks.

"What just happened there?" Zane asked, his normally easygoing demeanor completely gone and replaced with a look of absolute concern for his two campers.

"I showed Lucas the truth," Shelly began, "about our parents. I tried to help them. I tried to do something. But I couldn't. I could only watch them wither away. I could only see them…"

She began to sob more hard and this time, to everyone's surprise, Zane knelt down and hugged both Lucas and Shelly.

"It's okay. *It's okay.*" Zane said the last part with great emphasis. "You both suffered a terrible loss. The kind of thing no child should ever have to face. I am so sorry for that."

Both siblings were completely mystified by this. Not only because of the tender way in which Zane hugged them, but by the uncharacteristic way he spoke. No jokes or the typical rudeness they had become accustomed to. Instead he carefully said each word as if he were making a complicated dish.

"It's not fair and it never will be. But you have each other." Zane moved backwards and cupped both Lucas' left cheek and Shelly's right cheek. "Help each other through this loss. This kind of loss can make or break you. You need to get through this not just for yourself, Lucas, but for the people who love you. Your sister loves you so much. I would have given my left kidney to have a sister like her."

Zane said this part so bitterly and with such remorse it was enough to make both siblings want to cry again. Then he cleared his throat and stood up.

"Ahem, if that's the end of the waterworks, it looks like we found a way out of the fog."

Lucas and Shelly looked at each other incredulously and did the one thing neither sibling expected of the other. They began to laugh in such a way that made their previous sobbing a thing of the past. Josh took this cue as his turn to join in despite not knowing the full circumstance and Devon seemed indifferent to this.

"Alright now, settle down. Don't bust a lung," Zane cautioned. "We're not out of the woods yet. Well, technically we are but you know what I mean. We need to get off this island."

When the fog around them cleared, the island itself appeared to be like a discarded piece of land forgotten by civilization. The clear blue sky broke through the clouds and the sun shone down its spotlight to the five companions. The wind picked up and with it Shelly could smell the ocean and the sand. It was so close and intimate she felt like she was swimming in the ocean.

I didn't realize how big the ocean really is.

Shelly looked at Lucas and wondered if he was thinking the same thing as her. Both siblings didn't speak about the memory, but Shelly knew her brother was thinking about it.

Some things about the memory were different than what really happened. For instance, I never grabbed my mom like that. They only said those words a few times before becoming catatonic. The words they said, I remember hearing them, but I don't think they said that. Something about the dream was not right.

The more Shelly tried to rationalize the memory with the way she and her brother saw it, the more confused she felt. She decided to let it go while Zane explained what was to come next.

"Ordinarily, we would use the skeletal cab drivers from this point to make it to our destination," Zane noted. "But since Henry wasn't able to call upon them this summer, we'll have to use this."

Zane pulled from his pocket what looked like a weathered stone that had a huge Z etched into the middle. Lucas noticed a tiny crack on it which wasn't an encouraging sign.

"This boys and a girl, is a sanctuary stone," Zane explained. "It will take us back to camp as soon as the mission is complete. That's what it is used for, only now we need to use it for a bit more than that. Which isn't recommended but desperate times. The good news is that there's five of us and that's the recommended limit for the stone usage. The bad news is..." Zane pointed to the small crack forming on the stone. "That's been happening since the last time I used it and that was pushing it. So I figure at most it only has a few charges left. Out of curiosity, does everyone have their beads?"

Everyone but Shelly and Devon nodded.

"Lucas, lend your sister some beads, and tell Josh to do the same for Devon. Avoid the specific colors or initialized beads."

Lucas handed Shelly a few beads from his wristband and Josh, having read Zane's lip movement, did the same with Devon.

"Alright so hold onto those until we get back to camp because without the beads, this stone won't register you."

Zane tapped the stone with his open palm like cymbals and all five of them were engulfed in a sudden rush that made Shelly think of a roller coaster ride. She felt her head splitting and her body taking on a different shape than she knew. She looked around and saw her brother, his friend and the small boy, all looked like expressionist paintings.

I probably look the same to them.

Instantly, all five of them were dropped off to a new location, which was sunny and humid like an open oven. Panting, looking around, Shelly tried to gather her bearings. She saw Josh vomiting next to a vase while Devon seemed unaffected. Lucas also looked calm, though his eyes looked like they were underwater for too long.

They look bloodshot…

"I've got some sodas in my backpack. Help yourselves," Zane instructed.

He handed them one can each with Lucas quickly popping it open and taking a steady swallow of his. Shelly mimicked her brother's gesture, while Josh gulped his down in seconds and took Devon's before the small boy could protest.

"Welcome to Domeworld," Zane announced. The giant sign became visible to Shelly and the rest. On the top middle was a huge dome-like sphere and underneath the sign words similar to Camp Supernaturals:

'When in Dome, do as the dome do.'

Chapter 23: Cabin Wars

Noah's eyes were staring at the camp pen where newly arrived animals were being tended to by children campers. The only one he knew by name among them was Sapphire. She was being escorted by Keira, the camp's psychologist-in-training, along with Betty who had a few child campers with her. He thought about going over there to pet some of the animals; there were a few dogs, some cats, one horse, and plenty of birds in cages. Some of the birds were the ones associated with the nature walk activity.

Noah was so distracted that he didn't notice when his friend angrily tapped on his shoulder. He turned to see the pouty look of Amy, who looked like someone woke her up too early. Her dark blue eyes looked murky right now, with brows that conveyed a sense of irritation at something Noah wasn't too familiar with. Her curly gold-brown hair was done up with little scrunches to make her look like she had small horns. She wore a red camp shirt which read '*Final Curtain*' and had a unique design which had her initials: 'AFD'.

"This is the fourth time today you've ignored me," Amy said with annoyance. Noah shrugged and tried to justify himself. Looking at the dozens of water balloons near his feet, he realized he had forgotten again what they are for. It was hard for him to retain information for long, and often he had to write crucial information down such as when he ate (and what he ate), and when to take his medicine (something he hadn't done in a while) .

I always lose stuff because I forget where I last put it.

"Those animals look so pretty," Noah told Amy, who was too busy filling up the balloons with the wet dirt they got from the small river they used as a beach in camp. "I wonder where the Camp Guardian finds them. I want to look at the birds. I like birds, did I tell you? My favorite are eagles, because they're big and can soar very high."

Amy sighed and shook her head.

"You tell me that all the time, Noah. No offense, because it was cute at first but now when I think of you, all I think about are birds. We need to finish up so you can get back to your cabin. I still don't know why the Obnoxious Offspring and the Jaded Jester are having this war at all. I thought you all had a cease fire or something?"

Noah knew Amy was the more level-headed of her cabin, with the rest of her cabin mates being what he privately called the cast of a Broadway Musical'. When he first met Amy, he feared she would introduce herself in some big outrageous way, the way another one of her cabin mates in Swan Song had when she tried to befriend him. Instead, all she did was introduce herself in a calm and friendly way; this somehow made Noah even more nervous. It wasn't until after the two continued to hang out that he became convinced she wasn't going to do anything to weird him out. Soon after, they eventually got together for arts and crafts and spent the time describing their disabilities and abilities.

"I have short term memory loss, like Dory, and I can create for myself realistic scenarios in my head like movie scenes," Noah mentioned.

"That's pretty cool. So you're a mental then? Not in a bad way, just that camp categorizes Alter Children as either having mental or physical abilities?"

Noah thought about it and ended up agreeing with the idea.

"I guess. The only thing that sucks about the movie scenes I make is I forget them. I only remember the feeling, not the moment."

Amy nodded and gave him an understanding look.

"Well regardless I still say that's pretty cool. Meanwhile I'm physical." She lifted her hand, showing that two of her fingers were fused together.

"Your hands are Vulcan," Noah said aloud, not meaning to sound insensitive.

Amy laughed at this and nodded.

"I'm more of a Star Wars girl but yeah. I have something called syndactyly. It's when the skin or joints are fused together but in my case it's just the skin. I was born this way and I consider it a cool thing when I can do this."

At first Noah expected her to do the Vulcan Salute, but instead Amy steadied her hand and emitted what looked like small, concentrated webs on the tips of her fingers. The webs entangled themselves on the sides of her fingers and looked like they made small burns but this didn't seem to bother Amy much.

"It hurt a lot at first but now it's not so bad. The webs are not strong enough to swing with or do the stuff Spider-Man is known for doing, but I can do this."

She focused and used her other regular hand to catch the webs she was able to emit through her fingertips. When there was enough web, she made a sticky ball and handed it to Noah. He feared it would explode when he touched it or reveal a spider inside. Amy saw the hesitance in his eyes and reassured him it was fine. He took the web ball and found that it felt like yarn. *Sticky yarn.* He bounced the ball up and down and it felt like handling a bouncy ball.

"That's really awesome," Noah noted in awe. "How do you make the webs?"

Amy gave him an embarrassed look and that was enough to make Noah regret the question altogether. Even so, he shook his head and affirmed his acceptance of the ability.

"I think it's even better than what *Spider-Man* can do."

He, of course, didn't mean it, but for Amy's benefit, he did.

Amy had blushed at this and thanked Noah.

Now, this was their second summer in Camp Supernatural and both friends were thirteen years old. They had kept in touch during their time away from camp while also discussing the different ways in which the Jaded Jester would terrorize their cabins. During their first year, around July, Jaded Jester got one of their cabin members, who can spit acidic vomit, to shoot tiny spittles around their Obnoxious Offspring, giving it small little holes that wouldn't expand beyond a certain point. Unfortunately, the holes expanded so much that when it rained (as it often did in camp) the Obnoxious Offspring ended up flooded and Jaded Jester were demoted severely.

The Obnoxious Offspring then retaliated, when one of their campers, Ricardo, who had the ability to turn anything he touched into zero gravity, made everyone in Jaded Jester begin to float like balloons in their cabin. The Jesters were unable to get down, until Ricardo was forced to let them down after Henry got word of their prank wars.

After this, both cabins were banned from future pranks. Another point Henry mentioned was that they were violating the rule of the camp which is not to use their abilities on each other (even though they were mainly on the cabins themselves).

With most of the campers out on missions, Noah and Mario, the lead cabin mate of Jaded Jester, decided to reignite their friendly, contentious rivalry by waiting for the first stone to be cast. The plan was for Noah and Amy to throw water balloons filled with wet dirt while the cabin mates of Jaded Jester are out at an activity. Amy had it on good authority that Mario and his cabin mates would not be back for a while.

"They're taking part in that canoe activity that's always popular," Amy had told Noah prior to them filling the water balloons. "I heard a rumor around camp that there's this kid who came back from a mission all messed up. I think his name is Mike?"

Noah knew Mike and thought he was nice if not a bit standoffish.

I offered to shake his hand once and he gave me this look like I had dirt on my fingernails or something. I didn't but it just felt that way.

After the two friends finished filling up the last of the balloons, Amy carried the lion's share in her arms and let Noah carry a few in case he accidentally dropped some. He ended up dropping a few but luckily only two popped. He gave Amy an apologetic look and she sighed. They took the small balloons to his cabin and it was during this time when Noah began to think about something he never thought of before. Despite having been friends with Amy for over a year, he found himself beginning to have confusing feelings about her that he wasn't sure about. He recalled talking to Raul about it, his older cabin mate, since he was dating a girl from Cathedral Cove.

"Sounds like you have a crush on her," Raul told Noah, whose face turned as red as an apple. "It's nothing to be embarrassed about. You're a boy, she's a girl, and you've been friends for over a year. I'd be more surprised if you didn't notice your feelings for her by now."

Noah didn't feel embarrassed about the realization of having a crush, but rather that it was on Amy and not someone else. He didn't make it a habit of talking to a lot of people, and always noted that the only reason Amy became someone he talked to was because she came up to him first. Even so, he found himself creating a scenario in his mind where he had the courage to ask out Amy and tell her how he felt. He replaced his own voice with Andrew Garfield's, who he felt was more in line with what a girl would like. Noah used Andrew's known accent rather than the one he famously used in his mainstream films.

Amy blushed and got so happy that Noah finally noticed her and nodded enthusiastically when he asked her out. The two held hands and when they hugged it was like two puzzle pieces coming together that fit perfectly.

"Try not to drop the rest of the balloons this time," Amy insisted. Noah came to his senses and realized where they actually were. They were inside his cabin, alone.

I'm a boy, and she's a girl. We're friends. I like her but I don't know if she likes me.

"Hey, uh, Amy?" Noah said aloud before he could stop himself. Amy had gathered up the balloons and moved them to a pile next to other objects that were going to be used for the upcoming prank war such as rubber ducks that emitted a loud screech when squeezed, yoyo's that splattered grease when used properly, and wads of slime that were guaranteed to stick on any surface.

"Yeah, what's up? Did we forget something?" Amy asked without looking at Noah. "You should really clean your cabin more." She was staring at his side of the cabin and looking at his messy small bed. He had comic books, a small radio, race cars of different colors, and a Rubik's Cube that was more for show than actual use.

I've only been able to do one side of that thing successfully before I forgot the rest, Noah told himself.

"No, I think we're good. It's just, well, what do you think?"

Amy was confused but answered him anyway.

"I think we've got some good stuff. I can't speak for Jaded Jester though but I'll ask Vicky. She can hear really well and has told me she's heard what Jaded Jester has been planning for a while now."

Noah shook his head, trying to muster up the courage to say what he really wanted Amy to know before his mind made him forget.

What if she doesn't feel the same? What if I make a fool of myself? Will she still want to be my friend?

"We've been friends since last year," Noah started out saying. He pinched his wrist to make sure this was real. It was. "Right, since last year. I think that's been nice."

Amy turned to look at him carefully and nodded.

"I think so also. Are we celebrating an anniversary or something?"

Noah blushed at this, not recognizing the tone in which Amy was using.

"I'm just teasing you," she said with a small giggle. The hand with her two fingers together went up to her face and Noah couldn't take his eyes off it and her.

"You're so beautiful," he murmured to himself.

Amy's eyes shot up and she was staring point blank at Noah now.

"What did you say?"

Quickly trying to recover, Noah turned his face and body in different directions as if he were directing traffic.

"What did I say? I don't remember what I said. I didn't say beautiful. I said 'plentiful'."

"I'm so plentiful?" Amy asked in a not-so-convinced tone. If anything she began to look irritated.

"Yeah like you have plenty to go around." Before he could stop himself, Noah added wood to that kindling of fire. "They say enough is enough but you go beyond that when you put yourself out there. Which is good, because your cabin is known for that. You're not like most girls either because you don't need to show off. You're already a natural."

Noah pinched himself again to make sure this was real and he felt he was on a roll. Amy, on the other hand, was beginning to feel very uncomfortable.

"I don't know what you mean by a natural or plenty to go around," Amy said in a leveled tone. "But I think you should stop before you say something else you'll forget but I'll remember."

"What's that supposed to mean?" Noah asked in annoyance. He began to feel upset at what he thought were kind words and gestures. "I'm just saying what I feel."

"I don't think you know what you feel." Amy sounded saddened by this, as if she did not want to say this but felt it was necessary. "Look, it's fine, I get it. You don't know what this is and sometimes it's best to just be honest with each other."

Moment of truth time. The crowd goes wild, cameras are getting ready to capture the big moment.

"You're my friend, Noah, and I care about you," Amy mentioned. Her eyes fell from his as she continued. "I just want you to be okay and I know sometimes you're not. You play it off because of your condition, but I know sometimes you still remember the feeling. So things get to you more than you let on."

Noah hesitated as he considered.

"I think we are missing something after all," he proclaimed. "We're supposed to have those small containers that carry salt and pepper. But we wanted to switch the two so that they think it's salt instead of pepper, which it will be."

Amy looked like she wanted to continue and waited for Noah to look at her again, but there was an awkward silence between them.

"I don't want to lose you," Amy finally said after a moment of silence between them. "I don't know how this works. What we're supposed to do."

Noah did the best he could to focus on the moment, dashing away the thoughts in his head that insisted he retreat to his imaginary realm where things were simpler, safer.

"We can just be as we are and see where that goes," Noah heard himself say, not as Andrew Garfield, but as Noah Baxter. "I think that's how it's supposed to work."

After a moment, Amy nodded at this and smiled.

"I'd like that, I think that would work very well."

The two friends nodded and Noah made to touch Amy's two conjoined hands.

"Is this okay?"

Amy nodded and looked at him with a soft smile.

"Don't forget this feeling," she whispered and planted a small kiss on Noah's cheek. He did not.

When they gathered up everything in one corner, Raul came in to inspect them and was pleased with the results.

"Excellent work you two. Did he give you any trouble, Amy?" Raul asked her playfully. Noah had forgotten the profession but the smile remained on his face.

"No, this was nice. I can't wait to see what all-out war is going to look like," Amy responded while giving Noah a shy reassuring look. "You be careful out there alright?"

Noah nodded and returned her look with one of his own.

"We also have another threat going on in camp," Raul noted, breaking the spell between the two friends. "That's why we need this; so much of what's been going on is a reminder that at the end of the day, we're just kids figuring all this out as we go. But we're not alone and I think if enough of us can come together, nothing can stop us, real or imagined."

Noah and Amy looked at Raul with agreement and Noah swore his cabin mate was the coolest guy he knew.

If he decides to become a Camp Counselor next year, he'll be a great one.

"When do we attack?" Noah asked Raul. His cabin mate looked at his watch and opened the cabin door as if to exit.

"The day is young and we are still figuring things out. I think we'll strike at first light, once the Camp Guardian's eyes are away from the cabins."

Amy pointed to the pile of traps they laid and carefully profiled before categorizing them.

"This will mark the most important day this camp has yet seen," Raul exclaimed with such charisma that Noah swore he'd follow him to a dragon's lair. "Jaded Jester thinks they have the upper hand because the campers there have abilities that could spin our heads out of our bodies. What they don't know is that we can out think them. Noah's imagination here is so vivid and real that I swear you'd be a hit if you wrote books one day."

Noah flustered at this and began to think about a career in writing.

I feel like I've thought that before. I remember in my notes somewhere I wrote about making short stories out of the scenarios I have. If only I could remember where I put them.

"At first light we strike then," Amy proclaimed and grabbed both Noah's hand and Raul's hand, lifting them up.

When the first light came, and the balloons flew through the air like doves, there were indeed tears. On one side of joy, and on the other side frustration. Noah did not forget the feeling he felt when Amy's lips touched his cheek, or how her conjoined fingers felt against his. When he looked at her laughing, smiling face, he knew those feelings were true.

That's my new favorite scenario, because I didn't make it up.

Chapter 24: When in Dome

"Time for a history lesson," Zane began. Lucas and the rest of the group followed closely behind Zane as he spoke. "Why did I bring you all to what looks like a theme park? It technically is but that's not all. Fun fact: this place was once where Camp Supernatural was based at. Henry decided to call it Domeworld because it was an easily trademarked name."

I asked what kind of idiot named this place. I'm going to take that question to my grave.

"How does Henry decide where the camp will be each time it moves?"

"Excellent question, Lucas' sister," Zane said. "I don't know the whole answer, but I know a part of it. According to Henry, there are parts in this world where an Alter Child's ability is amplified even more than usual. Take your phone for example. Seriously, I need someone's phone, mine's dead." Shelly reluctantly handed him hers, and he took it as if swiping it without her knowing. "Now take Lucas' sister's phone here. If I take it to a certain part of the world, it loses reception. Connect it to the internet, and its signal is boasted high. Certain abilities are stronger in different climates, places where there's more nature than people, and some abilities are physical, so these abilities require a specific place where they can flourish. Your girlfriend for instance, Lucas, needs a smooth area to run without falling over herself. Imagine if she were a car driving on a road that had bumps and rocks all over. She'd trip over herself more than she already does."

She's not my girlfriend, and I get the idea without him painting a picture for me, Lucas thought, his irritation feeling like an itch he wanted to scratch. He was happy Shelly interrupted Zane, which took his mind off his discomfort.

"By that logic, would I flourish in a place that features something to do with my ability to mimic what I see, such as gymnastics or sports related?" Lucas' sister asked Zane.

"Yes and surprisingly no. Yes because you're able to accurately mimic what you see and retain a photographic memory. On the other hand, it does hurt you because the more information you intake, the less you have to differentiate what you know vs. the new knowledge you are trying to process. You're basically like a computer that needs to reboot itself every so often when your input is too much."

Both Shelly and Lucas were simultaneously shocked by this.

There were nights when my sister crashed because she spent all day either studying, working out, or hanging out with her friends. Because of that, sleep came easier to her than it did to me. Where I struggled to rest, she just needed to close her eyes and in less than a second she'd be out cold. It also explains why she feels something was off about the memory she showed me. I wish I didn't know that…

"Now if you're done asking questions—"

"Why is there a giant Dome thing?" Josh asked, as if entering the conversation for the first time.

"Somebody fill him in before I zap some sense into him."

Lucas took charge and explained as best he could their situation.

"I've never seen anything about this place," Josh signed. "Are we going to meet someone here or have fun?"

"I thought someone filled him in on that part," Zane asked in annoyance as the four of them walked behind him.

Devon made hand gestures that were specific to him and of the other four only Josh seemed to understand him.

"His brother is here and he has something we need?" Josh said as if he were reading the words off a projector. Lucas and Shelly looked at the two in surprise, while Zane looked annoyed.

"That pretty much sums it up. Even though this person claims to have what we need, it's still up in the air."

Up in the air? What does that mean?

They made their way towards the security post in Domeworld. Two armed guards, one looking as tall as a stone statue, and another that was shorter but still just as intimidating with a plump unfriendly face. Both their faces were obscured by shadows.

"Let me do the talking," Zane insisted. "We're here on a field trip from Camp Goose. Your name is Buck (Lucas), Duck (Josh), Chuck (Devon), and Layla (Shelly)."

Buck, Duck, Chuck? Did we have the same mother?

"Did we have the same mother?" Lucas asked out loud. In a rare instance, he wasn't embarrassed to say his inside thoughts aloud.

"As far as Lumpy and Stumpy over there are concerned, sure. If it helps, I'm Martin. I wanted us to have generic names since we don't want to stick out. Even Shelly's name is from a song, so if nothing else, she'll be fine. Unless they listen to old music."

Zane said the last part as if he was hesitating to say something else.

I know what he meant; so if nothing else, she'll be the most suspicious out of the rest of us. Zane's idea is better to have one person stick out than everyone in the group.

When they were close enough to the entrance, the plump security guard stopped them.

"Hold it right dome," he said, with an eager hand going to his baton. "Are you visitors or lost?"

That's a very weird question to ask five strangers. What if we said we were lost?

Lucas was tempted, but allowed Zane to follow through on his plan.

"Greetings, good sir," Zane said in a more eloquent tone. "My name is Martin, no last name. I am a Camp Counselor from Camp Goose, as you can see on my shirt." Zane undid his jacket to show the word, '*Goose*', looking like graffiti on a wall. "I brought a small group of campers to this dome as a form of punishment. You should see the batch we get every year. This time we've got not only a kid who is deaf, but one who can't speak. Talk about cherry pickings, am I right?"

The overly eager guard laughed at this while the other joined in and noted the campers.

"Yeah they dome look like the sharpest bunch in the toolshed," said the shorter guard.

That makes no sense, Lucas thought to himself and momentarily felt Shelly think something similar.

"Alright, have a fun dome, just not a long dome. Talk in dome, and don't let yourself be caught speaking without the word." The tall guard gestured to a giant sign with small letters. The most notable were '**Speak in Dome when spoken to. Failure to comply will eject you out in dome.**'

Lucas was surprised when the guards didn't make Zane pay for them. Zane just responded with, "Right you are all the dome."

He took in the entrance and saw other people ranging from families, children, to even kids from school. One group were girls around his age who wore grey skirts and blouses and looked at him and his friends with curiosity.

They are definitely staring at us. We must stick out like how the guards suspected us.

While Lucas felt uncomfortable with the unwanted attention, Josh seemed to enjoy him, throwing the girls a wave and smiling. Around them were rides associated with domes such as the Merry go Dome, the Twisted Dome, and the Kicking Dome. This last ride consisted of a giant ball that kids kicked around to each other like soccer balls.

That's the stupidest ride I've ever seen. It isn't even a ride.

The dome itself was massive and looked like it encased everyone in the park like in an ant farm. There were not a lot of attendants but the few who were there looked either confused by their surroundings, or didn't seem to realize the strangeness of the place.

"Alright, before we get excited about the rides and," Zane paused, looking around carefully, "check to make sure we have enough dome. We need to find who we came here for and get the dome out of here."

Lucas was becoming annoyed by the constant use of the word but peered behind Zane's shoulder and saw the most peculiar thing he could imagine. It was a tiny spherical device that was hovering around. It had a light emitting from the middle which at the moment was green.

Something tells me any other color than green is bad.

As if to confirm this theory, Lucas heard an older man complaining about how much the concession stands were charging for a hot dog.

"Ten dollars for a freaking hot dog," the father told his child. "I should have saved my money and time by going to Disneyland."

The spherical device's light suddenly changed from green to red and began to channel a low frequency which sounded to Lucas like a silent alarm. Before the father realized what was happening, he was surrounded by two guards. Not unlike the ones at the gate, these one's faces were shown. Lucas was immediately unsure if it was the lighting of the place or his mind playing tricks on him.

One has the head of a lion and the other the face of a wolf. I'm definitely seeing things. The guards in the front entrance looked normal right? Right?

The animal-headed guards dragged the screaming father away, who began to blabber the word 'dome' to the point where his voice sounded like an echo. His son looked about ready to cry until one of the guards handed him cotton candy. The child ate it delectably and seemed to forget the whole situation.

That is the creepiest thing I've ever seen. Why are we here?!

"Okay that was crazy as dome," Lucas said impulsively and thanked the Gods that word came to his mind just then. The spherical drone whirred past them and seemed satisfied for the moment.

"You got that dome. Now then, if there's nothing else, let's discuss the plan. As you know, Devon's brother is here and he's not exactly expecting us all."

Devon nodded and did specific hand signals with his hands by clapping his shoulders and touching his nose with his index finger.

"I need to say dome?" Josh asked in that same enunciation. "I wasn't supposed to say that. Devon says if I speak out loud, like now, I need to say that word. Dome. Is that good enough?"

Zane sighed and nodded.

"Just don't do too much talking. Neither of you," he pointed at both Josh and Devon. "Now, back to the dome. We are here because as one of the notable places Camp Supernatural was established in, Henry decided to hide its location under the guise of a theme park. Now you might think, what the dome, how is that possible? Also what's the deal with those things that have animal heads and that weird flying ball? Don't think I didn't notice how dome that was."

Lucas and the others waited for an answer, until Zane continued.

"Okay so the flying ball is what maintains the illusion of the dome. The guards you saw are also part of that illusion, sort of. The best way I can describe it is there are things in this world that you are not aware of at this dome. Maybe one day in your travels you'll meet more like them, but I can guarantee these ones will be the friendliest you meet outside the dome."

Those were friendly? You could have fooled me?

"Besides that, everything here is mostly a rendezvous point set up by Henry for whenever we need to meet with someone in secret."

"Is it my turn to speak?" Shelly asked. "Because I only had one question and that is the purpose of the dome itself?"

At least she said it normally.

Zane looked like he was holding his breath and let it out in relief.

"I'll answer your question in two parts. The purpose for the dome is to have a contingency plan for the camp should it ever be destroyed or need critical repairs. Henry also has other places like this but dome similar. The other part is to meet up with people we wouldn't otherwise invite to camp. Because not everyone is dome the way Devon here is. There's a reason why Devon here is so good at it. Care to demonstrate?"

The small boy's features shifted and he suddenly looked different from before. His height remained the same, but his skin looked grayish, his irises had changed from their original brown to a golden hue, and his fingers became longer.

"What the dome just happened?" Lucas said suddenly. He was also, again, happy the word came to him so impulsively.

"Devon has a split personality, sort of like Dr. Jekyll and Mr. Hyde. This version is Daron. Don't mix the two up or you'll get an earful of dome."

Daron looked at Josh, Shelly, and Lucas like complete strangers and seemed like he was contemplating which to charge at first. Zane was preparing to use his electricity on the small boy when he suddenly shifted back to his original self.

"Is that why Jacob could never read his dome?" Lucas asked

Zane nodded and pointed at Devon's head.

"As a sort of defense mechanism, he'd switch to Daron and Jacob could never tell the dome. He never knew the kid had more than one dome in his head. Pretty useful in that case."

That also explains why I couldn't read his thoughts beyond whatever Jacob did to him. This kid is like some kind of anti-telepathy Alter Child.

"Now that you got that squared away, Devon here is our best chance in dome to make sure his brother is willing to play ball with us, or if he's preparing to throw a curve ball and pull a fast dome on us."

Zane pulled out what looked like cuff links but these ones had runes embroiled.

I've seen those before. In the Infinite Forest and in camp. What do they mean?

"With this guy's ability, these cuffs won't hold him for dome, but it will still hurt when he tries to take them off. Again that's only if we need to use them. Hopefully not in this dome."

The group nodded as they began to make their way through the crowd. Lucas saw another spherical ball swirl past them and was surprised at how fast it sped by.

Is this how Henry makes his money?

Lucas asked Zane this question, with the word dome, and he chuckled.

"He doesn't make any money from this, that's all I'll say at this dome. Honestly I just assume he came into the money because he knows how to play the dome."

I kind of thought that also, but now after seeing this place, I am beginning to wonder how much of what I thought I knew was true.

They made their way to the gift shop first. Zane purchased a black leather jacket and a shirt that read, 'All Dome And No Play'. Josh seized one for himself and stuffed it inside his backpack before anyone could call it. Shelly got a cap that read 'When in Dome' and Devon settled for sticker sheets which had funny puns like 'Don't give a dome' and 'Tell it to the dome'. Lucas didn't want anything so Zane got him a soda.

At least the soda doesn't say the d word. I'm already sick of it.

Zane paid for each item using a strange credit card with Henry's name on it.

I've seen the credit cards Shelly uses and that card doesn't look legit, Lucas observed with puzzlement.

When the cashier swiped the card, a strange symbol came across the computer and the thin man looked almost appalled when his eyes darted from

Zane to the computer. He tapped it a couple of times just to make sure it wasn't malfunctioning until Zane explained that it was a 'masters' card.

"It's old, still a bit rough around the edges, but should be good to dome," Zane insisted.

The cashier seemed to understand and nodded without another thought or word.

Lucas wanted to ask Zane about the card, but worried about what the response would be.

The less I have to say the word dome the better.

After finishing their purchases, they made their way towards one of the viewing places where people could watch the rides. Josh made a comment about wanting a hot dog until Shelly mouthed that it wasn't a good idea in this place.

Ten dollars is definitely not worth a hot dog no matter what kind it is.

Lucas spotted a tall person who he swore was no child. This person appeared to be roughly if not a teen close to adulthood. He wore a dark green hoodie and purple shorts with flip-flops. What hair Lucas could see underneath the hood was dirty blond.

He looks like a young version of that actor who plays Thor.

Zane instructed the group with hand signals to keep themselves busy while he and Devon chatted with their person of interest. Josh kept himself occupied by looking at a pinball-like ride where a dome (fitting up to four people max) was tossed back and forth against other dome balls. Lucas and Shelly stared at postcards which consisted of New York, Nebraska, and Illinois. The last one made his sister emotional and when reading her mind briefly, Lucas saw the reason.

I wanted to go to Illinois after I graduated High School so I could apply to the colleges there, Shelly thought. Lucas held back the pain that came with his mind reading and compulsively took his sister's hand. She squeezed it in gratitude.

A memory came to him then of a time when his family went to eat at a burger restaurant and Lucas couldn't stop crying over the mascot performer impersonating a clown. He had been seven and his crying caused such a ruckus that his family left without so much as to go bags. He received a sharp scolding from his parents and Shelly tried to deflect the blame by saying they should have picked another restaurant.

He kept his fear of clowns to himself from that day and when the thought came to him, he remembered his parent's harsh words to him.

You always ruin everything. You're not like other kids. Why can't you be normal?

Lucas spotted the girls in school uniforms again and they were eyeing Josh intently. He in turn seemed to be giving them too much interest and Lucas felt something off.

They remind me of this one story I read once about women who lure men into the bottom of the ocean. Is that what they are like?

Some of these girls looked in Lucas' direction but he didn't stare at them long enough to gauge their interest. When that didn't work, they turned their gaze on Shelly, who similarly ignored them.

Yeah something is definitely off about them, and this place in general.

Lucas walked over to Josh and turned his friend to look at him. Josh's eyes were transfixed and unblinking, as if he were asleep with his eyes open. He tried to shake him awake, but this only seemed to annoy Josh. The girls in uniforms continued to giggle and smile in his direction until Lucas did the only thing he could think of.

He bit his tongue and with all his might said, "What dome did you ugly girls crawl from?"

One of the girls in the group let out a screech and recoiled like a turtle in its shell. The other girls continued to act flirtatiously towards Josh.

"How many domes do you need to be pretty? Not enough to cover what you have."

More than a few girls shrieked at this and it wasn't long before only a few of the girls in the group remained. Shelly joined in Lucas' insults.

"I've always wanted to try this," Shelly whisper. "It's too bad your mothers aren't here to see what you've done."

The remaining girls snickered at this until Shelly delivered the final blow.

"With your hair."

The rest of the girls retreated and once they were gone, Josh came out of his daze and looked like he had just awoken from a peaceful sleep.

"Where was I?" Josh asked. Lucas mouthed the word 'dome' which made Josh rephrase himself by saying, "Where in the dome was I?"

Lucas sighed and explained the situation to Josh.

"You were being hypnotized by what looked like girls but I don't think they were girls," Lucas explained. "Maybe after this you'll stop hitting on every girl you meet?"

When Josh understood everything his friend said, he stubbornly shook his head.

That's what I figured.

Lucas heard Zane call out to the three to join him and Devon down below. Lucas took the lead and was the first to see Devon, Zane and the hooded man near one of the Dome's edges. He got a better look at the guy's facial features with his hood off. The only color he had on his face were his eyes, which were dark green. He also had no eyebrows and his pale chin stuck out against his disfigured cleft jaw.

That's the ugliest mouth I've ever seen, Lucas thought in revulsion.

The jaw itself looked like it had been broken a couple of times and looked almost as grotesque as his horrendous chin.

It looks like someone dropped him a lot when he was little.

Lucas half expected the teen to speak, but instead he began to use a similar silent language as Devon. The two silently communicated with each other while Josh watched them intensely.

"He's Mark something, I don't understand his last name," Josh noted. He was about to add the d word to his rephrasing until Zane gestured for him not to.

"We're safe from that ball here. This is the edge of the dome and they don't usually monitor this part of it. Now translate the rest."

Josh nodded and continued.

"Mark brought the item you asked for, but has a condition in giving it to you."

Lucas felt his skin prickle at this. Not only because of the way it sounded, but what his mind said. Unlike Devon, whose mind was a mixture of feelings and thoughts, Marks were as clear as someone speaking them out loud.

Jacob helped me. He showed me how I hated my brother but I still wanted him to love me. He promised my parents would love me if I did this. I had to wait though. Because of him.

Lucas wasn't sure who Mark meant by 'him' until he followed his eyes. They were pointing at Devon. That moment was when Josh revealed the final piece of the puzzle.

"Mark wants his brother to come with him, back to Jacob."

Everyone's hearts suddenly began racing like a ticking time bomb about to go off. Zane's face appeared unchanged.

He knew. That's why he wanted Devon to come on this particular mission.

Mark looked indifferently at everyone and continued to hurriedly throw hand signals in Devon's direction.

"He was a burden to mom and dad," Josh translated. "They loved him but could not control him. After I promised my parents to keep him safe in camp, I lost him. When I found him, he wasn't my brother anymore. He was someone else. Jacob told me everything and helped me see my own truth. I was a bad brother. I hurt him and he hurt me. I hated him and I wanted him to love me. It made me so angry."

Mark began to tremble and his skin was turning a similar shade to his brothers, only this one was paler. He controlled himself and sighed with no hint of sound.

"Give him to me," Josh continued to translate as Mark's hand signals increased. "Then I will give you the secret Jacob has. His way of talking with people."

Josh paused and scratched his head.

"I didn't understand the last part," he shrugged.

Lucas understood suddenly.

"The Shadow People," he murmured. Mark's eyes turned on him and he nodded. His hand signs were now directed at him.

"He spoke of you last year," Josh translated Mark's words. "He wants your help when the time comes. Separate you are enemies, together you can be allies."

Josh sighed. It was clear this was taking a toll on him. Mark turned his attention back on Devon and Zane. Devon used hand signals to respond to his brother, but while his hand signals were calmer, Mark's hand signals were becoming increasingly aggressive.

This is bad. If we don't do something soon…

As if Zane were reading Lucas' concerns, he shook his head and said, "No deal." He darted past Mark so fast that the large man didn't feel the zap in-between his head. He fell to the ground face first, his body seizing until it became still. His breathing was steady and his mouth drooped with drool.

"What are you all waiting for?" Zane said in exasperation. "Help me bring this hulk in."

Chapter 25: I See You

Mark awoke in what felt like seconds to him but was minutes for Lucas and his friends. He was restrained tightly and Zane stood behind him in case he tried to transform again.

"So you have a similar ability to your brother," Zane noted. "He becomes all Dr. Jekyll and Mr. Hyde and you become the Hulk? Only gray?"

Since Mark couldn't talk, and because of his restraints, he had no way of communicating properly. He seemed to relish this with a smile to himself.

"I wouldn't be celebrating just yet. You see we planned for this. Well I did, because it's best to keep all your cards in one deck instead of sharing it with too many people." Zane walked over to the side and leveled his eyes with Marks. "Now you can transform and we'll see how strong that power of yours really is, or you can give us what we came for without the aforementioned trade. I can put in a good word for Henry to possibly let you back into camp."

He definitely can't do that, Lucas realized.

Mark made a scoffing sound and shook his head, which seemed to be all the confirmation Zane needed.

"Alright, that's fair. I can respect someone who sticks to their guns. Sadly we do need what you have and if you're not willing to give it up, we'll need to take it by force." Zane turned his eyes on Lucas, who suddenly felt cold.

Is this why I was brought here? To be his torturer? I won't do it! Do it I won't!

Lucas shook his head.

"My powers haven't been working the way they used to. I don't know how to control them."

"Yes you do," Zane insisted. "Your ability is mental, meaning you control how you make yourself feel. You keep telling yourself you can't do it and that it isn't like before. Guess what? That's the end result. Clear that head of yours and get to work."

Shelly stepped forward in between her brother and Zane.

"Hold on, my brother shouldn't use his powers for torture, no matter who the person is. There has to be another way."

"Are you willing to take that chance, because Mark here can transform at any time once the sedative I gave him wears out. Those cuffs won't hold him for long."

Sedative?

Lucas recalled electricity knocking out Rick but only now just realized what he saw was Zane using a syringe at lightning speed.

I definitely need to get my eyes checked one of these days.

"I still won't do it," Lucas insisted. "I could damage him beyond repair."

"Who cares," Zane said to Devon's sudden gasp. "He's the enemy. He'd no sooner kill you and his own brother to escape than risk capture. Let me ask you this, kid. If you can protect your friends from this maniac and Jacob, would you? Even if it meant ruining a life?"

Lucas thought about it and realized he would. Something inside him kept trying to say it was wrong, but the way Zane said that last part made him also think maybe in some instances it was okay.

If I can't do that, then what are my powers for?

Still with great reluctance, Lucas nodded.

"I'll do it. But if I feel it's going too far, then I'll stop it. Regardless of what I get out of him."

Zane thanked him while Shelly protested.

"Don't do this to yourself, Luke. You don't know what's in his mind. What he will do to you."

Lucas gave her a blank look, his eyes still bloodshot from before.

"That's why it has to be me."

He knelt by Mark, who looked at him in a dour way, and began to seize up.

"The sedative I gave him should also make it easier to read his mind," Zane mentioned. "Just, you know, don't go roaming the halls for too long."

Lucas gestured with his hand to stop talking and closed his eyes. In seconds he was in another place. This place was similar to somewhere he had once been.

The trees were high and nearly touched the sky. The wood looked ancient and foreboding. And it was pouring heavily though not quite as much as on that fateful day when Lucas was lost.

The Infinite Forest. Why am I back here?

He looked around and saw a boy frantically searching for someone. He was shouting and his voice was filled with grief.

"DEVON! DEVON, WHERE ARE YOU!" Mark shouted. His voice sounded like it had just hit puberty. Based on this he had to have been around the same age as Lucas when he first went to camp. He wore a purple camp shirt but Lucas couldn't make out the words in this vision.

He looks so much older now. He can't be any older than Bill is.

"I CAN'T GO BACK WITHOUT YOU! IF I DON'T FIND YOU I'LL KILL YOU!"

Mark seemed to regret this choice of words and proceeded to apologize in a low voice.

"I'm sorry, Devon. I'm so sorry I was a bad brother. I tried but I can't control this. This hurts so much." He looked at his gray trembling hand, with the veins on it popping out and bulging with each shake of his hand.

Just then sounds began to emit themselves through the forest, and both Lucas and Mark were looking around to see where it was coming from. While the sounds came off as incoherent murmurs and whispers, Mark seemed to understand them when Lucas before could not.

I thought listening to them would kill a person. Why do I remember that?

Mark became so entranced with what he heard that he didn't notice when the man stepped in front of him. His hair was long and silver, his eyes severely bloodshot and his skin appeared very pale. He was shirtless and wore torn jeans. The rain did not seem to bother him and he was instead more focused on the boy standing in front of him.

"Lost in the dark," the man said. His voice scared Mark even more than the whispers from a moment ago. "They see a value in potential. No…

no… stop that! This is my song! I'm speaking now!" Jacob began to scratch at himself and groaned in frustration. When he tore a cut into the side of his head, he stopped and sighed. Mark gasped and was even more freaked out that the man didn't seem to show any signs of pain.

"What is your given name?"

"Mark, sir. I'm looking for my brother Devon. Have you seen him? Please, I need to find him."

The man shook his head and turned his back on him. There was a giant tattoo that decorated the man's back and blue veins that seemed to stretch in every direction.

That looks like a tree.

"Don't interrupt me again!" the man screeched. Mark wanted to say he didn't say anything, but the man continued. "It isn't enough to always know what someone wants. Sometimes they need the right motivation. More life is given when others fail."

The man turned back to Mark and gave him a crooked smile. His teeth were bent and misshapen, suggesting they had been broken a couple of times.

"Devon is here," the man pointed to his head, then to himself. "Devon doesn't need anything because Devon wants for nothing. Why doesn't Mark join Devon this way? It isn't painful. Only at first."

Mark shivered in the rain and his tears were mixed with the drops from the heavens.

"I was a terrible brother to him," Mark revealed. "I beat him because mom and dad loved him more. I got angry and turned into a monster. It's because of me he's scared of talking. Because I always told him if he said anything about what I did to him, that I would kill him. I wouldn't though. I'm not a bad person. I promise I'm not."

The man let out a dry laugh that sounded terrifying to both Lucas and Mark.

"Yes you are. A bad person," the man said in a matter-of-fact way. "Otherwise no pain would have come from the feeling of jealousy. Some say monsters are born and others created. There is an interesting combination of both in your eyes and that hand."

The man gestured to Mark's misshapen hand, which was trembling fiercely now.

"I just want to go home with my brother. I want to be better for him."

"Want is not the same thing as doing. A person may *want* to be a better brother but they don't mean it in their heart. The heart is honest and the emotion of jealousy is true. Accept that. Don't fight it."

Mark was crying now and he fell to his knees shaking and trying to deny this.

"I'm not a bad person. I'm trying to be better. Please tell me I can be better. I'll do anything to be better."

The man shook his head and laid a hand on Mark's scalp. His long fingernails dug into his scalp.

"Only by accepting the true self can that self-become all that is needed. If people allowed themselves to be as they really are, this world wouldn't be so full of ugly thoughts and liars. Everyone is a monster. Everyone is a hypocrite. Everyone destroys what they love and regrets the memory of it. Becoming one's true self eliminates that completely. When Devon sees his brother next, it will be as he is, and there will be nothing except the truth between them. It isn't enough to want to be better. There is no being better for one such as what you are."

This last part finally broke Mark and he fell into a fetal position and the rain was now drowning him and his cries. The man stood above him and watched as Mark was confronted with not only the words the man spoke but the thoughts entering his head. Thoughts Lucas caught glimpses of.

I hate my brother. I wish he was never born. I wish I could have smothered him in his crib. Mom and dad made a mistake with me. I was never meant to be born. I wanted things I didn't need. I'm not good and I don't need to be.

Lucas groaned and pushed through, trying to find the part he was searching for in this memory. He saw it was when he found it. The man, who he finally recognized as Jacob, was holding in his hands something that glowed and looked familiar. He suddenly became cold and still. With everything in himself he wanted to scream so badly. He knew exactly what that glowing object was.

No, it can't be! There's no freaking way!

Jacob held it up and the voices around him increased.

It's the orb from the Relic game.

Lucas was about to exit the memory when a shadow loomed over him.

"I see you," Jacob's voice told him. All he saw was darkness...

Chapter 26: Lost Control

Lucas came back with a scream. His whole body was coated in sweat and he looked in all directions as Shelly cupped his face and hugged him to her. He was panting and gasping so much that when his eyes met Marks, he felt tears coming from his eyes.

He feels nothing, Lucas realized. *Absolutely no guilt for his actions. If he did, those feelings are gone now. Replaced by Jacobs hive mind.*

The look Mark gave him back was like a mug shot where someone was too inebriated to know what was happening around them.

No, he feels like Jacob; he does not care about Devon. He never did and Jacob helped him accept that truth.

"You are a monster," Lucas spat out to Mark. The tied up angry boy gave him a blank look and did not look away. His attention was on Devon, who looked to be on the verge of tears. He began to use his hand signs again and the ferocity in which his hands were moving was like a person screaming. Mark's expression remained blank, but Lucas noticed something that began to make him fearful.

He's not doing anything because of the medicine. He's stalling…

"I know where the item is and he doesn't have it," Lucas insisted.

Zane turned to face Lucas uncertainly.

"How do you know what it is?"

"It's in camp, and it's been there this whole time," Lucas admitted. "It's that orb that we use in the Relic game."

This revelation seemed to be what Mark wanted, which Lucas realized too late because there was a certain word in that sentence that was a trigger word.

Prepare for the ***game.***

Mark began to grunt, his body seizing and his muscles rippling. The cuffs around his wrists etched onto his skin and sizzled like burnt steak.

"Those cuffs have runes that should stop an Alter Child's powers from working, but considering his strength, it won't last long," Zane explained.

Lucas looked at the river on the edge of the Dome and saw for himself how pale the water looked. It looked like it was sizzling and Lucas swore he saw bones protruding from the top.

Please don't tell me that's where people who don't speak 'dome' end up. If so, someone needs to consider a lawsuit against this place.

Mark continued to transform though it was slow and Zane did his best to slow him down by jolting him with electricity. The cuffs continued to dig into him and Zane turned to his campers and instructed them to leave.

"I won't be able to hold him back for much longer. You four will need to take him out. We can't let him leave here. The mission has changed. Kill or be killed," Zane declared.

Lucas felt himself get angry at this, and he began to fear what this meant for him.

Why am I feeling this way?

He turned to see his sister whose eyes were filled with sorrow.

"Don't be what others want you to be," Shelly said, not directly at her brother but for him, nonetheless.

Lucas looked at Devon, who gave him a silent nod. His eyes were shifting from their regular color to the one associated with his other personality.

What is he doing?

Devon walked over to Zane, put a hand on him, and put the other on his brother. Mark grunted and tried to fight but his body was shifting between his regular form and the stronger one he was becoming. He roared so loudly that Lucas swore it would shatter the Dome itself. It did something far worse than that.

Small spherical balls appeared and began to eye the group like cameras. The animal-headed guards that Lucas saw were preparing to attack with weapons like swords, spears, and axes.

"Get back you fools," Zane commanded. "For the love of the dome, do not interfere with Camp Supernatural business!"

One of the guards looked uncertain and motioned his head to begin advancing.

"I thought you said your camp was Goose?"

Oh darn, one of them is smart.

Lucas imagined Zane thinking this.

"Right, yes. We're whatever you want us to be so long as you leave us be. Sounds good?"

Zane tried to continue his concentration on Mark but the big adolescent was already free of his cuffs and had tossed aside Devon. His body was a misshapen combination of his original form mixed in with one that reminded Lucas of a mutated zombie.

If that's his version of the Hulk, *he looks more like one of those bosses in that zombie video game everyone loves.*

Mark roared again and this time the spherical balls tumbled out of the way and were sent hurtling towards the surface of the dome. For as fast as they were thrown, the dome barely had so much as a scratch on it. The animal-headed guards weren't so lucky. Some were thrown off the edges they were standing in and fell into the boiling river. They ended up joining the people they 'evicted' from this place.

Looks like they're not getting their severance pay. What is that?

The ones who remained aimed their weapons at both Mark and Zane, who were a few feet from each other. Zane dodged an attack from Mark's giant misshapen right hand. It wasn't long before another attack came from his left hand, which appeared smaller in comparison, but this hand was very quick and nearly took off Zane's head.

It still did some damage since Zane flew backwards and had a giant line appear in the center of his forehead. Blood began to ooze from this opened cut.

"Yeah we're in serious trouble now," Zane told the group.

We could have told you that. Wait who?

"Run to the Dome. Find a flanking position in case I can't stop him."

"We're not leaving you, Zane," Shelly insisted.

"Where's Devon?" Josh asked, looking around.

"Don't worry about him," Zane said with his back turned. "Worry about yourselves. You three are my responsibility and if I have to go back to camp without you, I won't go back at all."

That's the sweetest thing he's ever said. Right? Get out of my head right now!

Lucas beat against his own head, his thoughts becoming jumbled and incoherent. He realized the voices he heard were coming from around him and from somewhere else.

This giant freaks going to kill us all! We need to get out of here! When in Dome, they never say when out of the dome? Move those railings and save what you can. Everything else, abandon ship.

There was a warm trickle of liquid that fell from Lucas' nose. He realized it was blood and though he couldn't see how bloodshot his eyes were, he could feel it when he rubbed his eyes and how irritable they were becoming.

Tired of this game are you? A new voice interrupted. *Tired of lies given to you in the blanket of truth? Desire for more without knowing the question first. We will soon meet under the blood moon and carnage will follow. Or a compromise. That choice belongs to you, my opposite.*

Lucas groaned, his mental abilities going haywire again and he could feel his touch with reality breaking again. Shelly tried to stop him but when she touched him, she felt a burning sensation and fell backwards. Her hands went to her shoulders as she cried out in pain. Josh saw in confusion and moved towards Lucas in an effort to stop him. He emitted a small whistle-like concentration of his sonic wave towards his friend.

Lucas' hands went up to defend himself and he felt something going through his hands. A kind of vibration similar to Josh's only it became stronger the more he focused his attention on it. Unable to stop himself, Lucas flung a hand forward and accidentally sent both Josh and Shelly backwards. They hit a nearby wall and were knocked unconscious. He looked at his hand which didn't feel like it should.

What is happening to us? Me. I'm me! There's no one else here but me!

While Lucas was too busy focusing on what could be a newfound ability, Mark turned his attention to him.

Forget my brother, Lucas heard him think. *This one is the real prize.*

Mark loomed over him and with his attention on Lucas, he didn't notice when Zane jumped behind him, his legs tangling with his bare chest, and driving what looked like his hand into Mark's back. It came out the other side mere inches from Lucas' face. The bolt of electricity this time was so enormous and strong that Zane even felt disoriented afterwards.

"This is going to be one of those magician tricks folks where you can only do this once," he said, beckoning towards the boiling river. "If I don't see you all again, tell everyone in camp I rode the lightning. They'll get it."

Zane smirked and emitted more electricity and this time Mark's screams were so strong Lucas saw blood seeping from Zane's ears. The giant hulk/zombie hybrid staggered backwards, trying with all his might to batter Zane off of him. With the floor as wet from the humidity as it was, they both went tumbling down with Zane at the bottom. Lucas rushed to try and help but he was too slow.

He had just regained his bearings when he looked at his surroundings. The Dome guards were either unconscious or dead. Shelly and Josh were unconscious and mildly hurt. Devon was nowhere to be seen. He was alone with his thoughts and self…

Chapter 27: The Betrayal

Bill was tired. He had spent that afternoon listening to his own thoughts about what he had lost in the last month. His abilities, his status as Camp Counselor, and though his sister and girlfriend meant well, Bill wanted so badly to push them both away. When he brought up the idea of taking time apart from Shannon, she did not take it well.

They don't know what I need. Nobody does. I want my life back. What I worked so hard for.

He looked around his cabin, once his home in Camp Supernatural, but now it felt like someplace that belonged to another version of himself. A version who had more life to look forward to. A future as a Camp Counselor, guiding others to hone their abilities as he was taught. So much of his life was dedicated to what he believed was coming his way that he never foresaw any trajectory in this plan.

It's what I deserve. It's what you need. I know I deserve it. I know it's what you need.

Bill didn't really care that he was hearing two voices in his head. He had been hearing this since his capture and brief confinement with Jacob. Devon had warned him it would be a side effect of his influence. The best he could do was hope it would go away eventually.

You know what needs to be done. What he asks for. What was taken can be given again. You have the key. He is the lock.

Shaking his head furiously, Bill refused to entertain the notion.

He's been through enough. Please. Let me be the one who does this. It isn't right.

Was it right what happened to me? It wasn't supposed to happen to you. Think of this; with your power again, your dream can become reality. A means to an end is a new beginning for you.

Grinding his teeth and scratching at the bandages on his eyes was all Bill felt he could do to fight the voices in his head. His head throbbed so much that he didn't notice when Gary tapped him on the shoulder.

"What is it!" he shouted in a near delirious state.

Gary raised a hand and with the other was holding a plate of food.

"I was going to see if you ate anything, man. Have you looked at yourself in the mirror lately?"

Looked? Ha ha. Mirror? Ha ha ha. Is he making fun of me? He is, isn't he?

"Are you messing with me?" Bill said angrily. His bandages began to emit the glowing red associated with his new unstable ability. Gary took a step backward and dropped the food in fear.

"No, Bill. I was just worried about you. Everyone in camp is."

"Well don't be!" he shouted. "Because I'm fine. More than that. This new ability makes me a force to be reckoned with, don't you think?"

He began to laugh even as he wanted to cry but he knew his tears would hurt him as much as the beams themselves.

"Get out of my way, I need to go somewhere," Bill decided. Gary was cleaning up the food that had fallen when he asked where his cabin mate was going. "You don't need to know everything. Just stay out of my way if you know what's good for you."

Gary looked hurt by this but did not offer any kind of protest. Instead resumed his previous task of cleaning the food Bill denied.

I'll show them all that I'm not broken. I can be fixed. You deserve it. I want what is mine.

Bill left the cabin but immediately felt the overwhelming sensation of being out by himself without being able to see. He stumbled down the steps and nearly lost his footing. It took him a moment to realize he had no footwear and the cloth around his eyes was beginning to weaken again.

I'll get them to change it while I'm at the ward.

He tried his best to listen to the sounds around him but everything was mixed in with the voices in his head. Voices which suddenly shifted into guides of shorts.

Turn right. Avoid pedestrians. Fastest route. Go past three rows of cabins. Turn left, then you have reached your destination.

Bill sighed in relief and followed the instructions to the letter. He didn't notice the rocks he stepped on and that one bumped against the joint of his big toe. He was on a mission and that mission was to become whole again.

"I can do this," he murmured to himself. "This is what I want. This is what I need to be whole again."

There was a mixture of sound all around him. Laughter, screams, a few cries, giggles, shouts, and various greetings aimed at each other. Bill hoped no one would see him. That he would be as invisible as the air itself.

"This is what needs to be done," Bill affirmed. "If I can do this, I will begin to see again. He promised and what was taken can be given again."

He heard the doors opening for him to the ward and rushed inside. He didn't think anyone noticed him because no one beckoned him.

There were voices encircling all around him, but they either paid him no mind or genuinely did not notice him.

As the Saint once said, 'don't look a gift horse in the mouth'. Now go!

Bill made his way to where the voices instructed him to go. This is where he found Mike in his bed. He was asleep, or at least he thought so. He closed the door and locked it.

"Please don't make me hurt him," Bill begged.

If you're fast, it won't be necessary. Say the words as they come to you and say them with haste.

Bill sighed and waited. When the words came he nodded and tapped Mike's shoulder. He couldn't see his friend's face turn to him, but he could feel the smile that radiated from him. That same warmth he had for everyone he met.

"Hey, Bill. How'd you get here by yourself? Your feet are bleeding, did you know that?"

Bill shrugged and walked around the bed, encircling Mike like an animal about to pounce on its prey.

"Talk to me, man. You're scaring me."

Bill became fearful Mike would call out for help, but the voices in his head reassured him he wouldn't need to worry about that.

Their ears are muffled and this room is all that remains.

Nodding and reciting the words in his mind, he began to say them out loud.

"Forgive me, Mike," Bill said. Before Mike could ask why, Bill began reciting the words: "Cast…Below…Surface…Loom…Strewn…"

Mike began to seize and cry out for help but there was no response. Bill stood above him, wanting so badly to turn away, but the voices assured him he needed to own his handiwork.

This was your choice. It was offered and you accepted. This price must now be paid. Watch.

Bill was about to question the last part, but somehow in his mind he could see what Mike was going through and that caused him to fall back to the nearest wall and gasp in horror.

"No please stop this," Bill begged. He could no longer move.

When he had finished seizing, Mike sounded calm but hoarse, like he had just exhausted his lungs of all their air.

"Where is the camp?" Mike's voice said, but the sound that came out wasn't his. "Give me your location now."

Bill shook his head.

"I can't do this. I took things too far. I want to take this back."

He felt a force grab at him and it was beginning to choke the life out of him.

"You can't take back what was given freely," the voice said again in Mike's body. "If you won't give your knowledge with the same transaction, your mind will become collateral."

Bill grimaced and nodded. He considered very strongly undoing his bandages and letting out the force of his energy beams on the invisible adversary. But Bill's biggest concern was killing Mike.

Why did I do this? No power is worth losing someone over. Why is this happening to me?

"The coordinates now!" the voice rasped again. Bill thought them and the invisible force he felt choking him subsided. "Good, tonight will be a blood moon and that is when we will arrive. A compromise will be reached. Or carnage will ensue. That is up to your friend. My opposite."

Bill knew who he meant immediately and was coughing out spittle, feeling his throat hurt despite not feeling a hand or wrist when he reached out to grab it.

What have I done? This is a nightmare.

Bill cowered in a corner as Mike lost consciousness again. When he was able to gain his bearings, he escaped through the room's window and without knowing which direction his legs would take him, Bill made a run for what he hoped was the Infinite Forest…

Chapter 28: Erin

Lucas searched his surroundings, his head was pounding like two cymbals beating in between his head. He tried to focus himself and recall what had just happened.

Zane fell with Mark into the boiling river below. Josh and Shelly are unconscious. I don't know when or if they'll wake up. He had the sanctuary stone so without it we're stranded here. Stranded here…

Lucas looked up and saw the cracks in the dome that were beginning to become more notable than he initially thought.

I hope this place has insurance or they won't have a big enough Dome to cover the damages.

Surrounding Lucas were frantic guests who were too busy preparing to leave the park to pay any attention to him. He purposefully avoided the attention of the remaining animal-headed guards posted at the front, fearing they would recognize him.

He walked by an outside merchant and with the seller nowhere in sight, quickly swiped an oversized red jacket he saw and put it on. He wore the hood up and tried to look inconspicuous.

All I need is sunglasses and a backpack and I'm pretty sure what vibe that will give most people.

Lucas was looking behind him when he bumped into a girl who had wandered off from her own group. As the two fell to the floor on opposite ends, Lucas got a brief glimpse of her before her eyes could scan him. He suddenly became fearful she would be like the other girls who nearly entranced Josh.

The girl had long shoulder-length red hair that looked like fire in the sun's flares. The girl also wore a maroon shirt that said 'Kingdome' with a picture of what looked like an egg-shaped monument on the front. Her eyes were clear, emerald, and narrow, appearing both mischievous and prickly. She looked like a normal girl, but when she opened her mouth, it was as if a different person was speaking through her.

"Hey you! What's your problem? Why don't you watch where you're going!?" She shouted in a clearly agitated tone.

Her voice was thick with irritation and sprinkled with annoyance.

Like food that looks good but has too much salt on it.

Lucas made sure his hood was still on, apologized, and bowed. When he offered his hand to her, the red-headed girl rebuffed him and dusted herself. She noticed a tear on her shirt, and Lucas noticed that the price tag was still attached to it.

"Are you kidding me? I just bought this shirt and I don't even like it!" she said with a very loud and obnoxious voice.

This isn't good. She's going to draw attention to us.

"I'm very sorry. I'll get you another if you want," Lucas offered.

"Dome right you will. Wait I mean… well, you know what I mean!" she stuttered in annoyance. "You haven't said 'dome' this whole time. Where are the freaking eye robots?"

Lucas had no idea who this girl was, but already he was enjoying her company less and less. He read her mind and saw her thinking about losing her own group of colleagues. She was at the Domeworld for a summer program her school was having. As it turned out, she was in the same grade as him, although she was attending a private boarding school.

So she's normal then right? Like there's no animal head underneath a human head sort of trick. He was not about to test that theory.

"What are you looking at, weirdo. Are we going or not?" she blurted out as Lucas returned to reality.

He followed her towards the gift shop, which was now destroyed and reduced to rubble from a couple of the fallen eye robots. She groaned in frustration as soon as the shop came into sight.

"This is just great. Now I have to find my group and buy myself a new clean shirt." When she said this she was staring at the ruined shop, but her next words were close enough that Lucas felt as if she were about to bite his face off. "What's your deal anyways? Who the heck are you? Also why are you wearing a hoodie that is clearly too big for you? All you need is sunglasses and a backpack and you would give me Unabomber vibes."

If she hasn't drawn attention to us yet, she will soon.

She glared at Lucas square in the eyes and he swore that he looked very fearful in the reflection he saw shining in her eyes.

"Do you have something to do with all of this? Tell me who you are or I'm going to scream," the girl threatened. Lucas heard her counting down in her head.

"My name is Lucas Fargo," he said with his breath sucked in. "I'm looking for my friends and tour guide."

It was plain by the look of her face that she saw right through his deception.

"Oh yeah? What school are you going to? You're not wearing a uniform, unless you belong to a public school. Are you part of a gang, because your clothes say more wannabe than actual be," the red-headed girl babbled obnoxiously as she walked closer towards him with each word.

The girl towered over Lucas only by a few inches, making him feel like a tiny bug.

Part of me really wants to shut her up with my mind control. The other part of me knows that would be a very bad idea. On the other hand, I could just make her forget me altogether.

"Riddlesburg High," Lucas answered truthfully. He didn't think of the harm it could cause, but upon hearing her thoughts briefly, he witnessed his error unfold.

"I've been over to that place and they don't have any summer programs involving Domeworld. In fact, you guys don't even go anywhere beyond a local Zoo, and that isn't saying much for a field trip when it's within miles of the school itself."

Lucas gulped, as he prayed for someone, anyone to save him from this fiery-haired girl.

"They started doing big trips this year. You would know if you've gone recently," Lucas insisted defensively. The red-haired girl was unconvinced.

"Why are you really here? Are you in some kind of trouble? Are you a criminal? You don't look like a criminal, but you could be. Like that Ted Bundy guy. You do have that sort of look to you that has a charm with a darkness underneath. Like a stalker or something."

Lucas knew that the girl was beginning to suspect him. She scanned him carefully from head to toe and squinted her eyes at him. He began to hyper fixate on her hair, which he noted was the reddest shade he ever saw.

I wonder if she's a natural or if she dyes it.

"I told you, I'm here with my friends and tour guide. I lost them when the cracks started to form."

"Yeah about that. I saw you guys going through quite the commotion near one of the edges of the dome area," the girl revealed as she pulled from her backpack a small little camera with very well taken pictures of them surrounding Mark. The other pictures were of Luca's group being surrounded by the animal-headed guards and eye robots as she called them.

That's not good. Those pictures are very-professionally taken. Wait… Lucas noticed something in the picture. *The guards don't have faces? Can this girl see that?*

Lucas thought about asking her before deciding not to bring it up.

She'll definitely think I'm crazy if she doesn't already.

"Now I'll ask you again; why are you here and if you don't tell me, I think those guards over there would like to know who caused the Dome to crack like an egg. Maybe social media will get a kick out of this too. What do you think?"

Lucas knew her threat to be legit. Her eyes were looking behind him at the traffic of people trying to leave the park along with the two guards from before.

I bet I'd look real good on television. I wish I had brought something nice to wear.

"If I tell you the truth, will you keep those pictures to yourself?" Lucas asked in a last attempt to keep her quiet.

The red-headed girl nodded but threw her index finger up as if to poke him with it. The nails were not painted, but the edge indicated that she had been biting them.

"You swear to tell the truth, the whole truth, and nothing but the truth? Swear on that girl who was with you. She looked like someone important to you."

Lucas nodded.

"She's my sister."

"Swear on her then."

"I swear on my sister to tell you nothing but the truth," Lucas heard himself grumble.

So help me gods.

The girl nodded approvingly as they began walking away from the destroyed gift shop. She managed to find a shirt in the rubble that wasn't torn, but it looked to be smaller than her preferred size. When she noticed Lucas staring at her, she angrily ordered him to turn away.

"Pervert this isn't a peep show," she growled.

I wasn't even looking at her. Where are Shell and Josh? I thought they'd be right behind me.

He led them closer to where they were and began to tell her about the camp, about Zane, Alistair, the Alter Children and Mark. He also told her about how Zane sacrificed himself to save the group while taking Mark down with him. Lucas also mentioned Henry James and Boris as the Camp Guardian. The girl listened to everything he said, and sensed the sincerity in his words.

If she didn't believe me I wouldn't blame her, but I kind of need her to in this instance.

While she was reluctant to believe him, the girl nonetheless kept her word and deleted the pictures.

"Thank you so much," Lucas said with a sigh. He removed his hood and his hair became its ordinary messy self. She snickered at this.

"Alright, Shaggy. You were honest with me, now I'll do the same with you," she said plainly. "My name is Erin, and for a while now I've been able to do this."

She pulled out a slingshot from her backpack and put a small pebble on it. Once it was latched on tight, she pulled the string backwards and let go. The pebble went flying in a straight and fast line like a bullet. It never once waned in its course, flying like a paper airplane as the wind carried it away.

It's not the craziest thing I've seen today but it's probably top five material.

"Where'd you learn to do that?" Lucas asked Erin.

"YouTube mostly. I'm kidding, no I learned it because it helps me focus my brain with my eyes. I have ADHD so hand eye coordination somehow helps lessen the worst of it," Erin noted.

Lucas was amazed, but wondered how this girl was not in camp like everyone else he knew.

If she's an Alter Child, she should have received the invitation or at least been visited by a skeleton cab driver.

"Were you ever sent an invitation or did a skeleton cab driver come to pick you up?" Lucas asked.

Erin shook her head.

"No and I am pretty sure that's not a real thing," Erin said as if the question insulted her intelligence. "Is there a reason those things should have happened to me?"

"If you have these abilities, related to your disabilities, then you should have been invited to Camp Supernatural," Lucas explained. "It's where I learned to control my abilities and you can better control yours."

Erin seemed offended by this.

"I got a pretty good handle of it already thank you very much. The only thing that sucks is after a while I need to put on my glasses because my head starts to hurt. Does that ever happen to you?"

"Only when I don't get enough sleep," Lucas said nonchalantly.

That was an inside thought.

She chuckled softly and showed him her glasses in a case she had on the side pocket of her backpack. When Erin removed her contact lenses, Lucas saw her true eye colors were more hazel. It was a darker shade like rainforest grass.

"My mind and eyes don't always work together. I used to take medication for it but now I try this instead." Erin gestured to her slingshot. "The main thing is I always have a hard time focusing on tasks for long. Don't get started on how many papers I've turned in late for class. Like sometimes my mind will be here, then I zone out, or other times I get distracted easily so I forget stuff like… what were we talking about?"

I can't tell if she's messing with me or not. Then again I can never tell on any given day with anyone.

She put the lenses in a small little container and put her glasses on. Her eyes squinted again at him and Lucas began to realize it wasn't from suspicion of him.

"So are we good?" Lucas asked.

Erin shook her head, causing Lucas to worry.

What else does she want from me?

"Take me with you. I want to meet others like myself and I really don't want to go back to that boring school of mine. I doubt anyone is looking for me. My teacher doesn't even remember my name. Names with E's are the easiest to remember. Get it?"

Lucas was hesitant to trust this girl, but upon reading her mind, knew she was being honest.

She's not a Silent One, that's plain enough, but she could still be an accomplice, maybe a Silent-One-to-be. If that's a thing.

"Alright, but first help me find the others. The one I'm not sure if he's alive or dead is Zane. He can be nice, if he really tries, but he prefers to be a jerk most times."

Erin giggled.

"He seemed cute to me, you know, for an adult. Is he in a rock band by any chance?"

Lucas shrugged.

"What about that other kid who was with you? He seems like a bad-boy-type."

"You mean Josh?" Lucas scoffed. "The only bad thing he does is talk up a storm."

Erin chuckled at that.

"I saw another kid with you. What happened to him?"

Lucas shook his head.

"That guy you saw, the big one, was his brother, and he tossed Devon aside. I didn't see where he went because I wasn't exactly in my best state of mind when it happened."

Erin nodded and that's when Lucas sensed the uncomfortable question coming up.

"What's your superpower?" she asked him.

I was really hoping she wouldn't ask.

"Telepathic abilities," Lucas revealed, feeling like he just said something incriminating to himself.

Erin's eyes widened after he said this, and she looked as if she were preparing for a defense of some kind.

"So you've been reading my mind all this time, or how does that work? Can you control minds too? Have you tried to control my mine? I mean mind?!" Erin babbled fearfully and put her hands to her mouth. "Did you make me say that?"

It's this place I swear. It makes me confused with the words I am thinking about and trying to say, Lucas heard her think. He began to cry out in pain and fell to his knees. *Ugh! Why is that still happening?*

"Are you okay?" Erin asked, kneeling down to level with Lucas. He nodded and instead of getting up immediately decided to try and calm his mind.

"My powers haven't been working the way they used to since last year," he admitted. "I went through something that I don't want to talk about. I can only read minds for a bit before it hurts and controlling them hasn't happened so far."

Erin looked unconvinced.

"How can I know you're not controlling me to be complacent with you right now? You know, gain my sympathy with your sob story and tragic background."

"You don't. You'll just have to trust me."

Erin's thoughts betrayed her facial expression.

I want to trust him, but how can I trust someone with such a shifty ability?

Lucas focused less on her words and began to focus more on her emotions, which were more positive. Hopeful.

She's never met someone like me, just like I've never met someone like her. I don't know if that's a good thing yet.

He turned his attention from Erin and looked towards where he left his friends. Shelly and Josh were coming up the steps and they spotted the two almost immediately. They appeared dazed and walked in zig zags but were otherwise in good health.

What exactly did I do to them? How did I do that?

Lucas raced towards them with Erin running behind him. Shelly and Josh spotted the red-haired girl and grew weary upon seeing her.

"Lucas, thank goodness you're alright," Shelly exclaimed. As the two embraced, Shelly's eyes met Erin's. "Who's your new friend?"

"This is Erin. Erin, Josh and Shelly, my best friend and sister."

Erin smiled and greeted them amiably. It made Lucas feel slightly cheated considering their awkward first encounter where she yelled at him for the first couple minutes.

"For being your 'best friend,' that was a hard throw," Josh signed and said breathlessly.

Before Lucas could answer, Josh turned his attention to Erin.

"You're like us?" he signed.

Erin nodded.

"I guess I am. So where is your tourist guide?"

Shelly looked confused until Lucas mentioned Zane's name. She then shrugged, seemingly going along with it.

"We've been looking for him and Devon. Devon was thrown off the edge by Mark. I don't think he made it." Shelly said this last part through clenched teeth.

Josh filled in the blanks and nodded.

"They're alive," he asserted fiercely with his hands. "I believe it."

Lucas nodded but wasn't as hopeful as his friend felt.

"So what is this camp place? Your brother says that it's a safe place for people like us," Erin asked enthusiastically.

Shelly gave Lucas a wary look.

How much did you tell her? Can we trust this girl?

Lucas nodded, but then realized Erin had noticed that.

"What are you nodding about?" she asked suspiciously. It suddenly came to her. "Are you communicating with your minds?!"

Shelly rolled her eyes as Lucas slapped his forehead.

"Don't be silly. That only happens in movies. I just had a small headache that I'll make better by doing this."

Lucas slapped his forehead again, wincing in pain, as Erin gave him a bewildered look.

"You are really strange. It's a good thing I like strange," Erin said to Lucas in an almost flirtatious manner.

Shelly sighed and Josh looked at the girl in fascination. After registering the strange part, Josh took it as a 'pick up line' towards Lucas.

"I'm strange also. I can touch my nose with my tongue," Josh boasted with his tongue sticking out.

Erin giggled as Josh struggled to extend his tongue upwards and finally gave up after accidently biting it.

"Well now what do we do?" Shelly exclaimed. "If Zane's dead, then…"

Lucas saw Zane and Devon emerging from the same steps Josh and Shelly came from. Zane was clasping a mangled hand under an armpit and Devon looked seemingly unharmed. Zane's face was also obscured by some of the dried blood that was mixed with sweat on his face. Lucas' eyes focused on a makeshift cloth that was wrapped around his head to cover the giant gash.

That's going to be a nasty scar.

Everyone but Erin cheered at seeing the two emerge alive. Zane waved with his good hand and staggered against the small boy.

"That was a close one," he boasted. "Not going to lie, I would have been a goner if not for this kid. He was clinging to the edge of the river and managed to grab me with that Hyde arm he has. His brother wasn't so lucky."

Devon's eyes turned downward and it was clear the passing of Mark affected him deeply.

He loved his brother but he also feared him. He said something about being the reason Devon doesn't speak. So that means he can *speak, he just chooses not to.*

Lucas gave the small boy a sympathetic look, but Devon turned away from his gaze.

Is there something on my face?

"What happened to your hand?" Josh asked, pointing to Zane's mangled hand.

"Oh yeah, I mentioned this was a magician's trick you can only do once. My hand was the price in that transaction. Once we get back to camp, I can probably save a few fingers but it's definitely not going to hold anything solid for a while. Devon tried to patch it up with what little medical supplies we have." Zane flexed the bandaged hand and it was hard to tell how many fingers he would be able to keep intact.

Lucas felt guilty about this. He blamed himself and Zane seemed to notice this.

"Hey, kid. Don't beat yourself up. We all know missions can be life or death, that's just how it goes. But you and your friends did outstanding. I want you to know that. Just don't tell anyone else because I'll deny I ever said that."

Erin chuckled at this and became shy when Zane turned his attention to her.

"And who's this firecracker? Have you been seeing someone behind everyone's back, Lucas?" Zane's question made Erin blush while Lucas looked irritated by the insinuation.

"This is Erin. I met her while looking for you. She can do cool stuff with a slingshot and rocks." Lucas boasted as Erin nodded approvingly. Zane was interested now.

"Is that so? Alright, Erin, impress me and I'll take you to camp with us."

Erin nodded and immediately opened her pack, pulled out her slingshot, and fired. The shot and accuracy impressed Zane.

"I've never seen anyone with that kind of power. I think you'll make a welcome addition to Camp Supernatural," Zane said cheerfully.

Erin smiled and without warning, threw her arms around Lucas. He was caught off guard completely and thought she was going to suffocate him, but he was only half right.

"This is the best day ever," the red-headed girl exclaimed, as Lucas looked like he wanted to hurl from the way she was shaking him.

After she let go, Erin turned to Zane and asked, "So how do we get to this place?"

Before Zane could answer, his eyes turned stone cold, while he stared in fixation at something…… or rather *someone.* Lucas turned to where he was looking and saw Alistair. He was glowing in the sunlight with a dark robe draped over him, a cape that danced in the wind, and the blade that he used to cut down Richardson with was unsheathed and looked freshly painted. Behind him were the corpses of the animal-headed guards while the rest of the citizens had fled.

"No need to thank me, I just carved an exit out for you all. You're welcome. Such a shame that Henry's pet project didn't hold up the way he had intended," Alistair said with a sigh. He stabbed the blade to the ground, and when he sheathed his bone-like sword it was no longer covered in red.

Zane glared at him disdainfully and clenched his good fist with electricity.

"You didn't have to kill them. Is that all you're good for? If you're looking for a rematch I'd be more than happy to oblige you."

Alistair shook his head and scoffed.

"If I wanted to kill you, I could. You can test me and see how far that gets you."

Zane grunted and sighed, knowing he wouldn't be at his strongest until his injured hand was attended to.

Alistair eyed the rest of the group and noted Devon among them.

"Devon, you naughty boy. You were supposed to stay put in camp. I know you don't talk but surely you're not stupid either." He then turned his attention to Shelly.

"You must be the big sister. Such a lovely face, it would be a shame to ruin it," he threatened venomously.

If you touch my sister you're a dead man, Lucas wanted to say, but he still couldn't look Alistair in the eyes as he spoke.

Shelly realized who he was and her fists clenched so hard Lucas feared she would do something rash.

"You're the one who captured those kids."

Alistair did a mocking bow as if he meant to tip his hat to her.

"The very same. Your brother and I are already quite acquainted. After all, I did try to kill him last year but he's like a cockroach. He doesn't know when to stay dead."

This realization shocked all in attendance and Lucas felt like his suspicions had been confirmed.

He's the man in my dreams! He's the one I'm scared of.

His heart began to race strongly and he could feel that original dark urge from before. Those voices that tried to take control of him. He tried hard to shut them out even as they promised him power enough to get revenge on Alistair. Then Lucas felt a hand on his right wrist. It was Shelly's. Touching his left wrist was Josh while Erin, Zane, and Devon stood by him.

Alistair chuckled at this and tried to stop himself. His golden hair danced in the wind so majestically.

"This is just too funny. You're all so adorable. Perhaps if you hurry along and use your fancy rocks you might be able to get a front row seat to the show, it's called 'Jacob and his Silent Ones will be attacking your camp tonight during the blood moon.' It's sure to be quite the showstopper."

The five campers went dead cold at the sound of that.

Something about this doesn't seem right.

"Why are you telling us this? What do you want, Alistair?" Zane asked him.

If he wanted us dead, we wouldn't have even noticed him at all.

"I could tell you, but where's the fun in that? In any case, you all have bigger fish to fry than where you were just swimming," Alistair sniggered.

"Are you the bad guy or something?" Erin asked when no one else spoke up.

Alistair turned to her and gave her one of his famous knife-cutting smiles.

"Or something. I'm more the kind who gets his hands dirty and doesn't ask questions about it." Alistair sighed and threw his head backwards. "Well you best get on with it or you'll miss what is to come. It looks like that little traitor of yours has served his purpose after all. Don't be too hard on him. He was desperate and blind to the truth."

With that final word, Alistair vanished in an instant through a shadowy portal.

He tried to kill me? But why? I didn't get to ask him.

Zane hurriedly pulled out his sanctuary stone and began to palm his hand against it as much as possible. It formed a new crack, making the small one look more pronounced now.

"Destination, Camp Supernatural, and make it fast!" he commanded anxiously. "This is going to be a very tight fit so it might be the last charge this stone has to offer. Get on board, Annie, while the train is hot."

Erin groaned in irritation and murmured "I was waiting for that one."

Unlike the first time which felt like they were being shot out of a rocket, this time felt more like being in a sports car at full speed. It wasn't as strong but it was still disorienting.

It took what felt like seconds for everyone to regain their bearings when the camp manifested itself before everyone's eyes. Lucas didn't wait to be told anything. He darted from the group and made his way towards Henry's home even as those in camp who saw them tried to get his and the others' attention.

I've got to warn Henry, and fast!

Lucas burst through Henry's room as if a gust of wind came through. The Camp Director was sitting calmly in his chair reading through some notes.

“Lucas, you have returned,” Henry acknowledged happily, but the feeling was cut short.

“We don’t have much time, Henry. Jacob is coming and he’s bringing his army of Silent Ones. They’ll be here tonight during the blood moon!”

Chapter 29: Eyes of Vermilion

The camp went into full lockdown as everyone armed themselves and prepared for the upcoming assault. Campers, big and small, were given weapons that best suited them and their abilities. Boris manned the front gates as Zane was taken to the ward to treat his wounded hand. Despite his injuries Zane insisted he could help and, if given the chance, would ensure Alistair's timely defeat.

After watching him survive a near death fall, I believe he can do anything.

The campers and counselors who went out on missions were not back yet, so this meant the camp was going to have less of a defensive advantage.

Jacob and Alistair must have known this, or at least that the camp wasn't going to be at its strongest.

Devon went to the hospital ward and decided, once he was checked out, he would assist with the injured campers after the battle concluded. Henry approved and told Daniel to prepare the other counselors for the upcoming battle. Lucas noted how tense Daniel seemed to him, but even more so how conflicted his thoughts were.

It should be me… Why always him!

Erin was not given a proper introduction, which she understood without complaint. Instead of any of the traditional weapons available in camp, Erin chose what she brought with her, her slingshot with a bag full of marbles. Lucas' memory took him back to the previous year and the realization that Alistair was the one who tried to kill him.

When I met him last year, I led him to the camp. I'm trying to remember what else happened but all I can see now is his face, his shape, and the words 'One less thing for him to worry about. This is for him.'

A group of children assembled in the main pavilion of the camp and were put into groups to scout ahead. Along with Boris and a few seasoned campers, they would explore the front entrance area along with parts of the Infinite Forest. This group included Alexia, Daniel, Naomi, and Erin.

"You just got here, Erin," Lucas insisted when he found out she volunteered. "It's too dangerous."

"I'll be fine, Shaggy," Erin told Lucas playfully. "I appreciate your concern but I can handle myself as you've seen. When I get back, you owe me a proper tour of this place, and a Camp shirt. Size M please."

Lucas reluctantly nodded and watched as the four disappeared into the forest. The other group consisting of people he didn't know went through the front entrance. Since they were small groups, they were more likely to do recon and return safely.

No pressure.

Lucas went to Ashley's cabin to check on her. When he tried to enter, Hailey laid a heavy hand on his shoulder and glared at him. Ashley saw Lucas and asked Hailey to let him through. She did so reluctantly but her eyes never left him.

"Lucas, I'm so glad you're alright," said Ashley happily.

"We don't have much time. Alistair and Jacob are coming, and you need to get someplace safe."

It didn't take him long to realize they already knew.

"Daniel told us before you all came back. I want to help. I don't think I can run right now as fast as usual but I can still do something."

Lucas smiled and felt suddenly grateful for Ashley's presence in camp. As Ashley struggled out of her bed, Lucas was about to help when Hailey pushed him aside and declared that she would do it. Hailey threw Ashley's arm around her broad shoulders and walked her outside of the cabin.

The last words spoken by Alistair came into his mind suddenly: '*Looks like your little traitor has served his purpose after all.*'

He tried to imagine who could have done such a thing when he realized one name came to his mind.

Lucas ran to his cabin and found Vanessa inside. She was in tears.

"Where's Bill?!" Her face was tear drenched and it was clear that she had no idea what was happening.

"I don't know, Vanessa. I just got back to camp a few minutes ago. I was hoping you would know."

"I haven't seen him in two days. He was talking to himself and when I asked why he told me to mind my own business."

She said this part with so much pain that Lucas felt his own heart breaking.

She's talking to me so maybe she's forgiven me.

"Don't think this means I forgive you," Vanessa declared, dashing Lucas' hopes. "You're still a jerk for breaking up with me. I just want to find Bill and if we can do that then I'll try to look past you being a dumb guy."

Lucas sighed and nodded.

"I deserve that. I'm sorry for hurting you, Vanessa. I wish I could have done better and been better for you."

She offered no response to this.

After knocking on the door, Josh and Gary burst in.

"We have a really big problem," Gary declared. Lucas and Vanessa turned their complete attention on him. "Bill's gone and so is Mike."

Lucas' heart lurched from his chest and he felt it do a double flip in front of him.

"We knew about Bill but not Mike," Vanessa revealed. She, like Lucas, was similarly shocked. "What exactly is happening?"

Gary went on to explain that Bill fled after he began behaving strangely and that Mike disappeared without a trace. He also mentioned how Bill behaved when he last saw him.

That can't be a coincidence. If Bill's the traitor, he must have done something to Mike. The only question is what did he do?

"Bill was super scary," Gary was explaining to the group. "I've never seen him like that before and I didn't know what to do so I just did nothing." He said this last part with his head lowered.

Patting Gary's shoulder, Lucas said, "You couldn't have known. Where do you think they went?"

Gary thought about it for a moment before mentioning the forest for Bill and for Mike either there or he might still be within the camp.

Lucas nodded, beginning to see the pattern now.

This has to be because of what Mike told me last time. How strange he acted.

He decided instead of keeping the rest of the information in his head to share it with his friends.

"When Mike came back, he was different. Mike said Jacob isn't the person we think he is and he scared Caroline last time she went to see him. I think he was planted in camp as a homing beacon to guide Jacob and his group to us. As for Bill." Lucas looked at Vanessa before he continued. "I don't know why he would have anything to do with what is happening. The only thing I can think of is he wants his powers back and if that's the case maybe Jacob promised him he could give them back."

The other three campers looked at each other uncertainly.

"He can't though, right?" Gary asked Lucas. "I thought what happened to Bill was permanent."

"Henry says it is. Right now Bill's desperate enough to be open to any promise. Even if deep down, he knows it isn't true."

Vanessa began to cry now and she made a confession of her own.

"He told me he wanted his life back. Bill said he couldn't live without his old abilities," Vanessa confessed tearfully. "I heard him talking to himself about it and at first I thought maybe it's his way of coping with the trauma he's been through. I should have done something sooner."

The tears began to swell down like a waterfall as Vanessa hugged her chest.

"I have an idea. You're not going to like where we're going but you can't be alone like this, Vanessa," Lucas insisted. She nodded stiffly and followed him, Josh, and Gary out of the cabin.

In a few minutes they found themselves in front of Ashley's cabin.

"Can Vanessa stay here with you, Ashley?" Lucas asked. When he noticed Hailey he sighed and added, "Can Vanessa stay here with you both, Hailey?"

"Only if she keeps her mouth shut and behaves," Hailey said firmly. Lucas got tense at this and tried to remain calm.

"She's scared for Bill," he revealed in a leveled tone. "He's missing and we don't know where he is. I understand you don't like Vanessa and you don't like me right now, but please help her."

Hailey was glaring at him and looked about ready to sucker punch him when Ashley broke the tension between them.

"We'll do it," Ashley declared. "Vanessa can stay with us through this. Find Bill and stay safe out there."

Lucas was preparing to leave when Keira entered and revealed she was going to be watching over the Weeping Willow cabin along with a few others.

"Before the battle starts, I need you three girls and your other cabin mates to come with me to the grand hall. That's where we'll have the children and any Alter Child who are not equipped to fight."

Hailey threw her fist in the air and took a step forward.

"I can fight. I want to help the camp with the defenses but I don't want to leave Ashley alone."

The next bit surprised everyone in attendance. Vanessa stepped forward and put a hand on Ashley's shoulders.

"I'll watch over her, Hailey. You make sure the camp is safe, and Lucas and his friends will find my brother and Mike."

Lucas was about to leave when Vanessa called out to him.

"Lucas…please save my brother. Bring him home..."

Lucas nodded and rejoined Gary and Josh outside of the Weeping Willow.

"So what's the game plan?" Gary asked Lucas.

He thought about it and tried to think of ideas that would work well with what everyone else is doing.

Boris is securing as many people as he can. The counselors are divided and we have scouts checking the outer perimeters. What I would like immediate answers on are why that ball Jacob was using looked like the Orb in the Relic *game and why Alistair tried to kill me? I need to talk to Henry.*

The camp looked so different in that mid-afternoon light. Everyone was dressed in some kind of armor and holding weapons. A glaring problem became notable though; no one seemed prepared for this.

The last time we were attacked so many campers and staff were injured. I don't understand why anyone would follow Jacob. If they know what he is, don't they care?

"The plan is this," Lucas declared. "Josh, your ability is good to confuse and distract a good number of enemies. You should be with the first wave when they come. If you get too tired, pull back and recover." Josh nodded with no response. "Gary, I sort of remember what you can do, but can you do anything new?"

Gary nodded.

"Only this."

He thumped his chest rhythmically, made a motion like he was about to run, and began to pump his arms so fast Lucas and Josh were not able to see how fast his arms were actually moving. Gary sighed and something bright emanated from his chest as he began to shake rapidly. It had a similar color to Bill's beams only it also had blue intertwining it. He shot it out straight towards nearby trees. When the beam died down, a hole appeared on his shirt.

When did he learn to do that?!

"I was holding back that time but basically I can charge up kinetic energy from my body by moving a certain way. Once I do, the beam comes out and it can do a lot more than make holes in my shirt," Gary boasted.

"In that case you need to be where the fighters will be. I'm guessing you don't need a weapon."

Gary shook his head.

"I'll take armor though. I'm not about to test my luck like you, Lucky Luke."

Lucas smiled and the two clasped hands.

"Find Bill and Mike and bring them home."

Lucas nodded and Gary went to see where he could offer assistance. Josh was about to leave as well when Lucas communicated with him telepathically.

I don't know what's going to happen, but just stay safe out there and don't do anything stupid.

Josh turned around and gave his friend the kind of smile that is usually reserved for something stupid.

If you know me as you say, best friend, then you know that's exactly what I will do.

The two parted and Lucas tried to see what he could do in the meantime. The daylight was quickly dying away and the night was giving way to the moon's fateful appearance. It wasn't red, yet, but it wouldn't be long now.

Maybe I can find Henry. He owes me and everyone else some serious answers.

Lucas' search was in vain. Henry was not in his home and Boris did not know where the Camp Director had gone.

Well that's just great. It's almost like he knows I want to talk to him and he's avoiding me.

Lucas knew that wasn't the case, but it didn't help Henry suddenly disappearing before the moment of a big battle.

He sat down on the steps of his cabin, contemplating the summer and year so far.

"I came back here with so much hope," Lucas said out loud softly. "I wanted this summer to make up for the last one, but everything bad keeps happening to me. Just me."

He sighed and shook his head, berating himself.

"No, that's not true. Bill suffered. Vanessa suffered. Mike suffered. Ashley suffered. They all suffered because of me. I hurt them and I'm the reason this is about to happen. Aren't I?"

He wasn't sure who he was asking. What surprised Lucas most was when he received an answer through his mind.

Blame comes in many forms. Like the inside of a box. It's always the same shape, different contents. What determines how much it can take? Capacity or strength?

Lucas gasped and looked around frantically, trying to gain his bearings.

Do not be afraid, opposite one. This should be a familiar feeling for you. One that is experienced often.

Is that you, Jacob? Lucas asked himself.

It is as you say. Blood will be shed tonight and Henry will answer for himself.

Get in line. I have questions for him also.

Questions are meaningless when answers cannot be determined properly. Would you ask a liar for the time of day, or if you matter to them?

Lucas stiffened at this last part.

What are you implying? Is there something about Henry you know that no one else does?

To understand someone, ask them a difficult question. How they answer this determines their views.

Lucas considered what he would ask Henry from the questions he had, but tried to stop thinking about it when he realized Jacob could intercept his thoughts.

What do you want? Why are you doing all of this?

A question is posed and an answer must be given. It cannot be said, only proven through actions. It won't be long now. When we meet, you will see as I do.

Lucas felt the connection sever and he angrily thought, *what have you done to Mike and Bill? Where are they?*

No answer.

Seemingly the answer came in the form of a giant fireball similarly to the ones from the last attack. This one landed near the main pavilion and the stage where announcements were made caught fire. When this happened, the groups that left to scout ahead returned immediately. They appeared unharmed, which was a good sign, but their faces told Lucas what they were up against.

Alexia came through the front gates of the camp wielding her signature warhammer and clad in a sturdy breastplate, her *Braveheart* war-paint, and her curly brunette hair was tied underneath a half-helm that looked like some kind of Greek hairnet. She seemed to be the first to react to the incoming fireballs.

"We've got company, and they brought friends!" Alexia shouted.

Just as she was saying this, the front gate of the camp shook and from the sound of whatever was pounding it, Lucas knew they were in it.

The look on Alexia's eyes was bloodthirsty, like a shark that had tasted blood.

The way she's gripping that warhammer of hers, I pity whoever gets in her way. Unless it's Jacob, then by all means.

The gate shook again and this time Henry appeared from nowhere. He did not look in Lucas' direction but rather at the gate itself.

"Where are the rest of the scouts?" Lucas heard Henry ask Boris.

"They are reporting back. The Silent Ones have the camp surrounded in all areas, including the forest."

The Camp Director sighed and began to instruct those nearest him on what they needed to do.

He finally turned his attention to Lucas.

"I need you to stay away from this fight, Lucas," Henry instructed him. "Assist the younger children and do not under any circumstances get involved once Jacob arrives."

Lucas shook his head, putting himself in front of the Camp Director so he had to look at him.

"Bill and Mike are missing. What about them?"

Henry glanced at Lucas and sighed.

"If you insist on helping, keep to the back of the battle and go where there will be more defensive forces." He pointed towards the forest. "Go now!"

Lucas nodded and was about to leave when a roar shook the front gate. The only sounds he could hear was his own heartbeat and breathing along with those around him. Lucas looked and saw Alexia preparing for battle, Boris, Henry, and Zane who, despite his injuries, was in the field and ready to fight.

He gave Lucas a quick look and smirked.

"This is the splash zone, kid. If you stay here you'll definitely see a lot of action."

Lucas nodded and walked over to him so the two were side by side.

"That's what I'm hoping for."

Zane smiled and patted Lucas with his good hand.

You've come a long way, Lucas, he heard Zane think in his head. The pain that came with it was mild and he felt more confidence in that.

The day suddenly began to darken and when the sun disappeared behind the trees in the forest, the stars became visible. That's when the gate gave its final breath before sighing in defeat.

The thing that broke through the gate was similar to what Lucas and his friends encountered in Domeworld. Only this creature didn't have a human body and animal head; it was completely animal and looked like a gazelle mixed with a lion. Its horns were sharp points on its head and its teeth displayed a combination of sharp fangs and canine teeth that looked big enough to cut through a concrete wall. It wielded in its hands a warhammer similar to the one Alexia had. This sight seemed to excite more than intimidate her, who prepared to meet this foe.

"That's a Melron," Zane said with complete shock. "You remember those things we saw at Domeworld?" Lucas nodded. "Yeah those were tame in comparison to full hybrids like this. That thing looks like it has a scent and when they do they'll hunt down their target until their death."

The Melron's snout went up and it began to sniff the air, turning left, right, as the Silent Ones from behind were trying to enter the camp. It became clear that they were not able to.

"There's a barrier set in place between us and them. As long as it isn't broken we should be fine," Zane noted.

The Melron stopped sniffing and made a growling noise that turned into a roar. It stepped forward and crossed into the camp seemingly without effort or problem. Alexia prepared to charge for the creature when Boris stepped forward.

"This is my duty," the Camp Guardian announced. "Prepare for the rest when they break through." Boris gestured to the impatient Silent Ones. They looked like hungry customers.

The Camp Guardian rolled up the sleeves of his long camp shirt, to display a translucent forearm full of stitches and scars. He also tore off his bandages as the Melron roared again and charged towards him. It raised its warhammer up and prepared to bring it down on Boris when the monster caught it with one giant hand. The Melron tried with all its might to push the weapon down, even to the point where its hind feet dug into the ground and made deep indentations.

With his hand still on the warhammer, the Camp Guardian used his free hand, closed it into a fist, and drove it into the Melron's chest. The impact sounded like a thunderclap. Boris's fist remained in the hybrid's chest for the first few seconds. Then it burst through and appeared to pop out of its back. The Camp Guardian didn't seem like he had exerted too much force and instead looked like he had done this kind of punch before.

That looks similar to the same move Zane used on Mark. I wonder…

The Melron went limp, its eyes turning completely white and its warhammer dropped to the floor with a loud THUMP. Its body made a similar sound and Boris stood over it with a fist coated in black liquid.

"Who's next?" the Camp Guardian invited, raising his black crusted fist in the air. From behind, several campers began to emerge, including the rest of the scouts. They cheered on Boris and looked in astonishment at the dead hybrid creature.

The Silent Ones did not look as fearful as Lucas and the others might have hoped. Their eyes looked at the dead hybrid but did not seem to register the fact that it was a corpse. Their attention instead was on the entrance itself. They kept pushing each other to enter and it was clear that they were more afraid of what would happen if they didn't than of what Boris had just demonstrated.

An object appeared suddenly and made everyone pause. It was the orb from the relic game, and the person holding it made everyone stop dead in their tracks. He was dressed in a loose camp red shirt that hung on him, with shorts that showed his thin legs and an arrow wound. Mike held the orb and was walking towards them with a notable limp.

"What are you doing, Mike!" Lucas called out. Zane tried to stop him but he was too quick in wanting to see his friend. "Where did you get that from?"

"Don't try to stop me, Lucas," Mike insisted. His eyes were filled with tears and his body was shaking uncontrollably. "I have to do this. Jacob will let me see them again if I do. I'm forgetting them and I can't."

No, Mike, Lucas tried to project. *He's lying to you. If you do this so many people will get hurt including Sapphire.*

Mike looked unmoved by this and even when Lucas tried to project the thought of Sapphire, it did little to deter him.

"I'm doing this for her too."

Mike's hand trembled and he threw the orb to the ground. Shattering it. Immediately after the first Silent One put their foot in the camp's entrance.

Feet were running inside and past Mike. Boris ran forward and put himself in-between Lucas and the other kids. This time Alexia joined the Camp Guardian, swinging her warhammer and taking out a few of the Silent Ones who came in her direction.

One of the Silent Ones she attacked was able to dodge her weapon and stab at her armor. This ended up becoming a fatal mistake.

The first thing to pop into Lucas' mind when he saw the small little dot-of-a-dent was, *That Silent One is dead meat.*

He knew that Alexia would spend hours, and even a whole day just polishing her armor. She was especially stubborn about her warhammer and never allowed anyone to touch it, let alone breathe next to it. When she looked at her minimally dented armor, Alexia's nostrils flared and she seethed like an angry bull.

Alexia charged at the Silent One with such ferocity that he didn't even have time to process the moment. Faster than a millisecond, she slammed the giant weapon directly into the gut of the Silent One and sent him flying backwards as if he weighed nothing. The boy flew back so fast that he crashed into two unsuspecting Silent Ones like bowling pins.

Zane used his good hand, thrust it into the air upwards and shot out a bolt of lightning from the nearby night clouds. The night sky was briefly illuminated, showing the Silent Ones coming from the front gate and the ones entering now from the forest area.

Abilities were manifesting themselves like fireworks on the fourth of July. In a matter of seconds, everyone who could fight was engaging more than one Silent One. Josh took out a couple of them, sending them backwards to knock down a few more, while Gary's muscles began to ripple like ruptured water as his heart pumped like a machine. He emitted the beam from his chest again, taking out the oncoming Silent Ones. Some were sent flying back so far backwards that they crashed into the trees from the top and disappeared into the depths of the forest. Hailey was also with the defending crowd. Her steel form manifested itself. Even as she took hits, none seemed to bother her while she was throwing punches and kicks against anyone who came in front of her.

Lucas found it hard to focus, as more Silent Ones swarmed in like bees attacking in formation. Shelly was fighting as well, mimicking her kung-fu movie moves by delivering high kicks and swift upper fists towards the Silent Ones she faced. Erin and Alexia were fighting side-by-side, and complimented each other in passing.

"Nice shooting," Lucas heard Alexia shout in Erin's direction when she shot down three Silent Ones at once.

"Thanks. Nice swinging," Erin shouted back. She winked in Lucas' direction.

She's already made friends with the camp bully. She's got this.

Lucas' eyes diverted to a horrific sight. Shelly was surrounded by five Silent Ones. They had her pinned with her back to the cafeteria building which was now on fire from a recent fireball attack. She tried a series of palm and elbow strikes. However, these particular Silent Ones countered her every move as if in anticipation. She was outmatched.

Lucas was having his own problems fending off two Silent Ones who tried to tackle him. He tried to mind control them but his power wouldn't work on them. Instinctively, Lucas lifted his hand up, hoping the power he used before would manifest. It did not.

Good thing I can dodge because this would be over very fast.

Shelly looked like she was about to be pummeled by her foes when Boris intervened. The Camp Guardian clasped his giant hand around the throat of one of the hostile Silent Ones from behind. The feeble child gasped for air as his windpipe shut down. Just as quick, Boris tossed aside his body, making a soft thud sound. For the next four, the Camp Guardian proceeded to bump two of their heads together, and slammed the third one's head against the wooden walls of the burning cafeteria. The last one attempted to run, but Boris blocked his way.

The Silent One was so blinded by his own fear and anger that he began to rapidly attack Boris's chest. He didn't make a dent when the Camp Guardian used an open palm on the boy's shoulder. The attack left the Silent One unconscious and limp as a dead fish.

Shelly rose to her knees, fighting back the tears of pain and gratitude, as Boris helped her steady herself. He got in front of her and began repelling all who came in front of them. Lucas was grateful for Boris's help. Daniel came into battle charging, wielding a short sword with a rounded shield strapped to his left hand.

He looks like a gladiator preparing to fight to the death in some Roman arena, mused Lucas.

Naomi also appeared and began hurling charged up rocks at Silent Ones. This caused them to fall back as the rocks exploded within impact.

Daniel slashed against wooden shields and poorly crafted armor that one of the Silent Ones wore, but it wasn't long before one of them disarmed him by tangling his sword hand with their whip. Lucas recognized the Silent One instantly as the one who tormented Bill when he was being held captive. The pockmarked Silent One looked at Daniel with pale-emotionless eyes and pulled him in for the kill.

With no thought to his actions, Lucas darted forward, scooped up Daniel's discarded blade, slashed through the whip, and thrust the pommel against the boy's nose, shattering it. The pockmarked Silent One groaned with a hard grunting sound and retreated from the battle in agony while clasping his bloodied ruin of a nose.

I meant to take his head off with that move.

Daniel struggled to rise from the ground, but when Lucas attempted to aid him, he rebuffed him.

"I'm fine, you didn't have to help me," Daniel grunted.

Daniel gathered up his short sword and shield again and made his way towards more enemy combatants. Josh rushed towards Lucas and slid to a halt.

"Luke, we found Bill. In the forest. Come with us," said Josh as he and Gary made their way into the forest.

Before he could follow them, a Silent One lurched at Lucas from behind and wrapped him in a bear hug. The Silent One's arms tightened around his chest like a boa constrictor. Lucas tried to turn his head to look at the Silent One but the air in his lungs was going out. He couldn't call for help and he couldn't use his abilities to stop his attacker.

He's squishing my chest… I can't breathe…

Lucas was almost out cold when he suddenly fell to the ground and the Silent One who was choking him was in a bubble. The mute teen was gasping for air, suffocating just as Lucas had under his grip, while Henry seemed unyielding in his desire to kill him.

That look on his face… he's not holding back.

It wasn't until Lucas shouted, "Henry! Stop, please! Don't kill him!" that the Camp Director finally stopped and the bubble evaporated.

The Silent One fell and it was unclear to Lucas if he was alive or not. Henry only regarded him with a hard look full of pain and anger.

A sudden gasp was heard when someone recognized the unconscious Silent One.

"That's Connors," Shannon said. "You almost killed one of us!" The wolf girl looked at Henry with such anger and hatred, yet the Camp Director did not even glance at her.

"I'm heading into the forest to search for Bill," Shannon told Lucas. "I can sniff him out better than anyone else can."

Lucas nodded and followed right behind her closely.

I'll save Bill and Mike. No one dies tonight. I won't let them.

Lucas followed Shannon into the forest and when they entered there were all sorts of sounds surrounding them. Fighting, shouting, screams, cheers, and laughter.

"Who's laughing at a time like this?" Shannon asked, grinding her teeth. She began to bite the area below her nail on her left thumb. Lucas saw how her left hand- fingers and all- were covered with old and fresh scars alike.

She's definitely been doing that for a while.

"It sounds like laughter, but it's all mixed in together. This isn't a battle; it's a massacre."

Shannon composed herself. "His scent is this way. Do not fall behind."

Lucas did his best to keep up with her but found this difficult considering how fast she moved. It was also harder to see as the night sky became now a dark blanket that covered the camp. He looked up and saw that fateful blood moon nestled on the top of the sky. It looked like the sun but without any of the warmth it provided.

This feels like a nightmare, except I can die here.

Shannon noticed Lucas' distraction and called out to him.

"I won't do that again so don't fall back," Shannon warned Lucas.

He nodded and decided to ask her something when a thought entered his mind from her.

"What happened to you and Bill?"

She slowed down and momentarily went from running to walking.

"That's none of your business. If you know what's good for you, don't ask me again."

"Bill did something to Mike. He made him betray us to Jacob. At least that's what I think."

Shannon shook her head stubbornly.

"You don't know anything, Fargo. Bill would never do anything to hurt anyone in this camp. I thought you were his best friend."

"I am his best friend."

She shook her head in disbelief.

"Do you accuse all your best friends of putting others in danger or just the ones who were kidnapped because of you?"

He was about to say something when he heard someone coming from behind them. Lucas put his hands up, hoping not to get put into another bear hug situation. He felt a body slam into him and he nearly lost his footing.

"What are you doing here, Erin?" Lucas asked more harshly than he intended.

"I followed you and this person into the forest. Thank you so much for bringing me along. I can't remember the last time I had so much fun!" Erin exclaimed a little too enthusiastically.

The feeling was not mutual to Lucas or Shannon.

"This is not *fun*. This is a *battle*, not some playground school fight," said Lucas sharply. "Get out of here before you hurt yourself."

He brushed off Erin's shoulder and hoped she would go back to where everyone else was. She did not.

"Hey, don't you yell at me like I'm some kid. I'm a few inches taller than you and I can shoot your eyes out, Shaggy," Erin threatened.

She stamped her feet towards him until their faces were inches from each other. Shannon abruptly got in between them.

"I don't know you and I don't care to. I'm out here looking for my boyfriend so if you get in my way we are going to have a problem," Shannon warned Erin. The two glared at each other like teakettles about to burst. "If you want to help, don't get in our way, or go back where you came from."

Erin looked like she would rise to Shannon's challenge, only for her defiance to cool down and her senses to get the better of her.

"It looks like I'm sticking you two then. But when this is over, you and I are going to have a nice talk about this." She was looking in Lucas' direction.

Erin darted ahead, giving herself a good distance between herself and the other two.

"Is she the one who came back with you?" Shannon asked Lucas. When he nodded, she scoffed. "I don't like her."

She's not so bad when she isn't talking, Lucas wanted to say but kept this thought to himself.

"We've wasted enough time. His scent is this way."

The three of them ran at an even pace and when Lucas tried to talk to Erin, she ignored him.

She's definitely upset about what just happened. I do feel bad because I know she was just excited but I wish I had handled it better. Hopefully she gets over it soon.

They eventually caught up with Josh and Gary, who were fending off some Silent Ones they had encountered. Closer inspection showed Lucas how these kids appeared malnourished and fatigued. Despite how strong some of their abilities appeared, they didn't seem like they were threats beyond a few of them.

"Glad to see you catch up," Josh signed and said to Lucas.

They heard more shouting and screams in the other direction.

"I've lost his scent," Shannon said in a grunt. There was smoke in the woods that wasn't there before and Lucas felt himself beyond annoyed by this.

"Someone is setting fire here. Could it be the same person who is throwing those fireballs in camp?"

Gary shrugged.

"The fireballs are coming from this direction though. If we can't find Bill or Mike we should think about heading back."

Shannon shook her head stubbornly.

"I'll shift into my wolf form. I can't smell anything beyond that smoke now," she admitted. "If I find Bill, I'll let out a howl. If I don't, don't wait for me."

Shannon got on all fours, her nails extracting and digging into the earth giving her something to hold onto as her features shifted. In addition to her nails- now claws, Lucas noticed her ears turning slightly pointy, her teeth becoming sharper, and her legs snapping to an odd angle resembling more like hind legs. She sniffed the air and let out a short howl before running off into the forest.

"She's a werewolf?!" Erin asked in a high pitched tone. Lucas put a finger to his lips and told her to keep her voice down.

"She's not a werewolf, technically. I don't think so. But she has powers like one," Lucas whispered. "She's more like that one guy from that old black and white *Wolf Man* movie."

"First there's Frankenstein's Monster and now a wolf girl? Next thing you'll be telling me the Camp Director is a vampire or something. Is he?"

Lucas shook his head.

"By any chance can you track someone?"

"Not unless they have a phone on them," Erin said, shaking her head.

Lucas sighed.

"We should probably head back then or at least within a safe distance in case Shannon howls."

The rest of his group nodded and they made their way backwards. As they did, the noises began to get louder rather than decrease. One particular sound grew so loud that it caused the three of them to run faster. Josh had trouble noticing what was going on but followed Lucas' lead closely.

"I can't see anything and I can't hear anything which is nothing new," Josh remarked in his usual loud tone.

Lucas began to realize something as they were running through the forest. That familiar feeling of all those trees surrounding him. The rain was pattering on him. He didn't feel it physically but in his mind's eye he did. His memory was taking him back to that night. The night he tried to run away from camp.

He remembered how helpless he felt and how angry he was. Mike had tried to stop him and he pushed the boy's help away. Now Mike needed his help but Lucas didn't know if he could help him.

Mike might not want to be helped. Based on how he talked about him, Jacob is giving him something he feels he needs. Like those people who felt like they needed Jacob in the orphanage. How they must have felt deep down…

Lucas pondered that last thought, thinking about the thoughts he pushed away in the back of his mind. What he always thought about in his lowest moments.

No, no, no, that isn't me. I don't want that. I want to live but I'm scared.

When his eyes adjusted themselves, he saw a familiar face in the forest. Someone he didn't think about until now.

Sasha? Is that you?

Lucas looked at the frail girl whose expression was completely blank. Her hair was cut short in a clumsy fashion, her eyes blank canvases, and her physique just as malnourished as the other Silent Ones.

She had tears in her eyes and darted away from his direction. He ran after her and ignored the calls of his friends calling for him.

"Don't you guys see her?" When they didn't respond, Lucas ran after Sasha. He eventually caught up with her, but she was still outracing him.

"Sasha, stop running. It's me. Lucas. I can help you." He wasn't sure if he could but he wanted to try.

This isn't right. Something about this isn't right. But if it's her, I can't let go.

He did his best to keep pace but eventually found himself back in his memory again. The trees of the forest in that smoky hue and burning brightness looked as tall as totem poles and gave off an eerie feeling. Lucas rested his hands against a tree and came up with some sap.

Just like before.

He wiped it against his hands and tried to concentrate on himself. He forgot which direction Sasha had gone and was now sure he was in the heart of the forest just as he had been a year ago. Whispers entered his ear and began to play a tune just for him.

Heistheonewhocamebeforeandcomesagainnow. Likelynotknowinganythingorunderstandinghispurposetotheonewhocomesnow.

What?! What are they saying? I can't understand them! How can I hear them? Is it…?

Thebloodmoonyes. Itisthepurposeforwhichwestand. Thatallmustendasitbegan. Listenwellandnow. Wewillguideyoutohim. Asitmustbe. Itshallbeagain.

Lucas clasped his head and groaned in pain.

This is my mind, not yours! I won't be controlled by anything.

Won'tmattersnotinwhatis. Bettertoseewhatmustbeattainedthantothrowawaypotentialvalue.

Lucas focused and instead of pushing the voices away began to listen to them.

Therewearethereyouare. Donotfearusbecauseyoucannotseeus. Wearemanyandweareallhere. Findhimyouwillinthisforest. Hewillcometoyouandyouwillbecomeallies.

Lucas shook his head, understanding particularly the last part.

That won't happen. I will never join him or become like him.

Wewillsee. Andsowillyou.

The voices disappeared suddenly and Lucas was left alone now. He tried to think and his thoughts became just as jumbled.

WhyamIthinkinglikethis? Thisisn'tmeatall.

He groaned in pain and collected his thoughts.

These are my words, my thoughts, my feelings. If the blood moon is making the Shadow People stronger, what does that mean for Jacob?

Suddenly, Lucas turned in the direction of a loud voice and saw his friends surrounded by both Silent Ones and Alistair.

"Let us go, you crazy hipster," Erin told Alistair as she was restrained by two rather large Silent Ones. Josh and Gary were held together to the point where if either used their abilities it would be on each other.

"Crazy hipster?" Alistair answered back in a hurtful tone. "I can live with being called crazy but hipster. Young lady, I'll have you know that I have been in a number of fashion magazine covers since before your parents were born. Yeah, stew on that tonight if you're still alive."

Erin spit at him and he dodged the spittle expertly.

"Too bad your power isn't throwing good spits."

"I'll tell Lucas what you're doing to us. He'll kick your butts, all of you."

I hope I'm not a bad person for thinking this, but maybe I should just leave her here.

Lucas tried to concentrate his mind, hearing his own thoughts again.

It'shardtothinklikethis,evenwhentheideaisthere. What if?

Lucas recognized a hooded figure who revealed herself to be Shanine, the girl from his dream. Even in the darkness, he could see her purple hair and how it flowed down her left shoulder. She was beautiful except for how translucent her skin looked and the way her lips curled into someone with malicious intent.

Who is she really? Why is she here?

"You should be careful how you address us, girl," Shanine warned Erin. "We are the Chosen Ones. Chosen by the Gods to help the savior of humanity cleanse the world of darkness."

She spoke with such a sharp tone that her tongue might have been a knife being sharpened against her teeth. Meanwhile, Alistair snickered and laughed at the thought of Lucas 'kicking his butt' as Erin had boasted and ignored the rambling of the woman.

"Really, that mind freak is going to fight me? No, I think he's afraid of me, and that gives him more sense than you have." Alistair turned his attention to Shanine, who was mumbling to herself. "You be quiet. It's bad enough I have to deal with one maniac. My limit only extends to the one; you're just a passenger in this little entourage."

Alistair aimed his sword at Erin, and it was close enough that had she not been restrained, she might have been able to snatch it. As if reading her mind, one of the Silent Ones behind Erin tightened her grip.

"Do you know what this blade is called?"

Erin shrugged and examined it with her eyes.

"Did you name it after your mother?"

Alistair snickered at that and shook his head.

"No, this blade is far too sentimental for that."

When Erin didn't offer a retort, Alistair continued.

"It's funny how people who preach the word love to talk like they know everything. Reminds me of a supposed 'savior'."

"Do not mock the Chosen One," Shanine said in a near hysterical tone. "The gods chose him, and shone their light on me to lead him in our salvation. Without him we are lost."

Ignoring her again, Alistair went back to his original discussion.

"Anyways, I call my blade Spine, because that's exactly what it is. It belonged to someone who didn't need it anymore. It's indestructible and to the point."

Lucas hadn't noticed it before, but the grotesque blade had a sick curve to it, as if the very blade itself had been born with a terrible affliction. The sides looked broken and twisted, while the middle extended itself like a bony finger. The pommel was metallic and looked similar to an actual sword.

I've never seen a sword like that.

"Would you like an example of Spine's ferocity?" Without waiting for an answer, he thrust the point of the blade in-between her armpit across the Silent One's heart. He gasped and his grip suddenly loosened. Erin staggered a few inches, struggling to keep herself from falling, as the Silent One collapsed on the ground and ceased breathing. She stared motionlessly down on the fallen child, then back at Alistair in cold contempt.

"He was your friend. How could you do that to him?" Erin demanded with bitter disdain.

Alistair burst into a mocking laugh.

"Foolish girl, he was merely a pawn. One of many. In the final days of judgment the first to die will be the pawns, then the rest will follow like sheep to the slaughter."

Alistair rolled his eyes.

"Don't listen to her babbling. I barely understand half the stuff she says. In any case, he didn't mind. None of them have a mind of their own."

Alistair glared at the one who still held onto Erin by her one arm and the child gave no indication she had any fear or doubt. Her body shook and her face trembled but there were no other signs of fear or anxiety.

"These kids have no homes of their own. No families that miss them. Even your precious Camp Supernatural couldn't be that for most of them. They get more of a reality in their own heads than whatever life has offered them."

Alistair plunged the bony sword into the ground and after a few removed it to show that it was clean from blood.

"Look, you're new to the whole Camp Supernatural cult so I'll let you in on a secret," Alistair revealed to Erin. "The kids Henry fails, or the kids he doesn't even bother to train because they're abilities are too unstable, he sends my way, and I send them to Jacob. That's why they can't think for themselves anymore."

Erin stared sadly at the Silent One holding her and the ones that surrounded them. Lucas could feel her sadness and it was overwhelming.

"What about you? What do you get out of this? Is this how you get your kicks?"

Alistair answered back in a cautious tone.

"Keep talking like that and you'll find out how to become a Silent One through first-hand experience."

Just then, a shadow came up from the darkness of the forest, a tall man who looked like a human, but his behavior suggested something else. His long silver hair fell down his shoulders and appeared unruly. His bare chest showed even in the darkness how pale his skin looked and the blue veined tattoo on his back pulsed in the night. The tattoo of the dead tree looked haunting against the blood moon's light. On his feet he wore sandals but this did more to irritate the man than was the point. He was scratching at his head and his bloodshot eyes were looking maniacally forward.

"Who are these disposable ones? Where is my opposite?!" Jacob snarled.

It's him, Lucas thought with horror. *He looks a lot scarier in person.*

Jacob's bloodshot eyes stared in all directions as he continued to pound on the ground and removed his sandals forcibly.

Beware the eyes of vermilion… the words the Crow and Eagle told me. I want connection while Jacob wants separation.

"Here he is, in his benevolence and magnificence; the Chosen One of the gods, destined to defeat the darkness and cleanse the mortal world," Shanine declared with her hands sticking out in Jacob's direction. He was muttering about his feet and was scratching them against the ground.

HIM?! Lucas thought in horror. *He can't be. He's a monster. No, he can't be the Chosen One. There's just no way.*

"Spare everyone here when you're just as crazy as he is," Alistair spat at Shanine. He snapped his fingers and pointed his finger in the opposite direction.

"We caught that one trying to talk sense into your latest pet. She almost got through to him," Alistair told Jacob as some Silent Ones emerged and led Bill out.

His hands were tied and his eyes still bandaged while Shannon was restrained both with her feet, hands, and what looked like a tight muzzle around her face. Her shirt and shorts had small rips but were otherwise no worse for wear. Lucas watched all of this in horror.

Shannon let out a muffled protest and Bill appeared unmoved by her.

"You should have left me behind," was all Bill said to Shannon. Her fight went out and she glared at him with such disappointment it was tragic to see.

"I did what you asked for. You're in Camp Supernatural. I can lead you to Lucas. It's him you want, not me."

What are you doing, Bill? Lucas hoped his friend would hear his words in his head, but Bill didn't give any indication. Instead, Jacob seemed to perk up, but he appeared so out of it, Lucas wasn't sure what he was thinking.

"Then you can give me back my power. Please, you promised me."

Jacob nodded without looking in Bill's direction.

"What was given can be returned. It may not retain its same form, but it may yet gain a new one. My opposite one is not a priority right now. Take us to where Henry is."

Bill nodded and pointed forward.

"That's where the most sounds are coming from."

Alistair nodded and walked in front of Bill.

"It's not too late to turn back now. You may not be welcomed back to camp after this."

Bill shook his head stubbornly.

"Don't talk to me. It's because of you that I'm like this."

Alistair backed off while Lucas' attention was on his friends. They were no longer protesting or fighting. They all were on their knees, trembling and trying to keep themselves from falling over. Erin in particular looked like she was feeling sick.

"Why can't I think straight," she said in agony. She looked at Jacob and tried to rise but felt a burning sensation running through her. Lucas felt this as well and had to pull himself back from it.

Ugh! I'm boiling! This feels like I'm inside a sauna.

"Yearning for a place to belong, with no means of direct communication." Jacob said this part with such coldness it was like a therapist who wasn't trying to give helpful suggestions.

"You don't know anything about me," Erin spat back.

"I know everything. Your lives mean nothing to me and yet what I know can fill a blank canvas that others will insist is art." Jacob pointed a sharp nailed finger at her and was so close to her it was like he meant to stab her.

"Alright let's take this show on the road," Alistair beckoned. "Lead on, Lady Justice."

Bill grimaced and started moving forward. He let his hands and feet guide him. Despite stepping on stickers and rocks, he never once stopped walking.

Lucas watched his friends being led away and Erin softly sobbing to herself. The fight that was previously in her was gone now. Josh looked indifferent although Lucas could see in his eyes he was hiding his pain well. Gary was trembling and did his best to remain calm but he looked near his breaking point.

What is he doing to them? I can't read their minds, even their surface thoughts.

The voices returned, trying to make a residency in his mind. Before they could he reminded himself of his own thoughts and what they meant to him.

I'm not going to let them take over me. Nomatterwhattheydo. I'm me and that's all I want to be. They don't make methinkotherwise.

It was through Jacob and his followers that Lucas managed to find his way through the forest. The clearing came out not long after and he was back in Camp Supernatural with his friends who were still being held by Jacob's Silent Ones.

"Old grounds that feel foreign to these feet," Jacob reminisced. His bare feet dug into the earth and his bloodshot eyes looked around the camp. "We must gather our forces and meet Henry. Then my opposite."

Alistair looked around and saw the corpse of the Melron.

"What killed that thing? I wouldn't be surprised if it was that monster who guards this place. I knew we should have brought another one of those hybrid things. Too bad they're not the easiest to control."

Jacob sighed and started muttering to himself. He turned his attention to Bill.

"Find Henry and bring him here. He has answers to questions that will yield results." Bill nodded and made his way forward, stumbling as he went.

"Poor kid. What do you plan to do with him once he fulfills his end of the bargain?"

"No use for a vase that can no longer hold water properly. No glue or string to hold it together."

Alistair nodded, understanding.

From his hiding place in the back, Lucas fixated on Jacobs eyes.

Those eyes are… so RED… like blood… like the moon right now…

Lucas felt the wave hit him from Jacob's presence. It was the same foreboding feeling one felt when a strong storm was about to make landfall.

There is no way this guy is going to save anyone. He's hurting my friends just by being near them. I can't feel anything coming from him.

Bill returned with Henry and a group of others. Most everyone Lucas knew from his sister Shelly to little Sapphire, Daniel, Caroline, Zane, Naomi, and Keira. Thankfully Vanessa and Ashley were still gone.

Daniel saw Alistair and pointed a finger at him.

"What is he doing here? He tried to kill me!"

"Does that mean you're ready for round two?" Alistair told Daniel in a snide tone.

Daniel held back what he wanted to say as Henry moved forward away from the rest of the campers and staff.

"So nice to see you again, Henry, can't say time has been kind to you." Alistair called out to the Camp Director. "Did you like the fireballs display from before? Wasn't that a beaut? I would have knocked but your gate gave in before the thought could occur to me."

Bill rejoined Jacob while Henry addressed Alistair.

"My old friend, this is an unfortunate circumstance. Allying yourself with one such as this." He pointed a shaking finger towards Jacob.

"These eyes behold the one who once promised much," Jacob told Henry. "The years have ignored your presence, old master. How is this?"

Henry sighed and looked at Bill.

"Release him. He is of no more use to you, Jacob."

Jacob shook his head.

"All have uses when used properly. I was once useful to you and this place. Do you recall?"

Henry nodded. His gaze was fixed on Jacob but he did briefly glance at Alistair, who looked at him like he was waiting to be noticed. Jacob was beginning to become angry.

"You claim, old master, to help those who come here, to your precious camp. Yet so many end up with me and come from broken families with minds and hearts that need mending. Do you recognize any from those who remain silent?"

Jacob gestured to the Silent Ones both surrounding him, and near the campers who appeared ready to attack on command.

No… Don't tell me…

"These are the ones who were never saved by you, old master, but by me."

Jacob grimaced and began to grind his teeth.

"He knows. Yes he does. But deny it he will. Always taking silence when it's convenient."

"I failed you, Jacob. Just as I failed so many others. It was not my intent."

Jacob shook his head.

"It's not the intent of a dog to bark at something it doesn't understand. But it is a master's job to teach that dog to obey them and know better." The way Jacob said this was with such emotion that Lucas feared he would cause everyone around him to go back into a fighting frenzy.

Henry sighed and shook his head.

"What do you want, Jacob?"

His eyes darted in the forest and before Lucas knew what was happening, he was kneeling in front of Jacob. His arms on each side were being held by two strong Silent Ones. Lucas looked around at the surroundings. Shelly called out to him but Zane held her back with one arm and Sapphire was fearful as well.

What's happening to me? I feel something. I can't… I don't… ugh! Ahhhhhh!!!!

Lucas began to feel a burning sensation running through his body and he tried his best not to cry out loud, but his teeth gritted and his knees dug into the ground.

"It hurts the more resistance is met," Jacob explained. He exerted no force or energy whatsoever. "This is my opposite, is he? The one who is believed to be chosen?"

Shanine shook her head stubbornly, her purple hair glittering in the blood moon's light.

"I have spoken to him and he is a flawed imitation to your perfection, my beloved," Shanine told Jacob. She moved over to him, wanting to touch his shoulder, but he brushed her off violently.

Lucas wasn't sure what they were talking about when he looked in Henry's direction. The Camp Director looked emotionlessly at him. He calmed himself and directed his attention to Alistair.

"Why did you try to kill me last year?" Lucas asked Alistair in an accusatory tone. He stared at him and sighed.

"You weren't meant to be in the forest," he revealed. His tone sounded sad, even regretful. "You were at the wrong place at the wrong time. When I realized what you were, I couldn't let that mistake happen again." His eyes briefly glanced at Jacob, then Henry, and back to Lucas. "It's too bad really. Because you ending up where you did is how all this is happening now."

Lucas felt his body continue to burn and his will dying out at this answer.

"What do you mean by that?"

"The Shadow People. Jacob. They learned about you that day and decided that meeting you was what came next in the grand scheme of things. Henry had you well hidden, but you were too stupid to sit still it seems."

For the first time in what now felt like a predestined meeting, Lucas' eyes met Jacob's and the two looked at each other with such an intensity that Lucas tried to fight the ensuing heat he kept feeling. He tried to fight it as he had the voices from the whispers, but this force was much more powerful. He wasn't sure if Jacob made everyone he mind controlled feel the same way, because this felt like an invasion of a person's self.

Get out of my mind! Ouyr otn dssepup ot eb ni eher.

Jacob let out a dry laugh and displayed his crooked teeth. These went in great contrast to his otherwise handsome features which Lucas thought made him look younger than his age despite how gray his hair is.

"What a mind this one here possesses," Jacob admitted to Lucas. "You're like a child who has just discovered what fire can do and what a gun with bullets is capable of. Your mind is wielded this way."

Lucas turned away, feeling shameful at what was being implied.

"I don't enjoy hurting others. That's something I can never do."

"It can't be helped. Humans are so fragile about themselves that when they are confronted with truths, they cannot handle them. So I give them their own truths. Not lies because lies are created. Truths are given."

Jacob gestured to his Silent Ones who were stretching their hands out to him as he pointed in their direction.

"They want what I give them, even when I do not want them."

His followers silently begged him to stay and were on their knees now, tears welling in their eyes. They had released Erin, Josh, and Gary, but neither offered any kind of resistance. Henry made a gesture and the three of them came over to his side.

"That's quite enough, Jacob," Henry announced. "What is it you wish to discuss? Why come back now?"

Jacob shook his head and looked irritated at the absence of Lucas' friends.

"We are still discussing our differences, old master. Once that is done, the next phase begins."

Lucas did not try to fight the burning sensation even as it came and went.

"My mom and dad. Did you kill them? I need to know."

"They were victims, this is true. Not of this mind but of another. What makes a victim? It isn't a circumstance and it isn't life. It's this." Jacob stabbed a pointed finger to his head. He ignored whatever pain that caused. "This creates the illusion of being a victim. A sentiment many share and it is pathetic. It's why the human race is the lowliest of creatures that exist in this known world. They constantly try to pretend they know what they want by hiding behind their limitations. Instead of embracing that difference and being better, there is more comfort in that panic and confusion. I remove those inhibitions, that fear, that doubt. They're given a new purpose and one that allows for growth where none existed before. Can you not see this, my opposite?"

Lucas thought for a moment and for one terrifying moment, he did see it.

"It's there, yes, you feel it." Jacob looked satisfied, his head nodding to himself. "We are more alike than you want to admit."

"We're nothing alike." Lucas said this with such anger and pain in his tone from the burning sensation. He looked at the Camp Director when he said, "I am nothing like him."

"I know that, my son."

Jacob began to laugh that dry laughter again and walked up to Lucas. He cupped his face to examine his eyes.

"Both our eyes are the same. How fitting when one can be allowed to be as they truly are. That is true freedom from control."

Lucas shook his head but his thoughts were beginning to see the sense in what Jacob was saying.

"Why do his powers no longer work? The word 'trauma' swims around in that head like it has some place in there. What if it were removed? Whatever makes him hurt? I can take that away and we'd be equals. Should I do this, old master?"

Lucas started to feel hopeful about this. He was nearly close to contemplating it when he looked in Shelly's direction and hesitated. She shook her head and tears were running down her eyes.

Don't do it, Lucas. Please. You're better than that and you always have been. That's your true power.

"Your mind wanders to her," Jacob pointed to Shelly. She was suddenly thrust in front of him by Silent Ones. Lucas reacted so fast that the Silent Ones holding him gripped his arms tight enough to constrict the blood circulation. The burning sensation in him also increased exponentially.

"Let her go!" Lucas shouted in the loudest and angriest voice he had ever used. Jacob groaned and turned back to Lucas.

"She is the reason you are holding back," Jacob revealed to him. "Your powers cannot work so long as you remain guilty of the past. But if the obstacle is removed."

Shelly began to cry out. For a brief moment she fought the control, only for her expression to become transfixed. Lucas tried hard to struggle against the Silent Ones who held him, but their grip was so tight that both his arms became suddenly numb.

Blank eyes stared back at Lucas when he tried to get his sister's attention. She began to mutter, tears in her eyes. "Mom…Dad…I'm so sorry… Please don't leave me again…Are you there?... Yes please… I've come home…" She fell to the floor, her tears of horror turning into tears of joy.

"What did you do to her?!" Lucas screeched again. Jacob groaned and walked over to him.

"Your sister has been given what she wanted. The parents, alive and well. That memory, though false, will heal her heart and make her feel whole again. This can happen for you as well, then your power will be as it once was. Under the blood moon's dominance and the Shadow's influence, we could both be equals instead of adversaries."

Lucas was horrified by this.

This goes beyond manipulating people. Is this what he does to everyone? This is why no one wants to be without him. It's evil!

"Do what he says, Lucas," Shelly said in a dreamlike state. "Jacob has made it so that mom and dad are here waiting for us. All you have to do is let go and you'll be free as well."

Lucas shook his head and continued to fight. The burning sensation increased and surged throughout his body.

"Stop this, Henry! Make Jacob stop what he's doing!"

"The old master cannot," Jacob revealed. "He is waiting for the final outcome to be announced. So it shall be. It comes in two's as a reflection on a mirror." He scratched at his head and made a quick muttering sound before stopping. "The compromise is the boy comes with me and my old master with Alistair. The camp will remain unharmed although the lives of the Silent Ones lost will need to be reimbursed. Carnage will see the camp decimated and all who refuse to be free. The lives lost will not matter in the grand scheme. However, only one of us can exist should this unfavorable option be chosen."

Lucas looked at his friends, at his sister, at Henry. He tried to think of what kind of response he should say. He feared thinking at the moment.

"If I go with you, will you let my sister go? She can't stay like that and you have to free everyone under your control."

Jacob started to become irritable at this and began to stammer when he spoke.

"Do not make demands! That is improper! When you have guests over in the house, do you leave them to their own devices and resume regular activities? If they are content where they are, then leave them be."

Lucas shook his head in stubborn refusal. He stood up on his feet and did not feel the pain in his arms at all.

"I would rather die than let my friends and sister get hurt. If that means only one of us can exist, then so be it."

Jacob groaned and turned away, his hands scratching at his scalp and droplets of blood spreading across his head and fingers. Shanine ran to his side to help heal him but he was so upset that he slapped her with a free hand. She fell backwards and was clasping her blooded cheek.

"Foolish boy. An offer was made and the hand denied. There is too much intent in your heart. Easily manipulated, as mine once was. You don't know what real pain is yet but it can be taught."

Shelly's tears of joy became sorrow in an instant. She was throwing her hands forward, every which way and crying out for her parents.

"No, not again. Don't leave me again! Please come back. We need you. I need you!" Shelly collapsed and her whole body shook. She began to groan in pain and Lucas tried with all his might to use his mind control on Jacob. His nose began to bleed and he felt extremely lightheaded.

"The ability that is wielded through pain manifests this tenfold."

Lucas groaned and shook his head, trying hard to ignore the pain he was feeling.

"There's a darkness in you that is similar to this mind," Jacob gestured to himself. "Why do you hide your desire? So much pain, so much loneliness. Let it consume you so that you can see as I do." Jacob threw his hand backwards and the shadows seemed to shimmer.

Lucas pushed the thoughts back even as the thoughts called out to him.

I mean nothing to anyone. I'm worthless. I hate myself because I hate how I feel compared to others. I want to be happy but I don't know how. Sometimes I want to… want to… no, stop it! Get out of my head!

Jacob did not speak. His bloodshot eyes followed his opposite with great interest. He was encircling around Lucas as if he meant to pounce on him.

"You hide those thoughts well. Commendable. Caked in denial and illusion. But there is a memory that has become vulnerable and known now. This one is more accessible and…There it is." Jacob smirked as the memory came to fruition. Lucas fell backwards, the Silent Ones releasing their grips on his numb arms. He suddenly felt numb all over.

Oh no, no, not this again. I can't. No, I won't live like this.

"What was given can be taken away," Jacob murmured as Lucas screamed in fear. He closed his eyes and tried to command his body to move and convince his mind that this was a trick. Looking at his lifeless limbs again, he turned to look at Henry, who gave him an impassive expression.

"Help me please! I don't want to be this way again. I can't!"

Lucas moved his head sideways and felt himself become more frantic and terrified. A sudden feeling washed over him and caused Lucas to close his eyes as if he were drifting to sleep.

When he awoke, Lucas was in the White Room again. He was lying on his back and looking up as the Crow and Eagle hovered over him.

"He is beginning to see again, yes he is," the Crow cackled excitedly. "The face of the nightmares has been painted and now the eyes match those who came before."

The Eagle nodded and flew over to Lucas. It hovered in front of his eyes.

"Allow your mind to be as it once was, only stronger now. When you do not fear the pain that came before, it cannot be used to hurt you now."

Lucas shook his head. He tried to speak but his mouth along with his body were not working.

"Your adversary is a parasite who feeds off the life force of those around him," The Eagle revealed. "They become dependent on him and feel they cannot be whole without him. You resisted, which is a rare trait indeed. One that must be nurtured."

The Crow nodded eagerly and was now side to side with the Eagle.

"Indeed, yes. You must confront what haunts you. This feeling of powerlessness must be extinguished at its root core."

Lucas waited for them to continue.

"When you awake, your body will be your own once more, to a manageable degree. The only difference is you will be aware of the source, a known secret. To complete this transition, you must confront the memory that haunts you most which is aligned with your feeling of powerlessness.

"Your mind is capable of creating a place that exists within one's own self, but as a telepath, you can manipulate it as you feel is best for yourself. Do not linger inside for long, else the memory becomes more than the reality."

Lucas nodded stiffly.

The Crow laughed maniacally and flew off without another word.

Lucas awoke to the memory of the last day he saw his parents. He was standing atop the stairs while his parents shook uncontrollably. Their faces were turned away from him and were blanked out.

"Mom… Dad?" Lucas called out to them. The picture was similar to the memory his sister showed him, but this time he could make out the pictures on the walls and words on discarded newspapers. He walked up to his parents and they began to emit a stuttering sound the closer he got. "I wish I hadn't left. Maybe if I didn't, you both would still be alive. I don't know if it was my fault or Jacobs, or something else. But I miss you both so much and I'm sorry—"

Lucas was cut off with a fierce slap. He fought through this pain and tried to continue again.

"I'm sorry—"

He was slapped once more and that's when Lucas realized something.

The memory ends here. I never got to finish what I wanted to say. But I can try saying something different now.

"I wasn't a good son," Lucas continued. His mother's hand continued to tremble. "I know that now. You both deserved so much better than me and I tried to be good. I won't apologize anymore because the moment is gone. I rather move past this and make sure no one ever gets hurt again. Starting with those Jacob is hurting now."

His parents did not respond to any of this, but Lucas felt that aching in his heart, that desire to touch them. He put a hand on his mom's trembling hand and the other on his dad's face.

"I miss you both so much. I promise I'm going to be okay and so is Shelly. We have each other and we will always be there for one another. In the meantime, I'm going to make this life you gave me worth it."

To his surprise, his mother's hand reached out for his hand and his father's hand grasped the one touching his cheek. With their free hands they pulled Lucas into a warm embrace and the three of them began to cry. Lucas couldn't hear what his parents were saying, but he felt so much warmth from their touch that it didn't matter.

I'm not afraid… not anymore.

Lucas awoke and with a start his body was his own again. There was something else that wasn't there before. His mind began to hear the thoughts of his friends in the background and feel as they did.

There's no pain. I don't feel afraid anymore!

"What is this?" Jacob took a step backwards and clenched his fists. "How is this possible?"

"I saw my parents." Shelly perked up at this and looked at her brother with a longing like she was begging for something. "You need to let them go, Shell." Shelly shook her head and stubbornly beat against the ground.

"I won't let them go! I already lost them. I had to watch them die because you weren't there with me. I won't go through that again!"

"I know, Shell," Lucas said sorrowfully. "They understand and they promised to see us again."

His sister looked up at him, now with eyes of hope.

"Do you mean that? Can we see them again?"

Lucas shook his head.

"Not now, but one day."

Shelly buried her face in the ground. Her hands dug on the earth and she was crying out muffled sounds. As this happened, Mike emerged from the crowd, walking past his sister. Sapphire tried to get his attention but it was like he didn't see her. He was limping and moved past Shelly.

"I did it, Jacob!" Mike cried out. "I led you here. Just like I promised. Now where are my parents?"

Jacob was so preoccupied with himself that he swatted a hand in Mike's direction. Mike became angry and limped more aggressively forward.

"I want them back! I want to see them again!"

"Mikey, what are you doing?" Sapphire cried out. Twinkle was barking up a storm in her arms. Jacob groaned in pain and pointed a sharp finger at the dog's direction.

"Silence that infernal mutt or it will be beaten to death!"

Twinkle whimpered and Sapphire hugged him tightly.

"Don't hurt my doggie, you big meanie!"

Jacob moaned and tried to compose himself.

"A dog I was given once. For each lick it gave my hand, a hit was received by the other. One day, instead of licking, it bit the hand that hurt it. I felt no pain from this, no joy or sorrow. My mind reacted by making the dog suffer the pain it felt. This was also the first time I knew what pain was. This dog taught me that."

Sapphire began to cry and took a step backwards with Twinkle in her arms.

"You killed a puppy? You're a bad person!"

Mike fell to his knees. He groaned on the bad leg but the pain quickly became secondary to his main desire. His eyes were similarly bloodshot to Lucas' and Jacobs.

"Please, Jacob. I need to see them again. I'm tired of living without them."

Lucas felt his heart breaking.

He sounds like me last year when I was paralyzed.

Shelly looked upwards, her face covered in dirt. Both hers and Mike's hands were outstretching to Jacob.

"Help us please," they both said in unison.

Jacob's back was turned to them. The dead tree tattoo was like a closed door that wouldn't budge no matter how much it was pounded on.

Sapphire ran up to her brother and hugged Mike's arm.

"Please stop, Mikey. Please," she cried against him. Twinkle whimpered and moved out of the way when Mike rose to walk past him.

"I'm going to see mom and dad," Mike said. "I'll bring them here so you can meet them, Sapphire. We'll be a family again."

The little girl shook her head stubbornly and grasped Mike's wrist tighter.

"We're a family. I want you, Mikey. Just you." She cried harder now and it took all of her will to keep her power from activating. Someone emerged from the crowd. This person ran towards Mike, evading the nearby Silent Ones, and wrapped her arms around his shoulders.

Caroline!

She moved slightly to avoid hitting Sapphire.

"Your parents are gone, Mike. They loved you and Sapphire so much. You can always find them in your mind, but only as a memory. This man cannot give them back to you no matter what he promises you."

Mike was protesting and trying to move forward towards the annoyed and angered Jacob. One of his hands was still outstretched and the feeling of how close Caroline and Sapphire were didn't seem to bother him in the least.

Please Mike, you got to fight this. Don't give in. Lucas tried to project this thought onto his friend, but Mike's mind was closed to him.

After a brief struggle, Mike began to stammer and fell to his knees again.

"You don't understand. I need them back. Please!" Mike cried out. "I can't do this, mom and dad. I'm trying so hard and it's been very hard. I feel so alone."

"You're not alone," Caroline asserted. She buried her face on his back and Sapphire pressed her small body against the side of his. "Everyone here in camp cares about you so much. You have a family here and we won't abandon you."

Lucas felt how intensely Caroline's feelings for Mike were as they emitted from her to him like feedback from speakers.

"I love you so much, Mikey. You're my papa and mama."

Sapphire's power activated and she became translucent. The diamond light she emitted was so illuminating that it contrasted sharply with the blood moon's ominous glow. While everyone else shielded their eyes, Mike turned to his sister, as if noticing her for the first time. He began to cry. In Mike's eyes Lucas could feel a realization so deep and profound he found himself temporarily overwhelmed as well.

What is she doing to him? This is the most beautiful pure feeling I've ever felt.

Mike limply reached out his gloveless hands to grab both Caroline's arms and put the other hand on his sister's back. He felt himself shivering pervasively and cried softly against the girl he liked and the sister he loved. When the tears stopped and his face softened, Mike looked around as if recognizing his surroundings for the first time.

"Sapphy…Caroline…? Luke, Shelly? What's going on?" Mike asked in a near delirious state.

Sapphire sighed with relief and appeared exhausted. Lucas noted that her dark brown hair appeared lighter now, her eyes were turning more blue than green, and there was a small red shape that appeared on the center of her forehead.

That wasn't there before. It looks like a star.

Henry moved over to the three and shoved them backwards. He tried to do this to Shelly as well, but she fought back against him.

"Don't touch me!" Shelly protested. Boris emerged from the group and pulled Shelly to her feet. "Please, Lucas. I can't be without them again!"

Lucas sighed and turned his attention to Bill. He read his friend's mind and saw the torment there.

I didn't mean for this to happen.

"You can stop this, Bill," Lucas told his best friend. "Jacob can't give you what you want. Nothing can."

Jacob stopped shaking and panting.

"What is spoken is truth," Jacob told Bill. "What was taken from you was never stolen. It was given new life, and that new life cannot be as it was."

Bill shook his head furiously, his bandaged eyes emitting the red glow.

"No. That's not right. I can't do anything like this. I can't even see!" Bill was preparing to remove his bandages when Jacob threw a hand up.

"New life your power has, but it can become stable. So that sight returns to you."

Bill calmed down and looked in the direction of Jacob's voice.

When he asked how, Jacob pointed to Lucas.

"Kill Lucas, and I will make your power manageable."

Bill's breath stopped when he heard the last two words.

No, Bill, don't listen to him, Lucas projected into Bill's mind. *He can't do that either. He's feeding off what he knows you want.*

Bill did not seem to listen. He was preparing to remove the cloth from his eyes with the hand that was missing his fingertip joints. Alistair looked like he wanted to take a step forward but hesitated.

Bill walked over to where he could hear Lucas breathing. He ripped the cloth off and had his eyes closed firmly.

Alistair walked up to Bill, leaned against him, and pulled out his blade.

"If you unleash those beams of yours, you'll make a whole mess out there," he cautioned Bill. "This is cleaner and quicker. I'll stay here and make sure he doesn't move."

Alistair went behind Lucas and laid a hand on his shoulder.

"Don't move," Alistair whispered to Lucas. He turned to look at him and glared at the man hatefully.

What is this?

Lucas looked at his friends who were crying out for Bill to stop and Henry, who was watching everything without taking any action to intervene.

Bill was breathing hard, and sweat coated his face. It took all he had to not open his eyes.

"Don't do this, Bill. It won't change anything," Lucas pleaded as Bill leveled the sword towards Lucas. "Vanessa wants you to come home. She's waiting for you to stop and Shannon cares about you. She even forgives you for trying to break up with her."

This stopped Bill, with Shannon giving both Lucas and her boyfriend a sorrowful gaze.

He stammered and the bony sword shook in his hands.

"I…I…I need to do this. I need to do something."

When Bill brought the blade up, Lucas closed his eyes and felt his heart pumping hard.

If this is it, at least it's with a friend.

Bill swung the blade down as the other campers and staff turned away, shouting in protest. It took them a moment to realize that the blade hadn't cut into Lucas. Instead it was stabbed into the ground.

Was that on purpose or is it because he can't see?

"Get down," Bill said swiftly. He opened his eyes and the beams emitted hit Alistair, who was hit with the energy beam at full blast. He flew backwards like a baseball and was out of sight before long. Bill closed his eyes immediately, ripped a long piece of the shirt he wore and wrapped it around his eyelids.

All chaos erupted. The Silent Ones resumed fighting the campers who were being held back, while Josh emitted a sonic wave that blew away the ones near him, Gary, and Erin. The two were still dazed and unresponsive to the commotion. Shanine retreated into the woods, hiding away from the chaos. Meanwhile, Boris was trying to hold back Shelly from running towards where Jacob was. He was staggering and appeared weakened by Josh's ability. Shannon removed her restraints and shifted into her wolf form. She clawed at a few Silent Ones and scared off more. More of them made their way towards Lucas, who was prepared this time. When he threw his hands up, the Silent Ones flew to the side with such speed it was like the winds had grown a physical hand. Lucas gasped and looked at his hands in triumph.

It's back! Whatever I did before it is back again!

Another group came at him and this time he threw up his hand like he meant to swat at something and the attacking children flew into the forest. They hit both the trees and landed on the ground in a rolling tumbling synchronicity.

I can get used to this. Lucas flexed his hands and felt a sudden vibration coursing through the tips of his fingers down to his wrists like a numb muscle.

While everyone was fighting with each other, and Lucas admired his new ability, Josh took this opportunity to run towards Jacob in his weakened state.

Lucas saw something in Jacob's eyes and body. A primal animalistic look similar to a wounded predator readying itself to lash out against his prey. He pierced his eardrums with the tips of his sharp-nailed fingers and turned towards Josh.

"NOOOOOOOO!" was all Lucas could shout as he helplessly watched Josh opening his mouth and screaming in front of Jacob. Since Josh could not hear Lucas, he tried to mind control his friend and use his new ability on him. Neither worked.

Wait, why didn't it work? I thought my powers were working again.

Jacob, with his ears bloodied, thrust his left palm towards Josh's left rib cage. As his hand disappeared underneath Josh's shirt, a terrible sound soon followed. Josh screamed and staggered backwards, white-faced and coughing violently. He was suddenly having difficulty breathing.

Nooooooo, Josh!!! Ahhhhhhh!!!

When he collapsed on the ground, Josh was wheezing and sputtering erratically like a fish fresh out of water. Blood seeped out of his mouth with each cough. Lucas also fell to his knees and was coughing up spittle into his hand. There was no blood, only saliva. Lucas clasped his stomach area and groaned in pain.

Laying on the ground, Jacob prowled towards Josh. He was staggering but was otherwise able to make his way to the fallen camper. He began to savagely kick him until the same sound as before returned. Josh wailed in pain and tears were falling from his eyes. Another kick was followed by a large pop that sounded excruciating.

Stop it, stop now!

"Feel this do you?" Jacob asked Lucas. "Feel his pain as your own? Another folly, another weakness!"

Lucas felt every kick and each one caused him to fall backwards until he was lying on his back and gasping for air.

Henry finally walked over and with a watery whip, sent Jacob backwards. He crashed against a nearby tree, breaking it, but did not appear to be in any kind of discomfort. There was only that dry chuckle that came out of him. Jacob's hands touched his bloodied ears.

Shanine ran from her cover to Jacob and gave him two vials of water. Jacob took them swiftly and dumped all their contents into each of his ears. He cracked his neck and bit down on his crooked teeth. She put herself in front of him and flames began to emit from her back. They became wings and she was crying tears that fell onto Jacob's bare chest.

"Don't you dare come near us!" Shanine hissed, the flaming wings becoming more ferocious now.

Lucas was able to breathe again and strained to bring himself upwards.

"We need to get Josh out of here," Lucas told Henry, wheezily. The Camp Director nodded and lifted Josh up.

"The question was posed, not answered," Jacob called out to Henry in a weakened state. All around them Silent Ones and campers were still fighting, though it had evolved from abilities to fist fights between the older campers who were trying to subdue the bigger Silent Ones. "The truth must be told so all can be on the same playing field."

Henry turned towards Jacob, still holding an injured Josh.

"You asked about my years? You wish to know how old I am. Or rather wish me to say what I am?"

Jacob nodded stiffly and Lucas felt himself becoming lively.

In the pictures in the Grand Hall, he doesn't look any older than he does now.

"You know what Alistair is, and that is what I am," Henry told Jacob. "We have known each other for more than 100 years."

Lucas felt a proverbial bomb go off in his head. Any strength he had left was gone now.

100 years?! There's no way he'd be alive and looking the way he does now. Unless that's part of his power.

Henry looked at Lucas with a fixed gaze.

"Alistair and I are of the same, not species, but being. A state of being. We are Immortals."

As if his name summoned him, Alistair appeared via a portal that he had made. He looked unscathed by the energy beam blast, except his shirt had a hole in it that should have vaporized the skin underneath.

"That was quite the light show don't you think, Henry?" Alistair said in a snide tone. "Did I miss story time already?"

Henry, fearing where this was going, handed Josh off to Boris, who was still trying to keep Shelly back. Lucas went to his sister and took charge of her. She reached out her hands towards Jacob and continued to cry out for her parents. She fought against him but eventually stopped and began to cry against his shoulders.

"Mom…dad…I'm sorry…" Lucas patted his sisters back and hugged her to him.

"Alistair, you have crossed the line now. Allying yourself with Jacob and turning these children into his minions."

"Spare me the high road talk. How much have you shared? Our age? I can't even remember at this point. What about the truth? About that kid's parents?" Alistair pointed to Lucas. Lucas took a step back and looked at Henry, who was not paying attention to him.

"That is for me to say at the designated time," Henry insisted.

"Probably when no one is around to overhear how you justify yourself. Only I know you better than anyone living."

The two old friends were glaring at each other while Lucas and Jacob looked at each in a similar fashion.

"I had hoped we could settle our differences, Alistair," Henry noted in exhaustion. "Alas, I've come to realize we were both trying to chase after what is already past. It's time for us both to let go now."

The Camp Director turned to walk away. He beckoned for Lucas to do the same.

"That's it? After everything I've done for you, that's how you want to leave things? You're a coward and a selfish old man who won't let anyone get close to him because he's afraid."

Henry kept his back turned to them both.

"I'll never stop," Alistair called out. "Neither will he." He gestured to Jacob. "We'll keep finding you all and next time we'll bring more of those hybrid things you like so much. I killed the last ones you had in that Dome place of yours."

Henry stopped walking now and turned slowly towards his friend and Jacob.

"What have you done, Alistair?" His voice was so full of icy rage that Lucas feared an ice storm was about to happen. Even in the night sky, clouds began to form and a fierce drizzle was pouring down. It began to put out the flames that were still engulfing part of the forest.

"They got in my way. It's not like they were doing much else but guarding one of your many cover places. Those things are like rabbits and they multiply like them. Shouldn't be hard to find more."

Now the drizzle turned to rain and the Silent Ones still fighting became weakened. Their skins were sizzling and they ran towards the woods to retreat from the onrushing water. The campers, staff, and Lucas' friends were all unharmed.

The rain sizzled Alistair's body but otherwise did not harm him. The same was for Jacob, who appeared to be reaching his limit. He was no longer murmuring and was now recovering from the stunt he pulled with his eardrums.

"Nice trick with the rain. It didn't work last year and it won't work now. A Plus for effort though."

"Leave now, Alistair. Take Jacob and the others with you. This will be your final warning; if you return to camp again, I will kill you myself."

Alistair snickered at this.

"Promises, promises. You never were good at keeping them."

Alistair opened up a portal and a couple Silent Ones, Shanine, Jacob and Alistair himself were sucked through instantly. A few Silent Ones lingered but they hurried away in what looked like a confused state.

"Will they find Jacob?" Lucas asked Henry.

The Camp Director nodded.

"They will return to the source they feel they need. To be without it for long would mean death."

Henry said this with such sadness in his voice that Lucas almost forgot what he wanted to say.

"What's going to happen now? What does it mean that you and Alistair are Immortal?"

Shelly dashed past both the Camp Director and her brother, towards the woods. Lucas tackled her with all the strength he had left and held her back.

"Let me go, Lucas! I need to get back. Our parents are there waiting for us. Please don't keep me from them. It's your fault they're gone! They died because of you."

Lucas gripped his sister tight around the waist, biting back the pain those words brought him, and looked at Henry for help.

The Camp Director walked up to Shelly, lay a hand on her head, against her protests. Her eyes fluttered and she fell unconscious.

"Will she be okay?" Lucas asked Henry.

"Enough questions," Henry said this in a sharp tone. "Yes, she will be fine. Now we must return to Camp Supernatural. Take your sister with you. It's time I told you all the truth about me and this place."

Lucas lifted Shelly up by her arm, threw it over his shoulder and walked with Henry back towards where the rest of the campers were gathered underneath the dark rainy night. He spotted Shannon who was helping Bill walk. The two went behind them and did not say a word as they made their way back to Camp Supernatural…

Chapter 30: Immortal Eternal

The walk back to camp was silent. No one said a word, and nobody looked at each other. Lucas stared at Henry's back, and imagined a stranger staring back at him. Alistair's words echoed in his mind like a broken record.

Probably when no one is around to hear you justify yourself. What does he need to justify? He helped me when I needed it and has helped everyone here in camp. But the way he acted now, as everything was happening, was like the Relic game. The orb. What is the orb?!

Lucas looked behind him and saw Bill with Shannon, the two keeping to themselves. Neither made a motion to do much except put one foot in front of the other.

The remaining campers who came into view appeared either injured or huddled together in tears. Small children were holding small wooden bows and swords. The medical staff were doing their best to calm down some of the children but a few were preparing to keep fighting even when there were no more foes to face.

Whatever happens next, these kids won't ever be the same again.

It frightened Lucas how naive they had been, so cocky before the battle had started, and now so frightened that it's over.

Lucas gave Shelly over to Boris, who began to tend to her. She had a blank expression and didn't respond when Lucas tried to get her attention. She had stopped talking about their parents but reading her mind told him all he needed to know.

He's been lying to me and keeping secrets from me, Lucas heard Shelly think as her eyes looked at him with anger and sadness. *Jacob showed me the truth. All he cares about is his precious Camp Director. I only needed a little bit more time with mom and dad. Just a little. They took that from me.*

Lucas knew what his sister felt was going to take a while to fully recover from. It was similar to what everyone else was feeling.

That doesn't mean those words and feelings don't hurt. I know it isn't her, but deep down it's what she feels and never talked to me about.

The camp was in ruins, with the counselor's tents in flames, and the buildings either on fire or nearly gone. The cabins were mostly unscathed but many from the Majestic Meadow to the Imaginarium Illusion had damage that was caused from the fireballs and ensuing battle. The gift shop was destroyed and the livestock area where the animals had been previously was in ruins.

I hope the animals made it out alright.

Henry ascended the ruined steps of the pavilion as the remaining campers all gathered around the center. Lucas took his spot with his friends. Ashley and Vanessa moved towards his side without saying anything, while Erin came up from behind Lucas. She still appeared dazed but was slowly coming back to herself. More campers began clustering now, including the ones returning from their missions. They were horrified to witness the damage to the camp and the terrified faces of the campers who remained.

The Camp Director stared out into the crowd of people, his eyes looking even more tired and weary than they ever looked. The camp staff, which included Zane, Daniel, and Naomi, all stood in attendance but appeared to be more out of it than the campers themselves. It was so quiet that Lucas could hear the heartbeats and steady breathing of everyone around him.

"Good evening, my campers and staff. I apologize for what has happened today. The events of this battle will remain with us long after this summer has ended. Even so, the day is ours, and the enemy has retreated," Henry announced triumphantly.

Some of the younger campers began to weep, while the older ones solemnly looked at each other. They're eyes said more than any words could express.

This doesn't feel like a camp anymore.

"I feared this day would come, and I have done my best to maintain this camp in the years since its establishment. That being said, there is a truth you all must know now. Please know that no matter what happens, this will benefit you all as well as those who have yet to come," Henry asserted, "This knowledge that I am about to share with you all, once uttered, can never be forgotten again. I sought to find a way to halt this inevitability, a timeline that has been accelerated by Jacobs's interference. Before understanding this new threat, you must understand who I am, more specifically, *what* I am."

Henry paused for a moment as the newly arrived campers murmured to each other. Lucas felt this truth before the words were spoken and saw the features of Henry's aged face become like a melted wax figure.

"I am an Immortal. There are four Immortal's in this world, each who embody the four elements: water, earth, wind, fire. I am the water Immortal."

He demonstrated this as he lifted water from a mud puddle without lifting it with his bare hands and it flew to his left hand. It never touched his hand but instead just floated there as if gravity were suspended. The Camp Director also used his other hand to make it drizzle, with clouds appearing in the night sky as if they had been there all along.

"My purpose in creating this camp was to guide you all in having a chance at a normal existence. Those who have come before you were given a choice, to live their lives for as long as they lasted, or to know the truth. But this something of which you all unfortunately will not have. For this I apologize profusely. All of you exist and possess the abilities you have at a momentous price."

It was almost too much for many to bear. More of the smaller children began to cry, their echoing sobs reaching and affecting even their teen peers. Daniel swayed to Henry's side and whispered something to him but the Camp Director shrugged him off and returned his attention to everyone.

"I have lived in lies for too long, and I must speak the truth now so that you all can make individual decisions," Henry continued as the sobs died down and silence engulfed the camp. "I called you Alter Children, but you bear a true name, and once this name is spoken, you will all see the truth."

Hearts beating, breaths in, out, feet tapping the ground, finally, clenched muscles.

"You are all **Eternal** children."

When that word was said, each child in attendance, including Lucas and his friends, felt a giant wave hit them. The wave was so powerful that some children fell on their backs, others with their faces planted first on the ground. Lucas was on his knees, his eyes watery, his nose dripping with blood, and his mouth suddenly dry. When he looked around, behind the haze of tears, he saw his friends who appeared similarly. Everyone looked like a crowd that had been hit by tear-gas. Bill was struggling to keep the cloth around his eyes as the red beams emitted fiercely. Shannon hugged him, positioning herself in case his beams came out.

So many voices… so many emotions… I feel them all!

It took a few seconds for Lucas to begin seeing the visions that came to him. He wasn't seeing with his eyes, *my mind's eyes!*

Many images swirled into his head as if his brain had become a film strip. He saw what could only be described accurately as flashes that happened so fast he missed many the first time around.

Some of these images replayed themselves, with the most notable being a lone man on a mountain, clothed in the purest white. The sun radiated on him and bathed his pale body. This man was surrounded by others, all with shapes as solid and clear as statues. Eventually, they became shadows which engulfed this white man. When he was overtaken, another took his place. This person was shrouded in darkness and those who surrounded him were similarly shaded. Where one represented the light of a new day, the other represented the dark of a fallen night.

Lucas lucidly heard Henry continue. "All of you descend from an Immortal bloodline. It flows within each of you and allows you to have the abilities that you possess. Long ago it was decreed that any child born of an Immortal would be raised to take their place, lest their existence be short in length. An Eternal Child's lifespan has never gone beyond the age of thirty-three. When this happens the body shuts down and dies. There has not been a new Immortal appointed since long before the time this camp was established, and we have lost as many Eternal Children as have been gained throughout the years. Without an Immortal to control the elements, our world will fall into chaos and be destroyed as it was many years ago. Becoming Immortal has a steep price; you will forfeit your soul, an afterlife, and the possibility of rebirth."

The campers who had recovered from the information overload looked completely uneasy about all this. Looking at Daniel, Lucas could tell he had no idea about any of this and neither did the other counselors in attendance.

Why now? Why did he choose now to tell us all this? Why not others who came before us?

"I wish I could tell you all that everything will be alright, but I would be lying and I am so very tired of lying. The best outcome that you can all hope for is to enjoy the time you have with each other, and with your loved ones. If you wish to remain here, and continue on this next chapter of your lives, I will do my best to safeguard you all from any threats that may come our way. If you should choose to leave, I will understand as well and wish you the best in whatever form your life takes. We have all become a family in the short time we have known each other and like all families, we must be willing to let each other go for the benefit of the rest. I hope one day you all can understand why I chose to keep this information until now."

After ending his speech on a bittersweet note, the Camp Director made his exit and walked past sullen silent faces. Henry never looked in anyone's direction as he entered his home and shut the door behind him. A few minutes later life in camp resumed, but Lucas' mind was swimming with questions. What was the orb in the relic game? What did Henry have to do with his parents? Would Josh be okay from his injuries? What would be Bill's and Mike's fates for betraying the camp?

Lucas decided to make his first stop to visit his best friend. It was a horrific sight to see Josh attached to several machines, with a breathing mask over his mouth and nose. He was covered from the neck down with a blanket. Kendall cradled Josh's hand delicately and had been crying when Lucas entered.

"Hey, Lucas, I didn't see you there," said Kendall as she wiped her tears away. "I just got back from a mission not that long ago and all this happened."

Lucas walked closer and heard the steady but wheezing breathing of Josh's lungs.

He looks worse than I thought.

"How is he doing?"

Kendall shook her head.

"He's not doing so well. They said his left lung was punctured severely. If it had been closer to the heart, he would have died before he even reached the door."

Kendall turned her face towards Lucas.

"Josh won't be able to use his power anymore. They don't know for how long, but the doctor said it was a miracle he even survived. I don't know if it was his ability. It's possible that it helped because his lungs are stronger than an ordinary person's would be."

Lucas nodded and agreed.

"He will live and that is the important part."

Kendall looked very unsure.

"Is it? In the time that I have known Josh, he has always gloated about his power, how he loves it so much, and how he couldn't ever live without it. I just don't want to imagine how he will feel if it turns out he can't use it anymore. What that will mean for him."

If Josh can't use his power, he'll be like Bill where neither can remain campers nor become camp counselors.

"How did this happen to him?" Kendall asked.

Lucas explained what happened in the forest, and how Josh tried to attack Jacob but that he saw his intent coming before it happened.

"Josh should have known better than to do something so stupid."

I did warn him and that's exactly what he did, Lucas thought ruefully.

"He'll be fine. Josh is strong and if anyone can survive this he can."

Kendall nodded softly. The door creaked open as Ashley's head popped out. Behind her was Hailey, whose eyes were fixated on Josh.

"Hey, Lucas, how is Josh doing?" Ashley asked.

He explained Josh's condition, and as he finished, their faces looked grim.

"Without his ability Josh won't be able to stay in camp," Ashley said sorrowfully.

I figured as much, but still, I should try talking to Henry about it. Maybe he will listen to me, Lucas hoped.

Hailey moved forward into the room and stood at the foot-end of the bed, watching over Josh's unconscious body. Kendall was staring at her but neither girls smiled nor said anything to each other.

"There has to be something we can do," Lucas insisted.

Ashley shrugged.

"When he wakes up, just be there for him. He's going to need his friends now more than ever."

. *He needs to be healed more than anything else. Alright, time to go.*

Lucas left the hospital and made his way towards Henry's home. He wasn't sure what time it was but it must have been late enough that the night sky continued to persist and the crickets chirping were like the birds in the morning.

I don't know what I'll ask first but I need to make sure that Henry answers everything I want to know. No more secrets and no more lies.

To his dismay, Boris stood at the front of Henry's house and upon spotting Lucas stood in his way firmly.

"Lucas, I cannot allow you to enter. Henry does not wish to be disturbed by anyone."

Henry can't hide away from this. Not this time

"Please, Boris, this is important. I need his help for Josh, and I need to ask him about my parents. I think he knows what really happened to them."

Boris contemplated this, but ultimately shook his head.

"I'm sorry, Lucas. I cannot let you enter unless Henry says so."

"Then ask, please, Boris."

The Camp Guardian was only gone for a minute before he opened the door for Lucas to enter. When Lucas opened the door, he found Henry sitting in his chair impassively.

He doesn't even look like he cares. His body is there but his mind is a thousand miles away.

It took what felt like a few minutes for the Camp Director to notice him.

"Lucas, please come in. Have a seat."

When Lucas sat and looked at the Camp Director in the face, he was taken aback by his sudden appearance. Henry's smooth white skin was suddenly wrinkled, his eyes lined with crow's feet and his beard looked longer now. His sad ocean blue eyes looked even more melancholy in the light of the room.

We just saw him not even an hour ago and he looks like he has aged at least ten years in advance. No, he's not human; he's an Immortal. He's been alive for who knows how long. I don't even know who he is anymore.

Lucas sat there quietly as Henry poured him some water and got a glass for himself. As he did though, his hand trembled and his upper lip was quivering as if he were about to burst into tears.

What's going on? Why is he acting like this? This isn't like Henry at all.

"What can I do for you, Lucas?" Henry finally asked after the glasses were full of water. Lucas took a moment to compartmentalize his thoughts from what he wanted to ask and the various questions he had.

He hasn't helped anyone this summer from Bill, to Mike, now Josh. If he has some lame excuse about why he can't, I'm going to ask why.

"Is there something you wish to ask of me, Lucas?" Henry asked in that powerful but quiet voice that Lucas had become so fond of. At the moment, Lucas had mountains of questions for Henry, but he knew that the Camp Director would not answer all of them. If he was lucky, maybe two of them.

I want to ask about the orb in the Relic game, but even more than that I want to know about my parents.

"It's about Josh, Henry. I was just wondering what's going to happen to him at the end of summer?"

Lucas felt his stomach twist in a knot, and quivered at the answer he feared. Henry did not reply immediately, as he drank small sips of water from his cup. When he did answer, it was not what Lucas had hoped for.

"Depending on the severity of the damage, he may no longer be able to attend camp next year."

Lucas sighed angrily and kept calm.

"Can you heal Josh, the way you healed me last summer? I know you couldn't heal Bill, or Mike, but just this once, can you please make an exception?"

Lucas heard the words, but suddenly felt guilt for even asking. He brushed the guilt aside, hoping for a yes. To his disappointment, Henry refused.

"I cannot. I am sorry, my son."

Henry took another sip from his glass and laid the empty cup to the side of his table. Two no's in a roll shocked Lucas more than he showed.

Why is he being like this? What made me the exception to his power? Fine, time to ask why.

"Can I please ask why you won't help Josh? You didn't hesitate to help me when I asked you. How is this different? You helped me and Sapphire. How else was she able to leave the hospital like me?"

"I did not heal her," Henry revealed. "Her latent ability manifested and that's why she is here now."

He replayed the memory of Sapphire when she healed Mike and realized the truth in Henry's words.

She can't heal the same way Henry can though. That's why she's still as small and fragile as she is. Is she stronger than Henry is?

"Alright fine, you didn't heal Sapphire then, just me. So what was all that about Eternal Children, our short life spans, and having to become Immortals to live? And what about the orb from the Relic game? Jacob had one like it and Mike used it so the Silent Ones could enter camp. What is it?" Lucas blurted out too sharply.

He heard his voice rise with each word but Henry remained stone-faced. It always frightened him how the Camp Director never seemed emotional. The only time he could recall seeing emotion on Henry's face was when he woke up in the hospital and saw the tears on his face.

I thought they were tears but maybe they weren't.

"As I recall, Lucas, you promised me that no one would know how you were healed. However, you explicitly mentioned this in the company of Bill and your friends," Henry reminded him in a sharp tone.

Okay that's true, I admit it, but I didn't mean to.

"I cannot play favoritism. This is a camp full of children who are in equal need of guidance." Henry paused for a moment, inhaling slowly. "I will do all that I can for Josh, but healing him is out of the question."

Lucas did not understand Henry's logic.

He's making up an excuse, and a bad one, Lucas thought angrily. *All his talk about helping everyone here but what about Jacob? He was angry at Henry for a reason and he blames him for something.*

"Why did you help me then? Did you take pity on me because I wanted to go home so badly?" Lucas asked sullenly. "Or was it because you failed Jacob, used him, and when he didn't turn out the way you wanted, you decided to use me instead?"

Henry did not answer, but Lucas knew there was more.

He had to have known what my abilities were before I did. He nearly let me die in the game last year because he knew what it would take to make me unlock my power.

"The first day I came here you gave me your undivided attention. I didn't see you show any other camper their cabin like you did for me," Lucas pointed out firmly. "Did you do the same thing for Jacob when he was here? Did you show favoritism to him?"

Lucas had a hard time staying calm, his eyes fully on the Camp Director. He continued to talk for fear of being dismissed.

"It looks like you're playing favorites with me. I've seen how you are with Daniel. He's your son and you treat him like you don't want him around. I used to think Daniel was overreacting when he told me you would disappoint me, but I'm starting to think he was always right about you."

It didn't take him long to realize that the conversation was one-sided. Henry only looked at him with distant cold eyes, like he was there physically but not mentally. Nothing Lucas said caused the Camp Director to react in any meaningful way.

"Do you even want me here? Do you care about anyone who is here? I can't tell anymore when you just let things happen and let people get hurt in front of you. My sister and Mike could have died because of whatever Jacob does to people. You didn't care. I could have died and you didn't care. Is Alistair right about you, Henry?"

This time, Henry finally spoke.

"I have said it once and I shall say it once more, Lucas: Everything I have ever done has been for the safety of this camp, and the people in it. I only wanted to give you all a better life, but only now do I realize that by keeping this knowledge from you, I have condemned so many others and that is my fault alone…"

Henry's expression made his long face appear weathered and beaten down, like rocks eroded by saltwater.

He doesn't just sound weary, he looks it.

"That doesn't answer my question," Lucas pressed. "What made you want me here more than anyone else? Was it my abilities or what happened to my parents? And speaking of, what did Alistair mean when he said you know what really happened to them? You made me think Jacob had something to do with it, or worse yet, that I did."

Henry shook his head and brushed his hair backwards from his face as it fell in loose strands.

"I did not want to burden you, Lucas." When Henry said this, his tone was quivering, and his hands were shaking. "You made new friends here and gained a better grasp on your powers. I feared if you knew what happened to them, you might want to leave and never return. It was a miscalculation, and I apologize for it."

Lucas' heart lurched from his chest and his breath caught in his throat.

"Why would you do this to me? You knew I wanted to go home more than anything last year. Even with the friends I made, I was homesick and miserable. The only thing that kept me from going insane was the thought of going home and making things right with my parents. How could you lie to me and let me think that everything was fine when it wasn't? Why would you ever think that was the right thing to do?"

Lucas' volume was rising, and he was having a hard time containing the rage he was building up.

The Camp Director did not offer a response.

He's not the man I thought he was. Alistair was right; Henry is a coward.

Henry silently scoffed to himself, a gesture which made Lucas finally ask about his parents.

"What really happened to my mom and dad, Henry, and what am I doing here in camp? No more lies, no more half-truths. Tell me the whole truth or I am leaving Camp Supernatural and I'll never come back. I want to know everything you know and that's final."

Lucas heard his voice waver with his threat and felt his fists clench together. He was ready to scream, to break something if Henry confirmed his suspicions.

"Lucas… you have to understand. There was no other way," Henry revealed with emotion and hurt in his eyes. "Let me explain, my child…"

No… No… No… He did it… he…

"I am *not* your child. Don't you call me that ever again!"

He did it. He killed my parents…

Lucas stared at Henry with more anger and hate than he felt for both Alistair and Jacob. It took all the strength he had left to see this through now that it was here. This moment.

"I'm going to give you one chance to say it. One truth. Yes or no. Did you kill my parents?"

The Camp Director was silent again, so Lucas pounded on the table with his right fist so hard that the very floor quaked as if it were about to open up and swallow the two whole. Henry did not relent, even when Lucas was mere inches from his face, staring deep into his melancholy blue eyes.

"Yes. It was the only way to save you, Lucas," Henry explained unapologetically. "I lied to you before about what the price is for my power. The price is that I must take a life to restore a life. It took the lives of both your parents just to restore your life-force. But your soul remains fractured and that is a consequence for the manner in which you died."

Lucas shook his head in disbelief and slowly edged away from the Camp Director.

Died? I didn't die! I was hurt really badly. No, this can't be real. This is a nightmare.

"You did die and it is true. I can hear your thoughts in my mind. I've always been able to hear what you think since the moment you came to camp. That is how I knew where you'd be the day you fell. I was aware that you had plans to leave and I thought about stopping you. I could have intercepted you or let you remain lost in the forest. Instead, Alistair acted upon his own impulse believing your death is what would have benefitted me. This is the truth, Lucas, as you requested: I killed your parents, so that you could live, and I let Alistair kill you, so you would have to stay and unlock the potential of your abilities. My express desire is that you would take my place as an Immortal one day. Your soul is already fragmented, and without healing, it will only become worse, making the transition to becoming Immortal much easier…"

This disturbed him even more.

He is not the man I thought he was. He is worse than Alistair and Jacob. He's a monster.

"You're evil, Henry," said Lucas, loathingly. "You're a murderer and a liar! You killed my parents. You let me be killed by that psychopath so I'd be forced to stay. And you want me to take your place as an Immortal, meaning I'll be soulless like you; a monster like you. Do you hear yourself? Do you understand how messed up that is?!" When Henry said nothing, Lucas continued. "Do you know what Shelly's been through? What you've put us through. She's had to support us both, sacrificing everything, including the chance to finish high school, in order to protect me and keep me in school. Since losing my parents she has done everything for me and I took her for granted. No more.

"For so long I wanted to believe that our parent's deaths were an accident and that Shelly would eventually warm up to you, but this is all your fault! Everything you've done has been to push me away from the people who love me. If I had known that death paid for life, I would never have taken it! I would have rather stayed dead or paralyzed."

"That is why I never told you, because you are just like me."

"I am *nothing* like you. I am nothing like Jacob. I'm me and only me."

There was a time when I would have given anything to be like Henry. But now that my eyes are opened, I no longer see the man I thought I admired. I understand who he is now.

After a few seconds of silence, he decided not to hide his feelings anymore.

"I came back to camp for you," Lucas admitted, tears streaming down his face. "I missed your wisdom and guidance, but most of all; I missed you. I had so many questions that I wanted to ask about you. Now I don't care to know anything else about you."

When Henry did not respond, Lucas wiped away his tears and asked a hard question he feared the answer to.

"I have to know. My parents died from brain aneurysms. How did it really happen? What did you do to them?"

Henry did not hesitate when he answered.

"I mind controlled them and made it so that they treated you in a specific way. They tried to fight it, quite often, and this caused their minds to become weaker. By the time I used my ability, they were—"

"Stop, please. Please don't tell me the rest."

Henry nodded and continued to look at Lucas impassively.

The orb, from the Relic game. What was it really?

"The life force of Eternal Children," Henry revealed upon reading Lucas' mind. "Everyone who has ever held it, even for a few seconds, has lost a bit of their overall lifespan to it. Using the orb has various factors but the main one I've used it for is in shielding the camp. Jacob has one that is similar but not quite as refined. His orb allows him to communicate with the Shadow People without overwhelming himself."

There's more to it than that, but it's all I want to know right now.

"Is this all the questions you have for me?"

Lucas shook his head. He had one more question.

"When you asked me if I would erase Bill's mind from what he went through, why did you do that?"

"A person who is truly soulless would not have questioned me or hesitated even under threat. Instead you showed morality, which tells me your soul is still strong and you are still capable of great empathy."

Lucas made his final decision.

"I'm leaving Camp Supernatural," Lucas announced angrily. "I'm going home with Shelly and we are never coming back. I will never forgive you for as long as I live, Henry."

Suddenly, Henry's hidden emotions that Lucas had only glimpsed in his eyes manifested fully before him. There was pain and sadness in his face now. Henry's eyes dropped and he looked like he was ready to make a full-on confession.

"I must tell you something, Lucas. Please listen to me..." Henry's voice faltered.

But Lucas didn't listen.

"I have nothing more I want to know from you. I'm done with this camp and with you."

Lucas hopped from his chair and removed the camp beads from around his wrist. He furiously slammed them on Henry's desk.

"As long as you're here, I'm never coming back," Lucas said, his back turned to Henry, clenching his fists so hard that his nails dug into his palms. "I don't want you to read my mind to hear that. I want these words to be the last thing I ever say to you; I wish you had died instead of my parents."

Lucas reached for the door when he heard the Camp Director say something in a quivering tone.

"Lucas… please."

Lucas wanted to turn back, to look at him one last time. He wanted to forgive Henry and apologize for acting the way he did. He didn't want the last words he said to be in anger like with his parents. But when Shelly came into his mind, her tears and sorrow at having to live without seeing their parents again, Lucas opened the door.

This is the end for me. I'll never see Henry here again…

Lucas didn't realize it at the time, but he was right; this would be the last time he ever saw the Camp Director in Camp Supernatural…

Epilogue: Harbinger of Death

With August fast approaching, the camp was preparing to close down for the year. Repairs around the camp were beginning but would not be complete until the following summer. Campers without a cabin were bunked in the ward, which had extended itself to house various children, even ones who were not seriously injured. A few Silent Ones remained, though many left the camp before the end of that week. Devon continued to assist the hospital staff with the injured campers and remaining Silent Ones. He was even making progress with one, Connors, whose cognition was returning.

As long as he doesn't try to hug me again then we should be good, Lucas thought to himself.

Lucas hadn't seen Henry since that fateful night. There were whispers among the campers and staff that Henry had not left his house for anything, not even for Pizza Day.

I should not feel sorry for him, Lucas thought bitterly. *Just a few more days and I'll never have to see him again.*

He did not try to speak to the Camp Director or ask Boris anything about him.

Henry lied to us all. He kept so many secrets, and in the end we're all either going to die or become something called an Immortal? If it means becoming like him, I wish he had let me die instead.

Meanwhile, Erin quickly became a welcomed addition to the camp. Once she recovered from the effects of being near Jacob, she demonstrated her astonishing hand-eye coordination by hitting the bull's eye for every target in the training field using only her slingshot.

She enjoys it. Showing off. Makes sense why Alexia is her new best friend, Lucas thought with a smile. *I'm also glad for that. After the memorial, I realized Alexia isn't as bad as I thought she was.*

Weeping Willow only sustained minor damages but was intact enough to keep the campers inside safely. When Lucas went to check on Shelly, after giving her a while to recover, she no longer talked about their parents and was now beginning to accept the reality of their lives.

"I felt so empty when the connection was severed," Shelly admitted to her brother. "Jacob gave me a glimpse of something I knew was unreal, and even though I swore I knew, my mind convinced me I needed it. Sapphire tried to help me like with Mike but I don't think she can use her power on command. So I have to keep riding it out as much as possible."

Shelly turned to her brother and fought back the tears that were behind her eyes.

"I'm sorry for what I said to you. I knew and I didn't stop myself. It felt so easy to say and think those things without feeling bad about it. Now that's all I can think about."

Lucas hugged his sister.

"It's okay, Shell. I'm just glad I have my sister back. No matter what you said or thought it doesn't change how much you mean to me. It's just you and me and that's all I want going forward," Lucas said in a sorrowful tone. "When summer ends, we'll go home and we won't come back to Camp Supernatural."

Shelly was about to ask him why until she saw his eyes.

She knows. Of course she does. Shelly suspected Henry long before I did. Now I know why.

"I'm sorry, Lucas. I really wish I had been wrong about him."

Lucas nodded and squeezed his sister's hand.

"I miss them so much, Luke. I just never wanted to burden you with those thoughts and feelings."

"I feel I always knew anyway," Lucas admitted. "Not because I can read minds, but because I can feel other people's emotions. Going forward we should always be able to talk about how we feel and express concern where it is needed. I'm just glad I got to hug them before leaving."

His sister looked at him confused but became too tired to question him further.

Lucas then decided to visit Josh, who was now conscious.

I hope this doesn't change him too much. Life will become very boring if Josh isn't himself.

Upon seeing his friend, Josh appeared to be in better spirits, but was wearing an oxygen mask.

This really sucks, Josh projected ruefully in his mind.

Lucas nodded as his friend grinned back at him weakly. Kendall arrived a few minutes after Lucas and exclaimed happily at seeing Josh awake.

"Thank the Gods. I always had faith." Kendall wiped away tears of joy from her eyes. The tears had ruined her mascara but she still looked very beautiful.

"Josh is going back home for medical treatment in a few days," Kendall revealed to Lucas. "I'm going to become a counselor on a temporary basis next summer. Daniel mentioned being short staffed because Lucinda, Betty, and Margot resigned last week. Maybe you can ask if he'll let you also be a counselor to help out next year."

Lucas did not have the heart to tell Kendall or Josh that he wouldn't be back next year.

I rather not add on to the sadness in this room. The truth can wait, just a bit longer.

"Have you told Josh yet about it?"

Kendall shook her head as she turned to stroke Josh's uncombed hair. He frowned through the breathing mask and impulsively removed it for a moment.

"I'm...use...less," Josh wheezed drearily.

Lucas knew that even when the wounds healed, the scars never would.

The memory of waking up in that hospital bed, feeling my whole body paralyzed, with Henry next to me... no, I won't think of him. That's the same as seeing him and talking to him.

Abruptly, Hailey entered with a vase full of watered flowers. Kendall saw Hailey and warmly greeted her. Even though she knew of Hailey's feelings for Josh, she did not show her any form of hostility, and instead treated her with courtesy.

Her inside thoughts say otherwise. They're not worth dwelling on or repeating right now.

"Hi, Hailey. Do you want to leave those here for Josh?" Kendall asked amiably.

Hailey shook her head. When she saw Josh was awake, despite the happiness in her eyes, she leveled herself coolly at Kendall.

"I would like a moment please. If that is alright with you?" Hailey asked a little too bluntly.

Kendall reluctantly nodded and walked out of the door. Lucas left also as Hailey's eyes angrily glanced at him.

I don't blame her for being upset at me, but when will she forgive me already?

When she was alone, Hailey closed the door shut and walked over to Josh, who was lucidly conscious. He had trouble seeing her as his eyes squinted and were watery from both the machine and the tears that he was forming.

"Hey, Josh, it's me Hailey. How are you feeling?"

Hailey leaned in towards him and wrote down some of the words so he could read it. Josh responded in-between breaths how he may not return to camp anymore after his injury and how he really has nothing now without his power. He groaned in pain when he tried to speak often. He also tried to sign some of it and write down what was harder to say.

"I don't believe that's true," Hailey insisted. "You're the funniest guy I know. How many guys out there, deaf especially, can quote lip movement from movies by memory and even do the facial gestures right down to the smile or scowl?"

Josh grinned proudly after understanding what she said and coughed weakly when he tried to do an impression.

"How about the time when you once thought the school I attended was like the one from that Robin Williams movie. Except it's a school for girls not boys."

She began talking about past events with him using sign language. All of a sudden, before she could stop herself, Hailey burst into tears.

I thought I could do this, Hailey thought to herself. *I didn't want to show it, but this is so hard.*

"Please don't leave us, Josh, don't leave *me*," Hailey begged sorrowfully. "We'll find a way to make it work. You'll be alright, and we'll make Jacob pay for this," she vowed vengefully.

Josh looked at her tear streaked face and moved his hand as if to stroke her cheek. His hand hung in the air as if he were contemplating the idea. Taking this as her cue, Hailey stroked his cheek tenderly.

No matter how long it takes, I'll get stronger. I'll work harder than I ever have before…

Lucas' next destination was to see how Bill and Mike were doing. The whispers and gossip of them around camp was not good. Both were put in Atlas's Burden and were being closely monitored by Jeremy. He begrudgingly allowed Lucas to speak to them but was watching them carefully. He was no longer in a wheelchair but was using crutches on his injured legs. Devon was with Bill and he brightened upon seeing Lucas.

A smile looks good on him, Lucas noted with a smile of his own.

"Devon told me about your mission together," Bill mentioned. "I'm sorry about his brother but I'm glad he's dead. He wasn't a good person."

Lucas nodded in agreement.

"I'm guessing you know his secret? That there's two heads in there." Bill gestured a hand up where he thought Devon was. The small boy humored him.

"Yeah Zane mentioned it. But no matter what, he's Devon to us."

The small boy nodded in appreciation.

"Has Henry told you anything about what's going to happen to you and Mike?" Lucas asked Bill.

"Not yet, but odds are we won't be welcomed back. Shannon's not going to like that and neither will Vanessa. Did you hear that some of the counselors left? That means they'll be looking to fill those spots as fast as possible." Bill said this last part with some envy but also understanding.

Mike was spaced out and looked ashamed of himself.

"I don't deserve to be here," he said softly. "I betrayed everyone in camp. It's my fault Jacob and his Silent Ones came and anyone who got hurt is on my hands."

Bill shook his head and put his hand on Mike's shoulder. He flinched slightly, then relaxed.

"I told you already to stop beating yourself up about that. I was the one who made you do what you did. I'm so sorry, Mike." He turned his attention back to Lucas. "How's your sister doing, Luke?"

"She's doing better, but I know it still bothers her," Lucas admitted. "She never wanted to tell me what she was feeling so I guess seeing it made me realize that I was only feeling what I thought I wanted to feel instead of being honest about it with her."

"That's exactly how Jacob works," Mike admitted. "He knows exactly how to manipulate people and get them to do what he wants. He doesn't use fear but codependency, which is even more frightening."

"Who did you see when you were trying to walk towards Jacob?"

Mike hesitated and Lucas feared he wouldn't say. When he revealed the truth, Mike spoke so fast Lucas nearly missed what he said.

"I thought they were my parents, but they looked like shadows…"

Mike stopped, not wanting to talk about it further.

"I'm glad Shell is doing better, Lucas. It will take time. I still feel the residue but it's not as bad as it was a few weeks ago."

"I felt the same way," Bill acknowledged. "I wanted my powers back so badly that I was in denial they were never gone. It's now something new I need to learn to control. So it doesn't control me."

Lucas smiled at the obvious nod to the camp motto.

"We've forgotten that; everyone here," Lucas noted. "This camp has always been about our abilities and our disabilities, all of which are tied to us. They don't define who we are as people though and no one, not even Jacob, can change that fact. When we face him next time, we'll be ready." Lucas made a fist and threw it forward, touching Bill's fist. Mike followed suit and then Devon. The small boy looked up at Lucas and nodded approvingly.

"When you're ready to talk, Devon, I'll be ready to listen."

Devon touched Lucas' knees twice and tapped his own shoulders.

"I feel the same way," Lucas ended up saying and was surprised to realize he did know what Devon said.

Same goes for you, and thank you for helping me see Mark for who he always was. Some of that isn't completely 100% how he said it, but it's close enough.

"How's Josh doing?" Bill asked Lucas. "We haven't heard anything about him."

"Josh is not doing well. He might not be able to use his powers fully again and I don't know if he'll be allowed back in camp next year."

Bill shook his head stubbornly.

"No way, all five of us need to be back. You, me, Mike, Gary, and Josh. The cabin won't be the same without you all."

Lucas nodded, not having the heart to mention that he won't be back next year.

"I tried using my mind control on Josh to stop him when he attacked Jacob. I don't know why it didn't work."

Mike answered for Lucas.

"You mind controlled Josh last year when you made him listen to you. I know you've heard the phrase when one door closes another opens. In this case, when you did that, it made Josh easier to control, but because your abilities just got better, they weren't at their full strength. Even so, you may subconsciously not have wanted to have controlled him and the power always knows what is in our hearts better than we do."

"I developed a new ability during that fight. I think it's like telekinesis. I can't explain how it works. Only that it seems like Josh's power except it comes from my mind and body. They have to be a certain way and I feel vibrations when I use it."

"That'll be useful against someone like Jacob who I don't think can do that, but he is still not someone to underestimate."

Mike was going to say more when Jeremy cleared his throat and looked at Lucas impatiently.

"Before I leave, I wanted to ask two questions, one is for Bill specifically and the other two either you or Mike can answer," Lucas asked. He looked at Jeremy and knew he was pushing his presence.

"Last year you told me about the ladies in the cafeteria looking old and I know some of the doctors here are pushing thirty. Are they like us, Alter—I mean—Eternal children?"

Bill thought about it for a moment, then shook his head.

"Henry brought them here to help with the camp staff since not everyone who finishes their training here stays. A lot of us, including the ones I used to share my cabin with, all left and I never heard from them again."

"How do you guys feel about the whole becoming Immortal and only living to the age of thirty-three?"

All three pondered this. Mike was the one who answered.

"I don't believe it. I believe that Henry is Immortal. It would explain a lot and how much of this world we don't understand. For instance, Henry had a place that had humans with animal heads. So this world has more things than we've seen yet. Even so, I don't believe that our destiny is set at the age of thirty-three. That's when life begins truly for many. I believe there is a way to change that and now that we know of it, we can find a way past it."

Bill nodded, as did Devon.

"If it's a bloodline that means it's stronger in some and can skip generations. Especially when an Eternal child marries someone who isn't of an Immortal bloodline. So who knows? This isn't foolproof and I refuse to believe that this is all there is."

Lucas agreed with Mike and was satisfied with his answer. While Devon did not provide a vocal answer, he communicated this to Bill, who roughly translated.

"Devon says he believes if anyone can break this cycle, it's the best telepath he knows."

Lucas smiled to himself and promised to do just that.

Easier said than done.

Knowing his time was up and not wanting to be chased out of the cabin, Lucas said his goodbyes to his friends and briefly acknowledged Jeremy. The muscular camper did the same but his inside thoughts showed jealousy at knowing he was the object of Ashley's affections.

While I missed using my powers fully, now I'm hearing people's thoughts again and realizing how much they hate me behind my back.

Lucas passed by Erin and Alexia who were with her friends celebrating the end of the summer. Alexia was boasting of how many Silent Ones she incapacitated and Erin was expressing her excitement at returning next year to camp, assuming she could sneak away from her home. When she noticed him, Erin went over to where Lucas was.

"Hey, Shaggy, do you mind if we talk?"

Lucas nodded and the two walked away from where everyone else was.

"Stop calling me Shaggy please. My hair's not that bad."

Erin shook her head.

"I like it. Anyways, we have unfinished business from before."

Lucas knew exactly what she meant and braced for Erin's words.

"You're right and I deserve anything you have to say about it, so let's hear it."

"I understand tensions were high," Erin began, "but that doesn't excuse how you acted. However, I am willing to overlook it just this one time if you can guarantee me a place here in camp. I can definitely make a case for it with my dad, who will be happy enough for me to be out of the house. As long as I know I'll be welcomed here, then I'll trust your word and we'll be square."

Lucas nodded in agreement although he did not want to tell Erin about no longer being on speaking terms with Henry.

Maybe it doesn't matter because Erin has proven herself as having more than a place here. She should have been here all along.

Alexia beckoned for Erin to return to her group and gave Lucas a subtle nod. The red headed girl gave him a final hug and a kiss on the cheek.

"Thank you for bringing me here and for giving me a chance," Erin said with a shy smile.

Erin walked back to her group and Lucas heard her thoughts.

Was that too much? I feel like he's going to think so. He is kind of cute though and Alexia told me he broke up with his last girlfriend. I should ask him why next time.

Lucas couldn't believe he was entertaining the idea.

She's not all that bad, until she starts talking.

He felt a tug on his shoulder and turned around to see Gary.

"Hey, Luke, Mike wanted to see us both."

"I just saw him not even that long ago," Lucas admitted.

"Yeah and he mentioned we were going to want to see this."

Lucas followed Gary to Atlas's Burden and saw smoke coming from the opened windows of the cabin.

Is there a fire going on in there?!

A few campers were gathering around and Boris came as well. He prepared to break the door down when Mike flung it open. He was covered in soot and the only part of him that wasn't were the goggles he wore. He was holding onto the side of the entrance of the cabin, his limp leg causing him some discomfort.

"I did it," Mike said hoarsely. "After you left, Luke, I got inspired by something Devon mentioned. I wasn't sure how long it would take to make, but it turns out it took me only five minutes with my ability."

Lucas wasn't sure what Mike was talking about until he saw a small container in his hand.

"Oh, this took three minutes. It helps that there was a lot of crafting material in the cabin."

Lucas peered back to see the inside of the cabin. Some of the furniture was missing essential pieces and from the way Jeremy and his cabin mates glared at Mike, they were not pleased with their new décor.

What they're thinking is definitely not age-appropriate and not worth repeating.

Mike unveiled the container's contents and showed Lucas red tinted glasses that looked like ordinary sunglasses but the red hue looked like the blood moon did the night before.

"For the glasses I used bits from the beads I have in camp. I don't intend to become a Camp Counselor so it's all good. Then I combined them with some plastics I found here and light refraction materials, it's all very technical. But the point is these should help Bill see."

Everyone's attention was on Bill, who lay in a corner looking like he wanted nothing to do with the experiment.

"For how long will they work?" Bill asked, uncertainly.

"The idea is forever. Of course like any glasses you'll need to adjust them eventually and get a new prescription. Luckily for you the doctor is in." Mike pointed playfully to himself.

Lucas smiled big and wide and felt like hugging his friend.

It's so nice to see him back to his old self again. This is something Jacob could never appreciate; authenticity, who a person really is. Not what they think or think they feel.

Devon walked over to Bill, took his hand, and nudged him towards Mike and the glasses. He came hesitantly but still stopped.

"I don't deserve this, from you, from anyone." Bill tried not to sound upset but it was clear that he was beating himself up harshly.

"We don't know what the future holds, man. A lot of crazy stuff happened this summer and I missed most of it," Mike said and tried to add bits of humor in-between. "All I know for sure is whatever happens we'll face it together. You're one of us and regardless if you can control your abilities or not, you'll find a way. These will help as a starting point."

Mike extended his hand so Bill could take the glasses. He held them delicate by the temples and the hand missing his fingertip joints looked like it was going to drop the glasses. Lucas walked up to Bill and decided he needed to say something too.

"I'm sorry this happened to you," Lucas told Bill. With his eyes closed and still covered, Bill looked at Lucas and let him continue. "We'll make Jacob pay for this and for all the people he's hurt. Whatever happens you won't go through this alone. You have your friends, Shannon, your sister Vanessa—"

"And this camp," Daniel finished for Lucas. When he spoke, everyone parted ways for him like he was royalty. Daniel walked up to Bill, offering a hand for the cloth. Keira was behind him and remained with the crowd. "Regardless of what my father says, this camp needs to change the way it handles anyone who cannot control their abilities. It will be a more difficult road ahead, but if we face it together, it will feel less impossible. I propose this for Josh, Bill, and anyone else who feels their ability is unstable. That way no one will turn to a man like Jacob and will always have a place here in Camp Supernatural. The Silent Ones who remained will be given that same choice as well."

Bill began to cry and felt the stinging pain from his beams as he did this.

I didn't expect that kind of speech from Daniel. Maybe he will make a great Camp Director one day.

Feeling inspired, Bill undid the cloth from his face, handed it to Daniel, and, with his eyes closed shut, put the glasses on.

"If this doesn't work and the energy beams shoot out, try to run as fast as you can," Bill said both in a joking manner and seriously.

Everyone nodded while Jeremy and his cabin mates were already grimacing.

Not the cabin please, Lucas heard Jeremy thinking on repeat.

With a heavy sigh, Bill opened his eyes and the beams redirected themselves back into his eyes and his vision readjusted itself. For the first time since his powers changed he was able to see again. Even with the small bits of pain, the tears continued to flow from him and he rushed over to hug Mike harder than he had ever hugged anyone before. The smaller boy was lifted up off his feet and Bill swung him around as if he meant to break his back.

"Thank you so much, Mike. Thank you, thank you!"

Mike hugged Bill back just as tightly. The two boys who had been traumatized by Jacob were now bonded together through the deepest friendship there was.

Gary walked up and hesitantly extended a hand to Bill.

"I'm happy for you, dude." Gary said this with some reluctance and Lucas was worried that he was going to do something rash. Bill walked over to Gary after hugging Mike and took his hand.

"I'm sorry, Gary. I wasn't at my best self and I didn't know what I was doing."

Gary nodded but the hurt in his eyes still showed the lingering wound.

That's not going to heal anytime soon, but it's a start.

Lucas noticed Caroline in the crowd and got her to find both Vanessa and Shannon. When they came around and saw Bill's new miracle, they both hugged him really tight and Lucas swore they were going to pop him like a balloon. When they found out Mike was responsible for the glasses, they equally gave him a hard squeeze. By the end of it all, Mike looked like a deflated balloon. Not enough to deny his sister though when she came around and saw the exciting news.

"My brother is an inventa," Sapphire said in her squeaky tone.

Mike ruffled her light hair and noticed the change. Instead of asking about it, he kissed his sister on the forehead.

I think her hair looks nice that way, Lucas heard Mike think. The thought was not accompanied with pain, much to his relief.

Vanessa looked at Lucas and despite everything that happened between them, she gave her ex-boyfriend a hug.

"Thank you for keeping your promise and for bringing my brother home," Vanessa told Lucas through tears of joy. Their hug felt long but it was over before either of them could make any more of it.

"Thank you, Lukey, for bringing Mikey home," Sapphire hugged Lucas' leg. The small little girl looked so innocent that Lucas wanted nothing more than to protect her from evils like the Shadow People, Jacob, Alistair…and *Henry*. He shook his head, banishing the name from his mind.

Daniel quickly walked over to Keira who was crying tears of joy at seeing Bill regain the use of his sight.

"Keira, my love, the best part of my life has been with you and although I wanted to do this under different circumstances, the events of these last few weeks have made me realize how short and precious our time in this world really is. Especially for us, since now I know what we really are. That doesn't change how I feel and that I always intended to do this."

Keira wasn't sure what Daniel meant until he got on one knee and her hands flew to her mouth. Everyone who was watching them all gasped as well and took one step forward to see what was happening. Daniel unveiled a small box and in it was a ring with a special engraving on it.

"I used the sanctuary stone I had, a small piece of it at least, to make the center of it which is partly blue and partly green like my eyes. A mixture of emerald and sapphire." He turned to the little girl and winked. Lucas knew she had a hand in helping make that piece into its diamond shape. The engraving in the middle had the letter 'K' with a faded 'D' next to it. "That part was incredibly hard to do but so worth it."

Keira looked at the ring, then at Daniel and began to nervously laugh as everyone in camp saw them. Lucas looked around and spotted both Ashley and Hailey. Shelly was with them and everyone was looking at both Daniel and Keira with high expectations.

"Keira Elizabeth Lilly, I only want to love you from this day until the end of our lives. I only want to show you the love you have always given me through every moment since we've met. Will you marry me?" Daniel was also on the verge of tears and seemed to be holding them back depending on what Keira said.

She's definitely going to say yes.

Prophetically, Keira's head went up and down and she said with lungs so loud Lucas was sure everyone in camp, including Henry, heard her answer.

"Yes, of course I will marry you and spend my life with you, my beloved!"

A great big roar erupted as everyone began to clap their hands from campers and the few staff around alike. Daniel slipped the ring onto Keira's finger and held her hand in his. As they kissed, the nearby campers (specifically the girls) exclaimed, "*Woooooooo*" and began to clap their hands for the newly engaged couple.

Zane and Naomi were both with the crowd and in an uncharacteristic moment, Zane walked up to Daniel and slapped his shoulder with his good hand.

"Good on you, Keira, for making an honest man out of him. He doesn't always make the best choices but you are definitely one of them."

Daniel nodded respectfully to Zane and similarly patted his shoulder, thanking him.

Naomi walked up to both of them and although she had a troubled look on her face, she still hugged Keira and congratulated the two on their engagement.

Something is bothering her but she's either hiding it well, or trying not to think about it too much.

Ashley, Hailey and Shelly all came forward as well. Keira embraced Shelly while Daniel hugged Ashley. Then they switched places and Shelly thanked Daniel for everything.

When did they become on good terms, Lucas thought, bemused. *Well that looks like a wrap on this year and what a way to end. The first wedding in Camp Supernatural and it's with Daniel no less. Who knew what he had in him?*

Daniel blushed in embarrassment while Keira began showing off the ring to every girl nearby. Erin spotted the commotion with Alexia and the two girls looked at Keira's engagement ring with such admiration that Lucas swore both their faces looked the same. Ashley briefly saw Lucas and gave him the shy smile he was fond of.

Another celebration, this time bigger in size, soon followed. The whole camp boomed with music and cheers for the engaged couple. The only quiet spot it seemed was Henry's house, with the lights inside being turned off.

He's probably asleep or something. Do Immortals sleep? So what, I don't care.

Lucas ignored everyone and sat alone on a bench, admiring the stars.

Why did he lie to me for so long? Lucas thought bitterly. *If he had just told me the truth from the start, things would have been so different. Why did he have to be different from who I thought he was?*

Little Sapphire walked up to Lucas and asked him meekly, "Lukey, do you know where Camp Director Henry is? I want to give him this before summer ends." The little girl showed him a plastic plate with the words, 'Thank You Henry', written in macaroni. Lucas shook his head and tried to smile for the little girl.

She looks like herself again. That's good. But what about that red star on her forehead?

"He's probably busy, Sapphy. Why don't you go play with Twinkle or go see that nice ring on Keira's finger?"

Sapphire nodded and walked off to join the others, with the little puppy following at her heels. Lucas saw that Twinkle had also changed slightly. His fur was darker now and looked like copper instead of bronze.

Either that or I really need to get some sleep.

Feeling his social battery drained, Lucas decided to return to his cabin. When he entered his room, he found the scrapbook that Mike had given him for Christmas tugged away in between his bed and the wall.

With everything that happened this summer I forgot all about it.

He took it out and began to admire it. The blank pages reminded Lucas of the time he wasted worrying about his abilities and the fear he felt towards Alistair.

I'm still not sure what a scrapbook is for but I can at least add something to it. In case Mike remembers to ask about it.

Lucas started writing in it. One page became five pages immediately and he still had a lot of pages left. Looking at what he wrote, Lucas admired the way he compressed the whole summer into so few pages.

It makes feel like so little happened and yet so much has changed now.

He accidentally wrote the word 'Alter' a few times and scratched them off until the sentences read as '~~Alter~~ Eternal'.

"That's going to take some getting used to," he admitted out loud.

A knock came at the door and when Lucas went to see who it was, he was surprised to see who it was.

"Come with me," was all Zane said to him.

Lucas went with him obediently, although he questioned his own movement. It was as if Zane were controlling him, but Lucas knew it couldn't be so.

Why am I following him? I'm the telepath, not Zane.

They walked past the party and towards the training field, which was empty save for the two of them. It still had scorch marks from the fireballs and the weapons racks were all disarray.

Zane turned to face him and while he looked like he was doing better, Lucas could now see the mangled hand was no longer bandaged anymore. However, two of his fingers looked shorter than the others, similarly to Bill's hand. The line on his forehead didn't look as bad as when the cut first happened, but the scar it would form would still be notable.

Girl's like scars apparently so I doubt it'll stop Erin from blushing at him.

"A small price to pay for my life, wouldn't you say?" Zane asked Lucas. Lucas nodded and that was the end of that. "Thanks to Devon, I probably have more use of this hand than I would have had he not treated it when he did. At least I don't need to worry about cutting my nails with these two fingers."

Zane displayed them; they were his ring finger and index finger on his right hand.

"I also don't plan to get hitched like Daniel over there. Now then, after what happened a few weeks ago, I think you and I both know that things have changed for good," Zane told Lucas.

He began to feel uneasy, suspecting something amiss.

What is he talking about? Why drag me here away from the others?

"Even though I still think you have a long way to go, I must admit, you've grown this summer. Now the reason we're here alone, just the two of us, is because Henry has instructed me to begin the next phase of your training. I may still be in recovery, but that doesn't mean I'm going to go easy on you. So prepare yourself."

Lucas did not understand what Zane was saying until he emitted waves of electricity through his finger tips and sent a bolt in his direction. Wide-eyed and surprised, Lucas dodged the first shockwave easily enough, but the second had scraped a part of his left elbow and burned bits of his skin off. He felt the tingly sensation that followed.

"What are you doing?!" Lucas shouted distressfully as he cradled the injured elbow.

"Starting your training, now fight back. Use that new telekinesis ability of yours."

Lucas flushed red and threw his hand forward. He flung an empty weapons rack in Zane's direction. When he zapped it, it exploded into splinters that shot through his side without harming him. Zane grinned and prepared to charge towards Lucas, who began to rub his hands together.

As they trained, Lucas heard Zane's thoughts: *He's been through enough already and if he's going to survive what's to come, he can't be a kid anymore. I'm sorry, Lucas, but the future you have is not going to be an easy one. You won't be alone though, and you won't become Jacob. I'll make sure of that.*

Lucas pondered these thoughts, thinking about them as another voice entered his mind at the same time: *Now we are on the same playing field. Henry's lies are known and your eyes are no longer blinded. When next we meet, my opposite, only one of us will remain and the Shadows will have their Harbinger of Death…*

Acknowledgments

Thank you so much, fellow reader, for undertaking this amazing journey with me and for giving my vision for this series a second chance. Where I feel the first book functions as a prologue to the story and characters, book two feels more in line with what I was working towards with the set up and ideas I set forth. I also allowed my ideas to grow more on their own this time around and trusted a lot of the process to happen as it was. Even so, I also found myself coming to realize that I still have much to learn and that has enabled me to seek out more ways in which to inspire both my writing and growth as a person. Through reading various authors such as Stephen King, Brandon Sanderson, and Pierce Brown, I have begun to mold my influences with the style and themes I wish to portray in this series. Where book one is about Lucas discovering his powers, book two is about Lucas beginning to discover who he is without them as they were. Character development and growth is the core of my series and some of the themes I wish to explore is empathy and connection. The idea that everyone in this camp is different and while some may come from similar backgrounds, they all have unique voices to share. Before I close off, I would like to acknowledge and thank Dreamink Studio for doing the book art for both this book and the previous one. Thank you Naidelyn Ramos and Megan Johnson for editing my book and helping me to mold it into the form that it has now become. Thank you Mark Esperanza for helping me to publish my book and for always believing in me. Lastly, thank you to everyone who supported me through my first book. I hope you, fellow readers, enjoy the second installment as much as the first and are eagerly excited for book 3, tentatively titled The White Mourning.

Jonathan Solis lives in Rio Grande City, Texas, and began to pursue writing out of a love for storytelling and exploring the different aspects of the human psyche. He is the author of the YA horror fantasy series Camp Supernatural and has published the first two installments, Mind Over Matter and Eyes of Vermillion with the next three books pending. He hopes to write more stories one day and is inspired by the themes of creating empathy and connection through stories that talk about healing and bettering one's own self. He also holds a Master's Degree in Creative Writing and a Bachelor's Degree in English from the University of Texas Rio Grande Valley.

www.ingramcontent.com/pod-product-compliance
Lightning Source LLC
LaVergne TN
LVHW020646110826
845149LV00012B/1928

* 9 7 9 8 9 9 2 8 6 4 7 0 0 *